Amie

An African Adventure

by

Lucinda E Clarke

Amie

Copyright © 2014   Lucinda E Clarke

All Rights Reserved

This book may not be reproduced, transmitted, or stored in whole or in part by any means, including graphic, electronic, or mechanical without the express written consent of the publisher except in the cases of brief quotations embodied in critical articles and reviews.

All characters, locations and events in this publication are fictitious and any resemblance to real persons living or dead is purely coincidental.

Cover illustration by Peter Bendheim
peter@peterbendheim.com
www.peterbendheim.com

This book is for all those who know and love Africa and those who would like to learn more about this amazing continent. It's also for all those amazing friends who made me welcome in the various countries that became my home and which I grew to love.

Even after six years back in Europe, I am homesick for the wide open savannah, the majestic forests, and the soaring mountains. I miss the smiling faces, the hospitality that is second nature to the African races, the bustling markets and the high rise buildings in the cities.

Thanks to the best husband who has yet again lived through the time I was glued to the keyboard, and to those friends and fellow authors who, as always, are an inspiration.

While you may leave Africa, a part of Africa will never leave you.

Spain 2014

Contents

	PROLOGUE	1
1	AN UNEXPECTED MOVE	5
2	WELCOME TO APATU	26
3	SETTLING IN	47
4	PRETTY, TICKS AND ANGELINA	72
5	VISITORS AND A SAFARI	92
6	GOING HOME	117
7	A VISIT FROM THE COLONEL	139
8	BICYCLES AND SEWING MACHINES	159
9	PROPAGANDA FOR THE TRADE FAIR	182
10	A HORRIFIC SHOOT AND A VISIT	212
11	A SHOOT AND TELLING TALES	231
12	NOWHERE TO RUN	254
13	CAPTURED	270
14	DANGEROUS TERRITORY	290
15	THE LITTLE PEOPLE	310
16	BACK TO REALITY	323
17	THE RETURN	338
18	APATU AND BEYOND	358
	ABOUT THE AUTHOR	372

PROLOGUE

They came for her soon after the first rays of the sun began to pour over the far distant hills, spilling down the slopes onto the earth below. At first the gentle beams warmed the air, but as the sun rose higher in the sky, it produced a scorching heat, which beat down on the land with relentless energy.

She heard them approach, their footsteps echoing loudly on the bare concrete floors. As the marching feet drew closer, she curled up as small as she could, and tried to breathe slowly to stop her heart racing. No, please, not again, she whispered to herself. She couldn't take much more. What did they want? Would they beat her again? What did they expect to say?

There was nothing she could tell them, she was keeping no secrets. She knew she couldn't take any more pain, every little bit of her body ached. How many films had she seen where people were kicked or beaten up? She'd never understood real pain, the real agony even a single punch could inflict on the body. Now all she wanted was to die, to escape the torture and slide away into oblivion.

The large fat one was the first to appear on the other side of the door. She knew he was important, because the gold braid, medals, ribbons and badges on his uniform told everyone he was a powerful man, a man it would be very dangerous to cross. He was accompanied by three other warders, also in uniform, but with fewer decorations.

They unlocked the old, rusty, cell door and the skinny one walked over and dragged her to her feet. He pushed her away from him, swung her round and bound her wrists together behind her back, with a long strip of dirty cotton material. She winced as he pulled roughly on the cloth and then propelled her towards the door. The others stood back as she was pushed into the corridor and up the steps to the ground floor.

She thought they were going to turn left towards the room where they made her sit for hours and hours on a small chair. They'd shouted and screamed at her and got angry when she couldn't answer their questions. This made them angry so they hit her again.

She'd lost track of the time she'd been here, was it a few days, or several weeks? As she drifted in and out of consciousness she lost all sense of reality. Her former life was a blur, and it was too late to mark the cell walls to record how long they'd kept her imprisoned.

This time however they didn't turn left, they turned right at the top of the steps and pulled her down a long corridor towards an opening at the far end. She could see the bright sunlight reflecting off the dirty white walls. For a brief moment she had a sudden feeling of euphoria, they were going to let her go!

She could hear muffled sounds and shouts from the street outside. It was surreal there were people so close to the prison going about their everyday lives. On the other side of the wall, the early morning suppliers who brought produce in from the surrounding areas were haggling over prices with the market stallholders, shouting and arguing at the tops of their voices. Not one of them was aware of her, her pain or despair. Even if they *had* known, they wouldn't give her a second thought, why should they care? She didn't belong here. Only a few years ago she'd never heard of them or their country. The sounds drifting over the wall that were once so foreign, had become commonplace, then forgotten, and now remembered. She was aware of the everyday bustle and noise of the market, goats bleating, chickens squawking, children screaming and the babble of voices. But all these sounds could have been a million miles away, for they were way beyond her reach.

Hope flared briefly. Her captors had realized she was innocent. They'd never accused her of anything sensible, and she still didn't know why she'd been arrested. She knew she'd done nothing wrong. Her thoughts ran wild, and she convinced herself the nightmare was over at last.

All the doors on either side of the corridor were closed, as they half carried, half dragged her towards the opening in the archway at the end. The closer they got, against all reason, her hopes just grew, and grew, they were going to set her free. She was going home.

As they shoved her through the open doorway, she screwed up her eyes against the bright light, and when she opened them, it was to see they were in a bare courtyard, surrounded on three sides by high walls. As she looked around, she observed there was no other exit leading to the outside world.

Then she saw the stake in the ground on the far side, and brutally they pushed her towards it. She thought of trying to resist, but she was too weak, there was too much pain. It was difficult to walk, so she concentrated on putting one foot in front of the other, determined not to give the soldiers or police or whoever they were, any satisfaction. She would show as much dignity as she could.

The skinny one pushed her against the post and took another long piece of sheeting from his pocket and tied it around her chest fixing her firmly to the wood. She glanced down at the ground and was horrified to see large brown stains in the dust.

Not freedom, this was the end. She squeezed her eyes tight shut, determined not to let the tears run down her cheeks, but the sound of marching feet forced her to open them again. She saw four more men, all dressed in brown uniforms, with the all too familiar guns who lined up on the other side of the courtyard opposite her. They were a rough looking bunch, their uniforms were ill fitting and stained, and their boots were unpolished and covered in dust.

She was trembling all over. She didn't know whether to keep her eyes open to see what was going on, or close them and pretend this was all a dream. She was torn, part of her wanted it all to end now, but still a part of her wanted to scream 'Let me live!! Please, please let me live!!'

The big fat man barked commands and she heard the sounds of guns being broken open as he walked to each of them handing out ammunition, then with the safety catches off, they prepared to fire.

To her horror, she felt a warm trickle of liquid running down the inside of her thighs, at this very last moment, she had lost both her control and her dignity. They had not even offered her a blindfold, so she closed her eyes again and tried to remember happier times, before the nightmare started. Briefly she glanced up at the few fluffy white clouds floating high in the sky as the order to fire was given.

1 AN UNEXPECTED MOVE

The wedding day went without a hitch, and Amie, who was turning twenty seven in the summer, couldn't believe it had gone so well. It's not as if she really expected a 747 to make an emergency landing in the middle of the churchyard, or Uncle Oswald to get drunk out of his mind before the ceremony, but she had been worrying herself sick for weeks something awful would happen. Her mother was always teasing her about how much she worried about everything, but on the wedding day itself, the sun shone in a clear blue sky and there was hardly a breeze. No, not a single thing went wrong, but it was the calm before the storm. Life would soon take an abrupt turn and fate would redress the balance.

Both families approved of their new relations and on the day Amie and Jonathon exchanged their vows, friends and relatives from both sides had mingled well and enjoyed themselves. Even Amie's dad was secretly congratulating himself the bar bill was going to work out much lower than expected, thanks in part to the drink drive laws. Yes, all the planning and the time spent in preparing for Amie's great day had been worth it.

So far the biggest hiccups had been the usual dramas, finding just the right venue, the perfect dresses for Amie and the bridesmaids and compiling the guest list. Amie and Jonathon had decided to pay for most of the wedding themselves, this way, they had control over the event with minimal interference from other family members. This took quite a bite out of their savings, but Amie felt it was worth it and Jonathon was quite happy to agree.

As everyone raised their glasses to toast the bride and groom, life had been just as Amie had imagined it. Now, all she had to do was balance her career with having a family and somehow she would manage that as well. Other women had coped and there was no reason why all her future plans shouldn't work out just as perfectly.

While Amie had always hoped she would get married and have a family one day, she didn't consider herself just a permanent housewife and mother. The idea of being tied to the stove, barefoot and pregnant in the kitchen didn't appeal to her at all. To begin with she enjoyed her job and had hopes of being promoted in the near future. She'd always dreamed of working in the television industry, but after studying for three years in Technical College, she found it was an industry that was very oversubscribed with hundreds of 'wannabe' Steven Speilbergs and Richard Attenboroughs!

Following advice from one of the younger lecturers, after three years, working at a variety of temporary jobs, she had eventually managed to get employment as a receptionist in a video production house which made short inserts for television, and product launches and training programmes for large companies.

'This was the way into the industry,' she had been told. 'Work your way up, learn how things are done from the inside and make yourself indispensable. The mark of a prospective and successful director is to know how to roll cables correctly, and how to make a good cup of coffee, especially when everyone else around you is faint from lack of sleep.'

So, from day one, Amie sat behind her desk in the reception area and not only answered the phone, took messages and greeted visitors, she also offered to order tapes, help source props, book locations and liaise with the agencies that provided actors and extras. It was often frustrating for her, since she knew how to operate a camera, and how to edit, but for the moment, she had to watch everyone else rush off on shoot, while she was tied to a desk in the front office.

In the three years since she'd been there, no promotion had as yet loomed on the horizon, but she was hopeful she would be offered the job of production secretary while the present girl was away on maternity leave.

On the social side, she had known Jonathon since they had been in school. When he went away to University to study engineering, she had had several dates, casual friendships, but no one ever meant as much to her as Jonathon. Each vacation, they spent every spare moment together, and soon after he graduated, Jonathon took a further year to complete his studies. Amie was disappointed he would be away for even longer, as the course was held at another college much further north and he didn't come home during the usual holidays. She worried he would meet someone else and fretted when she didn't hear from him sometimes for several weeks. She never admitted her fears to Jonathon, but then he came back and got a job in their home town with a company that designed and installed desalination plants and it was as if they had never been apart.

It wasn't long before they decided to move out of their parents' homes and get a flat together and for the last three years, life had been very good.

Had Amie noticed that so far life had gone exactly to plan? To be honest, it wasn't a very exciting plan was it? Of course she'd had dreams like so many young girls do. She once thought of being prima ballerina with the Royal Ballet Company, but then she changed her mind. She would take up horse riding and win the Olympics and feature on the front page of the nation's newspapers. Or maybe become an actress and win a standing ovation and rave reviews for her interpretation of Ophelia in Hamlet.

But like most of us, she came back down to earth, and realized she would lead an ordinary life in the town where she'd been born, and as long as she was happy, that was all she could hope for. Part of the plan was for Jonathon to propose, which he did, and the other part of the plan was for Amie to accept, which she did.

Both sets of parents had been born in Castle Bridge, had their children in Castle Bridge Hospital and expected to be buried in Castle Bridge Cemetery. While Amie's parents both lectured at the local technical college, Jonathon's family owned a small chain of hardware stores.

So in all fairness to Amie she more or less accepted the same future. She did not yearn for distant horizons, she was happy as she was.

Amie's older sister Samantha was already married to Gerry who worked for the local council. They had two children, Dean and baby Jade and they also lived on the outskirts of town. Amie would often baby sit and she enjoyed spending time with her small niece and nephew, although she and Jonathon had decided to wait a few more years before starting a family of their own.

They had already started saving for a deposit on a house, perhaps over on the new estate they were planning south of the town, just large enough for the happy couple and the two children they were going to have.

But fate had quite a different future in mind for Amie, and the bombshell was dropped a few weeks after they returned from their idyllic honeymoon in Spain.

"What? Where?" shrieked Amie, as she almost jumped out of her chair.

"Shush," said Jonathon looking around the smart restaurant in dismay. "Don't shout, everyone is looking at you!"

"What do you mean don't shout, am I supposed to

whisper? What exactly did you just say?" Amie couldn't quite believe it.

"That the company has offered me a promotion?" replied Jonathon.

"No, that bit I understood, it's 'where' the promotion is," Amie whispered very loudly.

"Oh, that bit, well yes, it's in Togodo."

"Well where the bloody hell is Togodo?" asked Amie.

"I'm not sure of the exact co-ordinates, but somewhere near the Equator, along the coast, on the east side, I think," said Jonathon miserably. He'd not expected Amie to react quite so badly. He'd imagined this moment and he had persuaded himself Amie would gaze into his eyes and say something like; "How exciting, I knew living with you was going to be thrilling and adventurous, do tell me we're leaving soon."

Well that was the dream. The reality was somewhat different.

"I thought you'd be pleased," he added.

"Pleased! You mean leave here, leave England! Go somewhere I've not even heard of? Wait. The west coast of where?"

"Africa," replied Jonathon. "And I think it's on the east coast."

"Africa!" Amie took a deep breath. "Go and live in Africa?" She annunciated each word slowly and carefully.

"I thought you'd be pleased," Jonathon repeated. "It'll be a whole new experience for both of us."

"A new experience? Yes." said Amie as the realization of what Jonathon had just said really began to sink in. "Let's start again, just repeat what you just said. I don't quite believe all this."

"The company has asked me, well us of course, to go and open a new branch office in Apatu, that's the capital of Togodo, and get a new plant up and running....er..."

Jonathon fumbled for the right words. "It's the opportunity of a lifetime. I never expected to be a Project Manager so soon, even though they sponsored me through uni. It's a real chance for us. Oh Amie I thought you'd be as excited as I am!"

Amie looked at her new husband. She had automatically assumed he had the same plans for their future as she had. They'd talked about living in the town where they both grew up. They'd have a family, send the kids to their old school, socialize with the other people who'd also been friends since kindergarten, join the golf club, and look forward to the annual dinner dances. There was always the possibility of them moving a few miles away, perhaps as far as Scotland? But overseas, well that had never entered her mind.

"How long have you known about this?" asked Amie suddenly.

"Only since Tuesday and..."

"Two days! Two whole days, and you've not said a word?" Amie was astounded.

"I wanted the right setting, the right place to tell you," Jonathon tried to explain. "And you know how this place gets booked up and this is the first night they had a free table."

Amie wasn't stupid, she guessed Jonathon planned to tell her his news in a public place, it was a way of making sure she would keep her emotions in check. Not only that, but he'd chosen the most expensive restaurant in the area, everyone knew how exorbitant their prices were. Like a lamb to the slaughter, she'd followed him inside, wondering if it was an anniversary she'd missed, or a special occasion she'd forgotten, but no, it was to drop this bombshell.

Jonathon watched Amie carefully, trying to gage her reactions beneath the initial outburst. He thought he knew her so very well, they'd been together for almost ten years and known each other since primary school. His mind flashed back to the first time he'd really noticed her. It was in a science lesson in high school.

He remembered her sitting at her desk, lost in a world of her own, chewing the end of her pen and gazing out of the window.

"Miss Reynolds, from what you read last night, can you tell me who discovered the light splitting properties of the prism?" Mr Johnson asked.

Amie, was miles away and didn't hear a word.

"Miss Reynolds?"

"Uh yes Sir, what Sir?"

"What, indeed, and the answer?"

"Um," Amie played for time, she could hardly give the answer if she didn't know what the question was.

"I take it you were too busy washing your hair, or glued to the box, or on Facebook to study last night?" Mr Johnson's words dripped with sarcasm.

"Oh no, no Sir, Amie replied. "I read all about it, chapter six, kinetic energy."

"Really?" replied Mr Johnson, "the rest of the class studied chapter five. So next week when the rest of us have caught up with you, you'll be able to explain all about kinetic energy."

"Yes Sir, no Sir," Amie didn't know what to say.

While the rest of the class giggled, enjoying her discomfort, it was at that moment Jonathon fell in love with Amie. He looked at her long blond hair, big grey eyes, slender figure and vowed that one day he would marry her.

But it wasn't easy. She was a popular student and the boys would crowd round her at break time, and it was difficult to even get a chance to talk to her alone.

It took several months for him to pluck up the courage to ask her out, and was utterly amazed when she agreed to go with him to the bowling alley, he was so sure she'd turn him down flat.

That first date was a success, and so was the next one and the one after that, until they were acknowledged as an item and the rest of the testosterone laden hunters gave way and pursued other young ladies.

Jonathon worried himself sick when he went away to University, while Amie stayed home and attended the local technical college, but each vacation break reassured and reaffirmed his feelings. When he had to travel away on site visits, he also worried about all the famous people she might meet in the glamorous world of television. But he soon realized Amie seldom got to meet anyone particularly famous, and most of her day was spent not only as receptionist, but also as general runner, sourcing props, booking accommodation, filing log sheets, typing up call sheets and making numerous cups of coffee.

They had always got on so well, and they seldom fought, but Jonathon knew this was totally new ground, and he didn't really know how Amie would react. It was in this very restaurant that he'd proposed only a year ago, and although he'd been nervous then, it was nothing compared to how he felt now. They'd talked about their future and it seemed like most couples, they would continue to live and work close to family and all the friends they'd grown up with. It was expected they'd move out of the flat, buy a house, have a family and have a life like their parents until they drew the old age pension and bounced the grandchildren on their knees sitting in their rocking chairs on the porch.

Until now.

Amie looked at Jonathon, she hadn't been thinking about how they first fell in love, she'd been thinking about what she'd expected their future life to be, and going to live in some African hell hole was not part of her plans at all. She fiddled with her dessert spoon and fork.

"Look, I can turn it down if you're really unhappy about it," said Jonathon.

"You've already said 'yes,' haven't you?" Amie challenged

him.

"Well yes, but I can always change my mind, I can say no."

"But if you turn down this promotion, then it's not likely you'll be offered another one is it?" said Amie slowly.

"I'm not thirty yet, and I can always move to another company in a year or so, and…" Jonathon fell silent.

"You and I both know you've specialized in this field, and there aren't many companies doing desalination work and mostly, now I think about it, that sort of work is overseas?"

"I suppose so, but I never thought we'd have to move, I never thought working in the design office, and trips to site offices in Britain, I would be asked to travel overseas, and this came right out of the blue," Jonathon lied.

Amie sat quite still saying nothing and Jonathon couldn't gauge her reaction at all. Now she'd had a few moments to let it all sink in, was she pleased or horrified? He had to admit the offer coming so quickly had taken him by surprise, but when they asked him, it was in the board room, in front of all the directors. They all expected him to be thrilled and delighted and not for a moment did they even consider he would turn down the career opportunity of a lifetime. He knew what was expected of him, and he also admitted to a bolt of pure excitement in tackling a new project in a new place where for once, he didn't have to answer to anyone one else. It was like being given a charter which announced at last, you were a real, grown up, capable adult.

Now he thought about it, they never once mentioned talking to Amie about it. They just assumed he'd accept and she would pack up and follow him without a murmur. As an American owned company, their corporate expectations assumed all employees were willing and eager to climb the corporate ladder as far and as fast as they could. The job came first and last and family fitted in as and when convenient.

"Did they suggest you talked it over with your family first?"

asked Amie at last. The one question Jonathon didn't want to hear.

"Well, no, they just assumed…"

"Yes, I guess they would. I bet it never entered their heads at all. I suppose their wives would just pack up without a second thought and follow their husbands into the jaws of hell, but then they're all an older generation. 'Where I go, you, my wife will go.' Typical of that generation." Amie swigged the rest of her wine and held out her glass for more. A well trained waiter materialized out of nowhere, and refilled it to the brim.

"You're not going to get drunk are you?" asked Jonathon alarmed.

"I might and I might not," replied Amie starting on the next glassful. "How did you expect me to react?"

"To be honest I had no idea, I sort of hoped you'd be as excited as I am. It's such a wonderful opportunity, not only to do the work I love, but take a big step up the corporate ladder. They've offered a really good package, and it's all found. They provide the house, the car, pay the water and electricity bills, and our petrol, so all we have to buy is food. We'll be able to save lots and, if we decided to have a family…."

"In Africa, wouldn't that be fun?" Amie jumped in. "Lying on the floor in some filthy hospital where no one speaks English."

"Look, if you feel that way, we don't have to go." Jonathon replied. He was bitterly disappointed. He'd rehearsed how he was going to break the news, and had convinced himself, or rather tried to convince himself, Amie would be pleased, excited and very proud of him. He wanted this promotion really badly, and if he refused, then his future chances of moving further up the ladder were out the window. Hell, if the worst came to the worst, then he would spend the money and fly home every month, or, well he'd work something out. In the meantime, he'd play it cool.

The waiter placed the desserts on the table and walked

away. Amie studied the dish in front of her and silently began to eat. She said nothing until she had almost finished, then she looked at Jonathon.

"How long do they want you to go for?"

"Uh, it's a two year contract, and then if I, er, if we, liked it," he added quickly, "we could stay on for two more years. It will take some considerable time at least to get the plant built and up and running, and train the locals how to manage it and make repairs."

"And what happens if you, we, hate it and the plant's not ready in two years? Will they let you come home?"

"Um, I'm sure yes, I guess so." Jonathon hadn't the faintest idea, they hadn't discussed so many years into the future, but there was absolutely no question in his mind, of walking away from a job half done.

All Amie's dreams came crashing down around her as she pushed the last bit of her caramel custard around the plate. Now what was she going to do?

The next afternoon Amie drove across town to commiserate with her mother.

"But of course you must go!" exclaimed Amie's mother as she put the kettle on.

"Oh so you're on his side now are you?" snapped Amie.

"It's not a question of taking sides," replied Mary Reynolds, "I'm only stating a fact of life. The husband's career is always the most important. You can't base a marriage on the wife's career, what happens when she has babies and has to stay home and look after the children?"

"That's the way it was in your day Mother, things are different now. Women are just as important in the workplace as men."

"Ah, that's what you might like to believe, but I promise you, nature doesn't work that way. I know you don't believe me now, you're still young, but soon, very soon, you'll want babies of your own and you won't want to go off to work each morning and leave them with some stranger."

Mary filled two mugs with coffee, sugar and milk as she talked, while Amie perched on the edge of the kitchen table and glowered at her. She'd expected her mother at least to understand and commiserate with her, but it seemed as if she was quite happy to allow her younger daughter to go off into the deepest, darkest, wilds of Africa.

As if reading her mind, her mother continued. "And anyway, Togodo might be in Africa, but I'm sure it's quite civilized. It's a Commonwealth country for a start, and things are not as primitive as they were. I'm sure there will be lots of shops and hotels and a hospital and schools too. There might even be a shopping mall!"

"How come you know so much about it?" asked Amie suspiciously.

"My dear, when you lecture brash young teenagers every day, you have to be up on world affairs and know what is going on, even the names of the latest rap groups. My students are only too willing to think I'm over the hill at my age. Keeping up to date, also keeps you young." Amie's mother handed her a mug of coffee and sat down. "Don't you think you're over reacting just a bit?"

"Over reacting? How do you expect me to react?" Amie was beginning to wish she'd never come home looking for sympathy, it didn't look as if there was much on offer.

"My dear, all I'm saying is, this is a great opportunity for you both, to see a bit of the world and expand your horizons. Lots of people would jump at the chance. You don't realize how lucky you are."

"We can still see the world," replied Amie stubbornly. "We've already been to Spain and to France."

"That's not the same thing at all," said her mother. "For a few weeks, you were just another couple of tourists. No one gets to know a country in that time. It makes me mad when these politicians go on a three day 'fact finding mission,' when they're only shown what the government officials want them to see, and then shout loud and long about how to cure every ill in the place."

"Yes, yes," said Amie hastily. She had no intention of encouraging her mother once she got onto one of her favourite pet hate topics. "But I had it all planned out, I mean I'm happy here, I mean I never expected to well, go too far away…"

"You expected life would be very much the same for you as it has been for your Dad and me. Well it's not panning out that way is it? Goodness I'd jump at the chance."

"Then perhaps you and Jonathon should go," Amie said ungraciously as she stood up to go.

"Have you decided what to do?" asked her mother.

"I'm still thinking about it." Amie reached for her coat.

"Try to be more open minded," said her mother as they walked towards the front door. "At the very least, it's only a couple of years out of your life, Beech Avenue will be just the same when you come back, and I'm sure we can cope without you for a while, although we'll miss you both. And don't forget we can chat on Skype as often as you like."

"Yeah right," replied Amie, "I bet they've not even heard of the Internet over there!"

"Don't be such a pessimist darling!"

How uncaring, thought Amie as she gave her mother a peck on the cheek.

How I wish I was in her shoes, thought Amie's mother as she waved her daughter goodbye and watched her hop into her mini at the kerb, and I thought it was the young who were adventurous and raring to go these days. They never fail to surprise me. But there is no easy way to tell your children you did not have the opportunity or even the courage when you were young to look for exciting opportunities and experiences. Only a few decades ago, you just allowed life to happen to you and accepted what came along. She wondered what Amie would decide, would she have the courage to begin a new life in a new country?

As she drove back to the flat Amie was fuming, didn't anyone understand how she felt? How could her own mother not understand and commiserate with her? She parked the car under the car port and noticed Jonathon wasn't home yet. Good, that would give her time to phone Sam.

She unlocked the front door, threw off her coat and looked to see if there were any messages on the answering machine, but there was only one from the dry cleaners to tell her Jonathon's suit was ready to be collected. She punched in the numbers and sat back on the sofa.

"Hello, this is Dean, who do you want to speak to?"

"I'd like to speak to your Mummy please," said Amie. Usually she would chat to her five year old nephew, and ask him what he'd been doing at school, but today she was too upset and hoped he didn't recognize her voice.

"Mummy, there's a lady on the phone!" screeched Dean. Amie smiled, at least he called her a lady and not 'some woman' like he had last time. Sam must have spoken to him about that.

"Hello?"

"Sam it's me," said Amie.

"Oh, Dean didn't say…"

"Yes I know, but I'm too upset right now."

"What are you upset about? I'd have thought you'd be over the moon, just give me a couple of years in a hot country, away from all this traffic, grey skies, rain and coping with the kids indoors. Think of the fantastic tan you'll get. I should be so lucky! Working for the Council, Gerry will never be offered a job abroad. When do you go?"

Amie groaned, obviously her mother had been on the phone to Sam already and told her the news, and obviously

Sam wasn't going to understand either.

"So, when do you go?" repeated Sam. "Aren't you excited?"

"How can I be excited? It means missing all my friends and giving up my job and going somewhere I don't know a soul!"

"You'll know Jonathon," said Sam reasonably, "and you'll soon get to know people, you've never had a problem with that have you?"

"Well no," Amie agreed, "but I never expected…"

"Don't be such a stick in the mud," said her elder sister, "take it as an experience, especially before you get tied down like us with a couple of kids. And we can always come out and visit for a holiday, and nowhere is far away these days with all the cheap air flights."

"Ah, that's what you're thinking," said Amie sarcastically, "free holidays for the family somewhere hot."

"Sure, but then we only ever get a couple of weeks somewhere warm, just think, every day will be sunny and warm for you, you lucky thing."

"I'm still not convinced," Amie wasn't going to be persuaded that easily.

"Look, got to go, Jade is screaming for her next feed. Just be brave and say yes and go for heaven's sake. I'll miss you lots of course, but you can tell me all about it and show me all the photos when you're home on holiday and we can email. You'll have a ball!" and with that Samantha hung up.

Amie lay back and closed her eyes, no one understands. Why should I be uprooted just when life was predictable and secure and safe and I knew what to expect?

Going to hang her coat up, she noticed the pile of mail inside the front door. Picking up the envelopes, she ripped the first one open. The gas bill, hell, it was a lot higher than the last one. The electricity bill was up too. All the other envelopes contained demands for money. There was the car tax, insurance and a repair bill for the washing machine. It would be nice not to have bills dropping through the letter box each month.

At work they were very envious of Amie.

"Wish I was going somewhere exciting," grumbled one of the production assistants. "The most exciting location I've been on was to Worthing for some motorcycle gathering, in Worthing of all places!"

James who worked in the tape library was just as envious. "Wow, you lucky thing!" he exclaimed dumping a pile of tapes on the front office counter. "Have a word with Dave, he went out to do a piece on Kenya last year, he can tell you all about it."

"Jonathon isn't going to Kenya, he's going to Togodo," replied Amie.

"I'm sure one African country is much the same as all the rest," said James. "As I understand it, they're all hot, full of dust and flies and have lots of markets selling fruit and vegetables and hundreds of kids sitting around doing nothing. And that's the geography lesson for today," he said over his shoulder as he rushed down to Edit 1, balancing a pile of tapes and log sheets.

It's all very well for them to say I'm lucky, thought Amie, but they don't actually have to go and live miles from anywhere, with no television and no one who speaks English, and hell, it probably won't even be safe! African countries are always at war with one another, every other day on the news they show a war somewhere in Africa.

It wasn't easy to pin Dave down and have a few words with him. He was the best in-house cameraman at Video Inc. and he was always out on one shoot or another. Amie finally ran him to ground in the production office as he was pouring himself some coffee.

"Dave, what's Africa like?" asked Amie.

"Uh?" for a moment Dave looked a bit blank. "That's not an

easy question to answer in under two or three hours. Why do you want to know?"

"Jonathon's been offered a job in Togodo, and I know nothing about the place."

"Never been there, so I can't help you, but it'll be hot and dusty and lots of flies, but in my experience, most African countries have a civilization of sorts in the capitals, it will probably be more modern than you expect. Out in the bush, well that's another story. But hey, when you get there, keep an eye open for possible stories. We need good material for that series on young children born in this millennium and maybe I could twist Duncan's arm to include some from other countries too. Yeah, great idea," and Dave rushed out of the room leaving his mug of coffee on the table.

He's probably gone to bend Duncan's ear, thought Amie as she went back upstairs. It was fun working in the production house, but she envied the crews who rushed past on their way to this or that location.

"It's all hard work and no glamour," they told her at college, but Amie knew it had to be a lot more fun than sitting behind a desk all day, doing admin stuff and answering the phone. On the better days, she would be asked to source props or make appointments or get permission to film in places such as shopping malls or restaurants, but... goodness, what was she thinking, was she really getting bored in her job? Just how long would she have to wait for a promotion? A horrible thought struck her. What if they *didn't* offer her the production secretary's job when Michelle went on maternity leave, what then? It was all Jonathon's fault, thought Amie, if he hadn't mentioned going to live in Africa, then she would never have even questioned her current lifestyle.

After work, Amie decided not to go straight home. She walked over the road, into the park and sat down on a bench. She needed to be somewhere where she could think. There were very few other people around, just a couple of small boys near the central duck pond running away from their harassed mother. Amie glanced up at the trees which were already starting to lose their leaves. For a start, she needed to be honest with herself. Going to Togodo would be a whole lot different than sitting in the comfort of her own lounge watching Jane Goodall, or that gorilla lady battling her way through dense undergrowth in the deepest, darkest jungles. It was fine to share their adventures when you could get up, make a cup of tea and then fall into a cozy, warm bed. It was almost as good as being there without any of the inconveniences.

But, if she was honest, it wasn't likely they would be in the middle of the jungle, desalination plants were generally built on the coast, next to the sea. Most news inserts showed modern African cities with roads and cars and even high rise buildings.

Much as Amie was reluctant to climb out of her comfort zone, she was also aware other people only saw this as a great opportunity. They'd think her a total wimp if she stayed behind and let Jonathon go on his own. It wasn't as if she was running her own company or anything like that, they'd easily replace her at work. So why was she frightened of packing up and moving? Was it simply because life had thrown a curved ball she wasn't expecting? For the first time ever, Amie felt events were spinning totally out of her control. Was she in a rut? One day, when she was old and grey, would she regret not taking this opportunity to travel and see a bit of the world? She would miss her family terribly, and what if she gave up her job and then when they came back in two years she couldn't get another one? Jobs were not easy to find these days. And why was she the only one not excited about this opportunity? Was that simply because they were *not* being uprooted themselves? The whole idea of leaving scared Amie to death.

As the sun went down behind the trees, Amie shivered and walked back across the road.

"Your father and I, and Jonathon's parents, all got together and decided this would be the very best gift to give you," said her mother at the airport. "I wish it was me instead of you, but I'm so proud of you for being so brave. With this, we can at least share a little of your adventures."

Amie, Jonathon and both sets of parents, Samantha, Gerry, Dean and Jade were sitting in a bar outside the departure lounge at Heathrow Airport. Amie still couldn't believe she'd agreed to go on this crazy adventure. Even though she'd googled everything she could find on the Internet about Togodo, and there wasn't a lot, she was still unsure what to expect. Knowing how many tons of maize meal they exported each year was not going to be much help to her in her day to day life in a foreign country.

They had given up their flat, packed up all their belongings and put them into storage. They'd had millions of inoculations against all kinds of diseases she'd never heard of, and bought brand new suitcases. It was a done deal, all signed and sealed. There was no going back.

Jonathon took the box and looked inside.

"It's digital," explained his father, "and as we wanted to give it to you last minute, it's quite small, but we're assured it gives you pictures of almost broadcast quality."

For a moment Amie grinned, imagining Dave's reaction if she sent him a story back, complete with footage, she'd love to see his face as he read 'No need for you to travel out here, Dave, shot this this afternoon. Think you can put together a great insert from it!'

"Wow," said Jonathon, "this is really neat. Thanks, thanks to all of you."

"But high end video cameras are so expensive!" exclaimed Amie, she'd heard the complaints at work when the requisitions went in for new equipment.

"They've come down a lot in price, and it's not quite the top end stuff like they have at your work, Amie," said Jonathon's father. "But the guy in the shop was very enthusiastic about it."

"And it's a great way for you to keep in touch," added Amie's Mother. "You can set it up and send video letters home and also take pictures of the town and all the local places."

"I don't know what to say!" gasped Amie. "Thank you all so much, it's a fabulous present."

"The instruction book is in there," said Jonathon's mother, and it looks fairly straightforward."

Amie opened her mouth to reply and closed it again. Of course she knew how to use a camera, what did they think she'd been doing for three years at college?

"And don't forget, when you get connected to the Internet, you can surf and order books which will tell you even more," said Jonathon's father helpfully.

"The Internet," said Amie, "in Africa?"

"It's not going to be as foreign as all that," said Jonathon. "We'll have a link up just as soon as we get the office up and running, I need to keep in touch with London."

Amie hadn't thought about that, perhaps this wasn't going to be quite so scary after all.

"And that's not all," added Sam. "Gerry and I have got you a lightweight tripod and a small set of lights as well, so now you have the full gear. Oh and some tapes too of course."

"Wow!" exclaimed Amie. "I really don't know what to say, how can I thank you all? I really didn't expect this!" seeing his face, she added, "Jonathon, did you know anything about this?"

"Well maybe," he admitted with a grin. "That's why I've not checked in the large suitcases yet, as we will have to pack the tripod and lights in first."

Amie gave everyone in turn a big hug, but the tearful farewells were kept to a minimum, perhaps both sets of parents worried Amie just might change her mind at the last minute. It wasn't until they were on the plane, she realized that now there really was no way she could go back. For better or worse, she was on her way to Africa.

2 WELCOME TO APATU

On board everything was very civilized and Amie was impressed with the individual television sets which they'd never had on the short European flights. Jonathon smiled at her and squeezed her hand.

"Excited?" he asked.

Amie looked at her husband, over six foot tall, his fair hair was always flopping over his bright blue eyes. Even though he never jogged or worked out at the gym, he had kept in shape, and Amie had to admit, he was extremely good looking.

"I don't know, half scared out of my wits, and the other half is feeling none of this is real," replied Amie. "How do you feel?" For the first time she wondered just how nervous Jonathon was, moving to a new country, and setting up a new project, with lots more responsibility than he'd ever had before. He was young to be given such an opportunity.

"I'm fine," he said, "and I guess, a little bit nervous, remember, I've never traveled this far before either."

"No, I suppose Spain and France don't really count as 'abroad,' they're both so close to home."

"They don't even stamp your passport in the EU any more. We'll be fine, and we'll have fun, believe me."

"Yes," said Amie, tucking her blanket around her. She glanced up towards the overhead locker where they'd put the camera box. Maybe, just maybe, she could do something with that, she knew she was just as bright and creative as the rest of the production staff who'd been involved in making television programmes, and now she'd have the chance at least to practice. Then, when they went home, she could get a job as director, or at least as a production assistant and… on that thought, Amie fell asleep.

She woke as the plane began to descend rather steeply, but as they were sitting in the middle section of the plane the windows were too far away to see anything. All the seasoned travelers were gathering their things together as the plane flew lower and lower, but Amie wasn't expecting the hard jarring bump as the wheels touched the runway.

"Goodness," she gasped, "are they trying to avoid the pot holes in the runway?"

"You're not so far wrong there!" smiled one of the passengers in a nearby seat across the aisle. "Welcome to Africa, where the first world tries to meets the third, and generally fails!"

What can he possibly mean, wondered Amie as the plane taxied towards a long, low building in the distance.

"Is that the airport?" Amie pointed to the only building in sight.

"I guess so," replied Jonathon, "though I expected something much bigger for a capital city. Still, we'll find out soon enough."

"It's not much bigger than a couple of portakabins!" said Amie. She wasn't sure what she'd been expecting, nothing as large as Heathrow, or Gatwick, but this looked a lot more rural.

"Hush!" said Jonathon, "remember free speech is not as popular in other countries as it is at home."

They gathered their hand baggage and stood patiently waiting to leave the plane. As Amie walked slowly towards the door, she became aware of the heat. It was like no other heat she had ever experienced before, and when she stepped out of the plane, it seemed to hit her like a solid brick wall. She paused for a moment at the top of the steps and looked around for her very first experience of Africa. But there wasn't much to see, only one other plane next to the runway, which reminded Amie of one she'd seen long ago in some aircraft museum. The crush of people behind her gave her little time to see anything else, as she was half pushed down the steps onto the hot tarmac.

She followed Jonathon as the crowd spilled out over the apron and walked into the terminal building. By the time they reached it, Amie was sweating. She could feel small trickles of perspiration running down her back and her clothes clung to her like a second skin. She could also feel the strength of the sun on her head, like a red hot iron.

Inside the terminal it was a fraction cooler, due to the large number of fans mounted on the walls which were going full blast, but the noise and the crowds were overwhelming. Amie was used to orderly queues, but here, everyone was pushing and shoving to get to the counter where two bored looking officials were working as slowly as possible. It didn't seem to bother them there was a huge crowd of people waiting, as they took each passport, looked at it for an interminable time, asked a question or two and then lethargically waved each person through one by one. Every so often, they would stop and chat to each other, ignoring the people anxious to get through immigration, reclaim their luggage and leave the airport. Occasionally, the staff would simply get up and walk away causing the people nearest to their access point to push and shove sideways to regain their place close to the front in the parallel queue.

Jonathon grabbed Amie's arm just as she was about to get swept off her feet.

"Let's wait at the back, at least there's room to move. We're in no rush, and I doubt there will be many more planes landing in the next hour or so."

"Would there be room for another one?" asked Amie glancing back to look at the runway.

Slowly the crowd moved forward and by the time Amie and Jonathon reached the counter, both her feet and her head were aching. She put her hand luggage on the floor and reached into her handbag for a couple of paracetamol.

"Drugs?" barked the man behind the counter in a loud voice. Amie looked round, but couldn't see who the official was talking to.

"You, I ask you! What drugs?" The official pointed at Amie and glared at her.

"Drugs? Oh no, just for my head, only headache tablets," replied Amie. Out of the corner of her eye she noticed another uniformed official approaching, he was nursing a large gun. Amie began to shake, the only other times she had seen a gun was on television on the Antiques Roadshow, or in police and cowboy films.

"Show him the packet," urged Jonathon, "show him what they are."

Amie quickly dug into her handbag again and pulled out the canister of pills. She showed them to the official who took them and peered closely at the label, though it was probably doubtful if he could understand any of the pharmaceutical information. He shook his head and put them in his pocket.

"Hey, those are mine!" Amie was outraged. "Give them back!"

Jonathon grabbed her arm again. "Let it go," he hissed, "it's only a box of pills, just let it go."

"But it's the principle of it, how can they take my things like that?" exclaimed Amie who was very close to tears.

"Yes I know, I understand, but now is not the time nor the place. Just leave it."

The official behind the desk glared at Amie and waved his arm to indicate he wanted her passport. Amie reluctantly handed it over, nervous she would not get that back either.

The immigration official gazed at it for a long time scrutinizing each page and then began stamping it over and over again. Slowly, he returned the book and waved her past. Amie grabbed her passport and moved over to let Jonathon up to the counter. But the official wasn't finished yet, he barked, "Move on, go through," and Amie did as she was told. She hovered just beyond the barrier waiting for Jonathon who was whisked through, with barely a glance at his passport which received only one stamp.

"Male sexist pigs," thought Amie. She grabbed Jonathon's arm. "Did you see that man with a gun? In the middle of the airport! Are they expecting some trouble, Jonathon, Togodo's not at war is it?"

"No, I'm sure it's not, we would have heard."

"Not if it broke out while we were flying over, we were in that plane for nine hours," Amie replied. "I feel frightened."

"It's quite usual," said the same passenger who'd spoken to her on the plane. "They always have armed soldiers at the airport, and all the other border exits. Don't worry about it."

"Thank you," said Amie. "Do you live here? Have you been here long? What's it like?"

The man laughed. "We've been here for a couple of years now," he replied as they walked on through to the customs area, and waited for their luggage to appear on the carousel. Amie was both pleased and relieved to hear a friendly voice from someone who not only spoke English, but was also familiar with the country and its customs.

"We may have to wait a while, nothing moves quickly here, it is Africa, remember," he added.

"As if I could forget," Amie replied as the sweat continued to run down her back, soaking right through her shirt. The thick jacket she was carrying felt like a ton weight. It was difficult to believe she needed so much clothing to keep her warm in London.

"Once we landed around lunch time and had to wait nearly

three hours for the luggage to arrive," continued the English passenger. "Doesn't matter what's going on, when it's time to eat, then everything stops. At least they don't have a siesta here, and that's only because this was once a British colony. Mind, some people say it's siesta time all day in Togodo."

"Does that make it difficult to work?" asked Jonathon.

"Oh yes, but you learn to slow down and work at the same pace, though it's often very frustrating. Don't make the mistake of planning a week's work and expecting to meet your deadlines. The general rule is to think of a time frame and then double it or even triple it."

"Thanks for the advice," replied Jonathon.

"It's obviously your first time here?"

"Yes, first time in Africa, we've only traveled in Europe before," Amie said.

"Let me give you my card." Their new friend reached into his pocket and pulled out a business card. "Don't hesitate to contact me, and I'm sure my wife will be delighted to meet you, she'll give you lots of advice about where to go and where not to go and the best shopping places and so on. Where are you staying?"

"We're Jonathon and Amie Fish, and we're booked into the Grand Hotel for the first few weeks, while they get the accommodation sorted out," replied Jonathon.

The man laughed, "Grand it aint! You'll see what I mean when you get there. Ah, the luggage is arriving, that must be a record for here. Be seeing you, I'm Richard Carstens by the way and the wife's name is Diana. Take care!" Richard bolted for the carousel.

"There, I told you, it wouldn't be so bad," Jonathon whispered as they went to claim their suitcases. "Let me hold the camera, just in case there's a problem at customs. They appear to have less respect for the women here."

"You can say that again," muttered Amie as she grabbed the handle of her case. Meeting Richard had cheered her up a little, he was even taller than Jonathon, well built, smartly dressed and had an air of confidence about him.

The line to clear customs moved very slowly. It looked as if all those people who lived locally were simply waved through, but all foreigners were stopped and everyone had to open every case while the officials pawed through the contents.

When it was Amie's turn, she unlocked her case and threw back the lid. She watched as the custom's officer slowly examined everything, and it seemed to her, he was particularly slow as he held up her underwear one piece at a time. Inside Amie was fuming, as he peered at her thongs and lacy bras, but wisely she said nothing. She had already learned one lesson. The customs officer picked up her sponge bag and took out each item and looked at it carefully. He even went so far as to open the toothpaste, squeeze some onto his finger and lick it. Amie shuffled from one foot to another, her feet were aching, and her ankles were swollen after the long flight.

After an exhaustive search, the customs officer waved his arms to show he'd finished and Amie was left to re-close the case, not an easy task as it was full to bursting point, and now the contents were unfolded they took up a lot more space. Without Jonathon's help, she wouldn't have got it closed at all.

No one wanted to see beyond the top layer inside his case, ignoring the tripod and camera lights, and they barely glanced at the box containing the camera, nor at his lap top computer.

Once outside the airport, the heat struck Amie again like a furnace. She noticed everything seemed bigger, brighter and more colourful than it did at home. The sky was the most brilliant blue. She also noticed many of the women wore bright cotton dresses, which would have looked totally garish in London, but here they looked cheerful and blended in well with the surroundings.

Right outside the main airport doors was a row of decrepit

looking taxis with a driver beside each one, all shouting to attract the attention of potential customers.

"We're not getting in one of those surely?" gasped Amie. "None of them look roadworthy!"

"I tend to agree with you," replied Jonathon as he looked at the dents and scrapes on the paintwork. "Look, that one over there looks a bit better, we'll take that one."

The taxi driver helpfully opened the boot for them but left it to Jonathon to put their luggage inside it. Amie gave him a dirty look, but the driver just shrugged. Both the large suitcases wouldn't fit in the boot, so they piled one onto the back seat with all the hand luggage on top and Amie squeezed in beside it while Jonathon got into the front. The driver looked at him enquiringly.

"The Grand Hotel, please," said Jonathon.

There was an urgent knock on the window and Jonathon looked up to see Richard Carstens gesticulating. He tried to wind the window down, but it wouldn't budge, so he opened the door.

"Forgot to tell you, don't go anywhere without deciding on the price first," he said.

"How much should it be to the Grand?" asked Jonathon.

Meanwhile the driver was trying to start the engine, obviously bent on a rapid departure.

"Wait," said Jonathon, putting out his hand behind him. The taxi driver squawked as Jonathon's hand squeezed his upper leg. Jonathon turned round, horrified at what he'd done, while the taxi driver let loose with a stream of invective and jumped out of the car. He waved his arms and shouted as he walked round to the back of the vehicle, opened the boot, dragged the suitcase out and flung it on the road.

"How much is the fare?" Jonathon asked Richard again.

"Not more than twenty Togodo Dollars," replied Richard. "But it looks as if you'll have to get another cab, after your assault on the driver." He laughed. "Sorry I can't give you a lift, I'm being picked up in a compact, they're safer to use over here. Tell you what, we'll come over tonight and have a bite with you at the hotel."

"Thanks we'd really appreciate that," said Jonathon as he and Amie got out of the taxi. They dragged the rest of the luggage back onto the pavement and looked for another one, but by now, most of the taxis had departed, and the few left displayed the biggest dents, scratches and bumps.

"I guess we just take the nearest one," said Jonathon, and even he sounded less than confident. As he walked towards the next driver, Amie reminded him to agree on a fare first.

"I want to go to the Grand Hotel," said Jonathon to the bored looking driver who was busy picking his teeth with a dirty piece of wire. The driver nodded and smiled as he helped them stow the luggage

"I'll pay twenty dollars, no more," added Jonathon, as they all climbed in. The driver nodded and smiled again.

The driver raced the engine, and pulled straight out without so much as a look behind him. Had there been room to move in the back seat, Amie would have been flung from one side to the other. Hastily, Jonathon looked for a safety belt, but there didn't seem to be one, only a ragged hole in the bodywork where the factory had originally installed it. He clung to both sides of the seat and alternated between screwing his eyes tight, and opening them to see what hazards were ahead.

In the back, Amie didn't have a choice. She was wedged in so firmly with the largest suitcase, her greatest fear was the door bursting open and flinging her out onto the road amid the chaotic traffic.

If his passengers were about to have a nervous breakdown, the taxi driver seemed blissfully unaware of it. He used both hands to light a cigarette as they hurtled down the main road at over a hundred kilometres an hour. There was plenty of hooting and hand waving to other drivers and on one occasion, as they were approaching a back up of traffic ahead, he simply swung over to the side of the road and raced up the inside lane, which in most countries, is reserved for breakdowns and emergency vehicles.

Neither of the new arrivals had time to look and admire the scenery as they hurtled to their destination. Jonathon did notice there were several traffic lights along the way, but the local highway code seemed to be that whoever got there first went straight across, whether the lights were red, green or amber. Nothing the young couple had ever experienced before had prepared them for this journey. Never, thought Jonathon, will I ever moan about bad British drivers again.

In the distance, Jonathon could see skyscrapers, and other tall buildings as they raced towards the capital. The road widened out, until it became a dual carriageway with a grassy central reservation. Shops began to appear on either side, very few with plate glass windows, most were just holes in the wall with half the wares spilling out onto the pavement. The pavements themselves were narrow, so most of the crowds strolled in the roadway. The driver kept up a constant blasting on the horn as he missed the pedestrians by millimetres.

Amie was amazed to see large hoardings, advertising familiar products such as Omo, and Persil and other goods which she could buy in the supermarket at home. Here the difference was the people featured on the products were all African, with dark smiling faces, short black curly hair and brilliantly white teeth. Although many of the women wore long, brightly coloured, traditional robes, the younger girls wore short mini dresses and sandals and most of the younger men sported jeans or chinos. There was also a sprinkling of women covered head to toe in heavy black burkas.

The taxi screeched to an abrupt halt outside the hotel, throwing Amie violently against the back of the driver's seat. The building looked like a million other hotels anywhere at home, except for the man in a leopard skin loin cloth who leaped forward and opened the doors of the taxi. He welcomed them with many smiles, but his hospitality did not extend to helping them with the heavy suitcases.

Jonathon and Amie began to drag them up the ramp after giving the taxi driver twenty dollars and a ten per cent tip. The driver looked disgusted and began shouting and waving his arms around.

"We agreed twenty dollars," said Jonathon firmly, feeling less than confident inside.

"You steal from me!" screamed the driver. "Fare is fifty dollars."

"No, twenty dollars is what we agreed, and I don't have any more Togodo money," said Jonathon uneasily, as an interested crowd began to gather round them.

"You give me more money!" screeched the man. "I have wife and six children, I poor man, you cheat me!"

"I told you, I've no more money," Jonathon said again.

"Then I demand American dollars, or pounds, English pounds! You English yes?"

"Sorry, but no," and Jonathon turned to walk into the hotel. The taxi driver wasn't going to give up that easily, and he grabbed Jonathon's arm and tried to pull him back out onto the pavement.

A member of the hotel staff came to the door and shouted at the driver, who reluctantly let go and walked off shouting loudly how he had been robbed by these foreigners.

By now Amie was shaking. This was another new experience and it had given her quite a fright. Just how violent were the people in Togodo?

Inside, the hotel foyer was full almost to bursting point with crowds gathered at the reception desk, and it was quite a considerable time before Amie and Jonathon finally reached the counter and gave their names to the receptionist. Amie was surprised to see everything appeared to be computerized. The girl, whose name tag told everyone she was called Betsy, pressed the keys and gazed at the screen for several seconds before informing them there were no reservations for a Mr and Mrs Fish.

"But there must be!" exclaimed Jonathon. "My company made the reservations from London. We're booked in for at least three weeks!"

"Not here," replied Betsy with obvious satisfaction. "No reservations." She looked at the man standing next to them at the counter and smiled at him. "Can I help you?"

"Wait a minute," said Jonathon angrily. "Please look again, maybe it's under the company name." Betsy sighed.

"What is the company name?" she asked.

"Drenton Desalination," replied Jonathon.

The receptionist punched in several more keys and stared at the screen. "No," she said triumphantly, "no booking for them. Sorry." They could see from her face she wasn't the slightest bit sorry.

"Name?" Betsy turned to the next man.

"Name's Connaught, I've a room booked," and Amie and Jonathon watched in amazement as the man slid a note across the counter.

Without even looking at the computer, Betsy smiled, swept the note up and stuffed it inside the front of her shirt.

"Of course Mr Connaught, room 504, here is your key and please to have a nice stay."

"It seems that's the way to get a room," Amie whispered to Jonathon. "Try it."

"I don't have much local money on me, I think that was a hundred dollar note," he replied.

"Then try twenty quid, the taxi driver didn't seem to mind what currency you gave him. Perhaps they would even prefer having English pounds," said Amie. "Try, it, we must have somewhere to stay!" She was not only hot and bothered, angry over her treatment at the airport, scared out of her wits during the taxi ride, now she was hungry as well.

"Please look again," said Jonathon to the girl on the other side of the counter, and he slid a twenty pound note forward. It disappeared rapidly into Betsy's bra joining the hundred dollar bill, and she smiled brightly as the names came up on the screen.

"Oh, so sorry I not see it before!" she exclaimed in amazement. "You are on the fourth floor in 409 and these are your keys. Please to have a nice stay."

Amie picked up the keys and they made their way over to the lift.

"Whoever designed this building should be shot," muttered Jonathon as they waited outside the one and only lift. "This place is at least five floors and they only have one lift?"

When it eventually arrived, the lift was quite small which meant Amie and Jonathon could not fit themselves and the suitcases in all at once. It took two trips before they were finally able to unlock the door to 409 and fall into their room.

"At least the room is comfortable," said Amie bouncing up and down on the bed. "And they've provided us with everything."

"Except towels," said Jonathon coming out of the bathroom.

"Perhaps we should ring down and order some," said Amie pointing to the phone on the bedside table. But when Jonathon lifted the receiver, all he got was a clicking noise, and no matter what buttons he pressed it was obvious the phone wasn't working.

"I guess we'd better order them from Betsy at the front desk," he said glumly.

"Yes, with another twenty pound note to make sure someone is listening," said Amie. "Jonathon, if you can't get anything done without paying wads of money, we won't make a cent here, it'll all go in bribes!"

"I'd already thought of that," said Jonathon. "I'm putting it all down under company expenses! I'm sure Richard and his wife will be able to give us some good advice this evening though."

"I hope they remember to come," said Amie. "We really are going to need their help. When did you say the next Drenton personnel arrive?" she added.

"I hope within a week or so, when I've got the new office up and running," replied Jonathon. "We might have an opportunity to look around before they get here." He opened his wallet. "Heavens, I'll need to find a bank soon and draw more cash."

"Well, let me have a quick shower and let's get something to eat," said Amie heading for the bathroom. "I'll manage with the hand towel I brought, it'll be easy to drip dry in this heat."

"I'll see if I can get the air conditioner to work," Jonathon had only just noticed it on the wall, and it certainly wasn't providing any cool air. But although he fiddled with it and even took the front panel off, he had no success at all.

After putting in a request at the front desk for towels, along with another twenty pound note, they walked across the foyer to the restaurant. There was more chaos in here, with every table occupied and diners who seemed only to shout and not talk.

"Goodness, this is so different to any of the places we go to at home," said Amie.

"Yes, but the menu looks similar," said Jonathon. "Burgers, with or without cheese, toasted sandwiches, soup and salad."

"Soup! In this weather!" exclaimed Amie.

"Yes, but they also have steaks and omlettes as well. What do you want?" asked Jonathon as they made a dash for a vacant table just as the previous diners got to their feet.

"I'll just have a sandwich for now," said Amie, "especially as it's not too long until dinner."

Both were pleasantly surprised when the food arrived, it was hot and tasted good.

"Well I don't think we'll starve," said Jonathon as they drank their coffee, "Even the coffee is nice."

The combination of the heat, the food and the long flight, made Amie in particular very sleepy, so they went back up to their rooms and lay down. Within minutes they were both fast asleep and only an urgent knocking on the door woke them up.

"It must be the maid with the towels," said Amie as she walked over to open the door. Outside stood a bell boy, well that's what first sprung to mind as Amie looked at his Turkish styled hat and smart blue uniform festooned with gold braid. He was holding a silver salver with a note on it. Amie wanted to laugh, it reminded her of the period pieces she'd seen on television, when the butler approached the lady of the house with a similar tray. The bell boy bowed low as Amie took the note, nodded her thanks and closed the door.

"Didn't he expect a tip as well?" enquired Jonathon sitting up on the bed.

"Probably," said Amie opening the envelope. There was more furious knocking on the door and this time Jonathon went to open it, and sure enough, the bell hop was still standing there. Jonathon put a note into his hand and he bowed low again and walked away.

"I wonder how long he would have waited?" asked Amie.

"Probably until we went down to dinner," replied Jonathon "perhaps forever!"

"Thank goodness," exclaimed Amie. "It's from Richard, they're waiting for us downstairs in the restaurant. We sure need to talk to someone."

"Yes, life is going to be a bit more complicated than I thought," said Jonathon. "We'd better hurry."

Amie took to Diana immediately. She was at least ten or fifteen years older than Amie, but looked confident and capable, everything Amie was not feeling at that moment. Diana had short, dark hair, large brown eyes and was wearing a simple cotton dress and sandals. She wore no make-up, and looked cool and fresh. She was a little taller than Amie, about five foot six, had a slim figure and looked in the best of health.

"Hello, welcome to Togodo," she said as she got up to greet them. "Richard tells me you've only just arrived."

"Yes, a few hours ago," said Amie as she sat down at the table. "It's all so bewildering, so hot and so crowded."

"Yes, it can be quite a culture shock, especially if you've not been to Africa before."

"This is our first visit," said Amie. "It's so very different and yet some things seem the same!"

"Like this menu," laughed Diana, "exactly the same stuff you can get back home. We've even got a McDonalds on the other side of town."

"Goodness, really!" exclaimed Amie.

"Yes, but don't be fooled into thinking this is just like home, just as you settle in your comfort zone, something reminds you that you are really in Africa after all. Your home will be an oasis of England, on a very hot day of course, but venture outside and you'll notice the difference. Will you be staying in Apatu?"

"Yes," replied Jonathon. "The desalination plant is going to be just north of the capital, at least that's the plan."

"We badly need a more regular water supply. At the moment it's piped down from the mountains and the infrastructure is so old the water is always leaking out. In many places the locals deliberately break the pipes so they can siphon off the water to irrigate their crops," Richard remarked.

Amie gasped, she couldn't imagine anything like that happening in England.

Richard continued. "Where will the company house you?"

"We don't know yet," replied Jonathon. "Drenton suggested we find somewhere to rent, but they booked us into this hotel for three weeks to start with."

"Try to move out as fast as possible," Richard advised. "It costs for just about everything, and you'll get through money like water."

"We've already discovered that," said Jonathon. "We had to pay a bribe before they 'found' our room reservation, and we've had to pay to have towels sent to the room as well."

"That's a favourite one," said Diana, "they do that on purpose. Everyone is on the take."

"But isn't that bad for the economy?" asked Jonathon.

"None of them even gives the economy a thought," answered Richard, "here it's every man for himself, or herself for that matter. No one looks at the global picture. As long as the average African has food, clothes, booze and a woman for today, then that's all he worries about. Tomorrow can take care of itself."

"My dear, I should warn you," said Diana turning to Amie. "You will hear a lot said about the locals that will shock you. You'll be convinced we are all terrible racists. I can assure you all the values and opinions you were brought up with will be out of the window in short order."

"There's an old joke," said Richard. "What's the difference between a tourist and a racist?"

Amie looked puzzled.

Richard continued, "the answer is twenty four hours."

Amie was still puzzled.

Richard explained. "People travel with all kinds of preconceptions, and they judge another country by the standards, morals and values from their own country, and what they've seen on television of course. So, it doesn't take long for them to criticize what they see as bad behaviour, and then they're accused of being racist. Take the bribe you had to pay just for the room. The receptionist sees nothing wrong in lying to you and saying she has no reservation for you, she simply sees your arrival as a way to make some extra money for herself. She doesn't give a thought to the people who employ her, or the good name of the hotel, or allowing you to know she's lying. There's a whole new set of rules to learn."

"Yes, I see, well I think I do," said Amie slowly.

"Africa is still a wild and savage place, despite the new high rise buildings and the computers and the modern look of the place," added Diana. "We're not here to scare you just as you've arrived, but only to give help and advice."

"Yes, and we really appreciate that," said Amie. "We, well I, feel totally lost, like Alice, as if I've just stumbled through the looking glass, or down the rabbit hole!"

Diana laughed. "Well let's order first and we'll see how we can help you."

That evening, Amie and Jonathon listened as they learned where to look for a suitable place to rent, and the places to avoid, especially the down town areas. Diana told Amie never to put her handbag down, but always keep it on her lap and hug it tightly when she walked.

"They think nothing of cutting the strap and snatching it. And, although I don't want to frighten you, if you're held up at gun point or they wave a knife in your face, then give them what they want, don't put up a fight, it's not worth it. Life is cheap in Africa, and they will think nothing of committing murder. In theory, there is a justice system here, but I wouldn't rely on it being fair. There is also a police force, but again, it's unlikely they'll come if there's any trouble, they always tell you they have no transport. We'd advise you to employ a private security company to guard the house and if there is a problem, then you press the panic button and they will send out armed guards. But it's something you have to pay for."

Amie gulped. "It all sounds so dangerous," she said.

"Yes I know," Diana replied, "but I'd feel guilty if I didn't warn you, and you got hurt. Look it will probably never happen, but you must be aware. I've become so used to being on guard all the time, even if I walk down the road. I know who is in front of me and who is behind me at all times. I keep a careful watch in the car, especially near traffic lights and stop streets and when I'm coming in and out of the house."

"Look, the majority of the locals are good, decent, people in their own way," she continued, "but we can only just understand their levels of fear."

"But why are they afraid?" said Amie. "What have they got to be afraid of?"

"Well, people here are jealous of success, and those that do get ahead are viewed with suspicion. Surely you must have noticed presidential cavalcades, you've seen them on the television at home?"

Amie nodded. "I thought they were just showing off."

"Of course there's that too, but those in power are also very afraid, that's why they surround themselves with bodyguards and friends and relatives generally from the same tribes. That way they feel safer and they can hold onto their power." Diana paused. "The best way to explain is, say we have elections at home, free and fair of course, and the best or most popular man gets in. The loser puts on a brave face and accepts defeat and the worst he's likely to do is slag off the winning candidate in the press. Here, when you lose an election, the automatic response is to fight back, literally, with guns or whatever it takes. So, winning candidates surround themselves with plenty of protection. It just depends on how strong the opposition is, if it's worth the men in power killing them off, or if they have very little support and can safely be ignored."

She continued. "The next time it comes to elections, if the powerful ruling party think they might not get in again, or have a big enough majority, then they make quite sure the votes are not counted correctly, most of the ballot boxes are tampered with. If that doesn't work, the opposition party candidates are beaten up and killed, or their supporters' houses are set alight. Practically anything goes to make sure the man in power never loses his job and all the perks that go with it."

"It all sounds so brutal," Amie shivered.

"It is, my dear, it is. And yet there is something so endearing about the Africans who are not among the hierarchy, the ones, and there are plenty of them, who simply want to live normal lives; marry two or three wives, have a crowd of children and a large herd of cattle. What more can a man want?"

"I've already seen that women are not very high in status here," said Amie, remembering the fuss at the airport.

"That's very true," said Diana. "Women have a long way to go on this continent to get the equal status we're used to and which we deserve. Sure, you will see women working in banks and shops and driving cars and so on, but, if their male relatives say 'jump,' it's 'how high, when and where?' Yet despite all this, the average African has a lovely sense of humour, is quite happy go lucky and has the patience of a saint. You wouldn't catch me sitting waiting all day out in the blazing sun to see the doctor and accepting it with a shrug if he can't see you today, and that's after walking miles to and from the clinic. Generally Africans are quite fatalistic, most of the time they simply accept their lot in life. It takes a lot to upset an African but once he is upset, watch out. But my dear, I must be boring you with all this."

"No, not at all," said Amie. "I'm absolutely fascinated. "I've never even thought about this sort of stuff, and it's interesting. I really want to understand the people, especially if I'm going to be here for at least two years. I kept meaning to do loads of research on the Internet, but with all the packing and the sorting out and saying goodbye and all that, I didn't have time to delve very deeply, only the main sites and they didn't tell me all that much. It all happened so quickly. Are the people here so very different?"

"I don't think any of us have really got inside the heads of people with such a different culture. And this is an important thing to remember. I'm talking now of Africans, don't be confused and think I'm talking about all people with a black skin, that's not the case. There are plenty of black people who live in Britain who think and behave just like us, they are as British as we are. I'm talking about culture, a totally different way of looking at the world with different rules of behaviour and a totally different viewpoint. For example anyone with a white skin here, is thought to be extremely wealthy. We don't think we're well off, but then we've never lived in a mud hut with a leaking roof and no water or electricity. We have cars, so we don't have to walk for miles. But we've always had these luxuries right from birth, along with indoor plumbing, and electrical appliances and so on. So what we take for granted they aspire to."

Diana paused, "I think that's quite enough for one night from the podium, let's look at more practical things. We must meet up tomorrow and I'll show you some of the best areas to look for a house, I'll get Richard to provide a car and a driver and we'll go exploring."

"Thank you so much," said Amie, "you are really kind, I never expected…"

"It's not a problem, I'll enjoy it and I'm not so old I don't remember my first few months in Africa and how I wished someone had filled me in on the local scene, it would have made life so much easier."

But if Amie thought she was going to have an easy life in Africa, she was very much mistaken. In her wildest dreams, she could never have imagined the challenges she would face.

3 SETTLING IN

Amie had been wrong in judging Diana to be about ten years older than her; she was in her mid forties, almost twenty years older. She laughed when Amie mentioned this the next day and commented that perhaps it was due to not wearing makeup.

"It runs and melts in the heat," she explained, "and despite the hot sun, without all that stuff on your face, I really think it makes you look younger, besides which I save an awful lot of money not buying cosmetics. If you're wise, you will wear a hat at all times out of doors, even in the rainy season, and it's not good for either your complexion or your skin to let it get too tanned, skin cancer is a real problem in Africa. You can even get badly burned in cloudy weather as the sun's rays are so much stronger."

Amie smiled when she thought about Sam coming over to get a good tan. Diana had picked her up at the hotel at eight o'clock, just after breakfast, much to Amie's surprise. She was soon to learn in Togodo, the day began early and shops, offices and services already had their doors open by eight every morning. It made sense while it was still relatively cool.

They drove down the main street, with its high rise buildings on each side. The road was wide, with enough space for a centre island hosting a profusion of flowers. Amie recognized several well known banks and familiar company logos but no department stores. She wondered if the whole population of the capital was in town, as the pavements were already crowded with pedestrians and the buses were all full.

There were also plenty of suburban taxis, not the usual sedans, but minibuses which appeared to carry at least twenty or more people at a time. These stopped to pick up and drop off passengers when and where they wanted. Amie even saw one parked on a roundabout, as several large ladies with even larger shopping baskets squeezed their way inside. The traffic backed up behind them and there was much hooting of horns and screaming, but it seemed to lack aggression.

Most of the people looked happy and relaxed with smiles on their shining black faces. No one moved quickly, it appeared the whole pace of life was slower. While a few of the people were well dressed, most of them looked poor. Their clothing was clean but faded, and everyone was carrying at least one plastic bag advertising one of the local supermarket chains.

As soon as they left the main street, and went down the narrow side streets, there was more rubbish lying around, the shops were smaller, many looking decidedly seedy. The tarmac road had sunk in many places and their driver had to weave from side to side to avoid the worst of the sinkholes.

They passed a local market where concrete slabs were piled high with a variety of fruits and vegetables, many of them unfamiliar to Amie. At the far end of the market were baskets of chickens and a small herd of goats in pens or tethered to posts with bits of string, all bleating loudly.

Amie wondered at the cacophony of noise, and yet no one moved quickly and many of the people were sitting doing nothing at all. Past the 'down town' area as Diana described it, they followed the road out of the centre which led to the residential areas.

Amie was enchanted by the suburbs. They were now in a different world. The roads were laid out in a square grid pattern, and alongside the pavements were grass lawns and flowerbeds in front of most of the residences. All the houses looked enormous in comparison to those back in Britain, much, much larger than their parents' homes. They certainly could never afford to rent a place this size in Europe. She also noticed no two houses were the same, each one was individually designed and quite different to the neighbouring houses. The streets were wide, and quiet with none of the bustle and chaos of the city. There was a young black man walking a dog on the far side of the street and round the corner came a black nanny pushing a baby in a pram with a small white child holding her hand.

"It's a world away from the centre of town!" exclaimed Amie.

"Yes, it is. You know it takes a fair bit of water to keep a lawn going," said Diana, "but we Europeans like a grass lawn, it's what we expect in a garden. You need just the right sort, like Kikuyu grass, to grow in this climate, even then you must give it litres and litres of water, and we still persist, even though the water supply is erratic and expensive!"

"The gardens are beautiful," said Amie looking at the brilliant flowers and bushes.

"This area is called Spring Glen, and it's one of the suburbs I would recommend. We'll go on over to Brianwood later, that's on the north side of town, and you can see the houses over there, they're bigger and more expensive, so it will all depend on your budget. If possible, although it's a lot of work, I would recommend you get a place with at least a small swimming pool, it's a real help in cooling off in the hot weather. The first year I was here, we didn't have one and I spent a lot of time sitting in the bath and taking showers."

"Goodness I never thought about having my very own swimming pool before!" exclaimed Amie, "that sounds very posh indeed. And the Brianwood houses are even larger than these?"

"Yes," Diana laughed. "You'll get used to it, and a swimming pool is really more of a necessity than a status symbol," she added as the car swerved to avoid some local children playing in the road.

"They look so poor," murmured Amie.

"Many of them are, but the government is far too busy spending money on important things like palaces and new government buildings and armaments and, they're also planning to spend billions on a new airport. Lots will change in the next couple of years since rumour has it the Americans have found oil just off the coast, and the country is already awash with the money the oil companies paid for permission to look for the oil. No, that's not true, let me rephrase it. The ruling hierarchy is awash with money, but none of it has seeped down to these little ones and their parents."

Brianwood turned out to be an even smarter suburb, though like Spring Glen, all the houses were surrounded by high walls or steel fences topped with barbed wire.

"Yes, I know, they look like very upmarket prisons and to some extent I guess that's true," Diana remarked.

"They're watering the grass over there," Amie pointed over to the left.

"Garden boys, or I suppose we must learn to call them gardeners, though not one of them knows one plant from another," commented Diana. "The trick is to employ a guy who's been working for other Europeans, at least that way he won't dig up all your roses and leave the bindweed to flourish."

"Employ a gardener? I'd never thought about that either," said Amie.

"It's expected, we do our bit in employing at least two or three of the locals, even though they've become much more expensive these days. Your maid will probably live in and it's wise to pay her the going rate, even if you think you're paying her peanuts."

"A maid!! Goodness!! How much would I pay a maid?" asked Amie.

"The going rate is one hundred and fifty Togodo dollars a month, and then of course you pay for her food, her accommodation and her water and lights as well."

Amie did some fast mental arithmetic. It worked out to about £50 a month. "That's not very much," she said. "How can they live on so little?"

"Well the minimum government wages work out to thirty dollars, so you can see we are paying almost five times that rate. Also, you will find a lot of women will want to work for you. Most of the British and the Americans are respected for always paying their wages, and paying on time, which is not usually the case if they work for the locals. A maid will think she's doing well if she's employed by an expatriate."

"But why not pay more, I mean if she really works well?" asked Amie.

"Remember what I said last night about jealousy? If her neighbours find out your maid for example, is getting paid lots more than they are, they will be jealous and that puts her at risk. Her house or family might be attacked if she doesn't share this extra money or they might even put a spell on her. Either way, it doesn't actually improve her life."

"A spell? They surely don't practice witchcraft do they?" Amie was both amazed and horrified.

"Oh yes, witchcraft is alive and well, and I've known European friends who are even a bit wary. There's a lot about the mind we still don't understand, but most people go to the medicine man or witch doctor regularly and they don't come cheap either. Even the local doctors who've been trained in western medicine overseas and returned to work here, will visit the sangomas for a love potent or to cast a spell over a rival."

"You're kidding!" gasped Amie. "Do they work? The spells I mean."

"Those who are cursed certainly believe it, and I've seen a few cases where people just curl up and die, especially if they can't pay for another witch doctor to remove the curse."

"I have a lot to learn," said Amie. "I thought all those tales were just stories in books, definitely not real! And not in this century either!"

"Fact is often stranger than fiction," replied Diana.

After touring around the streets of Brianwood, Diana directed the driver to take them to the mall.

"There's a shopping mall here?" asked Amie in surprise.

Diana laughed, "It's not a very large mall, but there's a supermarket, a bookstore, computer outlet, a dry cleaners and about a dozen other shops, mainly clothes and it's all very clean and neat. It mostly serves the ministerial class and the expatriate community, so you'll meet lots of other people at the mall. My friend has a small coffee shop there, so we'll get some refreshments at the same time."

After all the horror stories she'd heard in the last few hours, Amie was a little re-assured when she saw the neat car park and the row of smart shops, similar to those at home, but they were less crowded and nothing like as large. However, the layout was familiar, and she saw many products in the windows exactly the same as she could buy at home.

"You'll find things a lot more expensive here if they're imported, but the fresh fruit and vegetables in season and the local meat you can get for practically nothing."

"This is like a little oasis of England in the middle of Africa!" said Amie as they took chairs in the courtyard outside the mall coffee shop.

"Yes, as you can see, Africa is a land of contrasts" replied Diana, picking up a menu.

Amie felt as if she were in the middle of a surrealistic dream. The sun shone so brightly it was dazzling, and the air was hot and close reminding her she was in Africa, yet she was looking at a very upmarket, British suburb transplanted almost in the middle of nowhere.

"What's Jonathon doing today?" asked Diana lighting a

cigarette.

"He was collected early this morning by someone from the company they are liaising with here, and then he mentioned discussions with some government minister I think," Amie answered.

"You'll probably find he works quite long hours," said Diana, "all the men do. So don't be surprised if he gets home exhausted in the evening."

Amie wasn't quite sure how to broach the question she'd been dying to ask. She took a deep breath. "What do the women do, do they work as well?"

"There are very few of us who can get jobs, difficulty with the language for one thing. I guess we keep busy entertaining and visiting the Expatriate Club and playing sports, things like that. A few of us help at some of the local schools, ostensibly with basic English lessons, although we spend more time teaching the teachers than we do teaching the children."

When the smiling waitress brought the coffee, Amie found it was the same as they'd had the night before. When she mentioned this to Diana, she was told they grew coffee on the slopes near the capital and prepared the beans themselves. No, they didn't export much, as firstly the yields were not high, and it was difficult to find labour to increase production. For a housewife, Diana was certainly well informed about what was going on thought Amie. She wondered if all the wives took as much interest in their adopted country.

"Now I've seen a couple of good areas to live, how do we go about finding somewhere to rent?" asked Amie.

"First port of call will be the Club, that's the Expatriate Club, to check on the notice board. Then if there's nothing there, the next option would be to ask around some of the larger landlords," replied Diana.

"Who owns all these properties?" Amie waved in the direction of the Brianwood houses.

"They are all owned by local people. Before independence,

all these houses were built by Europeans, but now the law states that within the capital, only Togodians are allowed to own property, but of course the vast majority of them can't afford houses like these in Brianwood."

"So did the government buy them from the, what would you call them, settlers, colonials?" Amie was curious.

"Goodness no," answered Diana. "They simply requisitioned them. It all happened overnight so I understand, although it was several years before we arrived. Suddenly, people who owned houses were forced to pay rent for them, it's bizarre isn't it? Most were given to government ministers and family members, so your landlord is likely to be a very wealthy and powerful man."

"But, but surely that's not legal is it!" Amie was horrified.

Diana laughed. "My dear, this is Africa, and if the government wants to do something they do it. There is no such thing as fair play, or abiding by the law. If they don't like the law, then they simply change it or ignore it. Remember any opposition party is in name only and all members of parliament do as they're told, so any bill put before the Assembly is sure to pass, especially when it's written by the President.

"So it's not really a democracy at all?" said Amie.

"Democracy the African way, one man, one vote, one time," replied Diana. "Remember, once you're in power, that's it, you stay there usually until you die, or someone bumps you off, or there's a full scale civil war."

Amie felt a shiver run down her back. "Could that happen here?"

"Sure it could, but at the moment President Mtumba is firmly in control and although the teaming masses are generally not happy with him, there's been no great disaster or upheaval to cause a serious threat to his leadership so far. What do you fancy for lunch?" said Diana changing the subject and handing Amie the menu.

Amie was further reassured to see there were quite a few European women doing their shopping in the mall, often with young children in tow and accompanied by a black nanny who was there to help push the trolleys and look after the little ones. Several of the women stopped to chat to Diana, and they all welcomed Amie into the community. It's almost like the first day at a new and friendly school, thought Amie as she said hello and told them where she was from, and Jonathon was here to work on the new desalination plant.

"We desperately need one," was the general comment, as the present water supplies were erratic at best, and often there was no water for days on end.

After lunch they drove to the Club and Diana introduced her to the Secretary and said that most probably Amie and Jonathon would be joining, and Richard and she would sponsor them.

"It's really quite easy to become a member," Diana whispered to Amie as they walked around the large swimming pool, "but everyone likes to keep up appearances, and you must be proposed and seconded and fill in all the forms. Unless you're one of the Great Train Robbers, you'll automatically be accepted."

The club house consisted of a large dining room, a smaller coffee shop, a bar, changing rooms that served both the pool and the small nine hole golf course, and two or three meeting rooms. There was a full time staff including gardeners, who tended the well kept lawns and flower beds.

There were three properties on the board for rent, two in Spring Glen and one in Brianwood. Amie wrote down the contact telephone numbers while Diana advised her to let Jonathon call the landlords, it was very unlikely the owners would negotiate with a woman. As Amie put the list into her purse she nodded. Her new life was going to take a lot of getting used to.

When Jonathon got back to the hotel that night it was quite

late. He looked tired, and admitted he'd not had an easy day. Apparently the land for the plant which had been agreed to in London was now all of a sudden 'not available.' They were now in the process of deciding where it could go. The previously agreed site was too close to the summer palace belonging to the President, and he might be disturbed by the building contractors during construction.

"It would be a lot easier to move the President's summer palace than re-site the plant," grumbled Jonathon. His negotiating skills had been stretched to the limit, but he had been promised a fixer, who would be working for him from the following day.

"What's a fixer?" enquired Amie.

"A Togodian who works for a foreign company and smoothes the way through government bureaucracy and red tape. He can obtain permissions, work permits, grease government hands, just about anything."

"So they do the actual bribing, so the foreign company isn't seen to," remarked Amie.

Jonathon looked at her in surprise. "I've never considered you a political animal!" he exclaimed.

"I think you need to be one to survive in a country like this," replied Amie. "I've learned more in one day with Diana than I ever learned in civics in school. It's all very different, and I can see it pays to be aware."

Jonathon smiled and took her hand. "Are you OK with being here? I mean, you don't think it's going to be too bad do you?"

Amie thought for a moment. "I can't honestly answer that right now," she replied truthfully. "It all takes a lot of getting used to. There is some good and some bad as well. I mean I wasn't expecting such large houses, you should see them, most of them are enormous. And I never expected to be hiring a gardener and a maid to do all the housework, that will be nice, and the shopping mall is great and everyone is so friendly. That's on the upside."

"And the down side?" prompted Jonathon.

"Well there is definitely an undercurrent of fear and poverty, and I wouldn't want to break the law here, and the police are useless and the houses are surrounded like fortresses with barbed wire and you have to hire a security company and the crime is bad." Amie paused for breath. "But that's all I've found out so far."

"Well you've seen a lot more of the country than I have," Jonathon laughed. "I've been stuck in an office all day, trying to keep my wits about me. I will admit the air conditioning was on high, well it would be in a ministerial office I guess."

"You do look tired," said Amie, as she rose to stand behind him and rub his shoulders. "I guess an early night is in order. Let's have a quick meal downstairs in the restaurant and head back up to bed."

"Great idea," agreed Jonathon. "It's more negotiations again tomorrow and I'm not looking forward to it."

"Then I am going to make sure you enjoy tonight," replied Amie as she began to unbutton her shirt slowly and let it drop on the floor.

"You're a tease," Jonathon smiled as he began to take off his own shirt.

"Uh, uh, you don't want to waste your energy now do you?" Amie released her bra and then led him to the bed. She gently forced him down and very slowly began to remove his clothes.

"Please," he murmured, "stop teasing!"

Amie smiled at him. "Are you hungrier for me than for a meal downstairs?"

"I think you know the answer to that," said Jonathon as he suddenly reached up to pull her closer.

"I thought most of this basic stuff had been sorted out," said Amie as they tucked into their steaks an hour later.

"That's the impression they gave me before I left," Jonathon replied. "I understood they had organized offices and the site for the plant had been chosen and all I had to do, was to complete the office set up, and then supervise the initial building to specification with the labour force that was waiting as soon as we stepped off the plane."

"So what has happened so far?" asked Amie.

"Absolutely nothing. The local company which was supposed to be sorting everything out, didn't even rent space for offices." Jonathon took a sip of wine. "We've made contact with the useless organizers here, and it seems as if nothing can be done at all without ministerial permission. You wouldn't believe how many ministers there are, and they are all jostling for position, it's one major power play. I was taken to some government office and most of the day was spent talking about where our offices were going to be situated, although why that should concern them, I don't know."

"What happens next?"

"Well, I think we'll be setting up in a building quite close to the city centre, I absolutely refused to construct an office building from scratch."

"They wanted you to put up a brand new building, for the company?" Amie was astounded.

"Yes, it's ludicrous! You only have to look around to see dozens of unoccupied buildings in the centre of town. I think," Jonathon paused for a moment, "they want us to put more money in, and invest in building an office block as well as the desalination plant. They showed me some lovely designs, basically another way of making us spend more. And of course, when the desalination plant is up and running, they will have a new office block to rent out."

"It doesn't look as if they can rent out the buildings they've already got," Amie remarked.

"I'm not sure what they own, but it seems we need one more decision, hopefully tomorrow and I can start getting the office set up. It's all a lot more chaotic than I thought it would be."

"So will this mean the Drenton people will delay coming out?" Amie asked.

"Yes, it's been put on hold. They won't arrive until the office is up and running, and that's going to take several days at least, maybe even weeks. Right now, there's nowhere for them to work. First we have to agree on the office location, then I must get the banking sorted out, so I can get the furniture and communications systems installed, and then, hopefully, they'll be on the next plane."

"Let's hope it won't take too long," said Amie as she finished her meal. She had to admit to herself she'd be a lot more upset if she'd not met Diana, at least she had someone to talk to, and she was certainly learning a lot about her new country. Amie dug into her bag and handed Jonathon the contact phone numbers for rental property.

"Diana says all the houses are owned by more government ministers and if I tried to contact them I wouldn't get very far."

"Why not?"

Amie took a deep breath. "Because I'm a woman," she hissed quietly. "Apparently they would refuse to negotiate with me."

"Oh dear," said Jonathon, knowing this was one moment when he dared not smile. "OK, I'll see what I can do. I'll phone them from our associates' offices first thing in the morning. What are you going to be doing tomorrow?"

"I'm meeting Diana again, and she's going to show me more of the area and the best places to get the stuff we need for the house," said Amie. "Even driving around for half the day is exhausting."

"I can believe it," said Jonathon, "it's not going to be easy to build a plant in this heat."

The next morning the sky was a cloudless blue as usual

and the sun was shining as strongly as ever.

"Is it this hot every day?" Amie asked Diana as they went into the hotel coffee shop for a drink before they ventured outside.

"Most days yes. We have two rainy seasons, called the big rains, from September to November at least around that time, and the little rains in March and April. But you can't always tell how long they will last and how much rain will fall, there has been a lot less recently, probably due to global warming."

"Um, my company was making a programme for television on that subject," Amie replied.

"You're in television!" exclaimed Diana, "how glamorous!"

"Don't believe a word of it," said Amie. "I was working in a production house which makes inserts for TV and the staff all agree it's mostly hard work, and on shoot you need to work very fast, you never know how long the rain will hold off." Amie felt a little guilty not mentioning her duties as a mere receptionist, but she hadn't exactly told a lie either. What Diana believed was up to her, and it was nice for other people to think she was part of the entertainment hype.

"You have no worries about that here, even in the rainy season it doesn't rain all day, but the moment it stops, the ground steams, the humidity goes up and you feel even hotter and all your clothes stick to you. In no time at all, the rain has disappeared, at least outside the city. Here in town there are no such things as storm water drains, so it runs all over the place and flows down the streets and generally causes chaos. No, what I miss most are the long summer evenings." Diana ordered a café latte from the waiter, while Amie settled for tea.

Amie struggled to remember long forgotten geography lessons. "What time does it get dark in summer then?"

"Practically the same time as it does in winter, we're close to the Equator here…"

"Oh yes, I remember now, day and night are about the

same length," Amie interrupted.

"Yes, and you won't notice much difference in the seasons either, except it rains more during certain months. Believe me, it can get monotonous."

"Really?" said Amie. "But think of all the British and the other Northern Europeans who rush to sit in the sun every year."

"True, but you can have too much of a good thing, and sometimes you long for a cold day and a chilly breeze and even some grey skies," Diana replied.

"I really can't imagine that," said Amie.

"Just give it time my dear and you'll feel exactly the same," Diana laughed.

"So what are we going to see today?" Amie felt a bit like a child about to go Christmas shopping.

"I thought I would take you and show you the markets. Once you have a maid, then you can take her and give her the list of things to get. Keep that in mind, because if you try to buy the produce yourself, then the prices will be triple or even more."

"Because they think we can afford more?"

"Yes, and it's really throwing money away. Not all African countries have this multi tier price system, but here they are so poor, they will grab anything they can get. They will assume you're a tourist and loaded with cash and charge you accordingly."

"Do you get many tourists here?" Amie asked.

"Very few, there's really nothing to see, and very few facilities, but there are a couple of horrendously expensive bush lodges which cater for rich Americans, and one of them caters for the hunting fraternity."

"I hate to think there are people who still want to kill animals," said Amie.

"It's big money business," replied Diana. "They pay thousands and thousands to go out into the bush, shoot some poor, luckless animal and then have their photograph taken with one foot on the dead body."

"Are there lots of wild animals out there?" asked Amie.

"Not as many as there were. I must admit we don't go out of town all that often, although there are a few expatriates who take to the bush whenever they can. I'm a bit too old now for roughing it in the wild. Give me a comfortable bed, water from the taps and electricity on demand, although both of those are pretty erratic here."

Diana had come to collect Amie in her own car, and as they walked down the front steps of the hotel, they were immediately surrounded by a group of noisy, dirty, children who all held their hands out and begged for money.

"No," said Diana sharply, "I've already reserved my car guard, see that tall one over there." As she pointed, an older boy, dressed in a scruffy t-shirt and ragged shorts got to his feet. He gave Diana a huge smile and held out his hand. Diana gave him a few coins and he bowed so low, his head touched his knees.

As they got into the car Diana said, "When you get your own car, you'll be asked for money every time you park it. Look around for the biggest boy, usually the leader, and give him a few coins. Promise him more, if the car is still there, or undamaged when you return, and always pay. If you don't, then you'll be lucky to get away without a broken window or two, a flat tyre, or several large scratches on the paintwork."

"It sounds like a protection racket!" exclaimed Amie.

"That's exactly what it is, the young learn early here. Everyone is on the take." Diana pulled into the flow of traffic. "First I'll show you the market I use, and then I thought you might like to visit one of the schools where we lend a hand."

"Yes, I'd like that," said Amie, though she had little experience of schools other than her own. Instead of taking the direct route through town, Diana drove past many of the important landmarks and Amie gazed in awe at the government buildings, tall structures constructed of steel and smoked glass, surrounded by bright green lawns and colourful flower beds. It seemed ridiculous that right on the boundary, street sellers were peddling their wares. Women sat on the pavements outside these tall, elegant buildings, next to plastic sheets covered with vegetables and cheap plastic toys and wooden carvings. In turn, these were surrounded with discarded wrappings, several pieces of rotting fruit, and other general rubbish.

"That sort of lowers the tone of the place," she remarked to Diana.

"That's typically African," her new friend replied. "They set up right next to the manicured gardens, and leave litter all around the place and do you see any toilets for them to use?"

"No. So what do they do?"

"I'll leave that to your imagination," said Diana.

To Amie it appeared the presidential palace was a cross between a Disney fairy tale castle and an English baronial residence. "It looks well guarded," she remarked. There were guards at the main gates which were firmly closed and topped with razor wire and there were CCTV cameras mounted on the walls every few metres.

"Yes, no one is allowed near the place, remember, the aim is to stay in power at all costs," said Diana. "You'll notice all the major buildings, like those for government departments and ministries are new and very smart, but they are seldom maintained properly. The Africans seem to have a mental block when it comes to looking after things. It's often easier to knock down the old building and start afresh. Some of these places look very smart from the outside, but look more closely and the plumbing probably doesn't work all that well, half the light bulbs are missing and in some cases, even the concrete cladding is beginning to fall off. The standard of building isn't very high, especially when you see how fast they're thrown together."

"What are they building over there?" Amie asked, pointing to a huge construction site where there was frantic activity."

"Ah, that's our new convention centre, to house exhibitions and shows and gala banquets. They've been building it for a couple of years now, but recently, they seemed to have increased the number of workers and it looks as if they will finish it after all."

When they reached the market, Amie was amazed at the size of it, covering the space of at least three football fields. There were rows and rows of women, she saw very few men, sitting on the ground next to the familiar plastic sheets and all of them were piled high with a wide variety of fruits and vegetables. Most were dressed in brightly coloured cotton dresses, and matching headscarves. A few of the ladies were sitting under bright umbrellas, advertising beer and Coca Cola, and some held pieces of cardboard above their heads, but most had no shade at all.

Many of the makeshift stalls were selling the same fruits and vegetables and Amie rightly guessed that all the produce on offer was currently in season. There were meat sellers too, guarding their piles of raw flesh covered in flies which they didn't even bother to disperse as prospective buyers approached.

"You don't buy your meat here do you!" gasped Amie.

"Not a chance," laughed Diana. "You'd need a very strong constitution not to get food poisoning from eating this stuff, but then the locals boil all their meat, they like it very well done."

Amie watched in disgust as an old woman haggled with the seller, before picking up a few pieces of stringy offal and slinging it into a plastic bag. She handed over a few coins.

"Eating meat almost daily is essential for most Africans," Diana commented.

The fruits and vegetables looked more appetizing, but there were several Amie didn't recognize.

"Most are members of the pumpkin or squash family," Diana told her. "They grow in all shapes, sizes and colours. Frankly I think most of them are quite tasteless, and the vegetables which are more familiar to us, like peas and green beans, you'll only get in the supermarket. This market is only for food, but I'll take you to the other markets which also sell clothing and baskets and household wares. Once you move into your own place, I'll draw you a map so you can find your way back here, but let's go to see the school."

Even at the market, there was a small crowd of young boys, crowding round asking for money.

"Don't start handing out coins," Diana warned Amie, "only pay if, for example they're guarding your car. Once you give to one, dozens more will materialize from nowhere and pester you."

"I feel so bad not helping them," said Amie looking at the large round eyes and thin bodies which showed through the holes in their clothing. Some of the children had scars on their faces, others had sores on their arms and legs.

"Yes, I know it's sad," said Diana as they drove away, "but you do learn to cope with it after a while. You have to be tough here to survive into adulthood. None of us can put things right, they must, eventually, do that for themselves."

Secretly Amie thought Diana was more than a little tough herself, she knew she would never get used to the poverty she saw, and her heart ached to see so much suffering.

The school was on the outskirts of town, reached by a dirt road, which caused a large cloud of dust to rise up behind the car. On either side of the road were rows and rows of shacks, built of a wide variety of materials, tin sheeting, wood from packing cases, a few bricks, old tyres and large pieces of plastic. Around some of the structures was an area of bare ground and a few even had makeshift fences to enclose the yard. Everywhere Amie looked, she could see piles of rubbish, old coke bottles, bits of paper and cardboard, rusty tins and old rags.

"Here we are," said Diana as they drove up to the school. To Amie's amazement, she saw the whole complex was surrounded by a chain link fence topped with yet more barbed wire. As the car approached, an old man carrying a large stick shuffled forward and opened the gates for them.

"It looks more like a prison than a school!" Amie exclaimed.

"Yes, but then theft is rife and once the word got round that the school was given three computers, it became a target. It often costs more to protect the equipment installed by sponsors and overseas donations, than the stuff cost in the first place," Diana replied as they parked by the main building and got out of the car. "These donations can be a burden in their own right."

Amie looked at the sprawling one story buildings linked by covered walkways. The grounds were bare earth, again, much of it covered with litter of all sorts, papers, tin cans, bottles and she even noticed a couple of used condoms. Here and there were patches of tall grass and a few bushes.

"Yes, it's a bit of a mess, and we have suggested they clear it up, but they don't really get the point," Diana remarked.

Many of the windows were broken, despite the wire mesh and steel bars protecting them, and Amie could hear dozens of young voices chanting as they walked towards the principal's office.

Amie's feet were soon covered in dust as they crossed the bare playground but before they had even reached the verandah, a lady rushed out to greet them, her face wreathed in smiles. Amie guessed she might be the school secretary as she was more smartly dressed than many of the local people she had seen so far.

"Ah Mama Diana," she shrieked. "You have come to see us and brought us a visitor too! Come, come, I will bring you tea."

Like a sheep dog with only two sheep, she herded them into a small room, assuring them the headmistress would be with them in a couple of minutes.

As they perched on the upright wooden chairs Amie looked around. The walls were covered with pieces of brightly coloured cardboard. On each of them, someone had written a phrase such as *'Always do you're Best,' 'God is Watchin You all the Time,' 'Always Tel the Truth*,' and the words were surrounded by pictures of flowers, birds, green grass and trees.

"You'll think me cynical, but that last one is a joke," whispered Diana with a smile. "If a lie serves you better, then it's part of cultural custom to lie."

Amie nodded nervously. She was more amused by the incorrect spelling and the interesting use of capital letters and the bold underlining of the phrases to indicate their importance.

A few minutes later the Secretary reappeared with a tray balancing cups, saucers and a plate of biscuits, closely followed by the Headmistress.

Diana introduced Amie to Mrs Motswezi. She was a cheerful, plump lady, smartly dressed in a bright purple polyester suit. She was average height, with large brown eyes and wore her straightened hair scraped back into a very short pony tail. She welcomed her visitors and ushered them into her brightly decorated office, which housed a desk, filing cabinet, three chairs and florescent red curtains. She poured the tea carefully and added milk and three sugars to each cup. Amie gulped, she didn't take sugar in tea, but was too polite to say anything.

"You have come to see our children?" enquired Mrs Motswezi handing the cups across the desk.

"Yes," Diana answered. "Amie has just arrived from

England, and I wanted to bring her in and introduce her."

"That is so nice. We are only a poor school, but we do our best, especially with the hostel."

"The hostel?" asked Amie.

"Here there are big problems with HIV/AIDS, and so many of our little ones have no parents at all. Some of the older children are now parents to the children, but those very little ones are all alone, so we use three of the classrooms as a hostel."

"So they live at school?"

"Yes, even in the holidays. They have nowhere else to go. They don't know their families, especially if their parents moved to town from the rural areas. Most of them have no idea who the father is." Mrs Motswezi shook her head sadly. "So often the men just run away when they hear there is to be a child. They know the mother will ask for money and they do not want to give money. Aiiieeee! They go and take another woman and they do not come back."

"How sad," said Amie. "Are there many of these children?"

"Yes, there are very, very many, but only a few we can help. The others? Who knows where they go, but they come to school many days and we teach them what we can. And," Mrs Motswezi added proudly, "we teach them in English, we know so much of the world speaks English and this is what makes our children to be so successful."

Amie managed to gulp down the sickly tea and crunch through a very stale biscuit, as the Headmistress described the children, the staff and the facilities she had already, and the plans she had for the future. As Mrs Motswezi gave them a tour of the school, Amie was part amused and part horrified by what she saw. There were a few posters on the walls, many of the words, all in English, were misspelled and the usual method of teaching was getting the children to repeat words and sentences by rote. She wondered if most of them had any idea what they were chanting. Each of the classrooms was filled to bursting point, with two or three children sharing a desk. There were only a few textbooks to be seen and no teaching aids at all beyond a blackboard and small piles of chalk. A few of the older children had an exercise book and they copied laboriously from the blackboard, while those without books waited patiently for them to finish writing. There were no science labs, no gym, no hall and the sports equipment was one deflated football and a set of mismatched coloured bands. What a stark contrast to British schools, thought Amie, as she watched one teacher sitting under a tree with her class of children grouped around her. It was all so very different to her own educational experience.

Mrs Motswezi swept them over to the furthest building next to which was a makeshift shelter housing a row of big, black, three legged, cooking pots, just like the ones used to boil the heroine in the old Hollywood films, Amie observed to herself. Piles of dry wood burned under each pot and three ladies were using large wooden paddles to stir what looked like porridge as it boiled and bubbled over the heat.

"We give the children vegetables for lunch," said Mrs Motswezi proudly, "and we grow these ourselves in our own vegetable garden, come look at it."

Amie thought there seemed to be a lot more weeds than vegetables, but she recognized a few cabbages and onion stalks struggling for survival against all odds. The garden also seemed very small for feeding so many children.

"How many children do you have at this school?" she asked the headmistress.

"Just over six hundred, but they don't all come every day."

Amie turned to count the number of classrooms, there were twelve being used for teaching. "So that means you have about fifty children in each class?" she asked.

"Yes, they are large classes," Mrs Motswezi replied, "but we have more in our pre-school, come we will go visit them next."

Amie gazed at the crowd of small faces who turned to look at the visitors as they walked into the pre-school classroom. Some of the children smiled and jumping to their feet came to crowd round the new arrivals. As in every other classroom they had seen, Mrs Motswezi told the children that Amie was a visitor from England and as one the children chanted "Good morning visitor from England."

Amie felt tears in her eyes as she gazed at the little faces. Some looked happy and eager, others looked sad and beaten, as if they knew, even at this early age, life was going to be one long struggle for survival. One child in particular caught her attention. Right at the very back was a small girl with the largest eyes Amie had ever seen. When the other children jumped to their feet, she noticed this little one was pushed to one side and she fell over before scrambling to her feet.

Mrs Motswezi saw Amie's face and beckoned the teacher to come over and they spoke for a few moments in the local language.

"That little one has no parents and she is not thriving," she told Amie pointing to the child she'd noticed. Maybe one day someone will take her and give her a good home, who knows. We don't know where she comes from, she was found by the gate many months ago."

Amie looked at the child again and wished she had something to give her. The child's filthy dress was much too small for her and was torn in several places.

"Does she stay here in the hostel?" she asked the teacher, but it was Mrs Motswezi who answered.

"Yes, she has nowhere else to go. She is called Angelina, but I think God has forgotten this little angel, we do the best we can for all our little ones.

In the car on the way back to the hotel, Amie was very

quiet.

"Don't get too emotionally involved, or it will break your heart," counseled Diana. "There are thousands of Angelinas in this country alone, and this is only one small country on a very large continent."

"It's just so different seeing this in real life," said Amie. "We see stuff on TV, but it's not the same at all. When you meet the poor face to face and see the suffering for yourself, it makes it very real."

"There is a lot of real suffering here," Diana replied, "but remember, Angelina is one of the lucky ones. She gets fed, and there is a chance of her getting at least some sort of a basic education."

"She's one of the lucky ones?" Amie exclaimed, "but surely her chances of ever getting out of the poverty trap are very limited."

"That's true," agreed her new friend, "and with the national life expectancy in Togodo of thirty to forty years, she may not have too many years to look forward to, poor little scrap. But I can't say it too strongly Amie, don't get involved, there is very little you can do to change the future for these children. Come with us by all means a couple of times a week to help the teachers and pass on ideas and so on. You can't take every child out of this environment and that is not necessarily the right thing to do. This is their country, their culture and their way of life. Yes, they are poor, yes many go hungry, but if we interfere too much we only impose our way of life on them and that might not be for the best in the long run. Don't get emotionally involved. You'll only end up breaking your own heart."

Although Amie did not realize it, it was good advice, but she had a sneaking feeling it was advice she was not going to follow. If only she had!

4 PRETTY, TICKS AND ANGELINA

The next few days were hectic. Jonathon remembered to phone the landlords and he and Amie went round to look at the three houses for rent. They were astonished at the size of them. They all had two or three lounges, one of which was referred to as the family room. There was also a dining room, three or four bedrooms all of which were en suite, plus at least one extra bathroom for visitors, and each property was surrounded by large gardens containing a swimming pool. In every back yard there was a separate building which they understood was the maid's quarters. The houses were furnished, basic furniture to be sure, nothing that would feature in *House and Home,* but the chairs, beds and tables were quite adequate for day to day living.

After looking at all three, they decided on one in Spring Glen, it was the smallest of the three and less expensive. They both agreed they would rattle around in the larger houses, and secretly Amie thought they would rattle around in this one. She couldn't wait to tell her family about the house, maid's quarters and a swimming pool! Arrangements were made for Jonathon to sign the lease and they could move in as soon as they liked.

Amie was really fed up living in the hotel. There were problems with the laundry, every bundle returned was short of several items, and although she complained bitterly to the management who were very apologetic, nothing ever came of it, and stuff continued to disappear.

The menu in the restaurant never varied and both of them were sick of burgers, omelettes, steaks and toasted sandwiches. Amie breathed a sigh of relief as a few days later they repacked their suitcases and moved out of the hotel.

An inventory in the new house revealed no vacuum cleaner, no washing machine, no kettle and no toaster.

"It would not be wise to let your maid loose with too many electrical appliances," remarked Diana who had come over for a visit and to have a look at the house. "She will do all your washing in the bath, and clean the floors by hand with a cloth and a bucket of water. Even if you buy her a mop or a squeegee, she will still get down on her hands and knees to wash and polish the floors."

"Do I *have* to have a maid?" asked Amie, the thought of letting someone else do all the housework was a bit daunting, she'd no idea how to handle a servant.

"Oh yes. It's expected. Most people will think it very odd if you don't, and you might as well enjoy one of the perks for living in a country where there are very limited resources."

"But where do I find one?" asked Amie.

"They find you, my dear, just look out of the window."

Amie walked over and pulled aside the net curtain. A large crowd of women had gathered at the bottom of the driveway, some standing, others sitting on the edge of the road. Most of them were chattering loudly reminding Amie of a large flock of colourful birds.

"Who are all those people?"

"Prospective maids, they're all hoping you'll employ them," Diana replied. "Word travels fast here, and already news is out a new white madam has moved in. It will be difficult to choose, but try to employ someone who has worked for a family before, though that's difficult to judge because they will lie about it. Oh, and only take on a girl who can speak at least a little bit of English."

"What about references?"

"I've tried to give some of my departing maids a letter of recommendation, but they don't see the point in them," Diana replied.

"You've had several maids?" asked Amie.

"Goodness yes, it usually takes a while to find the right one. Some steal from you, or borrow your clothes, or empty the liquor cabinet. On one occasion I saw Wonder walking down our driveway in one of my outfits. Of course she had to go!" Diana laughed. "Although it wasn't funny at the time."

"Will you stay and help me choose?" Amie was feeling a bit panicky. She would never be able to interview all the candidates. As fast as she talked to half a dozen, twelve more appeared at the bottom of the driveway. Most spoke very little English and it was difficult to turn them away. Faces which at first looked hopeful and smiling fell, and several of them begged to work for her, indicating they were hungry or had many children to feed.

At last with Diana's help, Amie chose a girl, although she was hardly young, and they agreed on one hundred and fifty Togodo dollars a month. The new maid's name was Pretty, although as Diana explained, most chose a European name as local names were very hard to pronounce.

Amie thought the name Pretty was perhaps not an accurate description of her new maid. She was short, had stocky legs, very short frizzy hair, a very large nose and a wide mouth. But as Diana pointed out, she was clean, her dress looked as if it had been ironed and Pretty at least did have papers, a torn and scruffy baptismal certificate which announced which province she'd been born in. It showed that Pretty was about thirty one years old. Privately, Amie thought she looked a good deal older.

Diana observed that it showed initiative to bring some sort of papers to an interview, and, if anything major happened they would have some idea where Pretty came from, if indeed the papers were hers in the first place.

It all seemed very hit and miss to Amie but she agreed to let Pretty work for her for a month and she would pay her weekly, as again, Diana had advised her it was possible to give her a week's notice if it didn't work out.

"At least," Diana remarked walking back into the house after sending Pretty out to tell the waiting crowd the Madam had engaged her, "she had the sense to turn up without any children."

Several of the women were obviously pregnant or held babies and small children, and the last thing Amie wanted was a whole crowd living in the servants' quarters in the garden.

"But there's only one bed, and the room is very small!" exclaimed Amie.

Diana looked at her. "Remember the shacks by the school? Your servant's quarters are five star in comparison, and Africans are used to living in large groups and would think nothing of crowding five or six into one room." She advised Amie to keep an eye open to make sure Pretty did not move half her family in there.

"You'll need a gardener as well," remarked Diana as they sat in the lounge drinking coffee. It seemed that was one thing Pretty could do. She never even looked for the kettle, but calmly filled a saucepan of water and put it on the stove to boil.

"A gardener as well? Are you sure I need a gardener?" said Amie in surprise.

"Unless you absolutely adore gardening, and would enjoy working out there in the extreme heat?" Diana grinned.

"Well no, I've never looked after a garden in my life, we always lived in an apartment but ...." Amie paused.

"It would probably shock the local workers to see you digging or cutting down branches," said Diana. "It's just not done by the Madam. Although cutting a few blooms for the house is acceptable of course."

"I feel so guilty and more than a little self conscious," said Amie. She surprised herself being this open with Diana, after all she hadn't known her all that long, but somehow Diana invited confidences and she was so easy to talk to.

"I do understand how you feel," replied Diana. "I've been in Africa for many years…"

"But I thought you said you'd only been here for two years," interrupted Amie.

"In Togodo for two years yes, but before that we were in Kenya and Botswana and Zimbabwe, in fact we've been abroad for the whole of our married life."

"Oh!" said Amie as the thought dawned on her that maybe one day she might be saying the same thing. Up until now she had only thought about this as a one off, two year contract and then back home to settle down as planned. Was this the beginning of a lifetime of expatriate living? She wasn't sure how she felt about that. Was she looking at herself in Diana in twenty years time? She wasn't sure she liked the idea at all.

In the meantime, Jonathon was making very slow, but sure progress. "The fixer is amazing," he told Amie. "Anything I want done, he just says 'Yes Boss,' and off he goes. I guess he must be bribing people all over the place, as his expenses are astronomical, but at least things are happening."

Jonathon took Amie into town to show her where the new offices were, nothing very exciting, there was little to choose from in the way of furniture, but at least the phone lines were working so would Amie like to phone home? Would she? Just give her half a chance!

She phoned her parents first and although there was a distinct delay on the line, she could hear her mother's familiar voice and she could picture her standing in the hall by the coat rack as they talked.

Amie didn't know quite where to begin there was so much

to tell, and how could you describe the heat, and the dust and the flies and the dirt and the poverty and the people and the bright sunlight and even the atmosphere of optimism among such degradation? It was all a million miles away from Beech Avenue on a cold, wet, overcast afternoon.

News from her mother was about people at home and who was doing what and the concert at the pre-school when Dean gave a marvelous performance as a cow. Sam had sat up half the night sewing the most amazing costume for him, complete with shiny horns. A brief image flashed into Amie's mind, thinking how different school was for Angelina and the thousand other children she'd been to see.

She phoned Samantha next, and as usual Dean answered the phone.

"This is Dean here, who is that?" he shouted down the wires, his voice distorting with the delay.

"It's Aunt Amie, I'm phoning from Africa."

"Are you coming to see us this afternoon?" Dean asked and then rushed on without waiting for a reply. "You didn't come and see me as the cow, I was so good, and it was a very important part, Mrs Fleming said so."

"I'm so sorry I missed it Dean, but I am living a very, very long way away and I will only be coming home once in a whole year," Amie replied, trying to swallow the lump in her throat as she thought of her family so far away. She heard Sam's voice in the background asking who was on the phone.

"It's Aunt Amie," Dean replied, "but I'm talking to her."

"Not any more, say goodbye quickly, overseas phone calls are very expensive," Sam said as she took the receiver away from her eldest.

"Hi Sam, it's good to hear your voice," said Amie almost tearfully.

"You've been gone almost four weeks and not a word from you, how's it going?"

"But I've written at least six letters," Amie cried, "didn't you get any of them?"

"No, nothing, we were beginning to get a bit worried."

"Look I don't know what the situation is with the office phone, but I will try and talk to you at least once a month, especially if we can't trust the postal service," said Amie, "and I'm sure I can make arrangements to come into the office and send emails from the computer at least once a week. Jonathon has promised to try and get Internet in the house, but it may take a while. Nothing moves quickly over here."

"That would be great, so what's it like out there, lots of sunshine? Got a tan yet?"

"Oh Sam it's all so different, it's hard to describe, but it's nothing like France or Spain that's for sure. It's kind of primitive, yet there are computers everywhere and all the trappings of the first world but they're not really used properly, and anyway we are expected to stay in the expatriates' cocoon and go to the Club and play tennis and generally live lives of the pampered married woman....." Amie wasn't quite sure exactly when they were cut off, but she suddenly realized there was no connection and although they tried several more times, it was impossible to get through to England again.

"Never mind," said Jonathon.

"I feel bad, you never got to talk to your parents at all," Amie said.

"I'll send them an email on Monday, or as soon as the lines are back up again. Anyway, time we were going or we'll be late for dinner at the Club."

During the next three months, Amie settled into her new life. There were early problems with Pretty, who insisted she had worked as a maid before, but Amie was dubious. At first she felt awkward and uncomfortable telling someone else what to do, she guessed that if you grew up with servants you knew how to interact with them, but Amie didn't even know anyone who employed domestic staff. She didn't like to ask Diana for advice, fearing she would think her stupid, but it didn't take Pretty long to figure out Amie was a novice employer. She pushed the boundaries as far as she could.

At first, Amie didn't notice how much bread, sugar and jam went missing, until it became so obvious even she began to wonder. Surely they'd never used so much food before, even with one extra mouth to feed? She was buying six kilos of sugar every week and several jars of jam. At first it didn't occur to her that Pretty was stealing it, surely one person couldn't consume all this extra food?

Plucking up her courage, Amie asked Pretty if she had helped herself to any extra food. She felt very guilty accusing her maid of theft, she had no proof after all, but who else could be taking it?

Pretty looked completely shocked and denied she had touched any of the food. She only ate what Amie said she could have and she would never, ever steal from the Madam who was so kind as to give her work.

Amie felt dreadful and apologized profusely for having doubted her honesty. But the food kept disappearing, if anything at an even faster rate. It wasn't until Amie saw Pretty sitting on the pavement outside the house one afternoon selling small parcels of sugar, and slices of bread covered in jam, that the truth finally dawned on her.

Amie was furious, mostly because Pretty had made such a fool of her. She flew into a rage and threatened to fire her. Much to her horror, Pretty burst into tears and promised never to take anything ever again. Amie was reluctant to get rid of her, it meant starting all over again with another girl, so for the moment, she relented. After that, Amie kept strict control over the foodstuffs, and even went so far as to lock the food cupboards. Now she knew why the kitchen cabinets came with keys and locks and even the fridge had a lock on it. She must get into the habit of putting out what foodstuffs were needed for that day, and keeping the rest under lock and key. She reminded herself that telling lies was an accepted form of behaviour and she should remember and not be so naive in the future. Still the incident upset her.

Amie had suggested that Pretty was to eat with them in the evenings, but the first night, the atmosphere round the table was uncomfortable. Pretty ate with her fingers, ignoring the cutlery she had laid out and Amie could only guess the loud slurping noises Pretty made were a cultural show of appreciation. Half way through the meal, Pretty got to her feet and removed both herself and her plate and disappeared into her quarters without saying a word. Jonathon breathed a sigh of relief and grinned at Amie.

"I guess she doesn't want to eat with us after all," he said. "Let's wait and see what she decides to do tomorrow."

"I was only trying to be friendly and diplomatic," Amie commented. "But perhaps you're right, it was a mistake."

"I guess we should try and remember those old movies on TV about the Victorian era and take a leaf out of their book, I don't remember them fraternizing with the servants, they ate downstairs in the kitchen."

"But surely these days it's different. We're always being told to be modern and more politically correct," said Amie gathering up the empty plates.

Pretty re-appeared as if by magic and firmly claimed the dishes by grabbing them out of Amie's hands and marched back into the kitchen. Amie sat down, and from then on, Pretty made it quite clear she did not wish to eat with them, and in fact took great exception to Amie even lifting a finger to do any housework at all.

Amie had to show her how to use the iron, and even though she explained slowly and carefully, Pretty succeeded in burning most of the clothes. Amie was forced to go out and buy more clothes, especially when Jonathon only had two unscorched shirts left to wear. Pretty's performance only improved when, in desperation she followed Diana's advice, and threatened to deduct the cost of the ruined clothing from Pretty's wages. It worked like a charm, and from that day on, no more clothes were ruined.

"What did you do with the ruined shirts?" Diana asked Amie.

"I gave them to Pretty, they were really too good to throw in the bin," Amie replied.

"See, it's an excellent way to build up your wardrobe, burn something and it's yours!" exclaimed Diana. "They think we have an unending supply of money, and you proved this to Pretty, since you just went out and bought more shirts. If she thinks she'll lose money by spoiling your clothes, she'll stop." Diana was right.

"Oh, and if you find food is disappearing, take the cost out of her wages as well. Another trick is to see what you don't use very often. You'll notice it gets pushed right to the back of the shelf, and if you don't say anything, then it walks out the door."

Amie turned red, but said nothing, she was learning fast. It seemed the stricter you were with workers the better they performed and Jonathon agreed the same principle worked with the labourers he'd hired to build the plant. Somehow, if you were seen as too kind, thoughtful and considerate, then everyone took advantage of you.

Amie was not happy with this state of affairs, she had no desire to be slightly aloof and tough with Pretty, but if it stopped her stealing and wrecking their clothing then maybe it was worth it.

At first, she had a lot less to do with William the gardener. He was always busy out of doors whenever Amie went in and out of the house, but she suspected, he sat down and did nothing the moment she disappeared from view. She took to making a list of things for him to do on the two days a week he came to work, and insisted she inspect everything before he left for the day. She discovered instructions were taken quite literally, for example, she told him to water the lawn every afternoon, and he did, even when it was raining. Amie couldn't believe her eyes, and rushed outside to stop him.

"You say water lawn," he grumbled.

"Not when it's raining!!" shrieked Amie. "Are you stupid or what?" She paused, horrified at what she'd said, but William didn't reply. Amie turned and walked back into the house, hoping there wouldn't be any repercussions, perhaps he'd not understood her, she could only hope his English was not that good.

Amie had to admit to herself that she really enjoyed having all the housework done for her, it was not something she had ever really liked doing, it was just one of those things which had to be done. When she wrote and told Sam about having help in the house, she didn't mention how much she paid Pretty. Already, Amie was beginning to realize it was going to be difficult to explain just how different things were; you had to experience it to really understand.

She fell into the routine of playing tennis two mornings a week, sitting and chatting with the other women and reading books borrowed from the small library at the Club. But after a few months, Amie began to get bored. As Diana had warned, Jonathon worked very long hours and was usually exhausted by the time he got home late at night. Amie tried to talk to him about his work, but he was not forthcoming, except to give her the impression that anything that could go wrong, would go wrong.

Several other members of the company had arrived by now, but they were all single men who stayed together in apartments in the centre of town, and Amie only got to meet them briefly. She swam every day in the pool, although on the days the gardener worked, she waited until he left, since she was uncomfortable with the way William looked at her in her bikini.

Initially, she had been keen to use the video camera, and took it to the Club one day to record for the family, but several of the other members warned her not to be seen with it in public, as the authorities took a dim view of cameras, and if she was caught filming a 'sensitive' location, she could get into trouble. For the moment, Amie confined her filming to the house, the garden and the Club.

While out shopping one day in the mall, she saw a computer for sale and on impulse went in and bought it. Much to her amazement, it was one of the latest models with a large memory and a CD drive, so now she had something to play her music on. She was also thrilled to discover the shop could order in more tape for her camera, and put in an order there and then.

There were limited Internet facilities in Togodo, and Jonathon and Amie didn't even have a telephone in the house, but everyone had a mobile phone, commonly referred to as cell phones. There were three cell phone companies with offices in the capital and they vied with each other for custom. If there was one thing the Africans loved, it was to talk. It seemed even the most poverty stricken people somehow managed to possess a phone and they could be seen pulling them out of their pockets, bras and knickers to answer the calls they received. Even Pretty had a cell phone, though as Diana remarked, it was most unlikely it had been bought at the store. Cell phones were top of the list when it came to robberies and muggings. Even if they were blocked, there were plenty of small workshops in the shack lands where enterprising young scoundrels could quickly convert them and insert a stolen SIM card.

Once Amie realized she could buy a data package to put in her phone, she was able to use it as a modem, plug it into her computer and connect to the Internet. She activated Skype and was able to call home. Not too often, as the data was expensive, but at least she could keep in touch more regularly. Not one of the letters she had sent to the family ever arrived.

At last she was back in touch with the outside world, and she sent dozens of emails to friends and relatives telling them about her new life.

She logged on to her page on Facebook and added more information and a few pictures she had taken with her mobile phone. It felt so good to be connected to home and friends, and it lessened the isolation and the feeling she was completely out of touch with the rest of the planet.

On impulse, she went on line one day and ordered an editing package from London and waited excitedly for it to arrive. She knew she was taking a chance, as no outgoing mail had succeeded, but maybe it worked better the other way round? The post took almost ten weeks, but eventually Amie received a notice in her mail box there was a parcel to collect at the post office.

When she arrived, the queue, if you could call it that, stretched out of the building and round the corner, and it took the best part of the morning to fight her way to the counter and hand over the slip of paper. The clerk looked at it for a long time and then shrugged his shoulders.

"Not here," he said, guessing correctly that Amie spoke English.

"But this was in my post box, it must be here," she protested.

The clerk waved her to the other end of the post office. He seemed to be indicating another window at the far end.

Amie sighed and moved over prepared to fight her way through to the second counter. No one else seemed to be in the slightest hurry, they seemed quite content to wait indefinitely.

When she finally reached the front of the line, she handed over the paper to the clerk who scratched his head and stood picking his nose. He stared at Amie for several seconds then slowly and reluctantly turned and disappeared into a back room.

Amie stood and waited, how could it take this long to find one parcel?

Eventually he returned carrying a box partly covered in brown paper. "What is this?" he asked.

Amie thought quickly, how could she explain an editing package? "It's a computer game," she replied.

The clerk stared at her for a while then announced "You must pay for it."

"But why...." began Amie then collected herself. "How much?" she asked.

"Three hundred and twenty dollars," said the clerk. It was an exorbitant amount, but Amie had learned not to argue. It was more than two months wages for someone like Pretty and she doubted if one cent would find its way into the revenue service, but when in Rome...

Reluctantly, feeling her anger bubble up inside her, she counted out the money and handed it over.

The clerk did not immediately hand over the parcel, but sat gazing at it for several more moments and Amie began to worry he might change his mind, or was he deciding to try and charge her more? Finally, he half flung the parcel over the counter and Amie only just managed to catch it before it fell onto the floor.

The next few days were spent getting to grips with the editing package. Amie had spent time after hours in the edit suite at work and together with her training at college, was quite pleased with her first attempt at putting together her first video. She had recorded scenes around the house, including Pretty who was more than a little petrified. Goodness, thought Amie, the family will think I beat her she looks so scared. She filmed the gardens and the pool, but took care to show William only in the far distance. The garden was also a good backdrop to show the colourful birds and insects that seemed to be everywhere.

Amie smiled to herself as the camera followed a large spider as it ran alongside the edge of the pool. Sam would have a fit when she watched that! Amie herself could hardly believe that only a few weeks ago she had shrieked and grabbed Jonathon's arm when she saw her first large lizard outside the lounge doors. When she spied her first snake, she had panicked and run into the house closing all the doors and windows and climbed up onto the dining room table. Pretty stared at her in disgust or amazement, Amie wasn't sure which.

Admittedly it helped when Diana took her to what Togodo was proud to call its National History Museum. It had two small rooms with glass cages, holding a moth eaten collection of stuffed, dead animals. There was not much to learn from those, but there was a brightly coloured chart on the wall showing the most common snakes found in Togodo. Amie took a surreptitious shot of the chart with her mobile phone and studied it carefully at home. She was now fairly sure she could tell the poisonous snakes from the harmless ones, though she would never willingly get too close to any of them.

Her first video also included scenes from the Club and a few sentences from some of the people Amie had got to know, and a few extra shots of the mall and the suburbs she had taken from inside the car. She had not forgotten the warnings about 'sensitive areas.' But, she reasoned there is nothing sensitive about a suburban street and my house and the people at the Club didn't mind. It's not as if I was filming the palace or the airport or the army station just outside town.

She had recorded her own voice, although there was a lot of background interference and she added music to the completed programme. She did not think it was too appropriate, but they had only brought a few music CD's with them, and it was better than nothing, certainly better than silence. She recorded the whole programme onto a disk and parceled it up to send home. Once again, she stood in the sweltering crowds at the post office.

The clerk behind the counter wasn't any friendlier than the one she'd first encountered, and he insisted on opening the package and peering inside. He frowned when he saw the DVD inside.

"It's a computer game," said Amie, hoping against hope the computer sitting in front of the clerk wasn't geared up to playing DVD's, but that was quite unlikely. After several minutes the clerk decided to allow it to be sent in the mail, and charged her fifty dollars for the postage, although the stamps he placed on the envelope only added up to five dollars.

Amie was about to protest, then thought better of it. The envelope was not sealed properly, but before she could point this out, he threw the package into a large basket behind him and turned to the next customer.

If it ever arrives, it will be a miracle, thought Amie as she pushed her way out of the post office. Thank heavens I kept a copy!

That night she could have kicked herself as Jonathon expressed surprise she'd not thought to put the disk in with the company post. Nothing ever went astray as they used an international courier service. Oh well she thought, if it doesn't arrive in a few weeks I'll copy it and send it home again through the office.

Amie went down with a bug. It was unlike any bug she had ever had before. Her head ached, her feet ached and all points in between ached as well. She was running a high fever, she hardly had the energy to crawl out of bed and when she tried to stand up she felt so dizzy she keeled over. Luckily she went down with whatever it was on a Sunday afternoon when Jonathon was home. He phoned the Carstens.

"Take her to the hospital," advised Richard. "You don't have a cat in hell's chance of getting a doctor to come out. There's a Dutch doctor there who speaks quite good English, if you're lucky he'll be on duty. But generally they are quite efficient. Let us know if there is anything we can do to help."

With Richard's directions in hand, Jonathon carried Amie to the car and drove to the clinic. It was the usual series of low level buildings constructed in the by now familiar style of linked bungalows, with verandahs running the full length down each side. Several patients were sitting out on the threadbare grass, many with drip poles next to them.

Again, the difference between an African hospital and one at home in England was striking. However inside, there was the usual hospital disinfectant smell and surprisingly, the place was spotlessly clean. Jonathon was told to bring Amie through and put her on one of the beds in the outpatient area.

They did not have to wait long before an eager young black doctor arrived. He took Amie's temperature, examined her eyes and then poked, prodded and peered closely at her feet and legs.

Jonathon was about to object strongly, what did Amie's feet have to do with her illness? She ached all over didn't she?

The doctor straightened up with a smile and sensing Jonathon's anger, he pointed to a small raised swelling with a black dot in the centre, just above Amie's ankle.

"Tick bite," he said. "She has tick bite fever. We can treat it with antibiotics and after two weeks she will be as good as new again."

Amie groaned, she could not imagine ever feeling well again, the small hammers inside her head had turned into wrecking balls and the world had taken on a fuzzy and blurred vista. She just wanted to die, the pain was so fierce.

But the young doctor was right. He may have looked sixteen, as Amie told Diana later, but it took him seconds to know what was wrong with her and prescribe the right stuff.

Diana, who had come visiting with the usual bunch of grapes and rather ancient magazines, agreed. She entertained Amie with stories of friends who had gone back home from Africa, and then had weird symptoms. Most local British doctors were not familiar with foreign diseases, especially those found in Africa, and they scratched their heads trying to figure out what was wrong. Even batteries of tests didn't help, unless you had some idea what bugs to test for. The best advice was to go for medical help in one of the big port areas, where foreign and weird diseases had probably been seen before.

As its name suggested, tick bite fever is transferred from ticks which are very common all over Africa and there are several varieties. Amie could easily have picked up a tick from tall grass, plants in the garden or even in the house, which had then fed on her and dropped off before she even had a chance to notice it.

The doctor's diagnosis turned out to be exactly right, and it took almost three weeks for Amie to even remotely feel her old self again.

The highlights of Amie's week were her visits to the school and orphanage. Several of the wives went every Wednesday and Friday morning, and helped in the classrooms. A couple of them had taught back home in England and much of their time was spent in helping and instructing the teachers.

It fell to Amie to interact with the children, playing simple games with homemade equipment. She was amazed at the balls made from rolled up tights, the cricket bats carved from old planks and the doll's houses made from old grocery boxes inhabited by clothes peg dolls. It was a far cry from the high street toy shops and the toys Dane and Jade played with.

The children were served breakfast at school, as Mrs Motswezi explained, even if the children had parents, many of them could not afford to feed their children. Amie watched as each class lined up and one by one washed their hands carefully with soap before rinsing them off and drying them on a hand towel. Only then were they handed a plate and allowed to join the queue for their spoonful of maize meal porridge with a few vegetables.

Once a week if there was meat available, the cooks made up a stew, though it looked to Amie as if they were using the offal and entrails she had seen in the meat market. The very thought of eating it made her stomach turn over, but either the children were too hungry to care, or they didn't expect anything else and were used to such fare.

On each visit, Amie noticed that Angelina crept closer and closer until one day she finally gripped Amie's skirt and refused to let go. When it was time to leave, she clutched the fabric even tighter and Mrs Motswezi had to pry the child's fingers apart as Amie was getting into the car. Amie was almost in tears as they drove back out of the school gates.

"It's difficult not to get emotionally involved," remarked Diana, as they turned the next corner.

"I just want to pick her up and cuddle her and take her home," said Amie.

"She's certainly taken a liking to you, but it wouldn't be wise to encourage it," Diana changed the subject. "Did you say you were getting a car?"

"Yes, Jonathon found a small Fiat, it belonged to the Connor family, but they're leaving to go on their next contract, and I should get it in a few days. It's a bit battered and bent, but the mileage is low and it seems to run well. I know we've been here almost seven months, but it takes a lot of courage to drive on these roads! I think I'm brave enough now."

"There's nothing like having a bit of freedom."

"I'm not sure how far I'll have the courage to drive in a place where no one obeys the rules of the roads."

"I think you've settled in very well, especially as this is your first overseas posting."

While Amie was pleased by the compliment, it gave her a shock to remember it seemed to be taken for granted that once you were overseas on a contract, then inevitably other contracts would follow, one after the other. Would she ever go back and pick up her old life where she had left off? A lifetime of traveling from one place to another, was she prepared for that?

She tried to broach the subject at dinner that night. It was seldom a family meal any longer, she was often so hungry by nine, she ate long before Jonathon finally got home.

"Do you think they will send you overseas to another place when this job is over?" she asked.

Jonathon looked at her in astonishment. "How the hell should I know?" he snapped. "I haven't even thought that far into the future, I'm having enough problems here right now, to worry about that." He got up from the table and walked off to the bedroom slamming the door behind him.

Amie bit her lip hard and dug her fingernails into her palms to stop herself bursting into tears. Jonathon was getting more and more irritable lately, was it all because of the job? Could he cope? She had no answers to these questions, but she did know they seemed to be growing apart and communication between them had all but broken down.

5   VISITORS AND A SAFARI

The rainy season arrived and driving became even more hazardous. Few of the cars had windscreen wipers that worked, and as well as careering down the roads like bats out of hell, they also weaved from side to side to avoid the enormous puddles which rapidly filled up and splashed muddy water over the bonnets. Amie felt particularly sorry for the poor unfortunate donkeys pulling the carts, which were a frequent sight around town. She had noticed some of them didn't have proper bits, but pieces of wire in their mouths which cut into the skin. Enterprising owners had manufactured harnesses from cut off pieces of old tyres, bungee cords, baling twine and anything else that would make do.

Amie drove slowly and carefully, trying to leave as much space between her little Fiat and the other cars and carts on the road. She giggled to herself when she remembered how irritated she became at her father's slow and steady pace. He drove like a formula one champion in comparison to the speed she was driving these days!

Since she now had transport of her own, she took to visiting the school two or three times a week. She told everyone she liked playing with the children and hoped she might, even in a small way, be making a difference. But if she was honest, the reason for the more frequent trips was Angelina. Each time she arrived at the school gates, Angelina was waiting for her, hiding in the bushes by the fence and

Amie wondered if she sat there every day.

As soon as Amie got out of the car, Angelina would scurry over and firmly grip Amie's skirt or trousers and from then until Amie left, the child didn't leave her side for a moment. Mrs Motswezi said they had no knowledge of where the child had come from and no one had ever come looking for her. She was just one of thousands of displaced children, presumably an AIDS orphan and even her age was uncertain.

While Amie played with the other children, Angelina would climb up on her lap, and just gaze at Amie's face. More often than not, she sucked her thumb, and refused to join in the games. She simply wanted the close physical contact and sat quietly for hours.

Amie arrived one day in the summer, to find Mrs Motswezi and her staff in a fever of excitement. A party of ladies was arriving from Ireland the following day. They were part of a church group which had sent money to help fund the orphanage in the past, and now they wanted to visit and see for themselves what had already been done and how they could help further.

Groups of children were gathered around the water trough as the teachers scrubbed their faces until they were almost raw, then whipped their shirts, dresses and shorts off leaving them stark naked, while they dunked the clothes in the water and scrubbed them hard with bars of soap. They sent the little ones off to pick up the litter, while the elder ones were put to work cleaning windows and sweeping floors.

In all the times Amie and the other wives had visited, she had never seen such frenetic activity, but with the prospect of more money, it was obviously worthwhile making an effort for this visit. Amie had been in Africa long enough to realize this was the only reason for the massive clean-up, the usual one, more money.

Not that she could blame them, the government gave little or no support and both school and orphanage were run almost totally on overseas funding. There had been a case recently in a neighbouring country when it was discovered that a group of ladies had been accepting money from several churches based in Europe, to feed and house orphaned and abandoned children. An overseas video crew had faithfully recorded the orphaned children who recounted heart breaking tales, such as when they had watched their parents murdered in front of their eyes. Others had told how they nursed family members through the last stages of AIDS and other fatal diseases.

Money poured in in huge amounts, especially from the United States when the video was shown over there. It was only when the same video crew had returned unexpectedly to do a follow up story, that they discovered the AIDS 'orphans' were all living at home with parents and family, the building housing the 'orphanage' had been borrowed for the official visit, and all the caring workers and the money had disappeared. So Amie guessed this was a check to see that Mrs Motswezi and her ladies were not operating the same scam.

Amie agreed to come back the following day and welcome the foreign visitors and also to film their visit so they could take the tape back with them. This would prove to the church members contributing back home, their money was not being wasted or spent elsewhere.

A little after eleven a minibus drove in through the main gates and six hot and bothered people climbed out. Amie grinned to herself, remembering her own culture shock when she had first arrived. There were four ladies and two men, and they blinked in the bright sunlight as they looked around the bare earth playground.

Mrs Motswezi ushered them inside with many words of welcome, and as they walked through into the inside courtyard, the children broke into song, moving gracefully in time to the music. Even though Amie had heard them sing many times before, the small, black, scrubbed and shining faces once again brought tears to her eyes. As they swayed and stamped to the music, one of the teachers came over to urge Angelina over to join the other children.

"Come, sing for the people, you know the words," she said, but Angelina, with her thumb firmly in her mouth shook her head and refused to leave her accustomed place by Amie's side.

As soon as the singing had finished, benches were brought out and placed on the verandah for the visitors to sit on. They sank down gratefully, mopping their brows with hankies and scarves. Amie also noticed with amusement at least half the ladies were wearing tights and shoes and she caught sight of a nylon petticoat under one dress. Had no one warned them of the heat, had none of them been to Africa before? Should she mention the only suitable clothing for Africa was made of breathable cotton, not heat trapping nylon derivatives? Mrs Motswezi was the only other person she knew who seemed totally at ease in her polyester suits.

After the usual refreshments of cool drinks and biscuits, they all refused the tea, they were taken on a conducted tour of the school and then the classrooms which were utilized as the hostel.

They gazed in horror at the thin little mattresses on the bare concrete floor, they examined the large black cooking pots and they toured the vegetable garden as some of the elder children proudly described each vegetable in great detail. They looked quite shocked at the lack of facilities in the classrooms, and realized that science laboratories, a school hall and a gymnasium were probably unknown to both children and teaching staff. They examined the pile of pitiful homemade toys and saw the absence of text books and even exercise books, yet there, in a locked cupboard next to the principal's office sat three brand new computers. The Headmistress explained they were kept there for extra security and each child had a lesson once a year. As the visitors left, they pledged to raise as much money as they could for the school. They shook Mrs Motswezi's hand, thanked her for her hospitality and said they would get right on it as soon as they got back to Ireland in a couple of days.

Mrs Motswezi looked puzzled until Amie explained to her the people were going to raise lots of money as quickly as possible. Mrs Motswezi smiled and passed this on to the other teachers who all laughed and clapped and ululated loudly.

Amie captured the highlights of the day faithfully on her camera and before they climbed back into the minibus, she took the tape out of the camera and handed it over to the visitors.

"It's only rough footage of course," she explained. "But you have a record of the school and the children...."

"....and especially the singing," the lady who seemed to be in charge interrupted. "That was truly beautiful."

"Yes, it was," agreed Amie.

As Amie drove out of the school grounds that day, she felt a lightness of spirit she had not felt for a long time. There were good people in the world and they were going to help and she was sure there were many like Mrs Motswezi all over Africa working tirelessly for the disadvantaged and those in need. As she turned onto the main road, she made up her mind not to listen to Diana and the other wives with their tales of doom and gloom, they were not necessarily right and they had a one sided view of life on this continent. Today, Amie had seen the other side and it was one that gave her hope.

At the weekend the mood at the Club was subdued, it seemed as if everyone was talking about the changes around town. Local people who had been helpful and friendly before, were now morose and sullen. No one was willing to talk and it appeared that almost overnight, many of the expats got the uneasy feeling they were almost regarded as the enemy. Amie was not comfortable with the atmosphere.

"Don't take it too much to heart," said Diana as they sat on the verandah drinking coffee after dinner. The men had gone into a huddle inside and Amie wondered if they knew something they were not telling the women.

"It's difficult not to feel a bit unsettled," replied Amie. "The butcher practically threw my meat at me yesterday and the girl on the till in the supermarket just stared at the counter and didn't even glance at me."

Her friend lit a cigarette and then said "This will happen every now and again. You think you are all settled and begin to feel almost at home and then something upsets the locals and you are sharply reminded you are still an outsider, and always will be."

"Have you any idea what's causing this?"

"No, but it could be all kinds of things. It's possible someone back home in Westminster has said something rude about the President and as a result, everyone feels insulted. It could also be some of the wannabe rising politicians in the local townships stirring the locals up for their own ends if they want to score a few points."

"There is not really any such thing as an opposition party here though is there?" murmured Amie.

"No, of course not, just a token few, and if they do get any popular backing, come next elections they and their followers are soon 'persuaded' not to vote against the current ruling party. Democracy African style, it's nothing like democracy as we know it."

"I understand that much better now," said Amie. "We've been here over eight months."

"Goodness, is it that long already?" Diana was surprised. "Time speeds up as you get older."

"I feel as if I've been here all my life!" said Amie, surprised at the sudden feeling. "Well of course, not really but you know what I mean."

"Yes I do," replied Diana, "I know exactly what you mean. Ah here come Anne and Kate. I wonder if they've heard anything on the grapevine, Anne's maid can never keep her mouth shut."

Amie had got to know several of the other wives, and although she felt closest to Diana, despite the difference in their ages, their circle of friends had widened considerably. It was a special kind of friendship, she was thinking, as the others dropped into a couple of empty chairs. Both Anne and Kate were in their mid thirties, and had lived overseas for several years. Neither had children and Amie had not liked to ask either of them why not. They were fun to be with and a lot of their time was spent together.

Anne brushed her short fair hair away from her face as she exclaimed, "I simply can't do a thing with my hair and would you believe it my hairdresser told me he could not give me an appointment for over a month!"

"What a load of rubbish," exclaimed Diana. "What's got into him?"

"That's ridiculous," said Kate. "You'd think he'd be glad to take your money."

"So come on Anne, spill the beans, what have you learned from Beauty?" asked Diana referring to Anne's maid.

Amie smiled, so many of the local girls had some very inappropriate names. Beauty made her think of a good name for a horse!

"Well," began Anne slowly, attempting to build up the tension as she smoothed her dress over her long, slim legs. "Beauty has been even more quiet than usual, but I think it might have something to do with the people in the far north."

"The M'untu tribe?" asked Diana. "They're the largest group up north I believe."

"Maybe, but there is definitely some unrest up there and the government is very nervous right now."

"We've had these scares before," said Diana. "Usually they blow over after a couple of weeks. It's unlikely the government forces will let it simmer."

"Most unlikely," agreed Kate. "Gives them the opportunity to send the troops out for a little action and maybe rape, loot and pillage as well. It keeps the soldiers happy."

"There's plenty of war like stuff around," said Amie. "I've seen plenty of soldiers with guns, and the odd tank, and there are the 'no go' military areas. They must spend a huge percentage of their income on weapons and the like, and that was before, when there was no whispering about unrest."

"Well I have some news which may cheer you up," Diana said. "We've all been invited to the game lodge at Nkhandla for the weekend!"

There were gasps all round.

"How did you swing that?" asked Kate with an enormous smile on her face.

"Not absolutely sure," Diana was smiling as well. "Blame Richard for the invite. He met up with the owners who were in town collecting supplies and they got talking and it seems there are not too many overseas visitors right now and the place has got a bit lonely maybe?"

While Kate and Anne seemed to know all about Nkhandla, Amie was totally in the dark.

"There are only two smart game lodges in the whole country," explained Kate, "at least that's what I've been told, I've never been there myself. Has anyone else?"

While Anne shook her head, Diana replied. "I've been once, almost three years ago now, not long after we arrived. It's quite beautiful up there and so peaceful. And, thankfully, they don't allow hunting in their area, not like River Bend, that's where the hunters make for. I know we're all going to have a wonderful time."

"When's the invite for?" asked Kate.

"This coming weekend, and for this, I am sure all

husbands will find a good reason to take time off work and prepare for a little game viewing."

"I thought when I came to Africa there would be wild animals everywhere, even lions walking down the street at night," said Amie without thinking, then stopped as she realized how foolish that sounded.

"Don't be embarrassed," said Kate squeezing her hand. "I had exactly the same expectations. It's true there's lots of dangerous wildlife in town, but it's all small and insect sized! All the big animals have learned a long time ago to stay well away from the towns and even the villages."

"So will we see the big five?" asked Amie. She at least had heard of those!

"Possibly, but you can never tell. Go on a game drive one day and you'll see nothing at all, except a few buck and there are always plenty of those about. Another day, you'll be lucky. Dirk owns the lodge and he and his trackers will have a good idea where the animals hang out, so keep your fingers crossed." Diana took a sip of her wine, she was enjoying the excitement her announcement had caused.

"If there's an invite for me, then I'm definitely going, even if Charles can't make it," said Kate firmly.

"Me too," agreed Anne. "Benjy can stay in Apatu and work if he wants, but invites like this don't happen every day."

"In Togodo they don't," said Diana. "Most other African countries have some sort of quite well developed tourist industry going, and most of the enterprises are run by old time families who farmed and worked the land during colonial days. Most countries set up wild life parks and associations after independence, but here in Togodo, the fighting that followed their freedom was bloody and protracted and most of the foreign landowners left."

Diana's words were a surprise to Amie. She'd been so busy learning about Togodo in the present day she'd never given its past a thought. Had anyone even put much up on the Internet about it? She must google it when she got home.

As if reading her thoughts, Diana went on. "You will get one account of the pre first Togodian election wars on the net," she said, "but when you meet Dirk and Helen, you will hear more first hand. They had a tough time for a while, until the Kawa were victorious and set up the first government."

"After the usual 'democratic' elections," giggled Anne.

"Yes, and we don't expect any other party to get in, not in the distant future, not as long as President Mtumba is alive."

Hearing the others chat about Togodo and Africa, gave Amie a sense of comradeship. She was learning most of the expatriates she met had the same views as herself, whatever their age. It formed a strong bond among those people who were all from one culture, but who had chosen, or been chosen, to live in quite a different one. No, they were not family, but there were times Amie felt even closer to her friends here in Africa than she did to her real family. That thought came with not a little guilt.

On Friday, for once, Jonathon was home early from work and they threw their cases into the car and they were off. Amie had packed and re-packed her case several times. First she had filled it with shorts, skimpy tops and sandals, but after listening to Diana's advice on what clothing would be suitable, she tipped the lot out and started again. This time she put in long sleeved cotton shirts, a fleece for winter evenings, long trousers, socks, sensible shoes, a wide brimmed hat and insect repellant. She hoped there would be enough space for her camera gear, but she kept it to a minimum, leaving the lighting kit behind and only taking spare tapes, the tripod and the camera itself.

"I'm becoming a real bush brat," she told herself as she added a couple of books she just might find the time to read.

They all met up at Richard and Diana's house and Amie and Jonathon, Kate and Charles, and Anne and Benjy all piled into the minibus Richard had 'liberated' from his company for the weekend.

Everyone was in high spirits as they cut through the centre of Apatu and drove out of town. The tar roads did not extend far out of the city, but Amie was surprised at the width of the gravel road. There was plenty of room for both the small number of cars and the large amount of pedestrian traffic and the frequent herds of sheep and goats that meandered from side to side.

Richard kept the speed down, since it was a long time since the road had been graded and in many places the stones had formed ridges which made for a bumpy ride.

Diana had brought flasks of hot coffee and rolls and pieces of quiche along for the journey. The lodge was over a hundred kilometres away and they would not arrive before nightfall.

"How will we find it in the dark?" enquired Kate, much to Amie's relief. She'd been dying to ask the same question, but didn't want everyone to think she was nervous about getting lost in the wilderness.

"With a little help from modern science," replied Richard swerving around a particularly large pothole, and then slowing down behind a donkey cart. The two men in the front gave them all a friendly wave. "Dirk gave me the co-ordinates," he continued, "and hopefully the GPS will put us right on the spot. Mind, the first time we went there we arranged to leave early and arrive before sunset. It's pretty much a straight road, only a couple of turnings off, but it's getting the right turnings that makes all the difference!"

Although Jonathon and Amie had been in Togodo for quite a while, this was the first time they'd been outside the city and the suburbs. Amie knew there were a few intrepid explorers who drove off most weekends, but she wasn't sure she would have the courage to do that. With her vivid imagination, her thoughts of getting lost and being eaten by wild animals were enough to make her very nervous indeed, but in the group of friends she felt much safer, and it was her first trip after all.

She hugged the camera bag and prayed she would get some outstanding footage. National Geographic, here I come, she thought, daydreaming while watching the scenery slip past. Close to town there was more subsistence agriculture, but the further out of town they went, the denser the vegetation. Despite this, Amie was amazed to see that every few hundred metres there were some signs of human life. A peasant woman walking along behind her husband, bent almost double under a huge bundle of firewood. An old man riding a donkey, who nodded solemnly at the minibus, a couple of young girls walking so gracefully balancing five litre plastic containers full of water on their heads. Further on there was a group of small boys playing by the roadside bowling along an old metal hoop with a stick.

"Health and Safety would have a fit," commented Charles and they all burst out laughing.

The sun disappeared below the horizon and it was pitch dark before Richard swung off the main road, and onto another, much narrower gravel road. Now the trees formed an umbrella over them and Amie kept telling herself to be brave. It was probably more dangerous in Castle Bridge when they staggered out of the pubs on a Saturday night.

Suddenly they caught sight of small lights twinkling ahead, one moment they were there, the next they were gone, until after sweeping round a wide bend, there was the lodge.

"Welcome to Nkhandla Lodge," Kate read the sign. "Hey, we've arrived!" she said. "I can't wait to grab a drink and a shower."

It was difficult to make out the complete layout in the dark, but from what Amie could see, it was a piece of Africa exactly the way they showed it in the travel agents' windows. There were several small, rough stone-built, thatched huts around a central courtyard, with a much larger building at one end, where she could see a reception area, next to a bar and tables laid for dinner on the wide verandah.

Far from being quiet, as she had expected, the African night was full of noise. Cicadas were chirping, the trees rustled, and in the far distance she heard roars, and some shrieks of pain. There were dark shadows beyond the huts and she was convinced she could see large, hungry animals moving outside the lighted area within the camp. It was only then she noticed she'd not seen any fencing. Surely that was dangerous? What was to stop the animals just walking through as and when they felt like it? She moved closer to Jonathon, feeling just a little safer being right next to him.

Dirk and Helen came down the steps, with two local boys who began to unpack the minibus.

"Welcome," said their host. "It's great to see you. I've put you in the three bandas on either side nearest to the bar and dining area. If you tell Jefri and Kahlib what has to go where, they will show you where to go."

Much to Amie's relief, their accommodation was the one on the left closest to the main building, even then, she reckoned they would have to walk several metres in the dark to reach the bar area which felt very dangerous to her. She scuttled behind Jefri as he carried their suitcase into the hut.

Once inside she stopped in amazement. It might look rustic and primitive on the outside, but inside, the floor was laid with terra cotta tiles, the furniture made from varnished logs, the enormous bed was tastefully covered with a Laura Ashley floral print to match the curtains, and the soft duvet and pillows looked very inviting. The bathroom was separated from the bedroom by a half height wall, and Amie was both amused and shocked to see it had a window which looked out onto the dark night. There was one small curtain to pull across the window and she hoped it would be wide enough to afford some privacy.

"It's absolutely beautiful!" she exclaimed. "This is the

Africa I dreamed about, this is what I imagined it would be like, not Apatu!"

"Even with the dangerous and wild animals roaming free, waiting to gobble you up?" teased Jonathon who had followed her inside.

"Don't you dare frighten me. I'll be right behind you, every step of the way. If they eat you first, they won't be hungry enough to eat me as well!" Amie giggled nervously.

"Come. Let's go over to the bar and have a stiff drink, that should help calm your nerves!" Jonathon was already on his way out of the door.

"Wait for me," Amie was right behind him.

As they walked across the central area, Amie saw Diana had thought to bring a torch with her which she was using to sweep the ground in front of her. Now why didn't I think about that she asked herself.

"Just checking I don't trip over a night adder," called Diana cheerfully. "Always like to see where I put my feet, especially at night."

"There are snakes out at night?" gulped Amie. She'd been too busy worrying about the large game to think about the smaller stuff.

"There are always a few, but don't look so worried," laughed Diana, they usually stay far away from any activity."

"Unless they're attracted by the food," added Richard who appeared from the darkness.

Amie reached out and clutched Jonathon's hand firmly and breathed a sigh of relief as they walked up the steps to the bar.

A few drinks later, the good company, and an excellent meal, and Amie began to relax, she was even beginning to feel a lot braver as well. After all, Helen and Dirk lived out here all the time, so it couldn't be dangerous, she was just being a baby.

Helen looked over and smiled. "Is this your first trip out

into the bush?" she asked quietly.

"Yes," said Amie.

"It can be a bit overwhelming," said Helen. "I was twitchy when we first came out here to live. Dirk's family have been here for generations, but I was born and bred in England."

"So you know how I feel right now?"

Helen reached out and squeezed Amie's hand. "Yes I do. It took me a while to get used to a totally unfamiliar environment, but now I feel safer here than I do in the city."

"Have you ever been in a well, dangerous…." Amie trailed off, she didn't know the right words.

"A couple of narrow escapes, but it's reassuring having Dirk around, he knows the animals and how they're likely to behave. They have their own code of behaviour, and I think it's probably more civilized than ours in the long run!"

"I guess it's the fear of the unknown. You must think I'm a total wuss," replied Amie.

"Not at all," smiled Helen. "Just very normal and in a few years you'll wonder why you were so anxious. Africa grows on you."

Once again, Amie was reminded when you started travelling and living overseas, it was taken for granted you would be doing it for your whole working life. She still didn't know how she felt about that.

Dirk was indeed a fund of information. He had some large charts showing the different animals they were likely to see. "It always helps to know what you're looking at," he explained. "We can all recognize a lion for instance, but did you know it's mainly the lionesses who do the hunting, and then make way for the male lion to come in and eat his fill after they've done all the hard work? It's amazing how the girls all work together, they spread out and if possible surround their prey, but their killing methods are very inefficient. They bite the throat of the victim and that can be tricky, jumping onto the back of say, a wildebeest or a water buffalo, and then stretching down to attack the throat or muzzle to suffocate it."

"Do they kill something every day?" asked Amie.

"Not necessarily. It depends how hungry they are and how large the pride is," replied Dirk. "A good kill might keep the pride going for a few days, but of course they don't always kill everything they attack. The prey may outrun them, or a lion may get injured by flailing hooves and if they're undernourished, they may not have the strength to hunt successfully."

"And if the lion is very dominant, he will take, as they say 'the lion's share' of the kill, leaving the lionesses and cubs with very little to eat," said Helen.

"Then they have to protect the kill from the hyenas and the jackals and the vultures too, so it's seldom they get to sit down to a leisurely meal, poor things," smiled Dirk.

"I'm beginning to feel quite sorry for them!" laughed Kate.

"Not sure I do," added Anne. "They're very successful breeders even in captivity and at least they're not on the endangered species list."

"True, but did you know the majority of lions in Kruger National Park in South Africa are infected with tuberculosis which has become a serious problem? It's had a big impact on the numbers of lions there."

"Do you have the same problem here?" asked Charles.

"Unfortunately there are no proper investigations run by the government, they show little or no interest in their wild life at all," replied Dirk.

"In theory there is a governmental department which is supposed to manage the wild life, but they seem to be totally inactive," added Helen.

"One of the biggest problems is they have no state vet at the moment," Dirk continued. "Without properly trained people, where do you start?"

Charles poured himself another drink. "It's common knowledge Africans don't appreciate the tourist opportunity they have on their doorstep, nor how much foreign currency it could earn."

"That's very true," said Diana. "Even Mrs Motswezi who runs a local school in the capital, was amazed to hear we don't have the big five in Europe or America or anywhere else either! I'm not sure she has a real concept of the size of the world and all the other countries, peoples, cultures and customs."

"Yes, it's too easy to assume the people we meet over here have had the same access to the knowledge which we take for granted with television and the Internet," added Benjy.

"Well, it's bed time for me," Richard said standing up. "I'll see you all in the morning."

Much to Amie's relief, everyone else prepared to leave, and she was glad they all walked through the compound at the same time. Safety in numbers, she thought as they disappeared into their cottages.

Amie was horrified to notice there was quite a large gap between the door and the floor, surely a snake could slither in underneath? She grabbed the coverlet off the bed and stuffed it firmly along the bottom of the door, hoping it would make any illegal entry impossible. She turned round to see Jonathon watching her, he grinned slowly and shrugged his shoulders.

"OK so you think I'm a cowardly baby," said Amie, "but you just need to remember what an active imagination I have and it doesn't do any harm to take sensible precautions."

"I never said a word!" protested Jonathon.

"You didn't need to I can read your mind! I won't be able to sleep a wink tonight, I'm going to freak every time I hear a noise or a clunk or a shriek."

"You can't read my mind," Jonathon said. "I have an idea which will help you to sleep very soundly, come here and let me show you."

Even after they had made love, Amie was still convinced she wouldn't be able to sleep a wink, she couldn't take her eyes off the bottom of the door to see if something was trying to push their way in. Then suddenly it was morning, and the first dawn chorus found her safe and sound and snake bite free.

Everyone had agreed they would simply relax the first day and take an evening game drive, but get up very early, at dawn on the Sunday to catch the animals by the water hole.

Sitting over a lazy breakfast, Amie found herself beginning to relax even more. While she understood the bush was alive with hidden activity, she couldn't help but let herself unwind. Helen was right, there may be dangers, but they were not man-made, they did not have to worry about the human element. She noticed the local Togodians who worked in the lodge were very different from those she'd met in the city and she mentioned this to Helen.

"You may already know there are three main tribes in Togodo," said her hostess. "There are the Kawas, the M'untus and the Luebos. The Kawas are the biggest and brightest tribe and the most warlike, and they are the ones you are most likely to meet in the capital and largest towns. The M'untus mostly live in the north and they are far more laid back and peaceful. Generally they get on quite well with the Luebos, apart from the odd skirmish now and then."

"Are all the staff here the same tribe?" asked Charles.

"Yes, and for that we are grateful. They are all Luebos. It's like a large family. Within each tribe you get large extended families, or sub tribes, and all our staff is from the one vastly extended family. If one member leaves, or dies then immediately another one appears, we don't have to advertise! And if anyone from another branch of the Luebos strays onto our land then they are chased away immediately."

"I suppose in ancient Briton we also had tribes behaving the same way," mused Amie, "but that's all so very long ago."

"Tribalism is alive and well in Africa, and in many ways it's slowing them down on the road to the first world. It also encourages corruption and greed, as tribes seldom get on, and there's always the fear lurking in the minds of those in power they might be overthrown one day."

"How can you tell one tribe from another?" Amie wanted to know.

"We might not be able to tell at first," said Helen, "but they know immediately, by the way they speak, the languages are different, the way they dress and of course by the tribal markings."

"Are those the scars you see on the cheeks?"

"Yes, you most probably thought the young men had been fighting...?"

Amie laughed. "Yes, I thought some had been a bit handy with the knives after a hard night's drinking, until I noticed more and more of them."

"Making score marks on the cheeks and arms is part of the initiation ritual of all the tribes in Togodo, but the more educated people don't always follow traditional customs nowadays. Or if they do, say with circumcision for example, they will go to the hospital rather than let some old man in the bush with a rusty knife attack their most precious possession!"

Amie laughed again. She liked Helen, she was down to earth, refreshing and more relaxed than anyone she had met so far in Togodo.

"How long have you lived out here?" she asked.

"Coming up ten years now," replied Helen. "And I wouldn't live anywhere else. I would be heartbroken if for any reason we had to leave. We take a trip into Apatu every other month and what I see there, I don't like. The capital seems to attract the worst kind of people, yet I can understand that many go to find fame and fortune, or even a better education. After a couple of hours I can't wait to get back out into the bush."

"Can your staff here read and write?"

"When they arrived, most of them couldn't, so I set up a classroom and taught them, though I have to admit I could only teach them in English. Dirk is quite fluent in the local dialect of course, I'm nowhere as good, but whether they have transposed those skills to their own language I doubt. There is not a lot written in Togwana."

"No, I guess not." It wasn't something Amie had thought about before. With a population of less than thirty million, most of whom were illiterate, there was not much call for books and magazines, and those she had seen were all in English.

"Another problem with the tribal system is that when Europe was carving up this continent, they took no notice of tribal areas and now you often have the same tribe, split apart by an artificial border, living in two neighbouring countries, causing conflict, tribalism against nationalism, not an easy one to solve."

"No," said Amie. "I'd never realized all that before. None of it is easy is it?"

"No, and I'm selfish enough to hope we're left here in peace and quiet, among the animals we love, with enough tourists and visitors to keep us going. What goes on outside, I really don't want to know about." As Helen went off to the kitchens to oversee the meals for later in the day, Amie found herself wondering if it was better to know what was going on, or was it wiser to hide your head in the sand? She thought she herself would want to know, so she had enough time to, to what, jump on a plane for London? But then, what if your home and everything you possessed were already here in Africa? She guessed there were probably thousands of non indigenous people who had survived various civil wars and government changeovers and still farmed their land. They had nothing to run back to in the old country. Everything they knew and loved was in what would always be a foreign land.

Diana had told her Helen and Dirk's children had been

sent south to boarding school in Johannesburg, but they returned every holiday to the lodge. Apparently they'd not lost their love of the African wilderness. I guess it's what you're used to Amie reasoned. But what of the future? Helen and Dirk were hardly knee deep in tourists, and any upset in the government would make that worse, how would a place like this support them, their children and their future families as well?

Amie looked around. Flame trees towered next to the bomas, with their brilliant red/orange blossom it was easy to see where they got their name, it looked as if the branches were on fire.

A raptor flew over her head, floating effortlessly on the warm air currents, looking for prey with its sharp eyes. Suddenly it swooped down out of sight below the neighbouring rocks and there was a brief shriek before it rose again, a small, furry creature struggling in its claws. It was a stark example of the harsh, unforgiving nature in the wild. Eat or be eaten, survival of the fittest. Live to eat and breed another day. How far modern man has travelled from these basic tenants, Amie thought. Goodness, less than twelve hours out of the city and I'm beginning to question the meaning of life! Maybe being close to nature does that to you? But man is not really so far from the raw, survival state, he is not so honest, he hides his intentions behind a thin veneer of charm, politeness and friendship.

Amie wandered over and sat at the far end of the pool. She was glad to have these few moments alone, she could feel her body relaxing as she stared out over the grasslands dotted with acacia thorn trees.

I'm so lucky, she thought, how many people have the chance to experience nature this way, to have time to sit and ponder the meaning of life and existence. She thought of the people she knew back home, waiting to catch the bus or train to work, then sitting in an office for eight hours, then home again to household chores and a couple of hours in front of the television. How shallow it all appeared in comparison to sitting here, surrounded by life on earth unchanged for thousands of years.

Amie was surprised to find she didn't feel as nervous as she had the night before. Obviously the daylight helped, but she was beginning to understand that out here, miles from the nearest town, there was a code of behaviour, an unwritten set of rules, which although harsh, were understandable and made sense. You only killed to eat, or protect your young. Animals took what they needed and no more, there was still a balance and a harmony to life.

Lunch was served on the verandah, fresh fruit, cold meats, hot bread straight from the oven with fruit juice to wash it all down. Then everyone went for a swim followed by a siesta in the heat until it was time for the game drive as the sun began to sink towards the horizon.

Amie was quite nervous as she climbed into the Land Rover for her first ever game drive. She wanted desperately to see Africa's wild animals close up, but she wished they were in an enclosed car, rather than a vehicle which had no roof or side windows.

Their first encounter was a pair of giraffes, placidly stretching up to nibble at the tallest leaves on an acacia tree, their bluish tongues curling delicately around the leaves. Amie looked up at their dark, liquid eyes and decided she had never seen anything quite so beautiful. Here in the wild, they possessed a dignity one never saw in a zoo.

In the far distance, they saw a small herd of elephants, but they were on the opposite side of a ravine and it was not possible to get closer to them. There were plenty of buck, several different species, including the Thompson's gazelles, which bounded away leaping high into the air as if they had springs on their feet.

Dirk explained that dawn and dusk were the most active

times for the animals, when they hunted or went down to the water hole to drink. He was a mine of information as he pointed out the different animals, their habits, life spans, gestation periods and what they ate.

"We try and interfere as little as possible," he told them. "It can be heartbreaking at times to see helpless, young animals dying due to drought, or lack of food, but although one life is lost, we remind ourselves it provides food for another species. Out here, nothing is wasted."

"It makes me so ashamed we waste so much of the world's resources," remarked Diana as they crossed a dry river bed in the Land Rover.

"I wonder if we'll wipe ourselves out as a species before we've destroyed all these other creatures?" added Jonathon.

Amie looked at him in surprise. Maybe the vast beauty of the wild was getting to all of them. She'd never heard Jonathon even mention such things before. One thing I do know, she thought, this is not the same as sitting at home on a cosy sofa and watching the animals on television. Being here, you felt a part of it all, even though technically they were outsiders, not only here in the bush, but on the continent of Africa. How long would the white man be tolerated here and when he was finally evicted, would anyone care for the wild animals which were left behind? Would they just be regarded as bush meat and slaughtered to extinction? Amie shuddered, it was such a privilege to know she might be one of the last generations to have these experiences.

They all set out again the next morning before the sun came up, and Dirk took them to a hide overlooking the water hole. A lioness prowled slowly close to several of the buck, and Amie was amazed to see many of the deer only moved a little way away. She would have thought all the other animals would scatter, but they appeared quite calm, as if they weren't aware they were in danger. Suddenly, from out of nowhere, a cheetah raced towards one small Grant's gazelle on the fringes of the group. The gazelle leapt backwards and took off, racing as fast as it could, but it could not match the speed of the cheetah, as it closed in. Both animals disappeared behind a row of bushes and it was impossible to see the outcome.

Shortly afterwards a group of buffalo came down to drink, scattering the other animals and on the far side of the water hole, they spotted a lone rhino for a brief moment before it moved out of sight.

They had a late breakfast when they returned from their early morning game drive the following morning, and Amie was amused to see they served up a typically English breakfast of bacon, eggs, sausage and tomatoes. When they'd finished, Dirk suggested they go for a walk and he would show them some of the plants and smaller species.

"Man existed here for thousands of years," he said as they walked over to the river bed. "He lived in harmony with nature and was careful not to destroy his habitat."

"It's amazing to think you can survive in a place like this," said Kate, indicating the savannah around them. "I mean there's no obvious food anywhere, and I can't see any water either."

"To us, it's invisible, but if you know your plants, how the animals behave, and how to find and store water, even this barren looking area of Africa can provide everything you need," said Dirk.

By the time they returned to the Lodge, Amie's head was full of information about the African wilderness. Like the extinct ancient peoples of this land, Dirk's family had passed down their knowledge from father to son. Small indentations in the sand which Amie couldn't even see properly, told Dirk a particular animal had passed by and approximately how long ago. He was in harmony with the other creatures which shared this small part of the continent with him.

All too soon the weekend was over, and reluctantly they packed up the minibus and headed back to the city. They had seen four of the big five, the shy leopard remaining elusive. Amie's first sighting of the elephants had been amazing, they were at least three times the size of those she had ever seen in captivity. In the zoo was it just the presence of the bars and the safety moat that made them seem so small, and made her feel so secure?

Amie was yet to learn that cities could hold a lot more dangers than the African bush.

6 GOING HOME

When they reached the city, the noise of the crowds and the traffic was deafening. Amie was amazed she'd never been so aware of it before. Even day trips out into the countryside back home had never had the awesome peace of the bush. In the open African savannah, you knew there was plenty of life around you, scurrying in the undergrowth, the occasional roar in the distance, even the odd scream or shriek, but nothing of man and the constant, infernal racket from his machines.

It took a few days for them to settle down but then life slipped back into the usual routine. Jonathon continued to work very long hours and Amie filled her time with visits to the school, playing tennis, having coffee with the girls and organizing dinner parties and events at the Club.

There was usually at least one special occasion each month, Burns Night, St George's Day, Guy Fawkes, Ascot Saturday, any excuse for a party to relieve the tensions caused by work, and the frustrations that cropped up every now and again in their day to day lives.

Amie had to admit she was enjoying herself. It was nice to have warm weather most days, to sit out for coffee and meals, it was seldom necessary to sit indoors. There was rarely a need to wear coats, scarves or gloves, nor to put on any form of heating even in the evenings when it cooled down.

It was also nice not to have to do any housework, something Amie had never enjoyed. Pretty just got on with her work each day and her cooking improved as Amie taught her to prepare more European dishes, the food she and Jonathon enjoyed. There were several things she couldn't get in the shops, but as time went by, they seemed to forget about the favourite treats she used to buy every week in the supermarket in Castle Bridge. In fact their diet was a lot healthier, as fresh vegetables and fruit were readily available, and although Amie didn't possess any bathroom scales, her clothes told her she'd lost a little weight and she certainly felt more energetic, despite the heat.

What to wear was a bit of a problem though, once the clothes she'd brought with her didn't fit as well. The problem was solved with the purchase of a sewing machine, borrowed patterns from the other ladies and yards of cheap, colourful cotton fabrics which were readily available. The material was so cheap, Amie didn't feel bad about depositing her first few attempts in the dustbin and starting all over again. With help and guidance, especially from Anne, who had trained in textiles, she was quite proud of the outfits she produced.

Amie did allow herself another indulgence, while forgetting one of the taboos Diana had warned her against. With Mrs Motswezi's permission, she took Angelina to the mall one afternoon and bought her three new dresses, new underwear, a jacket and a small suitcase to put everything in. Angelina just stood staring at the shops in the mall and Amie hoped she liked the clothes she'd chosen, as there was so little reaction from Angelina except her wide-eyed look and her firm grip on Amie's skirt. But when Angelina put out a tentative hand to stroke a small blue teddy bear, that went into the shopping basket as well.

The tensions that had been so obvious earlier in the year slowly dissipated, and once again the locals were friendly and smiling, although they never missed an opportunity to make something on the side. Amie was now used to paying for car guards and to pay to have her shopping bags carried to the car. No one was prepared to allow her to carry them herself, and there was always a price to pay to the urchins who clustered round grabbing the bags off the counter before she had a chance to pick them up.

The weeks flew past and turned into months, and it seemed no time at all before Jonathon walked through the door one night, and reminded her they had been in Togodo for a year.

"And," Jonathon added, "I have some news."

"What?"

"Annual leave."

"Leave?" Amie hadn't given it a thought.

"Yes, we're due three weeks holiday, flights courtesy of the company."

"For a brief moment, Amie thought of all the places they could go, but common sense told her they would fly home to see the family.

"To England?" she asked.

"If that's what you want," replied Jonathon.

"Well yes of course," said Amie. "When do we go?"

"Next month."

Amie could barely contain her excitement, she couldn't wait to see Sam and the kids and of course her mother and father as well.

"I'll Skype them tonight, after supper."

"Hello Mum, can you hear me?"

"Yes, you're fading a bit and I won't put the video on, should help to make it clearer. How are you both?"

"We're fine Mum, but just in case we get cut off, let me tell you quickly we are coming home...."

Her mother's shrieks stopped Amie in her tracks. "Home? Oh that's great. Is the desalination plant up and running then? All finished?"

"No, nothing like, no Mum, listen..." Amie tried to get a

word in as her mother continued to rabbit on about how they had missed her.

"Mum," she almost shouted. "It's only for three weeks, it's Jonathon's annual leave."

"Oh, oh I see," her mother sounded disappointed, then added more cheerfully. "Well of course you must come and stay with us, and I'm sure I can put you on my insurance for the car." She turned to shout to Amie's father. "Raymond, how much would it cost to add Amie on my car insurance?"

It would be a lot more tactful to put Jonathon on, thought Amie, I'm not sure he'll be too thrilled to be chauffeured around by me for three whole weeks. She decided to say nothing at this stage.

Mary turned back to the computer. "So when are you coming? Soon?"

"Next month, as soon as we've booked the tickets and have the exact dates I'll let you know."

"Oh it will be so good to see you both, it seems such a long time since you left!" From the tone in her voice, Amie thought it strange that her mother, the one who had practically poured her on to the plane to go and explore the world, now seemed disappointed they were only returning for their annual leave. Had they had second thoughts, or missed Jonathon and Amie more than they'd imagined?

"Thanks Mum," said Amie. "It would be great to stay with you, and maybe we can go shopping, or find a show on at the theatre, the sort of things that are not available here."

"I'll look to see what's on. Send me all the details by email, but I must go, Coronation Street is about to start. It will be so good to see you again. Bye for now," and Amie's mother disconnected the call.

Amie sat for several seconds staring at the screen. Well her parents seemed pleased they were going over, but the television took priority? She gave herself a shake, she was just imagining things, being too sensitive. She got up to go and tell Pretty she could bring the coffee in.

Flying back to London and landing at Heathrow, Amie was beginning to feel like a seasoned traveler. This time she knew the ropes. It took an age to get through customs and immigration, and she shuffled from one foot to the other as despite going through the 'nothing to declare' exit, they were stopped and two of the cases were searched.

"Blood diamonds, bars of gold and drugs," breathed Jonathon into her ear. Despite her anxiety to hurry through to arrivals, Amie giggled. She was disappointed she'd only packed a couple of her newly made creations, even though it was late summer, she needed much warmer clothes for England, and she was wise enough to bring as little as possible. She planned to pack for the return journey with as many treats and 'unobtainables' as she could cram into her suitcase, and Jonathon's as well if he didn't complain too much.

Looking at his face now, as they waited for the customs officer to finish rummaging through the toilet bags, she could see the last year had aged him. There were lines which hadn't been there twelve months ago, the long hours, frustration and responsibility were weighing him down.

When they were eventually released and walked through the sliding doors, the first people Amie saw were Jade and Dean. They slipped under the barrier and raced over shrieking with glee. It was big hugs all round as both sets of parents and Sam and the children had come to welcome them home.

"I told you to behave yourselves," muttered Sam as she pulled Dean away just before he was flattened by an overloaded baggage trolley.

"They're home, they're home," shrieked Jade. "Aunt Amie is back home."

"Yes but only for a short time, just for a holiday," reminded his mother. Was Amie imagining it or did there seem to be a slight note of jealousy in Sam's tone of voice?

There was some lengthy discussion as to who would travel back with whom and where the luggage should go, but eventually they all arrived back at the Reynolds' house. On the journey Amie shrank back into her seat, barely aware of her mother's voice as she went on and on about what people had been doing, who had got engaged to whom, who had lost their job and what a state the country was in and so on.

Although everything was familiar, the same streets, traffic lights still in the same places, shops and office blocks unchanged, somehow it all seemed overwhelming and perhaps a little threatening. My mind is playing tricks, thought Amie, but it's both familiar and alien at the same time.

The house seemed to have shrunk, and Amie suddenly realized her home in Apatu was considerably larger than her parents' house. Either that or it had become smaller in the last year!

After a quick cup of tea, Samantha left with the children, and Amie and Jonathon went upstairs to her old room and began to unpack.

"Am I going crazy, or has the house shrunk?" whispered Amie. "I can't believe I thought I had a big bedroom."

"I have exactly the same feeling," said Jonathon quietly as he squeezed past her to get to the wardrobe. "It seems like home and also totally foreign."

Amie breathed a sigh of relief, thank goodness Jonathon felt exactly the same. She had one of those warm, comfortable moments when she felt very close to her husband, they had shared so much together which was so far away from their comfort zone, or was it a rut? Goodness, how much had she changed in only a year! How much could someone change in only twelve months?

Dinner was the usual ritual, the same familiar plates, the exact food she had grown up with. To her surprise, it didn't quite taste the same there was a plastic quality about it she'd never noticed before.

"I remembered you liked these crumbed pancakes," said her mother as she cleared away their plates. "Thank goodness for the frozen food counters and pre-cooked meals, I don't know how I would ever have coped without them, with me working and looking after you girls, and the house."

Amie felt a slight wave of guilt. She had forgotten the long hours her mother put in at the Technical College, and she also had the cooking, cleaning, washing, ironing, shopping and children routine. Amie didn't have any of that, except the shopping of course which was the fun part. In comparison to her mother, and millions of other housewives throughout the country, Amie was a lady of leisure.

"I thought we could pop down to the shops and get in some of the things you like best," continued Mary. "You'll know what you've missed most, and I didn't want to decide for you."

"Thanks Mum, that's a great idea," said Amie. "Really thoughtful of you."

Leaving Jonathon listening patiently to Raymond complaining bitterly about the present government policies and how the current ruling party was intent on destroying the country, Amie put on her coat and accompanied her mother to the supermarket.

Once inside the mega store, Amie had a brief moment of panic. The dairy counter seemed to stretch for miles, and there were so many different products to choose from she just stared at the displays, unable to move.

"Is everything all right dear?" asked her mother.

"Yes, yes, it's just...." Amie wasn't sure how to explain it. She waved her arms at the freezer cabinet. "There are just so many to choose from."

"Oh," her mother looked nonplussed. "You've not been away that long, nothing's changed. Now what kind of cheese would you like?"

No, nothing's changed, that's the problem, thought Amie. But I've changed, and it's frightening to realize that. If I change this much in a year, what will I be like in five, or ten years?

"Cheese? What kind do you want?" repeated her mother.

"Oh, any really. We can only get one kind of cheese at home, I mean in Apatu," Amie bit her lip, hoping her slip hadn't been noticed. Of course this was home, here where she was right now, not some far away third world African city which didn't even have a reliable electricity or water supply.

By the time they had loaded the trolley and were queuing up for the check out, Amie felt a little less spaced out, but her coat collar was rubbing on her neck and she found the atmosphere stifling. So many people were milling around. Sure there were lots of people in Apatu, but here they seemed closer together and yes, there were a lot more of them. People everywhere, jamming the aisles, pushing past each other on the sidewalk, avoiding each other in the car park. She felt constricted and confined, and the low grey clouds didn't help either. Ever since they had landed, there had not been one patch of blue sky. It was almost a sense of relief to arrive back at the house and help her mother unpack the groceries, even though the kitchen too had shrunk.

"We've arranged a get together on Friday night with some of your old school and college mates, they're all dying to see you again and hear all about Africa," said Mary brightly as she put the kettle on.

"Oh, great," said Amie, although she was not sure it was.

"You're all meeting at the Grill House at seven o'clock. At least twenty said they would come, so it should be quite a crowd."

"Ah, right," replied Amie, though she mentally added, 'another crowd!'

The first evening was spent in front of the television which left little time for conversation. Amie had been expecting to chat about the new house, the city, the school, their trip into the bush, Angelina and her story, and day to day life, but somehow she never got a chance. After East Enders, there was a documentary about people on benefits followed by a drama where the main characters had extra marital affairs every five minutes, and then it was time for bed. No one had asked anything about Africa and Amie didn't know how to start telling them.

As she snuggled up to Jonathon that night, she wondered just where she belonged now.

The next day Amie went over to visit Sam. The moment the door opened she realized how quiet the house was.

"Where are the children?" she asked.

"At school and playgroup," replied Sam cheerfully, giving her a big hug and then going to put the kettle on.

"I can't believe how silent it is!" said Amie, "and I'd forgotten Dean is school age now, when did he start?"

"Just after Easter, and I was lucky enough to get Jade into crèche, and as soon as I start work, Dean can go there after school, and I'll pick them both up on my way home."

"I thought you weren't going back to work until they were both in full time school, and maybe not even then."

"Ah, well not being here, you'll not know how much prices have been rocketing, the bills get bigger and bigger, but salaries don't. We're struggling on what Gerry brings home each month, so I will have to go out to work."

"That is such a shame," said Amie thinking of several of her friends who not only didn't work but had a full time maid as well. Pretty had asked her once or twice where her children were and if she was going to send for them so she could look after them.

"Believe me life is a struggle," said Sam and Amie noticed her sister looked quite frazzled.

"It's a real trial to get through each day. The kids are

impossible, they are always underfoot. Maybe I'm old fashioned, but everyone else's world seems to revolve around their kids. They don't do anything without consulting them first, always go to restaurants where there are child centred facilities, the little brats are never expected to sit up and shut up!"

"Like us," replied Amie with a smile.

"Oh, do you remember Great Aunt Mitchell's place? I used to dread those visits."

"Me too. No toys, we were only allowed to take a colouring book and crayons and we had to sit quietly…"

"….while the grown-ups talked and talked and talked for hours, and hours…."

"… and hours." They both laughed at the memories.

"But it's all changed Amie, now you can't even spank your children, you are supposed to reason with them and put them in the naughty corner and get them to apologize and explain *what* they have done wrong and *why* it is wrong. But they don't tell you what to do if they won't stay in the naughty corner. I've spent hours picking Dean up putting him back time after time after time to the corner, and I promise you he has masses more energy than I have. I'm worn out long before he is."

"And you can't put him in the bedroom?" asked Amie.

"No, you dare not lock them in, even if the bedroom door had a lock. But now he can reach the door handles there's no stopping him. I wouldn't mind but no one else has the same problem and I think that's because they just give in all the time and the children get exactly what they demand, and they're allowed to behave exactly as they like. It's the only way the parents seem to survive. But that's not the worst thing Sis, they all seem to enjoy making themselves complete doormats for their kids. I feel so out of step."

Amie put her arms around Sam as she began to sob. She had not been expecting this as a homecoming. Sam had always been the capable one, the one who multi tasked with confidence, the elder sister always urging her on to be braver, more decisive and more adventurous. Now the roles were reversed, Amie felt like the older, wiser sister.

"What about Gerry, how does he....?"

"Oh, he's working all hours, I think he avoids us as much as he can. Who would want to come back to two monsters after a hard day's work and have to listen to me screaming at them?" Sam cried. "I'm so tired and so fed up, how will I ever get a job looking like this?" and Sam dissolved into floods of tears.

Amie didn't know what to say. Ever since Sam had been married she had always seemed so sure, so composed, so self assured, she took everything in her stride. All Amie could do was to hug her and murmur meaningless phrases such as, "It will be all right, things will change, the kids will settle down. It's just a phase right now."

Sam sat back in her chair and poured out another cup of tea. "It's Gerry I am really worried about," she said quietly.

"Is he not well?" asked Amie.

"No, not in that sense, but I think," Sam paused, "I think he might be, you know..." she paused.

"Gerry! No! Never! He's so solid, so dependable," Amie was shocked. "You don't mean..."

"I don't know for certain, but I think so," said Sam miserably. "He has never worked so late at night before, and his job hasn't changed. I know he's got more responsibilities, they've not replaced several staff who've retired. Not that they're paying him a penny more of course, it's always the same excuse. 'We've got to cut back, don't you know there's a recession on, the Council's deeply in debt and so on.' I'm sick to death of hearing how poor this country is!"

"Tell you what," said Amie. "While we're home, why don't you and Gerry take next weekend away and Jonathon and I will look after the kids. Well it might just be me at the weekend, as Jonathon is popping up north to see a couple of friends from his post grad days."

"Don't you think I'd have dumped them on Mother and taken off for a few days?" wailed Sam. "Thanks for your offer, but we honestly don't have the money right now. Annual holidays are a thing of the past, at least until I'm working as well, and who knows how long it will take me to find a job?"

By the time Amie left, Sam had calmed down and at least agreed to Amie and Jonathon babysitting one evening, and allow Amie to treat them to a meal out, hopefully a romantic dinner."

"Look where previous romantic dinners got us!" Sam grimaced.

It only occurred to Amie as she drove back to the house, that not one word about her new life in Africa had been exchanged. She had a fund of stories to tell, and no one seemed to want to hear them or had really shown much interest. Maybe when they got together at the Grill House tomorrow evening she would have an opportunity then to tell everyone about her new life.

The restaurant was surprisingly empty when they first went in, before it had always been a hive of activity.

"Have we got the right day?" asked Amie.

"Yes, I'm sure your mum said Friday night, replied Jonathon. "Ah, here are Vanessa and Larry now." There were hugs all round as one by one, or in couples, their friends arrived and settled round the large table.

"Thirteen, fourteen…." counted Jonathon.

"Gail and Hadrian can't make it, they couldn't get a baby sitter," someone said.

"Yes and we all know Gail is wise not to let Hadrian out of her sight!" Everyone laughed. Goodness thought Amie, would I have laughed at that a year ago?

"So, tell us all about your new life then," said John.

"Well where to start," replied Amie, thinking that at last someone was taking an interest. "What can I tell you? We're on the edge of Apatu the capital of Togodo, in one of the nicer suburbs and the house is quite large we have room to move, which is great. The garden is not enormous, with a pool and...."

"You have your own swimming pool?" interrupted Stephanie.

"Yes, and I swim most days," said Amie.

"Lucky you, imagine being able to swim in your own pool, here it's much too cold."

"Yes, it's the local swimming baths for us."

"We've not been since that big outbreak of athlete's foot. Every time we went we caught it again, it cost us a fortune in medication, so I said enough is enough," said Stephanie.

"How long are you back for? Or are you finished out there now?" asked Peter.

"Just three weeks, that's all they give us at the moment," Jonathon answered. "I could honestly do with longer."

"The longer the holidays the better," said Bella, "but it's getting back home and coping with all the laundry...."

"Yes, and cleaning a house you thought was quite clean when you left," Debbie added.

"That's one thing I don't have to worry about," Amie responded cheerfully. "Pretty will have the clothes washed and put away in no time, and after I threatened to cut her wages every time she burnt holes with the iron, she is amazing..."

Before Amie could finish, Debbie butted in. "You have a servant?"

"Well yes, but we call them maids. Everyone has one. It's expected."

"Oh, no chance of us having one," Bella sounded quite jealous. "Does she come in every day?"

"She lives on the premises so she's there all the time,"

replied Amie.

"She stays with you in the house, she lives with you all the time?" Stephanie was curious.

"No, she has her own quarters at the back of the house."

"That must take a chunk of your salary, a full time maid," Peter addressed Jonathon.

"Local labour is quite cheap out there so it doesn't cost much. Even if Amie wanted to do her own housework it would be frowned on." There was a brief moment of uncomfortable silence.

"So it's rather colonial is it? The white madam and the cheap black labour? Sounds as if things haven't changed much in Africa despite all the democracy and own governments," Adrian spoke for the first time.

"Well of course we weren't there before they got independence, and I'm sure there have been massive changes. But we're not unkind to Pretty or the gardener…."

"A gardener as well!" exclaimed Ben.

"As I was trying to explain, we pay Pretty and William the going rate, just like everyone else, and for them their wages are good and they can buy everything they need." Jonathon found himself on the defensive.

"Ah, but of course they don't have the same standard of living as the whites do they?" Peter wanted to know.

"No, of course not, but your average domestic worker in England will have a lower salary than someone say in management."

"I remember," Stephanie said quickly, "when my mother needed help when Grandpa was so ill and couldn't get around, she had to pay megabucks for home help, and the lady arrived every day in her own car and her house was just as nice as ours. Pretty and William don't have cars do they?"

"No of course not," Jonathon was trying hard not to get angry. "Things are very different there, people are just glad to get a job and receive a regular wage. They often send most of it back to their villages to support their families."

"There are plenty of rich black people," Amie tried to explain. "In fact those in government positions earn way more than Jonathon does, and they make lots more on the side through corruption I'm sure." She paused as she took a sip of beer. "And neither Pretty nor William feel hard done by. You should have seen the long queue outside the house stretching into the distance with people wanting to work for us."

"Unemployment is high in Britain as well, but people are not forced to queue for hours to work for very basic wages," Peter said.

"Well of course there are no unemployment benefits or anything like that, although they are talking about child allowance and maybe some free medical stuff as well...."

Stephanie cut in before Jonathon had finished. "And they have to pay for all their medicine too poor things!"

"If you say everyone pays merely basic wages so every worker only earns a pittance, then aren't you perpetuating the role of the downtrodden peasant? How can they improve their lives if they don't have money? Don't you feel rather guilty?"

"But you see Peter," Amie jumped in, "if we pay more, two things happen. Firstly we could not afford to pay them at all, so they would have no work and no money. Secondly if they get more than other maids and gardeners for the same work and hours, then they will only invite jealousy and they could easily be killed if anyone found out, and at the least, other family members would take it away from them."

Fourteen pairs of eyes looked at her from around the table. They just don't understand, she thought miserably. How can they, if they've never been there, or, more importantly lived there and experienced things for themselves.

"Well I feel sorry for them," Bella said with conviction. "We see so many on the television, poor starving babies with no fresh water, not enough food, condemned to a life of sheer misery."

"Yes, if it wasn't for the donations people send in, many of them would be dead by now," said Peter.

"Don't you realize most of the money goes into the pockets of the fat cats in charge, and never gets anywhere near those who really need it?" By now Jonathon was trying very hard to keep his temper.

"Well we see plenty of news inserts showing doctors and aid workers and they are certainly dishing out the food and medicines, so some of it gets through. Don't you think the stereotype of the black politicians and the corruption and fraud is mainly propaganda really?"

"I think a lot of what *you're* shown on television here is also propaganda, only you don't realize it because you don't see both sides of the situation."

"Anyone for another drink?" asked Ben quickly, trying to defuse the situation.

"Make mine a half and a lemonade for Stephanie, she's driving tonight," said Peter.

The conversation then turned to a drama series currently being shown on the television and all further talk about Africa was ignored. The girls started talking about who was pregnant and who had just had a baby, and the price of food and the latest plots of their favourite soaps, and Amie sat and said nothing. She felt like a stranger watching a play in which she had no part. She had nothing to contribute.

The guys were talking about politics, social injustices and football. No one had asked them about other aspects of their life abroad, there was no opportunity to tell them about Diana and Richard and the trip to the game lodge, frankly no one seemed interested. She caught Jonathon's eye across the table and he gave her a slow wink. She knew what he was thinking, how soon can we leave?

The evening dragged on and on, but at last the group broke up with hugs and handshakes all round and lots of 'we must get together again before you go back,' and 'we'll see you before you fly out,' but there was very little sincerity in the words.

"So, what went wrong?" asked Amie as they drove out of the car park.

"I'm not sure, I'm in mild state of shock," replied Jonathon. "Steve did ask me on the side what it was like to work in Africa, and said he would like to apply for an overseas job himself."

"Oh!" Amie was surprised. "So he's going to…"

"No, he said he wouldn't be able to leave the family, and it was all right for some, who could just take off," said Jonathon gloomily.

"I just don't understand it Jonathon! These are our friends, the people we went to school with, grew up with. How is there such a …. a chasm between us now?"

"Beats me, and it's only taken a year! Have we changed?"

"No, I don't think we have, oh well, maybe we have. I do look at things differently now, I can see both sides of the situation in Africa. Maybe our eyes have been opened more than we realize."

"You do want to go back don't you?" he asked Amie.

"To Togodo?"

"Yes."

"Do you?"

"Of course I do! The people I'm working with can be so frustrating and I know I'm bad tempered at times and I work long hours, but I feel we are going to achieve something in the end. It's important work"

"It is important," said Amie. "Your desalination plant will provide clean, safe water for thousands, which is a hell of a lot more value than a few pounds sent in to buy a bag of rice."

"That's a good way to look at it, but in the meantime are we now alien to what we left behind? And do you want to go back?"

Amie didn't even take a moment to think about it. "Most definitely, yes. Do you know, I feel closer to Diana and Anne and Kate than I do to the old crowd tonight. Let's go back and make a fortune on the backs of the poor, down trodden, black workers!"

"Now if they all heard you say that and believed it, we would never be able to show our faces in this town again!" said Jonathon which had them both in fits of laughter.

Despite Jonathon's support and his understanding, Amie was deeply upset about the evening, so the next day, when Jonathon and her father had gone off fishing, she broached the subject with her mother.

Mary Reynolds listened carefully to her daughter as she described how the conversation had developed the night before.

"So Mum, what went wrong? Do you have an answer?"

"Did it occur to you both the others might have been jealous?"

"Goodness, no! But I don't think that's the answer. We told them so little about our lives over there they didn't have anything to be jealous about, except for the maid, gardener and the swimming pool."

"That might well be enough, along with the beautiful weather of course," her mother smiled.

"But it's not all perfect. There are lots of things we have to do without. We don't have a really good shopping mall, no chain stores, I've had to learn to make my own clothes, and getting sick can be a bit scary. Then there are all the diseases we have over there, and the roads which are so bad in the rainy season and....."

"That's enough," laughed her mother. "I must admit, I never thought when we encouraged you to take the job it would have this sort of repercussion. It never occurred to me."

"Well that's what's happened, and I'm not sure if we will

ever fit in again," Amie was quite despondent. Then seeing her mother take the ironing board out of the cupboard, she recounted the story of Pretty burning the clothes and how she had then threatened to cut her wages unless she took more care. Although it was only a fleeting moment, Amie saw her mother's face and sensed she disapproved of her behaviour. She changed tack immediately.

"I must also tell you about friends of ours who drove out into the bush and had two punctures, one after another. They were stranded, and the sun was going down and they were by the river and they could hear the animals getting closer and closer and they were just so scared....."

Her mother broke in. "What a coincidence! We had a puncture too, on the way to Torquay and your father had to walk over a mile before he found a garage which would send someone out to help us."

Amie realized her mother didn't really understand either. There was just no comparison between breaking down on a busy tarred road and breaking down in the middle of the bush, no comparison at all. She swiftly changed the subject and asked about the rising food prices.

All in all, Amie decided it was not a very successful holiday. There never seemed to be any time for cosy chats with her mother round the kitchen table. While she had been so looking forward to recounting all about the school and the club and how her cooking skills had improved, other everyday events took priority. Just as she began to talk about her life in Africa the phone would ring, or a neighbour popped round to say hello. Not, to ask about Amie's new life but to bring Amie up to speed on events in Castle Bridge.

It was also early in the academic year and her mother had test papers to mark and deadlines to meet, so on a couple of occasions, Amie either went shopping on her own, or met up with some of her girlfriends for a coffee. Even then she found she was out of the loop. Taking care not to mention her maid, the size of the house, the swimming pool or anything else which seemed out of place in her home town, she found her mind drifting off as the conversations included the train ticket increases, or the new tax laws, worries about redundancies and the like. Nothing, in fact, that had any impact on Amie's current lifestyle.

She also had the worry about Sam who seemed genuinely depressed and convinced her marriage was on the rocks. Even the night Amie dragged Jonathon along to babysit her niece and nephew, they arrived to find Sam all dressed up and ready to go out and no Gerry.

"Is he still at work?" asked Jonathon.

"I have no idea where he is," moaned Sam, "but he promised to be home early tonight, just for once."

Gerry eventually appeared, over an hour later and Amie could hear them arguing loudly as they got into the car and drove off for their romantic dinner.

"I don't think their evening is going to be a great success," she muttered to Jonathon as she chased the children up the stairs and into the bathroom to pop them into the bath.

"This holiday has been a disaster," said Jonathon after they had told the obligatory bedtime stories and kissed Dean and Jade goodnight. "Next break, we will go somewhere else, Paris, or maybe Venice."

"Wow, that would be fabulous," replied Amie, "but how can we? Everyone will expect us to come home and they will be angry with us if …."

"Let's cross that bridge when we come to it," said Jonathon looking through the paper for something to watch on TV. "Goodness what a lot of rubbish! Do you want to see people losing weight, real life drama with the police, or one of the soaps?"

"None of the above," said Amie. "Did we really sit and watch this rubbish night after night after night?"

"I guess we must have done, it all seems a world away,"

said Jonathon looking for a suitable CD to play instead. And that is exactly where my thoughts and heart are, Amie realized, a world away. She was thinking of Angelina and wondering what she was doing. Did she stand by the school gates every day waiting for Amie to arrive? Was she thrilled with her new clothes?

Amie had tried to explain she would not be coming to the school for several days. She held Angelina's hands and showed her that for each of her fingers Amie would be far away with her family.

"One day for every finger on your right hand Angelina, and then a day for each finger on your left hand, and then one more time on your right hand again, and then the left and the right. Then I will come and see you. It is twenty one sleeps until I am back." She wasn't at all sure Angelina understood, but it was the best she could do.

"I think your folks seem more interested," said Amie. "At least they asked lots of questions."

"Um, yes, but mostly about work and the difficulties. I just get the impression they are looking for ammunition to prove we're not having a good time and whenever I try to explain the problems, changes of agreements, or when the government moves the goal posts, they don't fail to remind me 'it's not the way they do things in Britain.' There's lots of implied criticism, though they haven't come out openly and said anything I can put my finger on."

"What I can't understand," said Amie as she cut the cake Sam had left out for them, "is that this time last year they almost pushed us on to the plane, insinuating we were total wimps for not jumping at the chance." Then seeing Jonathon's raised eyebrows she added, "well all right, I was the wimp, not you."

"Maybe they had second thoughts and now they see us in a different light. We have changed you know."

Amie thought for a moment. "Yes, I suppose we have.

We're more confident, more adult, and we have seen another side to life. I am a bit nauseated by the reports on television about Africa, and the backlash about the damage we did when we were in power over there in the great days of the British Empire."

"Well let's forget about it for now and try and enjoy the last few days off work. We have no idea what's gone wrong while we've been away. We might be in for a shock!"

7 A VISIT FROM THE COLONEL

Amie and Jonathon gave a sigh of relief as they kissed everyone goodbye and jumped into the taxi that arrived outside the house. It seemed too much disruption to ask people to take time off work just to take them to the airport. When they were first leaving England it was understandable, but now they were seasoned travelers it wasn't necessary.

As they flew in low, approaching President Mtumba Airport, Amie could see the shanty towns surrounding the capital on three sides, wide areas of scrubland and savannah, and beyond, the dark green, dense forest with patches where the land had been cleared for firewood. A low cloud of smog hovered over the shacks, as the fires were lit for the evening meal. I'm not even going to think about what a disappointment our trip has been, thought Amie. I'll put it down to experience and know better next time.

But it wasn't possible for Amie not to be quizzed about her holiday. Next morning as she got out of her car in the mall car park, she could already see Kate and Diana waving to her from their favourite table outside the coffee shop.

"Welcome back," smiled Kate as Amie sat down. "So how was it, did you have a fabulous time?"

"We saw a show in the West End which was great, and we took a drive down to the coast and had an ice cream on Brighton beachfront," replied Amie.

"But you're glad to be back," Diana observed.

Amie looked at her, she had forgotten just how perceptive Diana could be. "You could say that yes. Yes I am glad to be back, in the heat and the flies and the dust and the screaming naked children running about and the ..." Amie waved her arms trying to think of all the other things she was delighted to see.

"Told you," said Diana to Kate. "She's got the bug. She's really one of us now," and everyone began to laugh.

"I'm not sure where I belong any more, it was all so foreign! One main topic of interest for example was the forthcoming nativity play at Dean's school at the end of term. They're going to have a real donkey for Mary to make her grand entrance. Mind, I must say they are being quite progressive having a nativity play at all, as many schools don't now because they have so many different faiths, it's not politically correct any more. But..." Amie paused to build up the suspense, "....guess what? Mary will have to wear a crash helmet and elbow and knee pads!"

"You've got to be kidding," spluttered Kate. "Has the world gone mad?"

"Even here they're not that daft!" exclaimed Diana. "What kind of generation are they rearing these days?"

"I'm beginning to wonder if we're looking at the real survivors of the human race," observed Kate as she pointed to a small child rummaging in a nearby bin for leftover food."

"If he reaches adulthood, he's going to be tougher and stronger both physically and mentally," Diana observed wryly.

As Amie described the parents' lack of interest, and the alienation she had felt among previously close friends, and even Sam's marriage problems, somehow she didn't feel disloyal. It was amazing that after only a year, she felt closer to the people she now called her friends than any comradeship she'd experienced before. The days stretched out ahead, with the promise of warm sunny days, get-togethers at the Club, stimulating dinner parties and long, cool swims in the pool.

"Are you coming to the school tomorrow?" asked Kate.

"Sure, I've missed Angelina," said Amie. "Is she still there?"

"I haven't noticed her," said Diana, "but I'm sure she's fine." Diana did not approve of the interest Amie showed in one child, however cute she might be. It would only lead to trouble. She had gone so far and taken the liberty to mention to Mrs Motswezi, that perhaps Angelina was getting too fond of Amie, and in the long term there was no future.

But Mrs Motswezi was not too sympathetic. Her view was that if Amie wanted to give Angelina a home, then it was a good thing and could only benefit the child. Even though Diana repeatedly reminded her that most overseas expatriates were in the country for a limited period, and there was no chance of Amie ever getting permission to remove the child from Togodo, the headmistress's view was that even if it was for a couple of years, then at least Angelina would have a good life while it lasted. She did not seem able to think ahead to what would happen when Amie and her husband finally left, and were forced to abandon the child. It was the African way, think of today and let the future take care of itself.

In the end, Diana gave up and reasoned there was little she could do, and it was Amie's problem and something for her to work out for herself.

Within a couple of days, it was as if they had never been away on holiday and they were back in their usual routine. Amie was thrilled to find Pretty had made an effort and cooked some meals and put them in the freezer for when they returned. She had expected Pretty to slack off and do as little as possible while they were away, but she returned to a spotlessly clean house and William too had remembered to water the grass.

"But it rain one day Madam," Pretty told her proudly, "and I tell William no water then."

"Thank you, Pretty, you have done a good job, I am very pleased," and Amie had to restrain herself from giving Pretty a hug. That would be going too far!

Jonathon always left very early for work each day when it was cooler, and he could catch up on paperwork while the office was still quiet, so when there was a loud knocking on the front door a few minutes after he drove off the next morning, Amie assumed he'd returned for something and forgotten his keys.

She was still in her nightdress when she flung the door open and paused in shock to see a tall, thick set black man, in an imposing uniform festooned with lots of gold braid, standing in the doorway. He stared at her for several seconds and Amie had the impression he was enjoying her discomfort.

"I have the pleasure of addressing Mrs Fish?" His English was excellent and his accent would not have been out of place in a British public school.

"Er, yes," Amie felt uncomfortable and not a little alarmed. "But how, how…?"

"Ah yes, your gardener was kind enough to unlock the gate for me. I wonder if you would spare me a few moments of your valuable time?" He smiled, showing an abundance of bright white and gold teeth. But his smile was not reflected in his eyes.

Amie wasn't quite sure what to do. She didn't want to invite him in while she was still in her night clothes, yet to ask him to wait outside and close the door in his face didn't seem like a good idea either.

As if sensing her indecision, he turned away from the door and took a few steps towards the front gate. "I can wait a few moments while you …….."

"Oh yes, thank you," said Amie gently closing the door. She raced into the bedroom to throw on a t-shirt and a pair of trousers. She called out to Pretty to tell her they had a visitor.

As she ushered the man into the house, Amie felt uneasy. She'd heard enough tales to realize that authority in Togodo was generally trouble. Surely it was unheard of for an official to call on an expatriate wife, especially when her husband wasn't at home? She indicated for him to sit on the sofa, but he ignored her gesture, and put out his hand and shook hers so firmly, she felt as if her fingers were being crushed.

"I am Colonel Mbanzi."

"Well you know who I am," Amie replied nervously.

Pretty appeared in the doorway, her eyes swept over the visitor, she licked her lips nervously and then disappeared swiftly back into the kitchen.

"Can I offer you a drink?" asked Amie.

"Just a glass of water," Colonel Mbanzi said as he sat down.

Amie found Pretty in the kitchen, half way out of the back door. "A cup of coffee for me please Pretty, and a glass of water for the uh, visitor."

Pretty nodded her head reluctantly. She looked scared out of her wits. Amie walked back into the lounge and perched on the edge of the sofa. She waited to hear what Colonel Mbanzi was going to say.

"I have, uh, heard reports you have been using a video camera?" His eyes seemed to bore right through her.

Amie was unsure how to answer, but she could hardly lie, since he seemed sure of his facts.

"Well yes, but I only filmed the house and friends, things like that," she replied. She had a hollow feeling just below her ribs, hearing Diana's words in her head. 'Be careful with that camera, the authorities here can be very sensitive about filming certain things, even taking still photographs.'

"And other places as well I think?" the Colonel leaned back and stared at Amie.

"Oh no, I've not taken it into town, no government buildings or anything ..."

"Oh but I think you have, we recovered your tape at the airport."

Amie was puzzled. "But I've not been to the airport since I

arrived, apart from our leave, so how…? No, you must be mistaken."

"I can assure you I am not mistaken," the Colonel replied sharply. He put his hand in his pocket and brought out a familiar tape in its plastic case. Amie recognized it immediately. "I believe this belongs to you?" He looked less friendly now.

Amie suddenly understood. "Oh, yes I did record the visit to the school, when the foreign sponsors came over. They want to raise more money for the orphanage. It was for a good cause and they asked me to shoot, uh, film it."

"So, people outside this country will think we are not capable of providing for our own children, is that it?"

"No, no, well I guess…" Amie didn't know what to say. She had always assumed that countries, especially African countries, were only too happy to receive handouts of any amount, from anywhere, and from anyone who was prepared to give it to them.

"I thought, well these ladies, they wanted to show other people in their church the orphans needed some equipment, and wanted…." Amie didn't know how to continue. She felt with every word, she was only making things worse.

The Colonel sat silently for a few minutes and Pretty crept in with the coffee and the water, moving more quickly than Amie had ever seen her move before. It reminded Amie how afraid of authority the locals were.

Amie picked up the glass of water and pushed it to the end of the coffee table, then focused her attention on adding sugar and milk to her coffee. She was nervous, but tried hard not to show it.

"You know you are not allowed to just film anything? You know this?" asked the Colonel ignoring the glass in front of him.

"But I didn't, I mean it was just the school and the children and if it brings in money then they will all benefit won't they?

It's good for everyone, isn't it?" Amie was scared that whatever she said would only dig herself in deeper. Her mouth felt dry and she was finding it difficult to swallow.

"Some people might believe that yes," he replied slowly. "You take good pictures with your camera, sharp and in focus?" He twisted the plastic box around in his hand.

"Yes, I think so, I, uh, well I worked in a video production house in London where we made programmes for television," Amie replied, then groaned inwardly. That was the last thing she should have said, what an idiot she was.

"You are a professional film maker then?"

"Oh no, not really, I mean I'm not working here, here in Togodo. I mean I'm only here because my husband is building the desalination plant. I don't have a job or anything…"

"That is my point," Colonel Mbanzi picked up the glass of water and took a sip.

What point? thought Amie. What now? Oh please don't let this have any effect on Jonathon's work. He'll never forgive me if they throw us out of Togodo. Drenton would fire him and he'd never get another job and…. Amie's thoughts ran riot.

The Colonel sat silently for several seconds and then said, "I think you could be of help to us."

"Help? In what way?" Amie asked slowly. This was going from bad to worse.

"We want to show the people all the good things we are doing for them and I think if we have the pictures to prove it, then the people will be very happy. We don't need pictures showing bad conditions, this gives the world a very bad impression of us." He deliberately replaced Amie's tape of the school and orphanage back into his pocket.

"I really don't know how I can help," said Amie, what was he getting at? Every nerve in her body seemed to be on high alert.

"We would request you help us with the filming," he said.

"Me! Oh no, I'm not sure I'm that good! No, I couldn't!" exclaimed Amie.

"But you said you worked in a professional company in London, so I am sure you are being far too modest," as the Colonel smiled he displayed two rows of white teeth, but again, the smile never reached his eyes.

Amie didn't quite know what to think, but she did know she didn't want to get involved with any official department, no way.

As if reading her mind, the Colonel continued. "We would be most disappointed if you refused, especially when you are in a position to help us, as you, and your husband…." he paused to let his words sink in, "…are guests in our country." He smiled again and sat back waiting for her reply.

What a bastard, thought Amie, he's putting me in an impossible situation, what the hell am I supposed to say? Then she had an idea. "I'm not sure my husband would be at all happy about me working, you understand of course?"

"But he allowed you to work in London, no?" The Colonel continued to smile.

"That was different, most women work in England, you need two salaries to live and…" Amie was fast running out of ideas.

"We like to think we are just as modern and forward looking as you are in England," the Colonel replied.

Yeah, right, thought Amie. He has to be joking, has he ever travelled to a first world country?

"And we have no problems with women working, I'm sure you've seen many yourself, like the lady at the orphanage for example? And I'm sure when you explain to your husband how necessary this filming is, then he will benefit as well."

The Colonel smiled again and rose to his feet. "I'm sure we can come to some arrangement which is mutually beneficial to all of us. Here is my card, and I will expect to see you on Wednesday afternoon around two?" The Colonel turned and walked out of the house without waiting for Amie to show him out.

As soon as the Colonel's chauffeured Range Rover had disappeared from sight Amie went and sat back down on the couch. What had she got herself into? There was more than a hint of a veiled threat in the Colonel's words. If she refused, then it sounded as if there might even be problems with the desalination plant. He had said as much. Amie decided to wait and talk to Jonathon when he came home.

It was unfortunate that when Jonathon returned from work even later than usual, he was in a particularly bad mood, and Amie didn't think her news was going to improve his frame of mind. From the revving of the car engine and the loud slamming of both the car door and the front door, she could tell his day had also not gone well. She decided to wait until he had eaten before mentioning the Colonel's visit. But it didn't work out that way, she just couldn't wait to talk to him.

"How did your day go?" she asked as Jonathon flung down his briefcase on the couch.

"Like most days, bloody awful," he replied. "The equipment is still stuck in the docks, and it's one excuse after another as to why they won't release it. I wish I knew what was really going on." Jonathon dropped onto the sofa and closed his eyes.

"Well I don't know if it's connected in any way, but I had a visitor early this morning," said Amie slowly.

Jonathon opened his eyes and frowned. "A visitor? How on earth could that be connected with my work?"

"I don't really know, but there was a sort of threat that if I didn't…" Amie wasn't sure quite how to explain events. Perhaps her imagination was working overtime, but then she recalled the feelings she'd had earlier.

"Didn't what?" Jonathon sat up and gave her his full attention.

Amie sat down beside him and tried to gather her thoughts together. "This Colonel came to see me," she said. "A Colonel Mbanzi, who suggested I help him to make the country look good by taking videos."

"Mbanzi, that name rings a bell. Think he's pretty high up, has the ear of the President. Videos of what?" Jonathon was puzzled.

"Videos of all the improvements the government has made for the people, though so far, I've not seen anything that looks as if it's improving any lifestyle. I've never seen so much poverty."

"I certainly haven't seen anything, and I'm not sure how it could have been much worse before for most of the population," snapped Jonathon. "And where are you supposed to do all this filming?"

"I don't know, but I'm supposed to go and see the Colonel on Wednesday. He left me his card." Amie got the Colonel's business card out of her bag and handed it to Jonathon.

"Do you want to do this?" he asked her.

"No, not really. But I don't think I have a choice. He was very insistent and, well, this is how it may affect you. It was almost a veiled threat that if I didn't co-operate then things would be more difficult for you. He didn't say so in so many words Jonathon, but it was there, well his exact words were, 'And I'm sure when you explain to your husband how necessary this filming is, then he will benefit as well.'"

Jonathon leaned forward and put his head in his hands. "Look," he said after a few minutes, "you don't have to do this you know. I could always send you home, or, we could even leave together. I don't want you in any danger."

Not for a moment was Amie tempted, not after the fearful holiday, and it would be just too humiliating to slink home now. She could imagine people laughing and whispering about how they'd made a terrible mistake leaving in the first place.

No, her friends were here, she enjoyed her life and she thought of Angelina, and the school and Diana and her new friends at the Club, and the wide open spaces outside the city. There was something about Africa, it was almost as if she was under a spell. It came from walking on the ground with the feel of drum beats beneath your feet and she recalled hearing once you were in Africa for longer than ten years, then you could never leave, you always carried a piece of the dark continent within you.

"Look, I won't come to any harm, I'm sure I'll be all right." She pushed her fears to the back of her mind. This was just one more psychological hurdle to get over. Why was she being so silly? If someone in England asked her to go and film something, she'd be over the moon, so why should it be any different because this was another country? Amie stood up and walked towards the kitchen to fetch Jonathon's supper which had been waiting for him for several hours.

"Don't even think about either of us leaving," she said in a firm voice. "I'm just being ridiculous. I'm sure the Colonel will make sure nothing awful happens. I mean, what could go wrong for heaven's sake?"

"I'm sure you're right, a new environment just takes a bit of getting used to," said Jonathon and yawned widely. "This Colonel would lose a lot of face if you got hurt or anything, so perhaps we're over reacting."

"Sure," replied Amie as she returned with Jonathon's dried up dinner out of the oven.

How dangerous could it possibly be?

Amie tossed and turned in the early hours of the morning. Despite the whirling of the overhead fan, she found it impossible to sleep, as images tumbled round and round in her head. She didn't dare say no to what the Colonel had asked, but she was fearful. It was more than an unspoken rule among the expatriate population, you did not get involved in government and official business, especially if you were only temporarily resident as a wife. It was fine to visit a school and do a little low key charity work, and play tennis, attend parties and gatherings in your own home or the local Expatriate Club, but nothing more. Even trips out of town were not really encouraged, since there were several 'sensitive' areas, which were generally rumoured to be military training camps or possibly storage areas for weapons. There were the usual urban legends of one or two of those more curious people who had driven off one day never to be seen again.

Yet another hot, tiring and frustrating day at work ensured that Jonathon lay comatose and snoring quietly beside her as Amie worried what the following days might bring. At least she could talk to Diana and get advice from her, and that was the only decision Amie had made before the early birds began to chirp in the pre dawn light.

"Oh my dear, what a terrible position to be put in!" exclaimed Diana. "I must admit this is a first. I've never heard of a situation where the wife was asked to get involved with official business before."

Amie had phoned Diana on her cell phone first thing, and now they were sitting beside the pool at the Club sipping an early morning cup of coffee.

"I feel I'm damned if I do and damned if I don't," explained Amie miserably. "I know I didn't imagine the veiled threat that things wouldn't go well for Jonathon if I refused. I would never forgive myself if I stuffed up his big chance."

"It's certainly a problem," Diana replied. "The only thing I can think of is you 'drop' the camera so you can't do the work."

"I've already thought of that," Amie replied. "but similar cameras are on sale over the Internet, and I guess they would simply replace it. But why me, Diana? Why ask me to film for them? Surely there are plenty of other people here who are just as capable, if not more so."

"Well," her friend replied slowly. "Remember what I said about lack of trust. Perhaps, if they feel they can totally control you, then you will film exactly what they want. Also, remember now it's known you've had professional training, and you were trained in the country known worldwide for having excellent television, well that makes you a natural choice." She went on, "if they had looked at the footage you took at the school and were impressed with the quality, then it makes sense."

"I was rather proud of the bits I filmed on the visit," Amie said. She still didn't want to admit even to Diana she was only working as a receptionist for the production house in London, but on the other hand, she had received three years training in television and video production in college. If it wasn't such a popular profession then she might well have got a job as a camera person or an editor. But it was one of those industries you had to work your way up from the bottom. Now it looked as if she had leapt from the reception desk to full blown producer overnight.

"Maybe we're getting too hysterical about this," said Diana with a smile. "How bad can it be? All you have to do is make a short film of the things they point out to you. Play along with them and then later, when you're back in UK, use some of the footage to tell the real truth. Hey, you could become famous, get on National Geographic even."

"Now that's an idea," said Amie cheering up a lot.

Diana leaned back and lit a cigarette. "It would be an opportunity to try and explain what it's really like here in Africa. Pictures tell a thousand words, show the poverty, but also show the ignorance and the hard working mothers and the lazy, absentee fathers. Highlight the corruption and the wastage of foreign aid, it will give donors a chance to see how contributions can be given that will really help. No good sending lots of food if it's left on the docks to rot, or sold to the starving for their last few cents. Many people are not aware of this, and they give willingly, not realizing all they are doing is lining the already bulging pockets of those few at the top of the regime."

Amie listened to her friend in dismay. "But Diana, is it always as bad as that?" she protested mildly. "There are a lot of good, honest people here surely."

"Yes, there are," said Diana as she stubbed out her cigarette, "but those are not the people at the top. Not the people who run and control events. Strength is admired on this continent and you have to be tough and ruthless to get to the top and stay there."

Amie sat up straight and decided to look on the bright side. Perhaps it would be fun filming, at least she was the only foreigner who could do it openly and with government blessing. There must be strict rules even for overseas television crews, and no one had ever heard of anyone ever being given permission to film. No one took much interest in Togodo, it wasn't a particularly large country and it didn't have any developed natural resources worth fighting over.

It was only a couple of days later, when Amie and Jonathon were attending a function at the Club, she was to recall her thoughts that morning by the pool. Formal dinners were held at least monthly, it was an excuse to dress up, get together and relieve the monotony of a society without the usual television, cinemas and theatres. Some of the more active members of the Club organized beetle drives, a movie, quiz evenings, talent contests and so on. Amie thought of it as a flash back to the old Victorian days. In fact the evenings were fun, so perhaps those Victorians knew a thing or two.

Tonight, there were about twenty odd tables laid out in the main room of the Club. With ten people to a table, Amie reckoned nearly all the British expatriates were there, plus a couple of French and Italians as well. There were not too many foreigners in Togodo Amie realized for the first time. A few fairy lights had been strung round the walls and the waiters were wearing their best uniforms.

"What's the special occasion?" Amie asked Diana as they took their seats.

"I really don't know," Diana replied, but I do see a couple of strangers.

As in any small, tightly knit community, everyone knew everyone else, at least by sight, and new arrivals were greeted with interest. Amie remembered their first evening at the Club, when it seemed she met almost a hundred people all at once, and at the end of the evening, could only remember one or two of them.

As Amie and Jonathon took their places with Diana and Richard, they were also joined by a couple of the Drenton crowd, the single guys who shared an apartment in town. There were two vacant places at the table and it was towards the empty chairs that Leonard was propelling the two strangers.

Leonard, the present Club President, introduced their guests. "These gentlemen have just traveled down from up north where they've been on a hush-hush mission prospecting for, what were you guys looking for?"

The taller, sandy haired guy laughed. "Anything, anything at all Leonard, but of course, our findings are very hush hush."

"Naturally," replied Leonard. "This is Simon Walters and Eric Goodman, and they have two more nights to go before leaving for good old UK." Everyone laughed and clapped as the guests sat down and the waiters started serving the first course.

"Diana and Richard Carstens."

"I'm Jonathon and this is my wife Amie," everyone shook hands.

"Pleased to meet you, and great to be in civilization again," replied Simon. "And what line are you in?"

"Trying to get this desalination plant built and running, though it's like trying to swim through quicksand," Jonathon said pulling a face.

"We know what it's like," said Eric. "But in our case, because the government was so eager for us to get our report in on time, they pulled out all the stops."

"Why should prospecting be such a secret?" Amie asked Simon who was sitting on her left side.

"The balance of power, that's what it's all about. If you have something important buried beneath your land, then it changes everything. If there's nothing there, no gold, no platinum, no uranium, no oil, then no one takes any interest in you as a third world country. But add those magic ingredients and all of a sudden you're the flavour of the month."

Amie could have kicked herself for not realizing the importance of natural resources. "But there's no mining here in Togodo is there?" she asked.

"No, not yet." Then realizing maybe he'd said too much, Simon quickly turned to talk to the person on the other side of him.

The man sitting across from Amie claimed her attention. "You're married to a real high flier young lady. I hope you appreciate him!" he teased her.

"Jonathon?" Amie was surprised. "Well I know he's young to have such a position in the company."

"A very young company and this is their first venture abroad, did you know that?"

"No, no I didn't," replied Amie and wondered why Jonathon had never mentioned it to her. She turned to tell Diana but she was occupied with the guest on her other side.

"Tell us how you find stuff, how do you know what's hidden metres and metres under the ground?" Diana asked Eric as she picked up her glass of wine.

"Basically, we send sound waves into the ground and measure the speed they return and that gives us the depths and densities of the underlying rocks. From the data, we can work out what minerals the sound waves passed through." Eric buttered his roll, gave Diana a slightly lecherous look and nodded at Simon. "He takes it a lot more seriously than I do, but I can tell you that…" Eric dropped his voice to a whisper and Amie didn't hear the next few sentences. Watching them, Amie thought it was a good thing they were leaving in a couple of days, Eric in particular will be after the wives, and he seemed particularly taken with Diana. Amie hoped there wouldn't be any trouble. But the dinner passed pleasantly enough and it was long after midnight when they finally returned home.

"That was a good evening," said Jonathon, who seemed in a better mood than he'd been in for a long time.

"Yes, I enjoyed it too," Amie responded. "But I must admit I was curious about what Eric was telling Diana and I felt an awful fool asking why mineral prospecting was such a big secret. Simon didn't talk to me again the whole evening."

"Well that suits me fine," Jonathon grinned. "Since you were the prettiest girl there, I have to take extra care of you."

Amie laughed, pleased at the compliment. "Hardly the prettiest, but certainly the youngest wife. Have you noticed that groups abroad get on because we're all from the same background and age doesn't seem to matter?"

"Yes," Jonathon said as he ripped off his bow tie. "It's so very different from home, where all our friends were pretty much the same age as us. Here we mix as easily with fifty and sixty year olds as we do with those only a little older."

Amie threw the coverlet and sheets back off the bed. "Well we have a lot in common with them. We're all in the same boat together, and I quite like it, it sort of widens your interests and your horizons."

Jonathon nodded. "Funny, back in the UK, we would of

course be polite to older people, but we wouldn't possibly think to ask for their advice so often." Jonathon tossed his socks in the direction of the washing basket, but they fell far short. He continued. "We were lucky to meet Richard at the airport that day, he's been such a help."

"How long will it take to build the bridge?" Amie asked. She knew Richard's company was constructing a double lane highway over the river estuary.

"At least five more years at the rate it's proceeding. Like everything else, time means nothing in Africa." Jonathon yawned and fell back against the covers. "But it's no use changing the subject, come here and play your proper role as a wife."

Amie almost asked Jonathon to repeat what he said, it had been such a long time since he had any energy at all, and bed had been strictly for sleep and nothing else. Cheerfully, and now wide awake, she jumped into bed beside him with alacrity.

It wasn't until late the following afternoon that Amie had a chance to ask Diana about the previous evening and what had been going on between her and Eric. They chatted in the changing room before their tennis game.

"Well I know I shouldn't gossip," said Diana, ignoring the fact that that's what most of the expatriates did most of the time; "but he was telling me they found large uranium deposits up in the northwest and some other rare minerals which will be highly sought after."

"Will that make any difference to anything?" Amie asked.

"I don't know, well, yes of course, in time, but no one knows how soon. If these deposits are as rich as Eric suggested, then it could catapult Togodo into a whole different league. Once the word gets out, then the larger mining companies will be beating a path to the door, and it could even upset the balance here, if neighbouring countries try and claim tracts of land up in the far northwest."

"Are there any claims?" Amie enquired.

"I wouldn't be surprised. President Muwaba would love to expand his empire."

"He's the President of Budan isn't he?"

"Yes, and as I understand it, from what Eric said, the deposits are close to the northern border and probably extend into Budan. Still, I'm sure we'll all be out of here long before all hell breaks loose. Let's hurry, we've only got an hour before it gets dark, and it's not as nice playing under the floodlights, *if* the power doesn't fail."

Amie was hoping Wednesday wouldn't come too quickly, but it was impossible to hold back the days and she woke in the morning with a sinking feeling in the pit of her stomach. She got out of bed reluctantly. Jonathon was already in the kitchen, finishing off his coffee as Pretty hovered nearby waiting for instructions.

"Good morning Pretty," said Amie. "Can you please wash the windows today, and take the living room carpet out and give it a good shake."

"Yes Madam," replied Pretty as she poured a cup of coffee for Amie.

"So, today is the day?" remarked Jonathon.

"Yes, but please don't remind me. I'm not looking forward to it at all." Amie felt very nervous.

"Where are you meeting the Colonel?" asked Jonathon.

"He didn't actually say, just that he would see me about two this afternoon."

"Then wait for a driver, I'm sure they'll come and collect you."

"I guess I'll have to sit and wait. He didn't tell me where his office is."

"Nothing on his business card?" enquired Jonathon.

"No."

"If there is a problem, or you're at all worried then call me," said Jonathon giving her a peck on the cheek. "I'll keep my cell phone on all day." He picked up his lap top case and was out of the door before Amie could reply. As she watched him climb into the car she had the uneasy feeling he had already forgotten all about her and was concentrating on the day ahead. What was this living overseas doing to their marriage? Would it have been any different if they had stayed in Castle Bridge? Ambition had not entered their world before, but now Jonathon seemed driven and determined to succeed. Amie had to admit to herself that this was an admirable quality, especially in a husband, but it was certainly a downside for the wives. Many hours alone, an exhausted husband every night, and even when Jonathon was home, she suspected he was thinking about work most of the time. Maybe the only answer was to be as involved in your own work, and feel equally satisfied with your own career.

A couple of years ago Amie would have jumped at the opportunity of making programmes, but now the chance had come, she was nervous and wary. She was venturing into unknown territory and she was not looking forward to it at all.

8 BICYCLES AND SEWING MACHINES

Amie spent most of the morning wandering around the house, trying to keep out of Pretty's way. She checked and rechecked her equipment again and again, making sure she had enough tape, the batteries were fully charged and the camera was in running order.

She tried to read a book, but gave up after reading half a page and not taking in any of it. She put on the radio and fiddled with the dial trying to find some music, but all she got was garbled voices. She walked around the garden, holding her mobile in one hand in case Colonel Mbanzi phoned.

She wondered what the rest of her family was doing right now. England was two hours behind time wise, so Dean would be at school and baby Jade at the crèche. Sam would probably be doing the washing or some baking if she wasn't out at a job interview, and Gerry would be working away in the Council offices. Both her parents would be at work as well, trying to cram a bit of knowledge into unresponsive and belligerent young minds. No one would be thinking of her at this minute that was for sure.

She had lunch early, partly to settle her stomach which was churning like a cement mixer, and also to be ready in case a car came for her on time. But two o'clock came and there was no sign of transport, and by two thirty, Amie was feeling a bit panicky. What if the Colonel had expected her to drive to his offices, although she hadn't a clue where they were. Would he see it as a sign of non co-operation on her part? Should she have used her initiative and found out where he was based? What trouble could this cause for Jonathon and Drenton's desalination plant?

It was nearly three o'clock before a large car drove up outside the house. Out climbed a young black man in unadorned military uniform. He rang the bell and Amie walked down the front path to unlock the gate.

"Mrs Fish?" he enquired.

"Yes, are you from….?" she began, but he cut her off.

"Colonel Mbanzi sent me. He said you had equipment?"

"Yes, yes, it's just inside the front door," Amie replied.

Without waiting for permission, the driver walked into the house and picked up the boxes and started back to the car. "We must hurry," he said. "We are late."

Amie followed him, thinking she was not going to take the blame. She had been ready, the driver was late. She had been waiting all day.

The drive into town reminded her of the first trip from the airport, although this time many of the cars moved out of the way quickly. Although there were no official markings on the vehicle, a clean, un-dented, large, black car, screamed power and importance. No one in their right mind wanted to get involved with officialdom, including me, thought Amie bitterly.

They screeched through a pair of large gates set in a high wall not far from the Presidential Palace. Perhaps when it was first built, the three storied steel and glass construction would have been quite imposing, but now it had an air of neglect. There were weeds growing in the cracks along the walkways, and it was a long time since any of the windows had been cleaned, if ever. Several of the blinds inside hung at strange angles, obviously broken, but Amie had little time to take a closer look. The young driver quickly opened the back of the car, and grabbing the equipment boxes indicated she should follow him.

There were guards at the gate, and more guards either side of the main entrance. They stared at Amie insolently, but made no move to open the door for her, as she ran to catch it before it swung back in her face. She had quickly learned that in Africa, men do not allow women to walk in front of them. The explanation was men would check first if there was any danger, with the idea of protecting their wives and sisters. Amie suspected it was more to do with male dominance and a refusal to follow first world customs. Had women here even risen to be third class citizens? For the men, their cattle were their most prized possessions, followed by the wife or several wives, which were added to the asset list as part of the household contents.

With Amie behind him, the driver began to climb the stairs. Feeling hot and flustered Amie looked longingly at the lifts, and wondered if they were still working. As they turned left on the first landing, Amie saw the floor was covered by a dirty, red carpet which muffled their footsteps as they walked down to the far end. Stopping at the last door, the driver knocked and waited.

"Come," shouted Colonel Mbanzi from the other side and opening the door almost reverently, the driver pushed Amie inside. He placed the equipment just inside the door and beat a hasty retreat.

It was probably one of the largest offices Amie had ever seen. It was expensively furnished with an enormous desk, a separate seating area with armchairs grouped around a coffee table, and what looked to her untrained eye, several expensive paintings on the walls. Along one side of the room was a floor to ceiling bookcase unit crammed with books, a cocktail cabinet and a very large flat screen television.

Colonel Mbanzi looked pointedly at his watch before nodding to a plain, uncomfortable looking chair placed in front of his desk. Amie was about to protest her driver had arrived late, but decided it might not be wise. She didn't want to make enemies at any level.

"So you are finally here," the Colonel said with a smile,

which again did not reach his eyes.

"Yes …." Amie paused, she had no idea how to address him. Was she supposed to call him Sir, or Colonel or try and respond to him on a more professional level, seeing him as an equal? She decided not to give him any title. She hoped he would not sense she felt quite afraid of him, but she had her doubts.

"And I hope you are ready to start work?" He raised his eyebrows as he annunciated each word slowly and carefully.

"I'm not sure I understand exactly what you want me to do," Amie also spoke slowly, in an effort to stop her voice shaking. Now she was here, in this obviously important office, she was determined to behave as professionally as possible. What was the worst that could happen to her anyway? She'd pretend she was back home and this was just another assignment for her. She was her own MD, CEO and Chairman of the Board of her imaginary company, so she might as well act the part from the beginning. It gave her a little courage.

"As I explained, before…." Colonel Mbanzi gave the impression he was speaking to a mentally disabled child, "… I want you to record some of the many projects we have put in place for our people which have benefitted their lives, uplifted their standard of living and contributed to their well being."

Amie wondered briefly if he always used 'official speak' and for a brief moment she tried to imagine him at the breakfast table pontificating to the rest of his family. She gave herself a mental shake and tried to concentrate on what he was saying.

"You did not need to bring all that equipment with you today," the Colonel waved dismissively at the camera boxes on the floor. "Today's meeting is just to discuss some of the projects we have earmarked for publicity purposes."

Amie reached into her bag and took out a pen and a notebook.

"First there is our excellent bicycle project. We furnish the schools with bicycles to lend to their pupils who would be required to travel a long way to school each day. We are proud to call it the 'Shova Shova Bicycle Project.' You would need to show the pupils benefitting from this expanded mode of transport."

Bikes to and from school, wrote Amie.

"Then we would like to showcase our State Funded Bed and Breakfast Scheme for tourists."

Now he has to be joking, thought Amie. In all the months she had been here, she had not seen a single, solitary tourist.

"We would like you to illustrate our excellent training facilities, and then film some of the successfully run establishments." Without pausing for breath the Colonel continued. "We are also wanting you to record the computerization within our educational establishments. We are among the first in the world to provide such an excellent service to our young learners."

Is he serious? thought Amie. Well maybe she had a lot to learn, maybe she should wait until she actually saw these excellent facilities? They certainly were not obvious to the expatriate community.

"We must not forget our advanced hospital service," the Colonel droned on. "Togodo is highly regarded in the field of medicine and we wish to show our people what advances we can offer those whose health is not of the best. In particular the neo natal ward and the latest in diagnostic equipment of which we are rightly proud."

A knock at the door interrupted his flow, as a very beautiful young Togodian girl appeared balancing a tray with tea and biscuits. The Colonel nodded at her, though Amie detected something of a leer in his expression. Without lifting her eyes to look at either of them, she placed the tray on the desk and quickly left the room.

The Colonel put three spoons of sugar into each cup and

pushed one towards Amie, who did not take sugar in her tea, but did not like to mention it. Maybe at a later meeting she would find the courage.

"We need you to make a movie about our excellent electricity services, and show how we have connected many of our people to a regular and reliable supply of power thus enabling them to build up small industries within their own homes."

Amie hoped these small industries had a more reliable electric supply than she had in her own home. Most days they lost power for a good couple of hours.

"These are just the start of the projects we want you to record. There are of course, many more, but these will do to begin with."

Amie took a sip of the very sickly tea. "And your target audience is…?" she asked.

Colonel Mbanzi looked puzzled.

"Who do you want to show these projects to?" she simplified the question.

The Colonel waved his arms expansively. "Why, to everyone of course! Our people, overseas visitors and we plan to exhibit them in other countries as well."

"And do you have a timeframe for production?"

"We are holding an International Trade Fair here in the capital in two months time and we would expect you to be able to produce them by then."

"All of them!" Amie failed to mask her horror. "Two months is a very short time to produce six programmes!" she exclaimed.

"You can't accomplish it in time?"

Again, she recognized the underlying threat in his words. This was a man who was not used to being questioned about his orders, that was very clear.

Taking a deep breath Amie stood her ground. "I will certainly do my best, but there is a lot of work in making even one programme, research, scripting, shooting," she saw his face and added quickly; "by that I mean filming, then logging the scenes to be used and editing them in the right order, together with the voice over and the music which all has to be in sync. It all takes time." Hopefully I can blind him with my in-house speak, she thought, but the Colonel seemed quite unfazed.

"They don't have to be so long," he replied missing the point entirely. "Perhaps an hour each should be quite adequate."

"I think that would be far too long," replied Amie. "Research has shown adult concentration begins to diminish after twenty minutes, so I would suggest, with the benefit of my experience, fifteen minutes for each of these would suit your purpose much better. They would have more impact and thus further retention." Goodness she thought, I'm beginning to speak like the Colonel now! She continued. "You are hiring me for my expertise, so along with my ability to make videos for you, I can bring extra knowledge about the running time of the finished product. I do know what I'm talking about."

The Colonel looked totally unconvinced and more than a little annoyed, but he shrugged his shoulders as he said "Well if that is all you can manage in the time, I suppose it will have to do."

Amie bit back the sharp retort, she may have won her point but he had twisted it to make it her failing, her being unable to do a good enough job. It was obvious he was inferring she was short changing them.

"As you have indicated you will be under so much pressure," he continued, again emphasizing his words, "we will of course assign a student to help you, and, if necessary, translate for you."

"Thank you," said Amie. "And language, do you want ....?"

"English of course," Colonel did not wait for her to finish speaking. "It will be more beneficial for the overseas market and potential investors. So, you will start tomorrow morning and maybe choose the Shova Shova project. I will send a car for you at eight." The Colonel stood before continuing, "I hope you will make yourself available and not keep your driver and assistant waiting."

Amie was so tempted to say she had been on standby all day, it wasn't her fault, had she been given an address and used her own transport, she would have been knocking on his office door precisely on time. She thought better of it, and bit her lip and said nothing.

The Colonel put out his hand and shook hers with yet another smile which looked insincere, and waved towards the door to indicate the meeting was over.

If she had hoped to make a graceful exit, Amie was out of luck. By the time she had picked up the camera and other bits of equipment, Colonel Mbanzi was already on the phone barking orders to some hapless underling. But she could feel his eyes on her as she struggled with the door knob and made an undignified retreat.

She was wondering how she was going to get home, when the same driver materialized from an office half way along the corridor and with a sweep of his head, indicated she was to follow him. This time, he did not offer to help her carry the camera gear.

It was almost dark by the time Amie got home. When she was dropped off at her gate, again, she was offered no help with the equipment and she was grateful when Pretty appeared and helped her carry everything inside. She felt exhausted from the tension of the meeting and the uncertainty of what was behind her new career, if you could call it that. She found Colonel Mbanzi unnerving and she had to admit more than a little scary. If he hadn't the power to make their lives difficult, if not impossible, and possibly destroy Jonathon's career, she could have shaken the whole thing off and simply refused to co-operate. She had no idea how high up in government he was, but she was going to do her damndest to find out.

Amie would have preferred to kick off her shoes and spend a quiet night at home, but as luck would have it, there was another dinner on at the Club, one of Jonathon's bosses was over for just two days. Briefly, she wondered if he was enjoying the hospitality in one of Togodo's new bed and breakfasts run by a highly trained and efficient team. Somehow she doubted it.

It was a lot easier to entertain at the Club than at home, though Amie had hoped to throw the occasional dinner party in their own house. But although she had improved the kitchen facilities by buying a few gadgets, she still did not have sufficient crockery or cutlery or even serving dishes to feel she could entertain just yet. Pretty was just terrified of the food mixer and ran screaming out of the kitchen the first time Amie turned it on. It took a lot of persuading to entice her back and show her how it worked. What was more, Pretty did not seem to grasp the point of having a food mixer at all, and every time there were ingredients that needed mixing together, Pretty made it perfectly obvious she preferred to use a fork or a whisk. Guessing she was never going to change Pretty's mind, Amie gave up and let her get on with it.

Amie had met Brian Ford once before at a company function in Castle Bridge, but when she met him again that evening she was amazed to see there was almost a role reversal. True, he was Jonathon's boss, but he was out of his comfort zone and not as relaxed as he had been in the past. It dawned on Amie that while they had become quite familiar with the conditions, behaviour and atmosphere in Togodo, to Brian it was all new and strange. She realized she'd adapted to her new way of life and took most things in her stride.

Brian on the other hand seemed jumpy and ill at ease,

although a couple of beers before dinner, and a couple of glasses of wine during dinner seemed to help him relax. Jonathon had been dreading the visit, he knew he was weeks behind schedule and Brian had come over to see why they'd not kept to the timetable.

Since Richard was also at their table, Jonathon relied on him to perhaps explain how things were done, or rather not done here in Togodo. Coming from someone else, with years of expatriate living behind him would carry a lot more weight.

"I think Jonathon has done remarkably well," said Richard as the waiter brought their first course. "People in England have no idea how difficult it can be working in a place like this."

"I can appreciate there must be some differences," replied Brian. "The heat alone…"

"The practical things are easier to handle," continued Richard, "it's the people. When they sign the contract they promise the earth, but they are already calculating how much more they can get out of the deal, especially on a personal level. Take your offices for example. When Jonathon arrived, he was given to understand they had already been reserved for Drenton."

"Yes, that was part of the agreement right up front," replied Brian.

"But what do you say when they simply shrug their shoulders, tell you there was a misunderstanding and they have found a piece of ground where you can build brand new offices?"

"That was a tricky one to get round," put in Jonathon. "It took days and days to change their minds and find suitable premises."

"But we never agreed to building offices, that was never part of the plan!" exclaimed Brian.

"You know that, Jonathon knows that, but how do you convince the African officials? Remember they have their family and cousins on standby to erect yet another unnecessary building, with everyone getting a cut along the way. They can't wait to inflate your budget and their back pockets at the same time!"

"I can see this is going to take a lot longer than we had anticipated, probably double the time frame," said Brian.

Amie listened with interest. She had been hesitant about chatting to Jonathon about his work. If he wasn't tired, then he was in a foul mood when he got home most nights, so she tried to wait patiently until he was ready to talk. Unfortunately that did not happen very often.

"I am happy the office is up and running, but then there was this big debate about where to site the plant. I understood they were worried the construction noise would disturb the President, his palace is only a kilometre away so they wanted us to build it further up the coast." Brian sounded exasperated, he continued, "they don't seem to think it matters where it goes."

"How much does it matter?" asked Diana.

"It's probably not that critical," replied Jonathon, "but of course once they tentatively agreed on the new site we suggested, we had to survey the land to ensure the specs won't change for the safety of the building, the foundations and such and also the geology of the land where the pipes will be laid. But so far everything looks fine and we have started laying the foundations and the pipe work is underway."

"I see, and all the time your company is pouring in more and more money into the Togodian economy, which has to be good for them." Diana looked thoughtful. "Believe me, we've been in enough third world countries to know just how far and how fast you can push these governments and officials. Richard is constantly frustrated with missed deadlines and broken promises."

"I am indeed," agreed her husband, "but in the end you learn to take life more slowly, refuse to let your blood pressure rise too high, and just do the best you can. And that's what I keep telling Jonathon." He patted Jonathon on the shoulder.

It's amazing how we all stick together, thought Amie. Our little group living over here, are more in tune than we are with colleagues from our own companies back home. She reminded herself to thank both Richard and Diana for their loyal support. She was not sure Brian was wholly convinced about African business ethics, but if this visit helped to take the pressure off Jonathon even a little bit, that would be very welcome.

After dinner Diana asked Amie to come and keep her company while she had a cigarette out on the verandah. Even here in Togodo, you were not allowed to smoke inside a restaurant.

"I don't know what we would do without the Club," said Amie as they settled down on one of the large sofas. "I have never entertained any of Jonathon's bosses before, and I might have made a terrible hash of it."

Diana laughed. "I certainly did the first time I tried! I was so nervous, and we'd not been married all that long either. I had never learned to cook, my mother loathed cooking, so all I could do was heat and assemble from tins and packets. I knew how to prepare all the ready-made foods by heart and I never had to read the instructions."

"So what went wrong on your first dinner party?" asked Amie.

"We were in Tanzania, not in the suburbs, but a little way out in the bush. I'd raced into town to buy meat, but I forgot about the heat, and by the time I got home, the pork was reeking to high heaven." Amie laughed.

"Well I can laugh about it now but at the time I was frantic! No one had told me to take a cooler box with ice blocks in it when I went shopping. So I tried my hand at nut cutlets, which were not very successful, and for desert, I had to make custard for the first time from scratch, before I had always poured it straight out of the carton. It was a total disaster sadly, but everyone was very polite and Richard went overboard explaining how difficult and different things were in the African bush. Not at all like back home, no Sainsbury's just along the road."

"I was a little surprised and maybe upset, but Jonathon did not seem keen for Brian to come to our place even for drinks."

"I think he was wise, your husband is a lot more perceptive than you give him credit for."

"Whatever do you mean?" asked Amie.

"Well you heard them earlier, saying how behind schedule everything is," said Diana.

"Yes."

"Well you only have to look at the houses we have here, even bosses in England seldom have anything quite so grand, unless they're multi millionaires of course."

Amie looked puzzled. "But what does that have to do with anything?" she asked.

Diana smiled. "Jealousy, my dear. Seeing someone a lot further down the totem pole living in such grandeur, along with servants as well, and things behind schedule, it's all about perception. See what I mean?"

"Oh! They might think Jonathon is dragging his heels and extending his time here because we are living in the lap of luxury with everything paid for and, yes I see now."

"It doesn't matter where in the world you are, the basic human emotions are the same. We know Jonathon is working all hours...."

"Yes," agreed Amie. "He hardly has a chance to enjoy our mansion, which was the smallest on offer at the time. Oh dear, life is a bigger minefield than I thought."

"Make that *mind-field*," laughed Diana. "There are lots of good things about living overseas, but there is also the down side and we do not enjoy the same cosy, comfortable and safe life you find in most Western countries these days."

"Do you know, I think I'm beginning to enjoy the challenges," said Amie surprising herself, it was something she had only just realized.

"You'll do," said Diana. "Welcome to the world of the expatriates."

Since they were both very tired when they returned from the Club that night, Amie did not tell Jonathon much about the meeting with Colonel Mbanzi. But she did find time to show him how she had converted the luggage trolley to carry most of the camera gear. It did not look very professional, but it was much easier to drag it behind her than try and carry the camera, the small bag of lights, the tripod, the script and any other bits and pieces.

As she turned the light out Amie wondered what the next day would bring.

Up early, Amie was ready by seven thirty, and this time she was pleasantly surprised when a jeep drove up to the gate only ten minutes late. Much to her relief, there was a different driver, a slightly older, thick set man who smiled as she opened the gate. He was closely followed by a young man wearing jeans and a T-shirt with 'Guns and Roses' on the front.

The driver introduced himself as Themba, while the younger one said his name was Ben. Amie wondered if this was really his given name or he was using a Western one.

Ben took charge of the trolley, leaving Amie free to carry her clipboard and the log sheets. As they climbed into the jeep, Amie asked if they knew where to go. Yes, they assured her, one of the schools on the outskirts of town. Amie was relieved to see Themba was quite a careful driver, and apart from shouting insults at the other road users, he kept to a steady and reasonable speed.

It never failed to amaze Amie that although she didn't think of Apatu as a large place, nearly every time she went out, she saw different areas and even more shanty towns.

"We need to get general footage as well," she mentioned to them and they nodded their heads in agreement. She hoped their command of English was good, and they would understand at least most of what she said.

About half an hour later they drove up at the main gates to a school. It was a good deal smarter than the orphanage school, but there was still a gatekeeper, who at first seemed reluctant to let them in. There was quite a heated discussion with Themba before very slowly, the gates were opened, just wide enough for the jeep to scrape through.

"We go to see the Headmaster first," announced Ben.

"That is exactly what I was thinking," replied Amie looking round. The buildings extended upwards by three floors round a central square, the usual bare sandy area with not a blade of grass in sight. She noticed several broken windows, and decided to keep those out of shot if possible. There was the usual litter on the ground and the sounds of pupils chanting wafted out on the still, clear air.

Leaving the jeep close to the main door, Amie asked Themba if he would mind looking after the equipment while she and Ben went inside. He seemed quite happy to do this and immediately settled down in his seat and closed his eyes. Amie hoped he wouldn't really go to sleep, he was supposed to be guarding valuable camera gear.

Inside the main doors, there was no reception area, and no secretary, so they wandered down the corridor hoping to find someone to ask. It was not long before a teacher came hurtling towards them. He paused briefly as Ben asked where they could find the Headmaster. The teacher pointed briefly at one of the doors and ran off.

"Goodness, I've never seen a staff member running in school before!" exclaimed Amie in surprise.

"He wasn't a teacher!" said Ben, "this is a high school."

"But he looked at least twenty years old," replied Amie.

"That is quite possible," Ben replied. "If you fail to pass your exams at the end of a year in school, then you stay behind and repeat that year. Some of the children fail many, many times and it takes them a long time to finish school."

"So they don't have to leave when they are sixteen or eighteen?" Amie was surprised.

"As long as their parents can afford the fees, they can repeat school years as many times as they like."

It didn't make sense to Amie. "But," she persisted, "won't the new class be full from the year before you know..."

Ben shook his head. "No, learners drop out, and they leave room for the failed ones, as long as they can pay their fees. On sports days for the races we measure height, not ask about your age, and that makes it fairer for everyone didn't you think?"

Why am I not surprised, thought Amie as they knocked on the door to what they hoped was the Headmaster's study.

"Come. Come!" shouted a voice from inside.

Amie opened the door and peeped round to see a short, rather plump man sitting behind a large desk. In his hand he held a large cane and beside him stood a very small boy. Amie thought he didn't look old enough to be in any high school.

"Ah, the lady from the television! Welcome, welcome." He turned to the child. "And let that be a lesson to you. Today you are saved by this kind lady, what are you going to say to her?"

"Thank you, thank you Missy," said the child as he sidled quickly out of the room bobbing up and down at the same time.

"Sit down, sit down," said the Headmaster hospitably. "Now how can I help you? How can I help?" he asked as Amie and Ben perched on the hard wooden chairs on the other side of his desk.

"We have come to film the Shova Shova Project," said Amie.

"Ah, we must have tea, tea for both of you, yes?"

Amie wondered if he always said things twice. They both nodded. Amie had learned it was considered rude to refuse any offer of food and drink.

The Head got up and opened the door. "Tea for three, tea for three Mphula," he shouted down the corridor.

"Now, how can I help you?" he repeated as he sat down.

"The Shova, Shova Project?" said Amie.

"Ah, yes. The bicycles. Yes of course, the bicycles. What do you want to know about them?"

"We understand how the project works," replied Amie, "and we understand you were allocated...." She consulted her notes "fifty bicycles and we would like to show the children using them to come to and from school and maybe they can tell us how they don't have to walk such long distances. And, we would also like to see one of the training classes, where the children are taught how to look after their bicycles and learn about road safety too."

The door opened and Mphula appeared precariously balancing a tray with three teas in rather dirty cups. As she placed the tray on the desk, the Head briskly ladled four heaped spoons of sugar into each cup before Amie could protest. Inwardly she groaned, how long would it take her to get used to the warm, sickly, strong tea all the locals obviously adored.

"Yes, yes" said the Head.

"So can you show us where the bicycles are and introduce us to the children who use them?"

"Yes, yes."

Everyone sat in silence for a minute or two. Amie wondered if maybe the Head had not understood the question.

Ben came to life and spoke to the Head in the local

language. Amie had no idea what he said, but the Head jumped to his seat and smiling said, "Ah yes, I will take you to Mr Kumalo, he is in charge of the Shova, Shova project. Come, yes, he is in charge."

Amie and Ben followed him out into the corridor, almost running to keep up with him as he walked very briskly down the corridor. It occurred to Amie this was the first time she had seen anyone move quickly since she'd arrived in Togodo.

Mr Kumalo was a tall, slim man, and standing beside the short Headmaster, the image of Laurel and Hardy flitted briefly through Amie's mind. The Head left as quickly as he had come after very brief introductions.

"The Shova Shova Project?" Amie waited for the response. "I believe you are the teacher in charge?"

"Yes, that's correct."

"So can you show us the bicycles so we can film them?"

"Yes of course," Mr Kumalo smiled and called out one of the boys in the classroom. "This is Douglas, he will show you where they are."

Amie and Ben followed Douglas across the open playground to a store room at the far end of the buildings. There inside were two bicycles. Both of them had flat tyres, and the front wheel on one of them was bent almost at right angles.

Amie looked at them. "But where are the others? I thought the school had fifty of these bikes."

Douglas shrugged his shoulders. "Others gone," he said.

"Gone where?"

Douglas shrugged his shoulders again.

"Are there no more?" asked Ben.

"No, this is all," Douglas was obviously very uncomfortable he did not like to be the bearer of bad news.

"And the reflective arm bands, and the safety helmets? Are they somewhere else?" Amie was getting nervous.

Douglas reached in and picked up a cracked helmet from

behind the bicycles and underneath were two dusty arm bands.

Amie looked at Ben in horror. "What are we going to do?" she asked.

"Make it up," he said.

"Make it up! How?"

"We'll just have to use these two bicycles and pretend."

For a brief moment Amie considered going back to Colonel Mbanzi, then she thought better of it. She did not relish the idea of telling him forty eight bicycles had vanished from this, the best example of the project, and the two that remained were beyond repair.

"I guess you're right," she said slowly. "I'll just have to film carefully from er, different angles. I suppose we can pretend."

While Amie was wise enough to know they often cheated when filming commercials, and gave one sided views in many documentaries leaving certain facts out to make a point, she thought this must be a first. What she was going to show would be a complete lie from beginning to end.

By the end of the day when the light had started to fade, she had recorded a variety of boys on bikes supposedly arriving at school. Medium and close up shots of them "cleaning" the bicycles, and a mock up of a road safety lesson. She decided it would be easier to show this in the classroom, with chalk diagrams on the blackboard drawn by Amie herself, with a teacher pretending to explain the rules of the road. Later, she hoped to find a road safety manual in the book shop and insert a few shots of it as well.

It wasn't even easy to find candidates to pose as riders. While they were all keen to be seen on camera, not many of the children could ride a bike, even if the tyres were inflated and the wheels straightened out.

Amie began to wonder if the whole project had been a scam, but a few of the children assured her that yes, at least six shiny new bicycles had been delivered and helmets as well, but where they were now, no one seemed to know.

Amie asked if they knew which children had been given a bicycle so they could ride to and from school. A couple of names were mentioned. Could Amie talk to them? No, they were not at school any more. When had they left? The day after they had been presented with their new bicycles.

So that answers that question, she thought as she tried to film various children on the two wrecked bicycles without actually showing the bicycles at all. She wondered what Dave the cameraman back in Castle Bridge would say if he arrived to film this. She thought it might be wiser not to mention the hiccups when she emailed home. Best not to let everyone know she was visually telling lies, not a very professional approach was it? She would tell Jonathon and a few others here and leave it at that. Maybe in years to come she could laugh at this, but not right now.

It was hard work, and at the end of the day, Amie was quite exhausted. She had taken lots of general shots of the children, playing outside and working in the classrooms. She was hoping that maybe if she scripted lots of general chatter about helping children to learn, now they could get to school more easily, she could extol the virtues of the government's Shova Shova scheme, and practically ignore the bicycles altogether.

That night while waiting for Jonathon to get home she looked through the footage and logged the scenes she thought she could use. But she could not shake off the feeling she was a party to a pack of lies.

Things did not get any easier in the following weeks either.

A few days later Themba drove them to a rather dilapidated building on the outskirts of town, next to a small electrical substation.

And this is the 'state of the art' electrical system thought Amie in horror. Again they met the men in charge and as she filmed around the grubby and unkempt surroundings, she wondered if she could possibly Photoshop some of the shots. Walls which had once been white, now had the paint peeling off them and in places, large chunks of plaster threatened to descend on them any minute. One thing was obvious, the Togodians did not believe in repairing and maintaining any of their installations.

Even during the filming, there were two breakdowns in the electric supply and although Amie could continue to film as she was working with batteries, she did not want to show the personnel rushing backwards and forwards pressing switches and searching for broken cables while shouting and screaming at each other. As far as she could see, they were not at all embarrassed about the situation. Several of them grinned at her and waved to the camera, as they tried to rectify the faults. Again, she tried to get around the chaos by showing several workers in close up, hoping they would look as if they were concentrating and monitoring the supply, instead of trying to reconnect it!

The small industry chosen to show the advances electricity had brought to the business sector was a small breeze block garage where six women were using electric sewing machines.

When the crew arrived, none of the women were actually sewing, they had no power. Mrs Mosswara the lady in charge complained bitterly about the constant power breaks.

"I want machines you can work by hand!" she wailed. "Then we can work all day and not have to stop so often. But they tell us we must take these electrical machines which are not reliable."

"Yes, I understand," commiserated Amie. "Is there no way you can exchange them for manual ones?"

"Aieeeeeee. No! They said we are now a modern country and we must," she paused, "what was it now?" she looked at the other women.

"Move with the times," answered another lady who looked

totally fed up.

"We make school uniforms and we have to finish over a hundred dresses by the end of the week, and what are we supposed to do when the machines stop?"

"Yes, we have to come and work at night and at the weekends and leave our children so we can get all the dresses ready in time."

"And then the children get into mischief if we are not there to beat them when they do wrong." The women all nodded their heads in agreement.

And this is progress, thought Amie do they have any understanding of these problems in the government offices? Do they even care?

While the men at the school and the electricity station had pretended everything was fine, here Amie saw the women were not afraid to speak out and complain. But, she doubted if they would actually say anything to any male government official.

She took footage of the women and the sewing machines, choosing to show them arriving for work and then sitting down as if they were able to start sewing. They also found a small child, ripped her clothes off and put her in one of the school dresses to model for the cameras. Amie was amazed at the willingness of the women to act out parts and role play, with no signs of self consciousness. They were completely at ease, and by the end of the afternoon, she felt she had made firm friends with the women at the sewing factory. Despite their problems they were generally a cheerful bunch, but one comment made Amie stop and think.

"There is much unrest in the north," said one of the women very quietly.

"Is that serious?" asked Amie, also lowering her voice to match.

"Aieeeee who knows," whispered the woman. "The north is very far away, but the tribe there does not like this government."

Amie wondered if she should mention this to Jonathon, but he had enough to worry about at work. It might not be wise to upset him unnecessarily.

"Do you think there will be trouble from the north?" she asked Ben as Themba drove them back into town.

"The tribes in the north have always been a problem," he replied shrugging his shoulders. "But what will they gain by making war on the government? There are not so many of them and what good would it do them? No, there is nothing to worry about."

By chance, Amie caught a glimpse of Themba's face in the rear view mirror which startled her. He was smirking as if he did not believe a word Ben said.

9 PROPAGANDA FOR THE TRADE FAIR

It wasn't until the following Saturday when Amie was having a coffee at the Club with Diana that she had a chance to discuss her experiences.

"I've only filmed three of the projects, but they are all a disaster," she moaned. "I can make some sort of programme and get the point across in the audio, but honestly the pictures do not tell the same story at all!"

"Sorry to laugh," Diana was in stitches when Amie described the failed projects. "But I for one am not surprised. You will just have to do the best you can, deliver your 'efforts' to the Colonel and then hope he will leave you alone from then on."

"I hope you're right Diana. But one thing you told me I've now seen for myself. If this country is going to succeed it is because the women are prepared to work and support their children and see they are educated."

"Yes, that goes for every African country we've lived in. But unfortunately, women are still very much second class citizens and they are still dominated by the men."

"I always took my independence for granted," Amie said. "We expect our girls to be educated and able to have any career they want, and have an equal say with men. OK, I saw enough on television to realize it's not the case everywhere, but seeing it in action where we live now, well that's different."

"I agree, and at the same time, you learn not to speak too openly about any regime presently in power."

"I've already seen the corruption for myself," said Amie.

"They told me fifty new bicycles had been sent to the school yet only about six arrived, so quite a few disappeared somewhere along the way."

"Yes, resold I expect," said Diana. "There's always someone keen to implement his income any way he can."

"I think the bicycle project was a good idea, but what did it achieve? In fact it made things worse! Some of the boys who were lent the bicycles have not been seen since, so far from making it easier to get an education, they're getting no education at all! It's so frustrating."

"Welcome to Africa," smiled Diana. "But yes, I agree with you. Did I tell you about the water project in Zimbabwe?"

"No."

"Foreign aid poured in and it was decided to erect large steel fresh water tanks in this one village, which had been built next to a road, but far from the river. The men's decision of course, as it's not considered important if the women and children have to walk long distances to collect water, but it is important to be near the road for the convenience of the men."

"Shame," said Amie. "But I bet the women were pleased."

"Yes they were, now they only had to walk a few metres to fetch clean, potable water for their cooking, cleaning and washing. It made their lives much, much easier."

"At least that's one success story," Amie said with a smile.

"Unfortunately not. Within a week, the taps had been wrenched off the tanks and the water allowed to drain out. They were repaired and the water truck arrived and filled them again, but it was only a few days before they were vandalized again!"

"But why!" exclaimed Amie "Couldn't they see this was a benefit to everyone?"

"But it wasn't," said Diana, "that was the whole point. It did not benefit the young men at all."

"But they didn't collect water did they? I've only ever seen women and children here carrying water!"

"True, in Africa that's women's work, but when the young girls had to go to the river to fetch water or to wash clothes, that was the time when the young men would court them and flirt with them. If the water supply was nearby, they didn't have the same opportunity." Diana paused. "So while there were benefits, there were also drawbacks as well. The foreign aid workers had not done their homework, they did not foresee any problems."

"Then what was the answer?"

"I can't tell you what they should have done," said Diana. "After repairing the tanks several times, all I can tell you is that in the end, everything went back to how it was before, a long trek down to the river."

"That's so sad." Amie hesitated for a moment then, decided to confide in her new friend. "Diana, I heard there was trouble up north, have you heard anything?"

"I know Richard was talking to someone the other night, and they seemed to take it seriously. Tribalism is the scourge of Africa, and there will always be jostling for power. Right now, the government is all made up of the Kawa, they are the biggest and brightest of the tribes. They will do everything in their power to keep the other tribes subservient. Most countries are a mixture of different tribes, which no one in Europe took into account when they drew the boundaries on a map to delineate the different territories. They were too intent in their rush to grab land in Africa."

"How did they decide where to draw those lines?" asked Amie. "This is something they never mentioned in Geography or History lessons."

"They thought mountain ranges and rivers would make good boundaries," replied Diana. "Did you know they drew the borderline between Kenya and Tanganyika, to accommodate Queen Victoria and the Kaiser, as they each wanted a 'snow capped' mountain near the equator in their acquired empires?"

"No!" Amie was surprised.

"The boundary cut right though the middle of tribal areas to give England, Mount Kenya in Kenya, while Germany took possession of Mount Kilimanjaro in what is now Tanzania."

"So in Togodo, how big are the other tribes, are there many of them? Could they start a civil war?" Amie had fretted all week over what she'd heard at the sewing factory.

"Difficult to say," replied Diana. "Up to a couple of weeks ago, I would not have taken any notice of such rumours, there are *always* rumours. But if, and I say if, they have found a rich source of useful minerals in the north, then those tribes might have a much better reason to fight. It would depend if they can get backing from one of the super powers, to supply them with arms and military training. Up until now, they may have complained, but generally the Luebos and the M'untu's and I believe there are a few Tsaan as well, have been peaceful." Diana noticed the fear on Amie's face.

"Don't worry," she said. "Firstly, those three tribes in the north have to work together and it's most unlikely they will ever co-operate and they also have to find backing. Long before that happens, the desalination plant will be up and running and we will all be miles away from here."

"But what if it happens quickly?" asked Amie as shivers ran down her spine.

"Then that's where Her Majesty's Government comes in and rounds us all up, and whisks us out of here to the strains of 'Rule Britannia'."

Amie knew Diana was making light of the whole situation, but she resolved to listen carefully and see what other small pockets of information she could pick up. She would keep her eyes open as well.

When Amie got home that afternoon, it was to be greeted by piercing screams from Pretty who was standing in the garden next to what looked like an old bundle of clothes. It was William. He was lying on the ground and he was shaking from head to toe. Pretty was having hysterics, which was certainly not helping anyone.

Amie had a cousin who had once had an epileptic fit when they were playing in the garden, and she remembered her mother had put her on her side until the shaking stopped.

"Quick, get me a spoon," she said to Pretty.

Pretty stopped wailing long enough to stare at her Madam in amazement.

"Don't just stand there! Go!" Pretty ran off, while Amie turned William over and held his head. When Pretty returned with the spoon, Amie gently pushed it into William's mouth and held his tongue down. She wasn't absolutely certain this was totally the right thing to do, maybe it was a myth having a fit could result in swallowing your tongue, but it certainly couldn't hurt.

After several minutes William suddenly relaxed and then opened his eyes. He was horrified to see Amie leaning over him on the grass and began to gabble.

"Hush," said Amie, "You had a fit, but it's over now. Do you often have them?"

William's English was not as fluent as Pretty's, and in his current state, all he was able to do was mumble in Togwana. Amie turned to Pretty to help translate.

Pretty was keeping her distance and she was very reluctant to come closer, even though William was now lying quite still.

"He says he has this problem several times Madam," said Pretty, then added "but I have not seen before. Ah, the spirits have got him!" She began to retreat back to the house eying William with horror.

"Pretty! These are not spirits," said Amie firmly. "He had an epileptic fit and many, many people have this problem."

Pretty shook her head, she did not believe a word of it.

"Ask him if he takes any medicine for his problem," Amie

instructed Pretty.

Reluctantly, and from a safe distance, Pretty translated. "He says the sangoma gives him muti," she said. "But now it not work as many days, as he can only get a little muti as the prices are higher."

Amie looked at William. "Before the price went up, you had enough muti for the month?" she asked. "Now you only have enough money for muti for some of the month?"

William nodded, looking totally miserable. He struggled to get up.

"Right then, we are going straight to the hospital," said Amie. "Come on Pretty, you come too, I may need you to translate for me, or hold William if he has another fit."

Pretty wailed and walked backwards shaking her head. Nothing, not even her Madam's anger was going to persuade her to get into the car with William, much as she adored riding in cars.

William did not look too keen either, the word hospital put the fear of god, or maybe the fear of the sangoma in him, but he did not like to upset the Madam, he was sure she would fire him now, and then he would have no work. He decided it was best to obey.

Reluctantly he climbed into the back of the car and they set off for the hospital. This time the Dutch doctor was on duty and listened as Amie explained her amateur diagnosis. He disappeared into an examining room with William, and Amie passed the time reading the notices on the walls, primarily about AIDS, and basic health instructions, for washing hands and keeping food clean. There were lots of advice for pregnant mothers, urging them to use the hospital for pre natal checks, and the advantages of giving birth to healthy children. Most of the information was just plain common sense, but then Amie wondered just how much knowledge she had learned almost by infusion, as she'd been growing up.

For as long as she could remember, she knew to wash her hands, and how to use the bathroom, but what if her mother had not known about such things? She would not have passed the knowledge on, especially if they'd never had a bathroom, or running water and plenty of soap. The things we take for granted, she mused, are a new and novel experience for many.

When the doctor reappeared with a subdued William trailing behind him, he agreed further tests were needed, but it looked as if William suffered from epilepsy, and he was going to prescribe tablets which would keep it under control.

"How much are they?" inquired Amie. "I will pay for them."

"I don't think they cost very much, but take this to the hospital pharmacy and you can pay there. Oh, and William, don't lose the prescription, as it will give you pills every month, until we can arrange for the tests. Can I use your address?" the doctor turned to Amie.

"Oh course, I'll give you our post box number," replied Amie.

The doctor finished filling in the forms and smiled. "You should not have another fit as long as you take one tablet each morning and another each night. Do you understand?"

Still looking a little bewildered, William nodded vigorously.

It was quite late by the time Amie returned home. She had dropped William off close by the township where he lived, clutching his pill bottle tightly in his hand. Pretty was waiting in the kitchen and for once Jonathon was home first.

"William good now?" asked Pretty.

"Yes, he is fine, and he has muti to stop another fit," Amie told her as Pretty put the evening meal on the table.

"Pretty, you have never seen William having a fit before?"

"Oh no Madam, no, I would tell you so you could send him away! He is cursed by the spirits."

"No Pretty," said Amie sternly. "That is not true. William has a problem in his head, and now this medicine will keep him well. He will not have another fit as long as he takes the pills." Another thought occurred to her. "Pretty, do you know how much William was paying the sangoma every month?"

"I not know what for, but he pay one hundred and twenty dollars."

"That's almost....." Amie was shocked. She turned to Jonathon as soon as Pretty had left the room. "Do you realize that's almost all of his monthly wages?"

"Compassion is scarce in Africa," replied Jonathon. "But then you have to hand it to the sangoma. He must have diagnosed the problem and given him the right herbs or potions. There is more to tribal medicine than we give credit for."

Amie nodded in agreement. There was a lot about Africa which still made it the dark continent, many things, that coming from the so called civilized world, they simply did not know or understand.

The days went past quickly. Amie was out most days shooting, as she had decided to get as much footage in the can as fast as possible and then she would sit at home and edit it one programme after another.

For the programme to illustrate the state sponsored training facilities, Amie was only ever shown one project, but if there were more, she would have been surprised. The workshops were all inside a compound with small cubicles behind metal shutters. There was basket weaving, which as far as Amie knew, had been a local occupation for years and years. There was a pottery, where they were using wet clay dug from the river bed on the other side of the wall, to fashion small bowls of appalling quality. There was no furnace to fire the pots and no glaze. The finished, sun baked articles were rough, and certainly not of any standard to sell to the absent tourists. But the artists were quite insistent they made their pots for the tourists to buy.

There was yet another sewing group, but this time the machines were operated by hand and their productivity looked quite high, with lots of garments set out for sale. However, in the three days Amie and the crew were there, not a single customer approached the compound to even have a look, much less buy anything.

There was also a bead workshop, where another group of cheerful, chattering women were talking much faster than they were threading beads. There were a few completed necklaces, and bangles but Amie was puzzled by the lack of symmetry. Ben told her, in the past, young maidens had made bead love letters, the various colours each had a different message, and it told the young man who received it, what the girl thought of him. When Amie asked him if he had ever been given a bead love letter he looked quite offended, and said if he wanted to pass a message to someone he wrote it down on paper, or used his cell phone to send a text! Amie was not sure if she'd upset him, but he seemed sulky for the rest of the afternoon and stayed well away from her.

The woodworking shop was abandoned, and the only way they could identify it was by the few wood shavings on the floor, there were no tools in sight. The shutters were down on the last four 'training facilities' with no clue as to what went on inside when they were open.

Amie asked Ben to find out what they made and when they would be open, so they could come back and film them another day, but the only response he got was shrugged shoulders and shaking heads. Amie wondered if they were occupied at all. She had no idea how she was going to pretend this was a thriving training facility. No one was teaching anyone anything and there were no new or modern techniques or equipment in sight. Perhaps she could show it as a fostering of age old crafts and traditional handwork, although she had a good idea that was not what Colonel Mbanzi wanted. But there was a limit to what she could produce with so little to show. Could it get any worse, she wondered. It could.

The only bed and breakfast establishment they went to was a larger than normal house built of bare breeze block. Every time Amie brushed near a wall, her clothes got covered with a fine powdery dust. It fell over everything, and she immediately put a piece of plastic over the camera, afraid the dust would get inside it.

The proud owner of this fine establishment was Mrs Rabata, and she showed them around. There were three bedrooms in all, one for the family and the other two for guests. Rustic wasn't the word for it, well it would be the only truthful way of marketing it, thought Amie as she gazed in dismay at the metal framed, springless beds and thin foam mattresses. The covers were bright and cheerful and they looked clean, although the towels looked somewhat threadbare.

Mrs Rabata swept them into the kitchen to show off the facilities there. It was spick and span but certainly quite primitive, well maybe simple would be a better word, thought Amie feeling a little ashamed of herself. Her hostess was a cheerful, friendly lady and was quite happy to chat. She had been expecting them and as soon as they arrived, the tea tray appeared with the inevitable tea with three sugars. Amie decided to go with the flow, though she was not sure how guests to the bed and breakfast would react, to having their sugar put in their tea for them, especially three or four large spoonfuls per cup!

Amie asked how many guests had already stayed at the guest house, and Mrs Rabata told her cheerfully they were still waiting for the first rush of foreign visitors. Amie had to squash the thought that maybe they would have to wait a very long time.

And where had Mrs Rabata been trained in the hospitality

industry? The proud owner explained her mother had shown her how to keep a house clean, and repair the floors which were made from cow dung and mud. Her mother was also an excellent cook and she liked to prepare food that people enjoyed. The dishes she described were all local, and unlikely to appeal greatly to the average foreign traveler.

So did Mrs Rabata have any training from a government department at all? This question didn't seem to make sense to the landlady. No, she hadn't had any training, but she was given extra dollars to extend her house, with the idea of acting as a hostess when the tourism boom began.

Amie felt quite angry. She had expected so much more, and these 'projects' of the Colonel's were nothing more than a scam. Even with the most creative filming in the world, Amie knew it would not take a rocket scientist to see through the subterfuge and propaganda.

She took a deep breath and with a smile, suggested they first took shots of the exterior of the house. Perhaps while they were doing that, did Mrs Rabata have some friends who could pretend to be real guests, and did anyone have a couple of suitcases they could borrow for the day?

The school computer project was also a little tricky to show. Yes the large primary school they were taken to did in fact have computers, and Amie breathed a sigh of relief. At least she could show something real!

How many computers?

Three.

How many learners at the school?

One thousand five hundred, well, about that number it was difficult to keep track.

So did they have a special room where they kept the computers?

Oh yes, they were in the Headmistress's study, which was locked. In fact they were happy to find the keys and show how they had built cages to keep them safe.

Amie looked at the row of three desktop tower units with their monitor screens and keyboards all behind steel bars, and it was only then she noticed the candle on the Headmistress's desk.

Do they have frequent power cuts?

Puzzled looks all round. No, none at all.

They must be on a more reliable supply thought Amie.

Are they on Internet?

What's that? They asked.

Well could they open the cages and show the children working on them? How often did they have a computer lesson?

Well they had not started yet, we are waiting, they told her.

Waiting?

Yes.

What are you waiting for?

For the electricity of course. But the government had promised it would be installed possibly sometime next year. But in the meantime, the children had been working very hard and practicing their dancing, so would the visitors like to have a cup of tea and come and watch? The children were so excited they were going to be on television.

Amie's mind worked overtime as she watched the youngsters sing and dance beautifully. She would take footage of them and explain they were celebrating the arrival of the new computers to make learning more exciting and open up the world to enquiring minds. Then maybe get a truck to drive up and show the offloading of the computers. If they walked in with them three at a time, they could cut and walk in with 'another' three. Then close ups of the children's faces as they looked at the screens and she could take shots of her own lap top at home and cut them in between.

What am I doing? Amie asked herself, this is propaganda on an enormous scale! I am going to have to talk to the

Colonel and explain some of these difficulties. Even if I am *really* inventive and creative, these programmes would be a laughing stock if they are shown outside the country. But then, how am I going to explain that? She had a horrible feeling Colonel Mbanzi was not going to be the slightest bit interested in either her views, or her problems.

The last project to be visited was the hospital, and Amie hoped this location was not going to be a complete disaster. She had been there twice, once for herself and once with William, but this time she was looking at things from a completely different perspective, how was she going to tell the story?

She left Ben outside with the equipment, and asked him to walk around and find the best places where she could take a few exterior establishing shots. Amie mounted the front steps and went in the main door. She was impressed with the cleanliness in the entrance hall, and the lady at the reception desk was polite and directed her to the Matron's office. She knocked on the door and was amazed to see the woman sitting behind the desk was an Indian lady.

Matron looked up and smiled at Amie's obvious surprise. "Not what you expected I'm sure!" she said with a chuckle.

Amie was covered in confusion. "Oh, you must think me so rude, I'm so sorry…" she didn't know what to say without making things worse.

"No need to apologize" replied the Matron. "It's a very common response, you were expecting to see a black face?"

"Well, I er… "Amie took a deep breath and decided to be honest. "Yes, yes I was. In all the projects I've shot so far, there has not been one white face in charge, or even involved in a government project, so yes, I am surprised." Amie paused in embarrassment, Matron's face was more brown than white. "I've seen you at the Club," she added but I thought you were one of the wives." Please don't let her take offense, she thought.

But Matron smiled as she held out her hand. "I know, you must be Amie as I've been expecting you. I'm Sohanna Reddy, and I really am the Matron here. Come, sit down and let's have a chat first." Matron indicated a couple of easy chairs over by the window. "Tea, coffee?" she offered.

"A cup of coffee would be great," said Amie.

While Matron ordered the drinks, she looked out over the green lawns surrounding the hospital. "You must have the best lawns beside the bowling green in Togodo," she remarked.

"Gardens are a pet project of mine, and it takes a lot of hard work, but I believe if you are going to heal the body, then you must heal the mind at the same time."

Amie nodded in agreement.

"Let me give you a little background on the hospital. I've been here for almost two years, brought in with several other members of staff, when the President's son was dangerously ill. He'd received treatment overseas in America, but his father was unwilling to leave him in a hospital abroad. As you can imagine, it is not wise for..." Matron paused, looking for the right words, "...not wise to be absent from your country for any length of time."

Amie had been in Togodo long enough to understand exactly what Matron was saying. When you seized power by force, even under the guise of an electoral process, there were always those who were prepared to lead a coup and take over, by force if necessary, especially if the previous leader was absent.

"So, no expense has been spared here in the hospital," Matron continued. "We have an excellent staff, almost all of us from other countries and we have a lot of advanced equipment, such as MRI and CAT scans, an X ray department and two fully equipped operating theatres. We are most proud of our neo natal wards. In the last two years we have brought down the statistics on infant mortality to less than ten per cent among those who give birth in the hospital."

Matron looked at the expression on Amie's face as she scribbled in her notebook.

"I know that might not sound very impressive, but I can promise you that up until recently, the number of babies who died before, during and shortly after birth, was horrendous."

There was a knock on the door, the coffee had arrived and for once, and to her relief, Amie was invited to put in her own milk and sugar.

Matron smiled. "Are you getting used to strong tea with at least three spoons of sugar?"

Amie laughed. "You read my mind," she replied.

"This is not the first African country I've worked in, and customs do not vary."

Amie noticed Matron was not as young as she'd first thought. Her air of self assurance and confidence, together with a few white hairs, put her closer to fifty than forty.

Amie recalled the Colonel's instructions. "I would like to focus on the neo natal department, as I was told about that specifically."

"As soon as you've finished your coffee we can start. Although you might be in for a bit of a surprise!"

After collecting Ben and the equipment, they walked to one of the buildings at the far end of the hospital complex. The small ward was familiar, with six beds, all occupied by women, who looked to Amie to be in the early stages of labour. She was shown the labour room and the recovery room and next door, another room contained six incubators. Matron pointed to a hand dispenser on the wall for disinfecting their hands.

"Many of these little ones have not had the best start in life and are quite frail."

Amie gasped, inside each incubator, covered in a light blanket, coloured either pink or blue, lay the smallest babies she had ever seen.

"Many of our babies are born small and underweight," explained Matron. "Few of our mothers have a balanced diet and also, many of them work right up until they give birth. It has been quite a challenge to get them to come and give birth in the hospital. Many of them are frightened of what is strange to them, and too, the local witchdoctors do not look kindly on our work."

"I think I can guess why," said Amie as she wrote down the shots she wanted to get on camera.

"We are a threat to their income. We dispense most medicines for free, and of course the local sangomas demand payment for their services. Woe betide you if you upset a sangoma though, they are powerful people and are best avoided," Sohanna Reddy added.

Amie felt a shiver run down her spine. How would William's sangoma react when he realized she had deprived him of one of his best customers? She focused on what Matron was telling her.

"We encourage the mothers to come to our pre-natal classes, but that's not been the most successful part of the programme. We have a team I would like to introduce you to, who go out into the bush and look for young girls who may be pregnant. Some of them, poor dears, do not even realize they are pregnant."

"Surely not," Amie was amazed. "But their families must..."

Matron interrupted. "If they even suspect a girl has been with a boy, then they are often expelled from the family and the village. As far as they're concerned, she is now of no value and cannot command a good lobola or bride price. She is damaged goods." As she spoke Matron checked the monitoring devices attached to each bassinette.

"Often these poor girls are not wayward, but the victims of rape, many as young as twelve or thirteen, a few even younger than that. They are sent out into the bush to fend for themselves as best they can, and even though their tummies begin to swell up, they are not really aware of the cause."

"Africa is even more cruel than I thought it was," murmured Amie.

"It's a very different culture," Matron agreed.

"But what happens to them if your team do bring them in?" asked Amie.

"I think they should tell you themselves. Come, they are waiting for us over at the unit."

Outside in the small courtyard shaded by two acacia trees, Amie was introduced to Nomsa, Thuli and Marga who greeted her with broad smiles.

"Welcome," said Thuli. "You want to know more about what we do?"

"Yes please," replied Amie. "I have been asked to make a film about the hospital and all the things you are doing to help, especially the neo natal unit." As she spoke, Amie noticed the glances which passed between the others. They did not seem quite at ease, or was this just her over active imagination?

"We go out to the small villages around the city and talk to the people and try and find out if any of the young girls in their community have been expelled from their homes," Marga explained.

"It's not easy," continued Thuli. "Often the families are not willing to talk to us, they are very suspicious."

"Yes, so often it is the sisters of these poor girls, or a teacher in the village, who gives us information and then it is up to us to explore the bush and find them," Marga added.

Nomsa went on. "Usually they don't wander too far away from their village as they are scared of wild animals and unfamiliar places. But sometimes they will hide from us, and it is difficult even when we do talk to them, to persuade them to come with us."

"But if you are offering them food and shelter and comfort...?" Amie could see no reason for refusing help in such circumstances.

"It's the fear of the unknown," said Matron. "From being part of the community, living in a family group, suddenly their world changes, and they are chased out to fend for themselves."

"We can't help all of them," Nomsa added. "We know many of them die in the bush, if they can't find enough to eat, or the baby comes too soon. It is very sad."

"How, how many do you rescue?" asked Amie.

"We brought in forty two last year," answered Marga.

"And what happens when you bring them into the hospital?" Amie wanted to know.

"Ah, that's the part we are most proud of," Matron smiled. "Come, we will show you the hostel."

They all walked over to a low building, which consisted of a large dormitory, a central living area, a communal bathroom, and an area at the side under an overhang which served as a kitchen.

"We give them a bed and check them out medically and feed them of course," said Thuli indicating the large cooking pots.

"But the hard part is teaching them about their pregnancy," Nomsa cut in. "Many of them have no idea…"

Amie interrupted. "But surely they see babies being born all the time, and they have animals all around and…" she simply could not fathom anyone being pregnant and not knowing it.

"Sex is not a subject that is talked about," Matron, answered her. "It is not part of African culture to give any sex education at all. It also makes our family planning work difficult as well. Most of our women are very passive when it comes to being told what to do by the men. It is not their place to say no if a man wants favours."

"And if they refuse or are not willing, many times the man will beat them into submission," Thuli added.

"This also makes our work with the HIV patients difficult,"

said Matron. "We tell the women to encourage the men to wear condoms, to prevent the spread of the disease, but the men refuse, they don't like to wear condoms, so they don't. And now this is another form of power they have over the women."

"Do you know how many of the women in the hospital are HIV positive?" asked Amie. Again, she noticed uneasy looks between the other women.

"Officially, we are not allowed to test for AIDS, even with the consent of the patient, and there are no official records or statistics of how many people are infected."

Amie picked up on the word 'official' and took a chance. "I won't put this in my film, I won't even mention AIDs, but do you have any idea of … how many….?"

Matron looked round before she answered. "At the moment, one hundred percent of our pregnant and nursing mothers are HIV positive," she said quietly.

Amie gasped. She had no idea how bad the situation was. "And the government is not collecting figures at all?"

"How can you, if you are not allowed to find out who has AIDS and who hasn't?" asked Nomsa bitterly. "Until the government acknowledges there is a problem, then no one is going to do anything about it."

"We are not even officially allowed to encourage the women to ask for condoms."

"And we get nowhere talking to the men of course."

"What a difficult job you have!" Amie was horrified.

"But, on the brighter side," said Matron cheering up, "we have helped lots of our young bush mummies give birth to healthy newborns, and then we teach them how to breast feed and look after their babies."

"Because few of them can read and write, we teach them through song and dance, and some of them are going to sing for you and show you what they have learned," said Thuli.

"That will be great," said Amie, thinking this would make

the programme much more visual and interesting.

"We keep them as long as we can, and try to find a place for them to live, and work too if possible. But it's not easy. There are always more young mothers than we can accommodate."

By the end of the day, Amie was pleased with the footage she had in the can. She was sure this would make the best of all the programmes on her list and for once, there was some real truth in it. She made arrangements to go back the next day to interview a few of the patients and show some of the diagnostic equipment in use. The Colonel had not actually mentioned the mother and baby unit, only the neo natal ward, but Amie felt this was a vital part of the good work being done by the hospital staff, so she hoped he would not make any objections when he saw the finished programme.

On several occasions, Ben was surprised and puzzled by some of the shots Amie took, they did not seem relevant in his mind to the subject matter, but Amie was determined to have footage to use when she returned to England and put together what she saw as the truth about life and everyday happenings in Togodo. Her programme would not tell the same tales as those she was being coerced to make by the government, but for the moment, her version would have to wait. The Colonel's demands came first, and she only had two months to prepare all the programmes he wanted.

Amie had never thought of herself as an evangelist in any way, but she was beginning to have a burning desire to try and explain the way of life, the culture and the beliefs held by African people. She had already heard many stories about the wastage of foreign aid to third world countries, how most of the money and supplies went into the back pockets of the top, rich, ruling, class and how few of those who really needed help ever received any at all.

Did you really have to experience it here on the ground to understand people behaved differently, acted differently, thought differently? Yes. You could not even start to understand them unless you lived among them.

The moment Jonathon walked in the door that evening, Amie knew he'd not had a good day. He threw his briefcase on the sofa and only put his lap top down a little more gently.

"Bad day?" Amie enquired unnecessarily.

"Usual nonsense," he snapped as he made for the dinner table. Hearing the door bang, Pretty had rushed to take his plate out of the oven and bring it through.

"Nothing is ever simple," grumbled Jonathon as he sat down. "Everything you ask for, or try to organize, becomes a massive problem."

"Even with the Fixer?" asked Amie.

"Even Alfred is finding it uphill. It seems everyone is rather preoccupied at the moment. There's something going down, but no one can put their finger on what." Jonathon paused, then stood up and walked over and held out his arms.

"Come here, I need a hug. It's so good to be home and I will try not to be so grumpy, I promise."

"I understand," Amie replied giving him a big squeeze. "Life here can be so frustrating."

"But there are moments when it's extremely rewarding as well," and Jonathon smiled.

"It's all part of the experience," said Amie as she poured him a glass of wine.

"Not tempted to start the expatriate drinking are you?" Jonathon grinned.

"No, we're hardly in the 'White Mischief' class," giggled Amie. "Anyway, I have to admit that while I'm so busy at the moment with all this editing, I don't have a spare moment to get into any kind of mischief at all."

"How's it going? How many programmes does the Colonel want again?" asked Jonathon.

"There are six altogether, the bicycle project, the hospital, the computers in schools, the small business modules, electricity supply and the bed and breakfast. Frankly, the hospital is the only one I think will make a good programme, and I have a sneaky feeling the Colonel will not be at all pleased with it."

"Why, if that's the one you think is really good?" Jonathon was puzzled.

"He wanted me to show the new neo natal ward in particular, and it does have some really up to date modern equipment. But what really impressed me was the scheme they have for finding young pregnant girls who are thrown out by their families, and left to fend for themselves in the bush." Amie described how the girls were brought in, safely delivered, and then taught how to care for their babies.

"I can see why that might not please him," said Jonathon as he ate hungrily. "That's a throwback to more primitive times, and he wants you to show Togodo as a modern, upmarket, first world county."

"Exactly, and it most certainly is not, and there is no way I can get the camera to record those images, they're just not there," Amie complained.

"I wish you luck. What's for dessert?"

Even though time was extremely tight to get the programmes ready for the Trade Fair, Amie was determined to meet her deadline. To start with, she kept up her twice weekly visits to the school, but even those went by the board as she devoted every waking moment to the project. The days flew past as Amie sat up late every night, doing her best to edit the footage she had captured, to tell stories that were simply not there to show! She recorded the voice overs herself, often in the early hours when there was less external noise, and just hoped the cicadas chirping outside the window, would appear to be natural sounds recorded in the filming. There was no way she could stop them from rubbing their legs together, as she told quite enormous lies in her commentaries. She was dreading her meeting with Colonel Mbanzi on the due date for delivery.

The whole city was buzzing with the excitement of their first ever International Trade Fair. Even Jonathon had been diverted into setting up a booth with pictures, plans and information about the desalination plant. The newly built, and not quite completed, conference centre was the focal point of everyone's interest, and work continued day and night to try and get everything ready on time.

When Amie drove to the government building housing the Colonel's office, she couldn't stop herself from shaking. This is worse than a trip to the dentist, she thought. She needn't have worried, for although she'd made an appointment, the Colonel was nowhere to be seen, and his secretary had instructions for Amie to leave the disks with her.

Hopefully they'll get lost, thought Amie as she got back into the car. The show opens in a couple of days, and if he doesn't like them, then there's not a lot I can do about it now. She had tried to see her employer, if that was the right word to describe the Colonel, several times as she'd completed each of the programmes, but he'd always been far too busy to waste his time seeing her. Well that's his problem, but I know he'll make it mine somehow, even if it meant lying about his instructions to her.

That afternoon at the Club the buzz was all about who was going to come to Togodo to the Trade Fair. People were laying bets as to how many visitors would actually fly in, and how many the government would boast had come to the show.

"I'm not wasting my money on any wager," said Diana as she came over to join the others on the verandah. "But you can't lose if you bet the official statistics send the numbers through the roof."

"Can we go and have a look, is it open to the general public?" enquired Kate.

"I asked Jonathon to try and find out," said Amie.

"They won't just let anyone in off the streets," said Anne. "Can you imagine, crowds swarming in from the informal settlements and mixing with the overseas business elite?"

"What informal settlements?" asked Diana. "They simply don't admit they're there, though of course they are plainly visible as you fly in on the approach to the airport. And have you noticed how empty the main streets are?"

"Yes, now you come to mention it, when I drove back from the Colonel's office this morning, town looked quite deserted!" Amie was surprised, she hadn't given it a second thought. "What's going on?"

"They've rounded up all the street children and the beggars and the youths who normally hang around, and I was told they were loaded up into cattle trucks and driven off miles into the bush. By the time they find their way back to the city, the overseas visitors will be safely back in their own homes," Diana informed them.

"That's so cruel," cried Kate. "How can they do that?"

"Very easily," Anne was more cynical. "No one is going to refuse to jump in a truck, it's either co-operate or spend a few weeks in jail."

"And we all know you don't actually have to break the law here to end up in jail," added Diana. "Just cross the wrong path."

Yet again Amie felt shivers run down her spine. Just how angry might the Colonel be over her filming efforts? But, she reasoned to herself, I am a European and that gives me some protection surely. Wouldn't the British government kick up a terrible fuss? She wasn't so sure. She thought about the number of people who'd been kidnapped, imprisoned or spirited away while abroad, and only every now and again, did their families jump up and down and scream, and bring their plight to the attention of the media.

"You look thoughtful Amie," remarked Diana.

"Oh, nothing, just day dreaming," Amie replied.

"I tell you what we can do though," said Kate with a giggle. "They can't stop us going for coffee in the hotel and getting an idea how many extra visitors they have."

"Yes and how many different languages we can hear."

"Brilliant idea. Let's all meet there tomorrow at three."

"Of course, most could be staying at the chain of bed and breakfasts the Colonel asked me to film," laughed Amie.

"Shame," said Diana. "One day I'm sure there'll be a thriving list of good accommodation places to stay, but not yet, and not unless they get their act together, get the fraud and corruption under control, and start building up the country."

"That's all in the future yes," agreed Amie. "What makes me mad is the pretending it's all in place now, when it's not."

As if to give credibility to her words, just then the electricity went out and it was several minutes before someone got the generator up and running.

Amie felt very guilty she had not been to the school for several weeks. Her deadline was too important not to miss, even if Angelina wondered where she was and was missing her.

So the next morning Amie set out to visit, smiling and waving as Dodo the gate keeper waved her through. Angelina was nowhere to be seen. She was not in the usual classroom where the little ones were taught, nor was she in the hostel, nor hanging round the ladies who were cooking up lunch in their huge, black, iron pots under the overhang.

Amie retraced her steps to the classroom and hovered in the doorway until the bell rang for break time.

"Aieeee, we have not seen you for such a long time!" exclaimed the teacher. "We think you have gone back to your own country and forgotten all about us!"

"No, no I have been busy, the Trade Fair...." her words made Amie feel very guilty.

"Ah the Trade Fair! Ah that is good then. We are all so proud of our new hall and they say thousands and thousands of people will come to show what we can give to the world." The teacher, whose name was Olive was certainly enthusiastic.

"Yes, I'm sure it will be a big success," replied Amie, and she hoped she sounded sincere.

"You are looking for Angelina?"

"Yes, I can't find her anywhere and she always used to wait by the gate."

"Naughty girl, I tell her about that often, she should be in class learning her lessons, not waiting around for you."

Amie realized Olive did not mean that unkindly. "So, where is she?"

"No one knows. One day she is here, and the next, she is gone."

"Gone! But have you told the police, reported her missing or....?" Olive's expression already answered Amie's question.

"These little ones, they come and they go. We did look for her, around in the bush close to here, and we ask many people, but there are so many little ones." Olive shrugged. "If she wants to, she will come back. She knows we are here."

Amie stayed at the school for the rest of the morning. She had brought several packs of coloured crayons with her to teach the children how to colour in. She drew large simple pictures on blank paper, and when that ran out, used a couple of old cardboard boxes she found abandoned in the playground.

Although she stayed until after the children had had their lunch, in the hope Angelina would turn up with her little plastic plate and mug, she had not appeared by the time Amie drove back out of the school gates.

The lobby of the Grand Hotel was as chaotic as Amie remembered it, as the girls pushed their way through the mêlée and into the coffee shop. It was definitely more crowded than usual, but the familiar comments about 'no bookings showing on the computers' was still in operation! Amie wondered just how much extracurricular money the receptionists would be making over the next few days, and how sad it was that the very visitors they were trying so hard to impress, would be disgusted at this unwelcome and blatant example of corruption and fraud.

The coffee was still good, although the service was slower than ever. They all agreed there were larger than normal volumes of guests and wondered how some of the smaller hotels were coping. The Grand was the top one in Apatu, and none of them had ever visited the others, as they were considered very down market, and possibly not even safe.

It was there that Jonathon found them a little later and gave them invitation passes to the exhibition hall. The exhibitors had been given hundreds each and it was highly unlikely they would need even a fraction of the thousands they had printed.

When the girls walked into the entrance hall of the new exhibition centre, they had to admit the building itself was very impressive, lots of smoked glass, and a brightly patterned carpet on the floor. The ceiling stretched up way over their heads, as they admired the sweeping central staircase and the elegant décor.

"I had no idea this was going to be so grand," said Kate as she craned her head back to look at the modern frescoes up near the ceiling."

"No one did," replied Diana. "It was just a lot of banging and hammering behind miles of metal fencing."

"Which no one thought would be completed in time!" exclaimed Amie. "This is amazing!"

"It's astounding what can be achieved when people work

together," commented Diana as they walked into the main hall.

There were about fifty stalls set up, showcasing Togodo's culture, the handicrafts and the different products manufactured in the country. It was surprising to see that among the items made locally, were leather goods, baskets, various articles constructed from beads, and a wide range of plastic containers which they learned came from a factory on the edge of town. There was also a display showing tractors, which was an even bigger surprise to everyone.

"First I knew about this kind of heavy engineering," remarked Diana as they stood and stared at the bright yellow machines.

"Yes," said Richard who walked over to greet them. "Apparently there is a factory a few kilometres out of town where they screw on plates saying 'Made in Togodo.' But I am informed the tractors themselves are delivered from Russia just as you see them here!"

"All in one piece ready to use?" asked Kate in astonishment.

"Yes, but there are plans to leave extra bits off over a period of time, as the locals are trained in tractor assembly."

"Well it's a start I suppose," said Amie. "Do you know where Jonathon's stand is?"

"Yes, it's over here," and Richard led them down the adjoining aisle.

Jonathon's staff had put a lot of work into the stand, which was wall papered with brightly coloured photographs of desalination plants, and architectural plans, and a model of a working plant.

"Wow, this is impressive," exclaimed Anne.

Looking at the drawings, Amie was surprised at the progress they had made. She'd not been in that part of town recently, and it looked as if the plant was already half built.

"You didn't tell me you had progressed this far," she said

to Jonathon.

He smiled. "We haven't, our plant is only about a metre high, these pictures have been Photoshopped to show what it *will* look like when it is almost complete. Drenton sent over boxes and boxes of publicity material to show what we hope to achieve, in time!" Jonathon grinned and added, "in a long time from now!"

Although there was quite a lot to see, Amie noticed there didn't seem all those many visitors. Most of the foreigners she saw she recognized from the Club or had seen at various functions.

"I do hope the Trade Fair is a success," she said quietly to Diana as they stood admiring some of the bead work. They've put in a lot of time here on these displays, as well as building the hall of course."

"One can only hope so," answered Diana, "but where are your videos?"

"Goodness, I'd almost forgotten about them, how stupid! I guess they'll be on the government stand."

"But that was the large one as we came in, with the enormous poster showing the President, and I didn't notice a television or movies of any kind."

They retraced their steps to the entrance and this time they noticed a small television monitor right at the back, which was playing one of Amie's videos. It was the bicycle project, under a rather small poster showing the school, and a line of happy, smiling children standing next to new bicycles.

"Of all the projects, this one was the worst," grumbled Amie, "it doesn't really exist at all."

"And the other projects? I don't see them on the monitor," asked Kate as the programme came to an end and the Shova, Shova Project began to re-cycle through a second time.

"No idea," said Amie, "unless they're going to show them on another day."

"I'm sure you're glad it's all over now," Diana said to her as they left the exhibition centre.

"Yes, I just hope he never asks me to make any more programmes, and he is not furious about what I produced. I've had no feedback whatsoever, not even a telephone call to say good, bad or indifferent."

"I wouldn't worry," said Kate. "It's not as if you're here in Togodo to make videos for them. You're just a housewife here with your husband."

"True, but I haven't forgotten the veiled threats the Colonel made against Jonathon. His work is difficult enough already."

"Well you delivered, and on time, and you can only say you did your best," Diana tried to cheer her up. "Now what does everyone say to a drink at the Club, on me!"

It was the calm before the storm.

10 A HORRIFIC SHOOT AND A VISIT

Life settled back into the usual routine. The few overseas visitors went home, and Amie's trips to the school continued, though she missed seeing Angelina. There were plenty of other orphaned children to play with of course, but none of them struck the same chord.

Amie's tennis improved thanks to her frequent games, and she was becoming quite proud of her sewing skills. The days flew past, never enough time to fit everything in, even with a full time maid. Amie wondered how she would ever have coped back home if she had to do all the housework, the cooking and the washing and ironing. Certainly Jonathon would never have had time to look after the garden!

Just as things were going well, there was a knock on the outside gate early one morning, and when Amie answered it, she saw with a sinking feeling it was the Colonel. She hesitated before she invited him in.

It was impossible to tell from the expression on his face if he was friend or foe, but Amie was wary. Would he have waited all these weeks before coming to talk about the work she'd done? Surely not.

She indicated the sofa, but the Colonel didn't sit down but walked over by the window, with his hands behind his back. Amie couldn't see his face with the light behind it, and couldn't read his expression. She found she was holding her breath waiting for him to say something. Then she remembered not to offer refreshment was considered very rude when you visited, so she asked him what he would like to drink.

He bowed his head and declined. "You still have your camera?" he almost barked.

"Yes," said Amie quietly and waited.

"I need more work from you. I expect you to be ready for the car tomorrow morning, it will come for you early."

"To go where?"

"A little way out of town." The Colonel made a vague gesture with his arm, and from the tone of his voice, it was quite obvious he was not prepared to elaborate further. "You can inform your husband you will be well looked after, you will be with my men." He began to walk towards the door, "and you can give Mr Fish a message from me. The plans he was waiting for have been passed."

Amie was aware by now that co-operation could also be veiled blackmail, but cooperation could also bring rewards. Just as the Colonel reached the door, Amie asked, "will Ben and Themba be with me?"

The Colonel paused. "You want them too? They are a help to you?"

"Oh yes, an enormous help. I couldn't manage without them." Amie hoped she sounded convincing.

"I'll see what I can do," and with that the Colonel opened the front door and walked down the path to his car.

"I can't film without Ben's help," Amie repeated loudly and clearly from the doorway, but the Colonel gave no indication he'd heard her. His driver bowed his head deferentially and opened the rear door for him to get into the car. Amie noticed there was another uniformed man sitting in the front seat, and a second car parked close behind. Both cars drove off in tandem.

Amie knew one thing, she did not want to go anywhere and do any more filming in Togodo. She had the shots she wanted of their day to day lives, the shots she had not used for obvious reasons when filming the projects, showing the real side of Togodo, and a record of the school and Angelina. These were her own personal records of life here. After her recent visit home, she thought it unlikely anyone else, would be particularly interested, so she had simply decided to make a record of their first, and maybe only, posting abroad, for her and Jonathon to sit and watch when they were in their rocking chairs.

It had also occurred to her, if she tried to lift the lid on what really went on, by trying to get it on the national television channels, it might damage Jonathon's future prospects of ever working abroad again.

It was frustrating Colonel Mbanzi had not told her what he wanted her to shoot. It could be the tractor factory, or maybe another 'world class' scheme. But if she was to be prepared, then she needed to go and buy more tape. Hopefully the computer shop would still have some left from the large order they placed, after getting government permission to import extra stock from England. Amie suspected the Colonel was behind it, to make sure Amie could complete all the programmes he wanted.

As she drove into town, Amie wondered what to tell Jonathon. She didn't want to worry him, this was his one off career chance to get ahead in the company, and she was not going to ruin it for him. She decided she would just mention it in passing, and she wouldn't get into any of the Colonel's vehicles unless Ben was there. She trusted him, and they worked well together. At least there would be one person she knew, who also spoke the local language. Maybe she should write down what the Colonel had said just now, but no, she was getting paranoid. She had been living in Togodo for almost two years, and the worst that had happened was a burst tyre in the rainy season. No, she would just say she was going on another shoot for the Colonel, pass on his message about the plans, and leave it at that. However, she would tell Diana, to be a sort of back up.

"I have never come across a situation like this before," said Diana as they made for their usual table at the Mall coffee shop that afternoon. "It's most unusual. In my experience, the wives and children have always been ignored," she paused as the waitress put two coffees and a plate of cakes on the table. "Thank you." Diana smiled at the waitress. "As I was saying, we're always ignored and grateful for it."

"I'm not sure how I got involved in all this. It's not as if I was the only person out here with a video camera," Amie said miserably.

"Ah, but once they knew you were trained in film making, that's when the problem started."

"Yes, and of course at the airport they intercepted those tapes I gave the charity party."

"They were probably waving them around in the air, or asked if the scanner would damage the tapes." Diana helped herself to a doughnut. "Well at least we don't have a state television service here in Togodo yet," she continued, "though I have heard they're erecting a mast out on one of the mountain tops, so we'll be able to tune in to the Kenyan programmes."

"Diana! You're always the first to hear what's going on. You're better than the secret service!" exclaimed Amie. She could always rely on Diana to come up with some snippet of new information.

"Won't be for a couple of months, but a large container full of televisions, was unloaded at the docks last week, so they obviously expect to have a market for them. But you must make sure to take care of yourself, though violence against ex-pats is quite rare."

"I've said I won't go without Ben and I trust him. I'm sure I'll be fine, but if you could just phone me towards the end of the day to check, just in case Jonathon gets tied up and loses all sense of time?"

"Of course I will."

"There was one night when he came home so tired I'm sure he wouldn't have noticed if I was there or not! He tumbled straight into bed, ignoring me and his dinner and went out like a light!"

"Richard has learned to pace himself, and his company has worked in Africa for so long they have a total understanding of how slowly things can move. We're lucky there."

"And being much older, Richard has more experience…." Amie trailed off realizing what she'd just said. How rude that was, but Diana just laughed.

"That's exactly right. We're old hands at this game now. Richard works hard, but he's proved himself and he's learned not to let it get him down. Jonathon will too in time, just wait and see."

Amie didn't sleep well that night. She'd made a firm resolution not to get into any vehicle that stopped outside her gate the next day, unless Ben was already sitting inside. But what if they said they were on their way to pick him up and then didn't? What if the driver and passengers didn't speak any English? No, that was stupid, there needed to be one person to tell her what to film.

All too soon the dawn came up, and Amie felt as if she'd not closed her eyes all night. 'Early' in Africa meant any time after five, and Amie didn't think the car would arrive that early, but she was ready by six o'clock and much to her surprise just as she finished her coffee, three old and battered Land Rovers drove up and stopped outside the gate.

Much to Amie's relief, Themba jumped out and banged on the outside gate. Pretty let him in and Amie asked quickly, "Is Ben there as well?"

Themba nodded his head and picked up some of the camera gear. Amie stuffed her cell phone into her pocket and grabbed her coat, a packed lunch, her bag and the camera. She called goodbye to Pretty and followed Themba out of the gate.

I was such a fool to worry, Amie thought as she squeezed into the back of the second vehicle next to Ben. She was so pleased to see him she had to refrain from giving him a hug.

"Do you know where we're going?" she asked him quietly. He shook his head and looked away. Amie wondered if it was the presence of the soldiers which made him so quiet. Usually he was full of smiles and always ready to talk. There had been the odd occasion when she wished he would shut up if only for a moment.

Themba stowed the equipment into the back, climbed up into the third vehicle, and as soon as the doors were closed, they set off at quite a speed.

The driver and the front seat passenger both wore army uniforms, well Colonel Mbanzi had warned her he was sending his men. Amie wanted to twist round to see if all the others were also in uniform, but it was such a tight squeeze she couldn't move.

They passed swiftly through the centre of town and then, by Amie's reckoning, they headed north. The drivers took no care to slow down, as they bumped over the ridged gravel road, and Amie wished she could find a seat belt as they swerved from side to side, and slammed in and out of the occasional pothole.

They'd travelled for over two hours before the cars slowed down almost to a crawl. The soldier in the front leaned forward and brought his gun out from beneath the seat. Amie wasn't sure if it was an AK47 or not, it just looked dangerous. He removed the magazine and checked it before drawing back the breach to ensure it was loaded and ready to fire. Amie began to feel very uncomfortable. Why did they need guns? What was going on?

They came to an abrupt stop and the soldier jumped out of

the front seat and squatted down by the door. He was quickly followed by the rest of the soldiers from the other Land Rovers, and holding their guns tightly to their chests, they fanned out on all sides.

The driver turned round and indicated they should stay where they were for a moment. Amie had no intention of getting out any sooner than she had to, and she even tried to sink lower in her seat. Her heart was in her mouth and she was now beginning to feel very scared. She looked at Ben, but his face didn't give anything away and she couldn't even guess what he was thinking.

One of the soldiers who had gone ahead, returned and signaled to show the all clear, and the driver turned to Amie and indicated with a wave of his hand that she should get out.

She hesitated before slowly and deliberately sliding out, staying as close to the door as she could. Seeing no danger, the soldiers had relaxed, and some of them stopped to light cigarettes and chatter in small groups.

Amie looked enquiringly at the driver, he seemed to be the one in charge. He nodded and indicated they should take the camera equipment and get ready to film.

"I can't see anything here to shoot, can you?" Amie asked Ben quietly.

"It'll be close by," he whispered.

Grabbing the microphone, camera, cables and spare batteries, Amie, Ben and Themba reluctantly left the false shelter of the Land Rover, and followed one of the soldiers who beckoned them forwards.

Amie had no idea what to expect, but nothing had prepared her for what she saw when they walked into the clearing.

It had been a village until quite recently, but now most of the huts had been destroyed or set on fire. There was a strange smell in the air, not only the odour of burning but there was also a sweet, sickly taint. The empty dwellings had an abandoned feeling, but Amie could see that not long ago, it had been a hive of activity. A pot of maize lay on its side, a discarded clay doll, a pair of cast off sandals. Here the roof of a hut had been torn away, a calabash of local beer had been smashed, and the contents poured onto the ground. Clothes put out to dry on the bushes had been abandoned, and several pages of old magazines fluttered in the light breeze. There was no sign of anyone.

The driver walked in front of them, and began to point at the surroundings, indicating they take shots of everything they could see. Amie nodded to Ben who handed her the camera, and she began to record the desolate scene. The tape rolled on the empty huts, the abandoned preparation for the evening meal which had plainly been interrupted, forlorn pieces of cloth which had until recently been prized clothes. Amie could just read 'Columbia University' on a t-shirt which had once been white and was now a dark rust colour. In fact there were many patches of rust stained soil in the area and Amie wondered what could have caused them.

While Amie and Ben walked slowly round the village, faithfully recording what little was left of a once thriving village, the other soldiers went systematically through each of the huts, and grabbed anything that looked at all useful or valuable. They laughed and thumped each other, as they bartered over the little that was left to take.

"I think that is as much as we can capture," said Amie at last. "Can you tell the boss man we have finished?"

But the boss man shook his head and gestured for one of the soldiers to take them to the other side of the village and round the back of the furthest hut. As soon as she walked round the side wall, Amie realized where the sweet, sickly smell was coming from, and her legs almost gave way under her. She didn't have the strength to move away, as she gazed in shock at the tangled heap of dead bodies.

They had been covered over by a thick tarpaulin weighted down with boulders which the lowest ranking soldiers were still removing. There must have been at least fifty of them, men, women and children all thrown haphazardly one on top of another. The amount of blood suggested they had not only been shot, but hacked to death as well. There were several stray limbs lying beside the pile and Amie gazed in horror at the sight of a foot lying next to an arm, beside a head no longer attached to its body. All she wanted to do was close her eyes and back away, but you can't use a camera with your eyes shut.

Ben on the other hand seemed to take it all in his stride. Calmly he unwrapped another tape and handed it to her to put in the camera. Amie swallowed the bile which had risen in her throat, and told herself to pretend this was just a film set and the bodies were not real. She focused the camera while trying not to look, and pressed the record switch. There were maggots crawling out of the eye sockets of a child's face, and a myriad of small insects were disturbed as they scuttled away from the daylight.

At the bottom of the pile Amie could see a small arm belonging to a young child who could not have been older than six or seven. Its little hand still clutched one of the homemade balls of rolled up tights, probably a most treasured possession. For a terrible moment Amie wondered if it was Angelina. She knew she should move forward for the close up shots, but her legs refused to move. She zoomed in on the scene, but all she saw through the lens was a blur, as her eyes filled with tears. Without being sure of the quality of the shots, she let the camera roll and tried to pretend she was far away and this was all just an awful dream.

As soon as she had finished, she practically flung the camera at Ben, backed up behind the nearest hut and threw up and retched and retched until she had nothing left in her stomach. She bent over double gasping for air, as she tried to forget what she'd just seen. A couple of the soldiers saw her and made what sounded like ribald comments. Probably about how pathetic white women are, thought Amie angrily. Not one of the soldiers had shown any remorse, or horror or sadness at the horrific scene in front of their eyes.

Ben asked one of the soldiers a question and he replied briefly.

"What did you ask?" whispered Amie.

"I was surprised the bodies had not been dragged away by the animals last night, but they say a few soldiers were left here to guard them and they covered them up of course."

"But why not bury them? Why leave them like that? Have their families been told?" Amie had so many questions to ask she didn't know where to begin, although most of all she couldn't wait to get out of this place.

"They kept them here for us to film," replied Ben.

"Who are they?" Amie wanted to know.

"Some villagers or other." Ben seemed disinclined to talk, and he shrugged his shoulders and walked away round the corner and out of sight.

As she sank down onto her haunches as far away from the brutal carnage as she could get, Amie suddenly noticed two things. One was the number of vultures that had appeared overhead, attracted by the smell of blood and the second was the look she caught on Themba's face. For a brief moment she could have sworn he looked pleased, but when he saw her looking in his direction he quickly turned away.

"You finished, we go!" shrieked the main driver and everyone made for the trucks. Most of the soldiers were loaded down with whatever they had been able to loot from the village, and the sweet, sickly smell now invaded the vehicles as well. Amie was sure she was going to throw up again. Her legs still felt rubbery and her stomach was flopping over and over. She noticed she was shaking slightly and wondered how these men could feel nothing, nothing at all. Did a more austere upbringing deaden your senses? Amie had seen inserts on the news showing dead bodies, and documentary war films, but nothing, nothing had prepared her for this. In real life it was a totally different thing. This was the savagery of Africa right in front of her, and it scared her witless.

On the way back to the city, Amie could only stare down at the floor. She saw nothing of the scenery, nothing of the other vehicles they passed once they were back on the gravel road. What she had seen would haunt her forever. Every time she closed her eyes, all she could see was the pile of abandoned bodies, left unburied on the open veld for the animals to fight over. In a few days, all that would be left would be a few bones.

The brutality went further. Amie knew that not only had the villagers been brutalized, but they had been denied a proper burial as decreed by the ancestors. Their very existence into the next world had been jeopardized, and for an African, this was a fate far worse than death itself.

Once they reached the outskirts of the capital, the other two vehicles fell behind, but Amie's driver went straight to the government buildings that housed Colonel Mbanzi's offices. Outside they screeched to a halt and the driver turned and said something to Ben, who silently handed over the full tapes and told Amie they needed the tape that was still in the camera as well. She ejected it and handed it to Ben who passed it over.

It had not occurred to Amie to try and keep a tape for herself as she had on the other shoots. She wanted no reminders of what she'd seen today, and she never wanted to see anything like it again as long as she lived.

The driver jumped out and disappeared through the gates, reappearing a few minutes later without the tapes. Taking no care to even try and avoid the pedestrians in his path, he drove out to the suburbs and skidded to a halt in front of Amie's house. She looked at Ben as she struggled to climb out without falling over. Her legs still felt like large chunks of jelly, and she was still shaking.

Ben jumped out and helped offload the equipment, but as soon as he had finished, the Land Rover skidded away, leaving them both standing by the gate.

"Ben, what was that all about? Who were those people? What had they done? Who killed them?"

For a moment it looked as if Ben was not about to answer any of her questions, then he shrugged his shoulders and said slowly. "Just villagers. They believe they were killed by one of the tribes from the north."

"And were they?"

Ben shrugged his shoulders again. "Who can say?"

"And they want the footage to prove it happened, to help find the people who did this?" That was the only reason that made sense to Amie.

"To prove it, yes. But to punish...?"

"You don't think they were murdered to put the blame on the northern tribes do you?" Amie was shocked.

"We will never know. They wanted the tapes and they have them." Ben seemed to take this very much in his stride.

"Have you seen anything like that before?" Amie asked suddenly.

"Maybe," Ben was evasive. "But I must go now, my house is far from here."

Amie was sure this was just his polite way of asking for a lift home, but when she offered, Ben was quite emphatic he could walk, and catch one of the local taxis that ran along the main road on the edge of Spring Glen.

Once all the camera gear was safely inside, Amie sank down on the sofa and buried her head in her hands. Pretty appeared in the doorway looking distressed.

"Madam, you are ill?" she asked.

"No, not ill Pretty, just shocked," replied Amie. "Just bring me a cup of tea, a strong one." Pretty disappeared from view.

Amie got up and unlocked the liquor cabinet and poured herself a large brandy. She seldom drank before dinner, but it seemed like a good idea right now.

What should she do? Should she tell anyone? Report what she'd seen at the British Embassy? Should she tell her friends, or, what about Jonathon? She reasoned if he knew where she'd been, he'd put her on the next plane back to England. Did she want to go back home? No, her place was by Jonathon's side and if she was living safely back in Castle Bridge, she would never have a moment's peace worrying about him.

What if they both went to the British Embassy with the story? What repercussions would there be? Would they put all the British expatriates on a plane and ship them out? How many lives would be disrupted? How many projects put on hold?

It suddenly dawned on Amie she had no proof of what she'd seen. She had no idea where Ben lived, so could not prevail upon him to back up her story. The Colonel was even more likely to deny all knowledge of it, and the only concrete thing she could possibly prove, was that maybe Pretty had seen three trucks drive up outside the house early this morning and collect the Madam. Then one of the trucks had returned at the end of the day and deposited Madam safe and sound outside the gate again.

What Amie had experienced that day was horrific, but how could you weigh it against the chaos that might be caused by bringing it out into the open? The rules she was used to, didn't apply to Africa, they danced to their own tune, not live and let live, but eat or be eaten.

In the end, Amie decided to say nothing to anyone until she had had a chance to calm down and have a long think. She was not going to feel as safe now, knowing a massacre had taken place a mere two or three hours away by car, but there was plenty of security around the house and there was always the armed response to call out should she feel threatened.

For once she was not going to delay over dinner, but have a scalding hot shower and go to bed before Jonathon came home. That way at least she could avoid telling him anything.

Her dreams that night were full of bloodthirsty images, and she tossed and turned and tried to replace what she'd seen with memories of past birthday parties, her wedding, her first pony ride, anything to block out the nightmare. Jonathon, exhausted by another grueling day, slept right through and never stirred once.

Amie finally fell into a deep sleep just as the sun was coming up, but she had only been asleep for a short while, before she was woken up by Pretty, who was knocking loudly and repeatedly on the bedroom door.

"Madam," she shrilled, "come quick! There is someone here for you!"

Amie groaned and rolled over. Please don't let it be the Colonel, she thought as she reluctantly threw back the bedclothes and swung her feet onto the floor. Jonathon had obviously left early for work, his side of the bed was empty and the clothes he'd left on the bedroom chair were gone.

"They'll have to wait," she called back to Pretty. "I'll be a while. Tell them to wait in the lounge." Amie stepped into the shower, but even a second dose of steaming hot water didn't make her feel clean. She took her time getting dressed, and brushed her hair, before eventually making her way to the kitchen to grab the cup of coffee Pretty always had waiting for her first thing.

She walked into the lounge but there was no one there.

"Pretty, where's the visitor?" Amie asked as she went to look out of the front window.

"But Madam, I said to wait in the lounge, just like you

said," Pretty whined. "Maybe she has run away again!"

"Run away? *She*?" Amie wasn't sure she'd heard correctly.

"Yes, the little girl, she has been round here many times, but this morning I caught her, and made her tell me what she was doing." Pretty seemed quite pleased with herself over her decisive actions.

"It must be Angelina! But where is she?" Just then she noticed a shadow behind the sofa, and walking over she looked behind it. There, huddled into as small a shape as she could get was Angelina, her thumb still in her mouth.

"Where have you been?" asked Amie. "What are you doing here?" though she had a pretty good idea why the child was hiding behind her sofa.

"Come on out, you look very hungry. Do you want something to eat?"

For several seconds Angelina stared at her with her large brown eyes and then she slowly nodded her head. Amie put her arms round the child and lifting her up gently carried her through to the kitchen.

"I was so worried about you, I didn't know where you'd gone. I thought you had run away and I'd never see you again." Amie wasn't sure if Angelina understood her, but she was rewarded with a wide smile, which grew even larger as Pretty put a bowl of maize porridge in front of her.

"What has she told you Pretty?" Amie asked as they watched Angelina wolf down the food so fast, Amie was sure she was going to get a very bad tummy ache.

"Nothing Madam," Pretty did not sound very enthusiastic. "She very dirty Madam, she needs bath and clean hair." Pretty sniffed and looked disapprovingly at the child.

"Yes, she does," agreed Amie, wondering where the new clothes she had bought Angelina had gone. The child was wearing the same torn dress she had on when Amie had first seen her nearly two years ago, only now it barely stretched across her tiny figure, and there were even more holes in it.

As soon as Angelina had finished eating, Amie took her hand and led her into the bathroom.

Angelina's eyes opened wide as she watched the hot and cold water flow from the taps into the bath. She was even more fascinated when Amie squirted in liquid from a bottle which made lots of bubbles in the water.

The trouble began when Amie tried to remove her dress and knickers. Angelina began to kick and scream, fighting Amie as hard as she could. Her face turned bright red and huge tears poured down her cheeks.

"I'm not going to hurt you Angelina," Amie tried to reassure her. "But we need to get you clean. Look," she swished her hand around in the bubbles, "bath time is fun, and see, the water is nice and warm."

But still Angelina was not convinced, and in the end, it took both Amie and Pretty to practically force the child into the warm water and give her a gentle scrub. There were even more hysterics when they washed her hair, but having got this far, Amie was not about to give up. Angelina made so much noise even William lurked outside the bathroom window, calling out to see if Madam was all right.

Finally the ordeal was over, and Amie lifted the sobbing child out of the water, and wrapped her in a large towel. She sat Angelina on her lap and rocked her backwards and forwards as she gently patted her dry. All the time she murmured to her, telling her she was clean and smelled so nice, and there was one spare dress she had bought for Angelina and had kept for a special occasion.

Angelina then refused to leave the bathroom until she had watched every last bubble disappear down the plug hole. She even gave Amie a small smile as she gazed at the wonders of modern plumbing. It occurred to Amie she would also have to teach the child how to use the toilet and brush her teeth. So much we take for granted, she thought to herself, which these little ones know nothing about. Sure there was a tap at the orphanage, but no hot water, and there was a row of toilet 'long drops' the children seldom used, preferring to disappear off into the bush.

Amie had just finished dressing Angelina, and was trying to tie a ribbon in her tight, frizzy hair when the bell rang at the gate. It was Diana, who stopped in amazement when she saw Angelina.

"What is that child doing here!" she exclaimed as she perched on the edge of the bed.

"She just turned up," explained Amie. "Apparently William found her huddled by the gate post early this morning and she slipped into the garden before he could catch her. Pretty brought her inside. She was filthy and her clothes were in rags and she was near to starving. I've just given her a bath."

Diana smiled at Angelina and pulled a couple of faces which made the child giggle. "So what now? You can't keep her here you know."

"Well what am I supposed to do?" asked Amie.

"Take her back to the orphanage of course," Diana stated firmly.

"But they don't really care about her! When I asked Olive where she'd gone, she actually shrugged her shoulders and told me these little ones just come and go. If they want to stay they do, and if they don't, then they don't. It's perfectly obvious Angelina doesn't want to stay there. The other children were very rough with her. She was so miserable."

Amie was not going to admit to Diana she felt partly to blame for the misery, since she had exacerbated Angelina's problems by buying her new clothes, and the teddy bear. She had forgotten one of the golden rules Diana had been so emphatic about when she first arrived. Don't show any favouritism or you will create jealousy and do more harm than good. She now felt responsible for Angelina, for having made her bleak life even more unbearable. The least she could do now, was try to improve her life.

"Even Mrs Motswezi suggested I take her home as she seems so fond of me."

"She said much the same to me, and when you move on, then what happens?" asked Diana. "You can't just pass her along like an ex-pat dog you know. This is a human life you're playing with."

"I know," agreed Amie miserably, "but maybe I can find a solution before then."

"If you're thinking about the adoption route, forget it," continued Diana as they went through to the lounge for coffee. "One of the government ministers said the other day it was better for his people, that is, the Togodians, to live deprived lives, than be corrupted by western civilization and all its evils. He was absolutely positive about that. And what if Angelina's mother turns up one day and wants her child back?"

"I don't think that's very likely, do you?"

"Well, no I don't," replied Diana, "a chance in a million, but still a chance. You could be had up for kidnapping. You're on shaky ground here Amie."

Amie looked at Angelina, who was happily amusing herself playing with the teaspoons on the coffee tray. What was she going to do? She made one more argument. "Mrs Motswezi said it would be better for Angelina to have a couple of years of a good standard of living, than none at all. So even if we had to leave her behind when we go…." she paused, not sure how much of this conversation Angelina understood, they were talking about her as if she was a commodity to be bought and sold.

"Maybe," Diana continued slowly, "the best course is to take her along to Spring Glen Primary and talk to the headmistress there. They have good affiliations with several of the local churches and they may be able to organize an adoption or a family who will take Angelina in."

Diana's advice made good sense, but it was going to be hard for Amie. Her heart ached for the little waif who knelt beside her on the floor tapping two spoons together. Never before had another human showed such love and dependence on her. Angelina's eyes followed her everywhere, and looked at her with such worship, it was difficult not to respond and love her too.

"Yes, I could do that," Amie replied. "But I'll let her settle down for a couple of days first. I have no idea where she's been, or what she's suffered since she disappeared from the orphanage. I'll give her a bit of time to relax, feed her up and ....."

"Hmmmm," Diana was not convinced. Then she smiled. "I do see how hard it is. I've never seen such devotion from one of these little ones. They are very appealing but it is a dangerous road getting involved."

"Yes I know," replied Amie miserably. Was there no answer to the problem, surely she could work something out?

11 A SHOOT AND TELLING TALES

Several days passed. Amie did not socialize much but stayed close to home, and spent hours playing with Angelina. She was a bright child, quick to learn, absorbing each new experience like a sponge. As she gained confidence, she grew more responsive, with quiet cries of delight in the shop when Amie replaced the child's wardrobe with several new dresses, socks, shoes, underwear, a raincoat and toys. She also bought her another small suitcase, although Amie questioned her own motivation for this purchase. Was it to pack Angelina's possessions for a return to England, or was it to send with her to the new home one of the churches found for her? She pushed the thought to the back of her mind, and passed the money over the counter.

Watching Angelina's delight with all her new things, Amie tried to compare her response with that of her niece and nephew. Well baby Jade was too small yet, but Dean? She had never seen him show such delight over new clothes, or even the extra special toys he had asked for for Christmas.

It was impossible to put off the inevitable, and the following week, Amie took Angelina to Spring Glen Primary. The only similar aspect of this school, and the local one she and the other wives visited, was the chain link fencing round the exterior and the guard on the gates, who opened them as Amie's Fiat approached.

Spring Glen was the very best school in Apatu, so all the expatriates with young children sent them here, along with the local children from the government and ministerial families.

Most of the teachers had been trained in England or America, and they followed a syllabus similar to that in most international schools.

As Amie parked up, she noticed the well tended lawns and flower beds. There was not a piece of rubbish in sight.

As she sat in the secretary's office waiting for the headmistress, she noticed with wry amusement that all the notices were spelt correctly, and their internal electricity supply run by a generator outside, enabled the computers to function efficiently.

Amie had seen Marian Edwards several times at the Club, but they had not attended the same dinner parties and did not move in the same circles, so she was not quite sure what to expect. As she was shown into the Head's office, Marian rose from her chair behind the desk and held out her hand in greeting. She was a slim, pleasant looking woman in her late forties, with short, brown, curly hair and a cheerful smile.

"We've not really met properly before, but I'm surprised to learn you have a daughter! I didn't realize you have children. Please sit down."

Amie perched on a chair on the other side of the desk, while Angelina stood as close to her as possible clutching her dress tightly, as if she would never let go. Amie was feeling very nervous and was not quite sure how to explain the rather unusual position she found herself in.

"Well it's true I don't have children of my own," she began, "but I seemed to have acquired a local child, Angelina."

Marian Edwards looked at Angelina and frowned. "But that's not allowed here as far as I know. Have you legally adopted her, or are you fostering or ..... what?"

"No, it's not official at all. You know a few of us visit one of the local schools and orphanage over in Timbara?" Marian nodded. "Well this little girl, took a liking to me." Amie looked to see if she could read what the headmistress might be thinking, but Marian gave nothing away.

She stumbled on. "When we were away on leave, Angelina disappeared from the school where she'd been sleeping in the orphans' section. No one had seen her for two weeks, but what was so heartbreaking was they just didn't seem to care." Amie paused, she knew she was beginning to sound too dramatic. She took a deep breath. "No, maybe that's not fair, but they didn't seem too bothered at all. Then several days ago she turned up outside my house and now I don't know what to do. I know what I would *like* to do, but I understand that's not an option here."

"Any idea as to her background?" Marian Edwards asked.

"All they told me at Timbara was that she was found outside the school fence just over two years ago and no one has asked about her since. They think she is just another AIDS orphan."

"There are so many of them about, and the numbers are growing. But you do realize we don't have any boarding facilities here even if I could find a place for her. How old is Angelina now?"

"That would also be a guess. I took her to the doctor for a checkup and he thought she might be around six or seven, though she is small and undernourished for her age."

"What a tough life some of these little ones have," Marian was sympathetic. "So what do you want from us, how do you think we can help?"

"I, I hoped that maybe I could enrol her here, of course I'll pay her fees, while I follow up with any local churches to see if we can find her a good foster family or, maybe you know of a family?" It was a slight hope that as Headmistress, Marian Edwards had got to know local families and could make enquiries. It had dawned on Amie that although she was living in Africa she had not in fact mixed socially with any Africans at all. Her entertainment was centred round the Club and the various activities and the other expatriate families had become her extended family.

"Look, I can find a place for her in our first year class, that's not a problem, but I am worried about her circumstances. There could be a big backlash on the school if it came to the attention of the officials in government departments. So what I propose is we place her with a family first, and then we can offer her a permanent place. In the meantime bring her in on a temporary basis, she probably has a lot of catching up to do, to reach the standard of the other children her age."

Amie was disappointed. She had hoped to enroll Angelina officially, and then go and buy her her school uniform and a lunch box and all the other accoutrements necessary. But a temporary place was better than nothing.

Obviously the first step was to get her settled with a Togodian family, and get a firm grip on herself and her sentimentality. The longer they were together, the fonder she grew of the child, but common sense told her it would be impossible to adopt Angelina officially. Maybe she might think differently if she had children of her own? But she didn't think so. She and Jonathon had talked that over at length, and decided to wait a few more years. There was so much to get used to in a new county, and having children now, would be a complication neither of them was ready for.

Just as Amie reached the gate to her house, she saw William, who was heaping gardening rubbish in a big pile on the grass verge. He came over and handed Amie an envelope. It may have been clean and white once, now it was crumpled and covered in dust and William's dirty fingerprints.

"Where did this come from?" she asked him.

William did not look happy. "Man in army vehicle gave for the Madam," he mumbled looking at the ground. His body language told Amie quite clearly he did not approve. Locals avoided any kind of authority as much as was humanly possible. What was his Madam doing, getting involved with government and army people? Didn't she know how unwise that was?

Amie drove her car into the car port and sat for a moment while she looked at the envelope. She was tempted to tear it up and pretend she hadn't received it, but maybe that would get William into trouble, and that wasn't fair on him.

Slowly she opened the envelope and took out the single sheet of paper. As she'd suspected it was on official government paper and it was from Colonel Mbanzi. It ordered her to report to his office the next morning with all her video equipment. He would send a car for her. There was no please, or thank you or enquiry whether she was free, it was basically an order to be available on government orders.

Enough is enough, thought Amie. They don't pay me, unless I accept they are facilitating the work on the desalination plant. Jonathon had reported he couldn't quite believe the speed at which the project was moving forward. There was never any delay in passing plans or obtaining permission, and each morning all the workers were there on time, and worked with hardly a break. He was the envy of all the other contractors working in and around the capital. He was happy to take full credit for his achievements, but secretly, Amie was convinced it was her co-operation with her camera that was smoothing the path. Like all intelligent wives, she didn't breathe a word.

But this was getting too much. It was bad enough trying to fabricate sheer propaganda, but the last shoot out in the bush had shaken her badly. She still woke in the middle of the night sweating, as she recalled the mutilated bodies, the smell of blood, and the heart wrenching sight of small children, murdered before they'd had a chance to live.

Amie decided she didn't have an option. Doing as Colonel Mbanzi asked, made life a lot easier for everyone, everyone that is, except herself. What did they want her to film this time?

The following day was just as bad as the previous trip.

This time Amie reckoned they didn't travel as far to the scene where she witnessed more carnage. It must have been an ambush, she thought as the camera rolled. There were no huts or buildings, but several bodies lay scattered around in the bush. To her relief, she noticed no children seemed to be involved this time and the dead were young boys, soldiers maybe in their twenties. Most wore combat trousers and shirts, though there was a wide variety of colours and styles, and while some had what looked like army boots, others had worn shoes and in one case only a pair of flip flops.

It was a sad, desolate scene, but the government men who had accompanied Amie and Ben, seemed quite immune to the slaughter. They joked as they rifled through pockets and removed the better pieces of clothing that had not been destroyed by bullets. They showed no respect for the dead, as they rolled the bodies over with their feet to make sure they left nothing of value behind. Then they lounged against the vehicles and lit cigarettes and chewed gum, while Amie completed her grisly task.

"Aren't they going to bury them?" she whispered to Ben, but he only shrugged his shoulders in reply.

Amie shot the scenes as fast as she could and then walked over and went to get into the first car. Ben followed her quickly and pushed her towards the second of the three cars. In a low voice he warned her it was not wise to travel in the lead car in case of an ambush. Amie shuddered, it hadn't occurred to her that they themselves could be the target of an attack.

As usual Jonathon was working late into the evening, and after she had put Angelina to bed, Amie sat in darkness in the lounge and tried to think what to do. There was obviously some kind of armed struggle going on not too far outside the capital. Was this a common occurrence? Had it been happening all the time she'd been living in Togodo, or was this a new threat? Should she keep quiet or should she tell someone? If the fighting came closer they could all be in danger, despite what Diana said about the British Embassy rounding them all up and putting them on a plane. From what she'd been told, the British were usually the least likely to panic, and also the last of the foreigners to leave somewhere that was considered dangerous.

'Don't panic and keep a stiff upper lip. Carry on as normal,' seemed to be the British motto.

She finally came to the conclusion she should perhaps mention what she'd seen to someone in Her Majesty's Government, she couldn't take the chance innocent people might die because she didn't have the courage to speak up.

Having made up her mind, Amie got up to pour herself another coffee, when it struck her that the building housing the British Embassy was right across the street from Colonel Mbanzi's government offices. What if he saw her going in there? Not even him, but his secretary, or one of the soldiers or drivers, or any of the number of people who now knew Amie by sight. Perhaps visiting the embassy might not be such a clever idea after all.

She paced up and down, trying to find a solution. There had to be a simple way of telling the right people what she'd seen, and then at least her conscience would be clear. Just before Jonathon drove into the driveway, Amie found the answer, and wondered why it hadn't occurred to her before. She hurried to turn on the lights before Jonathon asked awkward questions as to why she'd been pacing around in the dark.

The next morning was Saturday and Amie set out early for the Club, telling Jonathon she was going to collect some things she'd left behind and she wouldn't be long. She left Angelina playing happily in the kitchen with Pretty, making a terrible row with a pile of saucepans.

As she walked in the main door, she had her fingers crossed the person she was looking for was there. She checked first by the pool, then the tennis courts and the verandah, but it wasn't until she looked in the dining room she saw the person she'd come to see. Taking a deep breath, she walked over to the table.

"Vivienne?" she asked.

A cheerful, plump, curly haired girl looked up at her. "Yes?"

"Hi, we've not met properly, I'm Amie." She pulled out a chair and sat down. "I think someone told me you work at the British Embassy?"

"Yes. Ah, you're Jonathon's wife! Mrs Fish?" Amie was surprised Vivienne knew Jonathon, he'd never mentioned it. But she didn't have time to worry about that now.

"Well I want to, I think I should...." Amie didn't know how to begin. Vivienne stared at her with a puzzled expression on her face.

"Er, what do you do there? I mean are you... do you know all the people who work there?" Amie squirmed, she was not exactly making a good impression, and the way Vivienne was looking at her made her feel very uncomfortable. She took another deep breath. "Look it's like this," and before she lost her nerve, Amie went on to explain how she'd filmed for Colonel Mbanzi, and briefly mentioned the programmes she'd produced for the Trade Fair, and then went on to describe the last two shoots. She described the massacre in the village and the remains of what looked to be an ambush with at least twenty dead soldiers, or whatever they were, freedom fighters, terrorists or maybe even dissidents. When she had finished she looked up to see one of the waiters was standing very close, waiting to take her order. She asked for a coffee and shuddered as he turned away. How much had he heard or understood? Most of the local staff here understood English quite well. She could have kicked herself for not being more vigilant.

Vivienne sat quietly and waited until the waiter put Amie's coffee on the table and returned to the bar before she looked around briefly and then began to talk.

"Why haven't you just come to the Embassy and asked to speak to someone?"

"Because the Colonel's offices are right across the road from the Embassy, and I didn't think it was wise to be seen," Amie explained.

"Yes, that was probably a good idea. But I'm only a secretary there, you need to speak to someone with more authority. Have you mentioned this to your husband?"

"Look, I don't want to make a big fuss about all this," Amie replied. "Maybe this happens all the time, and I have no idea why Colonel Mbanzi wants it recorded, and really I have no proof at all."

"You don't have the footage?"

"No, as soon as we get back into town, I'm ordered to hand over all the tapes. They've not asked me to edit it. So you see I don't want to start any sort of scare if this is well, 'normal' in this part of the world."

Vivienne gave a small grin and then looked serious. "Look, I'll pass on the information to the right people, but they'll probably want to talk to you themselves. Where can I get hold of you?"

Amie was about to give Vivienne her cell phone number when she paused. "Do they monitor our calls here?" she asked.

"As far as I know, their equipment is not that sophisticated, but I can't swear to it."

"Well I'm only prepared to talk to someone here at the Club. I don't want anyone coming to the house, or ...." Amie was not about to complicate things further by mentioning Angelina, and the fact she was a mother, albeit a temporary one, to a local Togodian child.

Vivienne thought for a moment. "If the high ups want to speak to you, I'll suggest they leave a note in your pigeon hole here. Would that be OK? They could mention they would like to discuss your opinion of the movie selection for the Friday night film programme."

"Yes, I guess so. This is beginning to sound like a spy novel, it's all a bit embarrassing, I mean I'm just an ordinary housewife here with my husband."

"There's more truth to some of those books than most people realize," Vivienne said with a smile. "I'll do what I can to pass on the word, but in the meantime try not to worry."

"I guess I am worried," Amie said. "I'm not cut out for the Mata Hari role."

"Leave it with me," answered Vivienne as Amie finished her coffee and stood up.

"Take care," said Vivienne as Amie turned to leave, and bumped into Diana who had just come in off the tennis courts.

"Hello!" she said. "I didn't know you two knew each other!"

Amie was struck dumb, but Vivienne smoothly answered for both of them. "Amie wanted information on fund raising for the orphanage," she replied brightly. "Keen to know where to try and access funds. But we all know how tight money is these days. Sorry I couldn't be more helpful," she addressed Amie.

"No, really, at least now I know where not to go! Thanks for the advice." Amie turned and taking Diana's arm she guided her towards the verandah and quickly changed the subject.

"Are you going to the Hunter's for dinner tonight?" she asked as they walked back outside.

"Yes, but we might be a bit late. Richard has a meeting at some ministry or other and they never turn up and start on time."

"I'll see you there then," Amie said in a rush. "Must go, just popped in for a moment and Jonathon is waiting to take us to the beach." Amie didn't give Diana a chance to open her mouth, but rushed across the lawn and jumped into her Fiat, and drove away so fast her wheels kicked up a cloud of dust.

Amie felt thoroughly miserable. Had she done the right thing? She wasn't sure. She hoped she hadn't made matters a lot worse by involving the people in the Embassy. She tried to shake off the feeling she'd somehow done something wrong, and tried to concentrate on the rest of the day. She would simply forget all about it and let events take their course. She also hoped Diana would not find out about her lie about going to the beach either, even though it was the weekend, Jonathon was working as usual. She had the dinner tonight to look forward to, and yes, why not drive over to Brianwood Mall and buy herself a new outfit on her way back home? Retail therapy, that's what I need, she thought as she drove away from the Club.

As she walked into the Mall she made a quick detour to the cash machine. Might as well get something really nice, she reasoned, if I'm going to cheer myself up I might as well do it properly. She pushed her card into the slot after making sure no one was loitering nearby, and wondered how it was, in a country that was so backward in many ways, there was such an excellent banking service. It offered more flexibility than her own bank at home. She withdrew her card and the money, and then turned back to collect her receipt. She barely gave it a glance as she put everything back in her bag and began walking towards her favourite boutique. Then she stopped and froze in her tracks.

Opening her bag she fished for the receipt she'd crammed in the back of her purse and looked at it again. That couldn't be right surely? Her balance was way too high. She went back to the machine and inserted her card again and pressed the buttons to print out a statement. The balance hadn't changed, and it showed there had been three deposits of over ten thousand Togodian dollars in the last two weeks!

There was no way Jonathon had put that sort of money into her account. He'd insisted she had a separate account, he was sensitive enough to know that now she wasn't working, she didn't want to feel like a kept housewife. He gave her money every month of course, but she had also brought in a little of her own from England. But thirty thousand dollars? That was more than Jonathon earned in three months!

Amie wondered if she should leave it for the moment, and hope it was a genuine mistake, and wait for the deposit to be reversed, it was obviously an error. Or, should she go back into town and visit the bank? Always someone who met problems head on, Amie walked back outside into the sunshine and climbed into her car.

There were long queues at the bank and the closer she got to the counter the more uneasy Amie began to feel. She tried to remain calm as those behind her in the line pressed forward, until they were practically leaning against her. She could almost hear Diana's voice telling her cheerfully that while personal space in most countries was at least twenty centimetres, here in Africa it was closer to twenty microns!

At last she reached the counter, and handing over her statement asked if they could identify who had made the three large deposits.

The teller squinted at the paper for several moments and then shrugged her shoulders as if to say why was she questioning it? "It does not say," she replied at last.

"Yes, I can see that, but isn't there some way to find out who did credit my account with such large sums of money?" Amie asked in frustration.

"You don't want the money?" the teller was confused.

"No, it's not that. I don't know who put those amounts into my bank account. I don't know where they came from and I want to know."

"It's a lot of money," the bank clerk remarked as she

squinted again at the paper in her hand.

"You must be able to tell me who deposited it surely!" Amie was beginning to feel more than a little exasperated.

"Wait, I go to ask." With that the teller stood up and walked over to a row of desks at the back. Amie watched as she showed the statement to another girl who looked up at Amie, stared at her for a moment, and then shook her head. She indicated the closed door of a nearby office. The teller knocked at the door and then disappeared from view.

The line behind her was getting restless, this was all taking a long time, and Amie felt the first trickles of sweat begin to run down her brow. I would be hopeless robbing a bank, she thought, it's nerve wracking enough just being puzzled about something.

A few minutes later the teller reappeared, and sat down behind the counter.

"It is correct," she said, pushing the mini statement back across the counter.

"But it can't be," said Amie. "I would know if someone was going to put that sort of money in my account, and why they were doing it."

The teller just shrugged as if to say that Amie was making a fuss over nothing.

"And you can't tell who put this money in my account?" Amie tried again.

"No," the teller shook her head decisively.

"Then can you print me out another statement please?"

Reluctantly the teller turned to her computer as if to indicate this customer was being particularly difficult, yet there was also a sense of unease too, or was Amie's imagination just running wild?

The teller slammed the statement face down on the counter along with Amie's card and then called out for the next customer.

"Wait," said Amie, "I want to speak with the manager."

"Manager not in on Saturday, or Sunday," the teller added to get the point across. "Managers don't work on weekends," she sounded quite bitter about this fact and deliberately turned to the next in line. Amie had no choice but to back away, as the large man pressing up behind her practically flung her to one side.

She looked at the statement and was horrified to see that in the time it had taken for her to drive from the Mall, her balance had increased by a further ten thousand Togodian dollars, making four deposits in all.

For a moment she hovered, undecided whether to insist on seeing the under bank manager, but realized it would be a waste of time, it's unlikely he worked weekends either. Options, thought Amie. One, Jonathon was unlikely to have credited her account, unless it was a tax thing, but she could easily ask him when he came home. Two, it was a genuine bank error and they were not going to admit that to her, maybe too much loss of face. So in a day or two the money would simply disappear out of her account and all would be well. A third option occurred to her. Was she being paid for her work for the Colonel? Had he credited her account? He had never asked for her bank details, but for a man in his position it wouldn't be difficult to find out. If that was the answer, Amie felt rather uncomfortable about talking to Vivienne this morning. Oh well, she would just have to wait and see what happened. She drove straight home, she was not in the mood to do any shopping now, she needed a strong cup of coffee and some more time to think.

The Hunters were renowned for throwing excellent parties. They always invited the most interesting people and Daphne Hunter had food parcels sent over from the States regularly, which allowed her to cook up more exotic dishes than could be assembled using only local ingredients.

Amie was seated between a wildlife photographer who

was just passing through Apatu, and he regaled her with stories of his experiences out in the bush, and a director who was over from Richard's head office. He wanted to know what the wives did all day while their poor husbands slaved away in air conditioned offices and raked the money in.

Amie laughed to herself. What would his reaction be if she replied she spent her time filming dead bodies, and may have been paid a fortune for it? She pushed such thoughts to the back of her mind and found she was thoroughly enjoying herself and had almost forgotten about her worries earlier in the day, when she overheard snippets of a whispered conversation across the table. She heard the words 'insurrection,' 'out of control,' 'Budan' and 'tribal differences.' She wondered if in any way it was connected with what she'd seen in the burnt out village and the ambush site.

As soon as everyone left the table she made her way as casually as possible to the two men who had sat across from her. Hoping she sounded offhanded, she asked if there had been any news of trouble further north, between the tribes maybe?

"Goodness no, it's as peaceful as peaceful could be. Togodo is a very stable country, despite its appalling government," the taller of the two said, but not before Amie saw a quick look of alarm pass between them.

"Well that's reassuring," she said brightly. "It's just that you can never tell in African countries can you? I mean they are so volatile if something upsets them," she added lamely as just as casually, she began to move away. She felt an idiot, but she was convinced she'd not imagined their embarrassment, and when she looked back across the room they were standing, still deep in conversation by the far wall, and once or twice they gave a quick glance in her direction.

"There you are!" exclaimed Diana. "I've been waiting to talk to you all evening," and she took Amie's arm firmly in hers as she led her out onto the terrace so Diana could light up one of her infamous cigarettes.

"So, what's up?" she asked.

"Why do you think....?"

"I've not reached my advanced age without being able to read people," Diana said briskly. "I know something is bothering you and if I can, I want to help."

For a moment, Amie was tempted to pour out all her worries. It would be comforting to confide in Diana, but at the same time, she didn't know where to begin or how Diana would react, especially to the atrocities she had witnessed, no more than witnessed, filmed! She might condemn her, insist on her telling Jonathon, suggest she be put on a plane home immediately, any number of reactions. For some reason, she had not confided in Diana in the Club that morning, so maybe her first instinct had been right.

"Oh nothing," she lied. "Just a bit down."

"Homesick?"

"No! Um, well yes. Yes a bit homesick." It was the last thing on Amie's mind, but if it satisfied Diana, then let her think that.

Her friend laughed. "I usually find three days back under overcast skies and pouring rain is the perfect cure for that. Then I can't wait to get back to Africa."

"Yes, it gets to you, I know that now," replied Amie, but not in the way you think, she thought to herself. Glancing at Diana's face she saw she had not been very convincing. The older woman looked at her thoughtfully for a few moments and then gave her arm a squeeze.

"Whatever it really is, you can rely on me to help, in anything, right?"

"Yes, yes thank you," Amie gulped.

"Remember out here close friends are your family. Well, surrogate family," Diana laughed.

Inside Amie felt really disloyal. She had information that might affect them all, and she was keeping it to herself. Was it fair on all these people who had been so kind and so welcoming? Would her silence put everyone in danger? But if she talked and started a panic, she could disrupt everyone's homes and work, maybe even their careers and their peace of mind.

No, she told herself firmly, you have done the best you can, so leave it up to the experts. We had a brief scare a few months ago and it all blew over. If there was need for an evacuation, then the staff at the embassy were the right people to handle it. She turned to greet Anne and Kate as they came outside to cool off and chatter about the local tennis championships, fought with just as much fervor as Wimbledon.

Amie, along with all the other dinner guests, would not have been as relaxed if they had seen Colonel Mbanzi and a host of other high up officials pacing up and down in one of the well appointed meeting rooms in the government offices of the Togodian Ministry of the Interior.

Most of the men looked very worried indeed. On the large conference table that ran down the middle of the room, there were maps of Togodo and several aerial photographs. There was a large screen against the end wall, and the group had just watched the raw footage shot by Amie a few days ago.

"This must not get out, you understand!" screamed the Colonel. "We can contain the rebels, they are just a bunch of ignorant peasants, Luebos and Tsaan!" he waved his arms in the air to show his disgust. "They don't know how to fight, and they do not stand a chance against our army. Captain Garuba!"

"Yes Sir," the Captain snapped to attention.

"I am putting you in charge in the field. I want these rebels stopped, stopped right now. Do you understand?"

"Yes Colonel. But if I may......?"

"You have a problem with that?" The Colonel glowered at

him.

"Oh no Sir, no Colonel. But my sources have indicated…" the Captain looked down at the papers he was holding and continued, "…have indicated they are not simply a bunch of rebels. They are well armed and look to have had a lot of training. And, they have formed a considerable force. It seems the M'untus and the Luebos and the Tsaan have all joined together."

"Pah!" replied the Colonel. "There is no way they have sufficient resources against our army. We are Kawas! Are you trying to tell me you are not up to the task?"

"No Sir, no Colonel," the Captain replied miserably. "I just wanted to report what my informers have seen so you know the true picture."

"The only picture I want to see is their dead corpses rotting on the ground," the Colonel snapped. "If you wish me to tell the President you are not up to the job, then you must let me know. You can easily be replaced and I can find some other post for you!"

The Captain shuddered, he knew exactly what the Colonel was implying. Slaughter every last rebel, or face his own slaughter. He had tried, but the Colonel wasn't going to listen, he certainly wasn't going to believe the rebel forces were well trained, well equipped and there were thousands of them. While the President and the Colonel were convinced the Togodian army was a match for any insurrection, the Captain was not so sure. He tried once more.

"Colonel, Sir," he began, "do I have your permission to include the Presidential troops for the assault? We are going to need every soldier we can muster, and we will need the surplus weapons and ammunition we have in the capital."

The Colonel glared at him. "Togodo troops are the best trained in the world, and there is no way I am going to withdraw the troops guarding the President. You have your orders," and with that, Colonel Mbanzi marched out of the room slamming the door behind him.

Those left behind looked at the Captain with either pity or contempt in their eyes. Each one of them was glad not to have been in the firing line, which was a certainty for the Captain if he failed to carry out his orders. If the Captain was worried, then just how big a problem was this unrest from the north? Did they have cause to worry for their own lives?

Across town Jonathon was worried about the progress, or rather lack of it, on the desalination project. For a while, things had moved quickly but then, almost without warning, things had slowed down and practically stopped. On several days the workers had not turned up at all and when they finally ambled into the yard they refused to say where they'd been or why they'd not been at work. He could get no sense from them.

There was also a change in atmosphere. The men spent a lot of time whispering to each other, and was it his imagination, or had they formed two distinct groups? Previously, they would all sit together at lunch time and at short breaks during the day. Now one group gathered at one side of the yard and another group made for the opposite end.

Jonathon felt faintly uneasy as he looked out at the workers from the site office window. Something had changed, but he couldn't put his finger on it and even asking Alfred his fixer threw no light on the situation.

Amie, on the other hand, was not aware of any change in atmosphere in her domestic situation. The school carried on as normal, Pretty and William worked away as usual, and the shops she went to most often that were patronized by the expatriate community, still served them all with a smile. The Club was an oasis of first world in the midst of a third world city and provided a home from home where everything ran as it should. The worst that ever seemed to happen was a shortage of tonic water, or late deliveries for the kitchen.

Since Jonathon had not confided in Amie, she was not aware of the heightened tension until she got chatting over coffee one morning with Kate, Anne and Diana on the verandah at the Club.

"Look, I don't want to worry you," Diana began, "but there are rumours there's trouble up north."

"From the other tribes?" asked Kate looking a little alarmed.

"Yes. It seems that for once the three northern tribes have banded together and are challenging the government."

"Who are all Kawa," stated Amie.

"Without exception. If you are not my tribe, then you are not my friend, and if you are not my friend then you must be my enemy. It's not possible to stay neutral." Diana had said something similar long ago and the truth of that had not changed.

Amie wondered if she should say anything about what she had seen, but decided to wait to hear what else Diana had to say.

"So what do you think the northern tribes want?" asked Kate gripping her coffee cup just a little more tightly.

"Who can ever be sure in Africa?" replied Diana. "But I've heard they want a larger slice of the cake. There's little or no development or upliftment outside Apatu, it's usually considered dangerous to make life more comfortable for the lesser tribes, because that would allow them to become a threat."

"Do you remember those engineers who were prospecting up north? You were talking to one Diana here after dinner that night. Didn't they find uranium and other stuff, and if so, could that be the cause of the unrest?" It made sense to Amie.

"You may well be right," Diana said thoughtfully. "I'd forgotten that. Well let's hope it all blows over soon. The only reason I'm mentioning it to you at all, is the fact that while it's bubbling under the surface, you may not even have noticed up till now…"

"Well I certainly haven't," Kate interrupted.

"It takes time for an African to get revved up so to speak, and these are very early days and it might die down. But it's good to be aware and on the alert. You might notice the young car guards getting bolder and more aggressive. Or, you might wait a lot longer to get served in the shops, or suddenly it's almost impossible to get a hair appointment."

"That happened to you a while ago, but it all seems fine now," said Kate looking at Anne.

"Yes," Anne giggled nervously, "and it all died down again and went back to normal. In fact there was all the excitement over the Trade Fair, and all those foreign visitors…"

"Not as many as they hoped I daresay," interrupted Diana.

"No, well it possibly doubled the number of us out here for a short while," continued Anne. "I must admit it was nice to see a few more white faces in the streets. There are times when I feel really outnumbered if you know what I mean."

Amie nodded, yes, she got that feeling sometimes as well.

"Anyway, I do have a hair appointment in half an hour," said Anne getting up, "so I will love and leave you."

Kate jumped up, too. "Amie are you busy this afternoon?"

"No," replied Amie, "well not until I have to collect Angelina from school."

"Then let's go to the Mall. I want you to help me choose a dress for the ball next month. Are you game?"

"Yes, good idea. I may have a look as well. We can use my car," said Amie.

"Just as well, I came in with Diana this morning, my car is in the shop," replied Kate. "Charles was in a good mood last night and he gave me a wad of cash, so let's go and blow it!"

Everyone laughed. Diana said she had to go and chat with Leonard about the arrangements for the Tennis Club Dance the following week, so Amie and Kate set off in Amie's car.

"Can we just stop off near the market?" asked Kate. "I need to pick up a few bits and pieces, and if we go to the Mall first, most of the stall holders will have packed up."

"Sure," replied Amie. "I could get some fruit at the same time. I forgot to give Pretty a shopping list this morning. Oh, and there's that Indian shop on the corner near the market, we could also look for dresses there before we go to the Mall."

"Good idea, but let me phone Charles first and he can meet me at Brianwood to take me home." Kate rummaged in her bag, but then remembered. "Drat, I left my cell on the hall table at home, can I borrow yours?"

"Sure," said Amie, as she handed it over." Kate dialed her husband's number, and waited for him to answer. She frowned, then looked at the screen.

"Your battery's flat," she said handing Amie's phone back.

"Damn! I forgot to put it on charge last night," said Amie. "I am sorry."

"Never mind, I'll call him from the coffee shop when we get to the Mall. Let's go buy clothes!"

They drove along the main street, past the smart glass and chrome buildings occupied by the banks, and Amie parked off in a side street close to the market. Immediately, a large group of small boys gathered round with their hands out. Was it Amie's imagination, or did they seem more threatening than before? She shook off the feeling and bargained with them, giving them a small amount of money with the promise of more, if the car was in one piece when she returned.

"The Indian women really know how to dress," said Kate as they flicked through the clothes on the rails.

"Yes they do, oh look Kate, what do you think of this one?" Amie held up an electric blue chiffon evening gown.

"It would suit you, why not try it on?" suggested Kate. "I like this lilac one and I think this pants suit is cool as well." The small shop only had one changing room, so Amie continued to browse as Kate disappeared behind the curtain.

"What do you think?" she asked Amie, reappearing a few minutes later.

Amie turned round to look at her. "It's a bit long, but I can help you take it up," she said. "Yes, it suits you Kate. I'd take it if I were you." Kate swirled round, peering over her shoulder in the mirror.

"It even makes me look quite slim," she chortled. "Wait until Charles sees me in this."

But Charles was never going to see Kate in her new dress, for at that moment there was a tremendous explosion, the walls shuddered, and the roof collapsed. The last Amie saw of Kate was the surprised expression on her face, then she screamed in pain, as the masonry fell on top of her.

12 NOWHERE TO RUN

Several bricks flew towards Amie as she froze, she was unable to move, and then she remembered nothing, as part of the wall behind her crumbled and buried her beneath the debris.

When she came too, she was covered in mortar and bricks and it took her several moments to fling the debris aside and surface. Through the cloud of dust she looked around wildly for Kate, but she could see nothing but piles of stones, bricks, wooden beams and here and there pieces of what had once been a collection of evening dresses.

Amie struggled to stand up. She was dazed and couldn't think properly. She swayed like a drunk as she tried to reach the pile of rubble where she'd last seen Kate. There was no sign of the Indian shop owner, nor her assistant. Then she became aware of more blasts from bombs dropping all around them. It seemed the whole city was under attack. What was left of the shop shook from the percussion blasts, causing Amie's head to spin and a loud ringing sound in her ears.

This isn't happening, thought Amie. What's going on? Are we under attack? No, I must get to Kate. Frantically she crawled forward and began trying to pull the bricks and stones from the huge pile of rubble. She worked in a mad frenzy, flinging the smaller stuff to one side until she had uncovered Kate's hand and then an arm. Tentatively, not sure what she was really doing, she felt for her friend's pulse, but there was nothing. Kate must have been killed instantly.

Amie fell back, with tears streaming down her cheeks. This is all a nightmare she sobbed quietly. Then she thought about Jonathon, and Angelina, and Pretty. Were they all right? She had to get home as fast as she could.

It took several minutes to orientate herself and inch her way towards the street. She had to dig through several piles of collapsed walls, and clamber over the remains of the metal shutters which had buckled and warped in the heat. Her hands and arms were bleeding and bruised from her frantic efforts to find Kate and clear a pathway to the street. She almost fell onto the pavement outside, and looking up she could see dozens of troops with guns. They were running in all directions, and firing indiscriminately in all directions, not stopping to line up a target before they let off another round of bullets. Amie ducked down behind what had once been a wooden door which was now hanging precariously by one hinge, and put her hands over her head. Instinct told her to stay as still as possible as she curled herself up as small as she could. There were bodies lying in the roadway, heaps of building material amid clouds of dust, where only a few minutes ago the street had been crowded with people going about their everyday lives.

Now the scene had changed to one of carnage and destruction. Those who were lying wounded were screaming in pain. One man was sitting dazed, staring at the leg he held in his hands. It was his own leg, but it was no longer attached to his body and his blood was flowing out into the dust, a few minutes later he slowly collapsed into a heap. A small child was screaming for his mother, running this way and that, looking for anyone who would take him away from all this. A woman was sitting in the road keening for the dead child she was cradling in her arms. She looked up at the sky and screamed abuse at the ancestors who had failed to protect them.

And still the soldiers ran wild, high on blood lust, whooping with delight as they found target after unprotected target to exact their revenge. It seemed to go on and on and on. Besides the soldiers in the streets and the gunfire here in the main street, Amie was aware of blasts from neighbouring areas.

It was probably only a few minutes, but it seemed like hours to Amie as she waited until the wave of soldiers had moved down the street. Tentatively, she crept out from her hiding place and immediately a strong hand reached out and clutched her wrist. She shrieked and jumped back. She turned to see a teenage boy, half his face blown away, he was pleading with her to help him.

"No, no, I can't," shrieked Amie, "I must get away. Look for your family!" She felt awful as she half ran, half crawled down the street towards the side road where she'd left her car. Her knees were bleeding where she'd scraped them on the ground, her clothes were torn, and her head was pounding.

Through some quirk, while the Fiat was covered with dust, and severely dented from falling bricks and rocks, it was still there! Amie was amazed to find that for some inexplicable reason, she still had her handbag over her shoulder. Crouching down, she fumbled inside for the car keys. Please let me drive away from here, back to Spring Glen, back home, she prayed. I must find out what has happened to Jonathon and to Angelina. And I must find Charles and tell him, how, how am I going to do that, what did you say to people about death? How can I tell him I watched his wife die?

It took the last of her strength to wrench the badly buckled door open, and her hands shook as she tried several times to insert the key in the ignition. The Fiat didn't fire the first time and Amie was beginning to panic as she turned the key again and again. Finally the engine turned over and purred. Amie was too scared to look behind her as she crouched down in the seat and engaged first gear. She was not about to turn round she would just drive straight, away from the city, away from the bloodshed, away from the burning buildings. All she wanted to do was leave it all behind her. Get as far away as possible.

She steered the car around the larger stones in the road, but ignored the smaller ones, as the car shuddered and jolted over the debris in its path. At the end of the street she just had time to swerve wildly to the other side of the road as a wall wavered and then collapsed into the road behind her. Everywhere she looked there was devastation, and destruction. The revolution is here, she repeated to herself over and over again like a mantra, as she peered over the top of the steering wheel. The revolution is here, the revolution is here. Although there were no soldiers in sight her back shivered, imagining a bullet winging its way towards her from behind that would end her life at any second.

At last she reached the outskirts of the city and drove towards her house on autopilot. Once clear of the centre, the world began to look more normal again. Please let Jonathon be at home, she prayed, please let him be there.

There was no one on the roads leading out to the suburbs. It was if all humanity had simply disappeared. Here the houses and shops were still intact and to her amazement, even the traffic lights were working, although this only vaguely registered in Amie's mind, and she deliberately drove straight though on the red lights. There were no other cars to be seen anywhere, she had the road to herself.

Amie had never been so glad to arrive home. Abandoning the car outside on the front lawn, she unlocked the gate and rushed into the house. It was deserted. Neither William nor Pretty was there and Amie realized Jonathon's car wasn't there either. She ran into every room, calling out for Angelina, for Pretty, for anyone, but there was no response. She ran back out into the garden and looked under bushes and ran round behind the trees but there was no one there. Part of her knew she was being irrational, but maybe she was still in shock, she just felt as if she had to keep moving, as if that would protect her from being shot or harmed. It was eerie her home seemed so normal, after what she'd just seen and experienced.

She paced around inside the house and even started to make herself a cup of coffee, but gave up half way through. She couldn't just stay here, she had to do something, but what?

They would fly them all out now surely? Somewhere safe, somewhere away from all this. Pack, yes, she should pack their most precious belongings and she would have them ready for when Jonathon came home. They could then leave immediately for the airport. Never had Castle Bridge seemed such a haven.

Still in shock, Amie collected a chair and climbed up to get down the suitcases from the top of the wardrobe. The large ones she threw to one side, the two smaller carry on sized cases would be easier to manage. She flung them open on the bed and then hovered indecisively for several moments. What should they take, what was most precious? She ran back into the lounge and picked up their wedding photographs from the sideboard and then realized how stupid that was. Her family had copies of those, they could be replaced. Underwear, yes a couple of pairs each, she talked to herself as she riffled through the clothes drawers. And a change of clothes and the passports of course and food, now that was sensible and a spare pair of shoes and money, yes as much of it as they had in the house and bottles of water and what else ....?

Amie knew she was gabbling to herself, and her hands and whole body were still shaking, but the constant running backwards and forwards round the house seemed to help. Then she had a brainwave as part of her rational thinking clicked back into gear. Her cell phone, of course, it was still in her bag! Why hadn't she thought of trying to phone anyone before now? She ran back into the living room and grabbed it. It took several attempts to press the right buttons, her hands were still shaking. Then she remembered the flat battery. She searched frantically for the charger cable, plugged it in, but the signal light didn't come on. It was only then she realized there was no electricity, there was no way she could phone anyone. She collapsed onto the sofa in defeat and tried to get a grip. What was the best thing to do? Stay at the house in case someone came back? Try to get to the airport and see if there were any embassy staff trying to round people up? Go to the Club and take refuge? Her mind went round and round in circles, and every time she closed her eyes, the image of Kate swam before her. Kate's final look of shock, the shop walls tumbling, the roof caving in and Kate being buried beneath the bricks and concrete beams.

Oh God don't let that happen to me, thought Amie, though she'd not thought of God in a long while, and it was even longer since she'd been to church. She began pacing up and down, up and down and it was then she became aware the far distant shots and explosions were getting nearer. Surely they were louder than they'd been a few minutes ago? She couldn't just stay here like a sitting duck, somehow her mind told her it was safer to stay on the move. She was so distraught she didn't even think to change her clothes, take a shower or clean up the scrapes on her arms and legs. She could only think about getting away. She'd try the school first, it was the closest familiar place, see what had happened there. Other people, she needed to be with other people, they would know what to do.

Still shaking, she dragged the two small cases out to the car, threw them on the front passenger seat and climbed in behind the wheel. She sat for a moment trying to breathe deeply, willing her mind to wake up and tell her what to do. Oh God, she must think clearly so she could make sensible decisions. She set off for Spring Glen Primary. The streets were still deserted and Amie couldn't decide if there were people hiding in the houses or if they had fled. Had they received instructions at home she had missed because she'd been in town? Or had the attack on Apatu taken everyone by surprise? As she raced down the street she wanted to kick herself. Why hadn't she thought of running next door and trying to find her neighbours? But logical thought seemed to have deserted her for now.

As Amie screeched round the last corner and slowed down outside the school, she was horrified to see it looked totally deserted. There was no guard on the gates which were wide open, and she drove straight in and up to the front door. Jumping out and leaving the car door open and the engine running, she ran inside the main building, calling out to see if anyone was there. She ran to the Head's office, but there was no sign of Marian Edwards, nor any staff and certainly no children. Was Angelina still here? Was she hiding out somewhere? How could everyone have vanished so quickly?

Her breath became ragged as Amie ran from classroom to classroom, hoping in vain to find some signs of life, but subconsciously she knew she was wasting her time.

Outside again she jumped into the car, and raced off towards the Club. It wasn't feasible to try to get to the British Embassy, that was right in the centre of town, and she had just escaped from there, so goodness knows what had happed to the building and the staff. The Club was her last hope. She couldn't be the only one left! Why oh why had they never discussed what to do in case of an emergency like this?

Without thinking about it, Amie had chosen to check out the school first as it was close to home, but the Club was much closer to the town centre. Briefly she wondered if it was wise to drive towards the fighting. Then she had another idea. The orphanage school, she would drive out to Tamara and try and find Mrs Motswezi, it would be safer than going to the hospital too, that was also close to town. Yes, she would keep her distance from the troops and the bullets and try and get help at the orphanage.

Amie did an illegal u-turn over a solid white line, not that she cared or was even aware of it, and took the road to Tamara. Ten minutes later she spied the grove of trees that surrounded the north side of the compound, which was now enveloped in a large cloud of black smoke. She jammed the brakes on in shock. Where only the day before yesterday, there had been a row of classrooms, the hostel and the office buildings, now there was nothing. The black clouds of smoke rose over the deserted playground, as fire consumed the last of the buildings. The whole compound had been torched and there was no sign of life. Amie noticed a torn exercise book lying by the gate and a melted plastic lunch bowl by the large tree which had miraculously escaped the flames. There was nothing left of what was once a school and orphanage, housing hundreds of small, friendly, cheerful little children, who never did anyone any harm.

Amie burst into tears. The bastards, the bastards, she repeated over and over as she drummed her fists on the steering wheel. What had those poor orphans ever done to hurt you? They must have been herded off somewhere, there was no sign of bodies lying anywhere and surely they could not have locked them in the classrooms and burnt them to death? But Amie was not convinced of this, she had come to learn the extent of the cruelty in Africa. It was a possibility, and she prayed they had not been slaughtered. For a brief moment Amie considered trying to drive into the compound to look for any survivors, but then rationalized if anyone had been there, surely they would have rushed out the moment they saw her car. Her eyes were stinging from the effects of the pall of black smoke and her throat was dry and sore.

Defeated she turned the car round and stopped to consider what she should do next. What if she drove around the outskirts of town and tried to get to the desalination works? The problem with that was if these were rebels from the north, the works site was also on the northern side of the city. She would drive straight into the advancing troops. Her mind wandered to Colonel Mbanzi. Where was he in all this? Where were the government troops? Were they fighting to defend the city, or had they joined the rebels? From the little Amie had seen in town, no one appeared to be defending the capital, it was a mindless slaughter of anything that moved.

That only left the Club. Amie didn't think it was any help trying to get to Diana's, Anne's or Kate's house, as they all lived in the northern suburbs, and if Spring Glen was deserted, then Brianwood was unlikely to be buzzing with activity.

No, the Club was the best destination, it was the central focus for all of the expatriates, so why hadn't she gone there first? Amie gave herself a good mental shake and put the Fiat into first gear.

The closer she got to the Club, the slower Amie drove. The noise from the bombs and explosions was a good deal louder now, and she could hear gunshots as well. She wondered if it might be wiser to leave the car and go the last part of the way on foot. She could hide by the road and sneak in, but then, she reasoned, if she were seen, she didn't have the protection of the car and the choice of flooring the pedal and driving out of harm's way. Why oh why can't I make up my mind about anything, Amie screamed at herself.

A sudden thought made her look down at the gauges in front of her. It was unlikely she could get very far, she was incredibly low on petrol, and if to confirm her discovery, the emergency fuel light lit up and winked cheerfully at her. Amie groaned, now she had less choice. No chance she could drive way out of town and try and sit it out. How long did these revolutions last, sometimes for years?

Gritting her teeth, Amie made her way slowly to the Club, it was already beginning to get dark, the short period of twilight that turns into night very quickly in Africa. She was only two roads away from her destination, but as she turned the last sharp corner, she drove straight into a manned barrier.

The troops had put wooden planks across the road with large nails protruding skyward and they punctured all four of Amie's tyres. The Fiat fishtailed to a stop, and immediately a large black face filled the driver's window and thumped on the glass, then the door was flung open.

Amie glanced fearfully at the small crowd of soldiers who were clustering round the car, and the one who looked as if he was in charge, indicated she was to get out. Initially, she shook her head and shrank back into her seat. Although her Fiat couldn't take her anywhere, it still seemed her one and only refuge.

Quite gently, the soldier took her arm and pulled her out of the car. He then gestured she should take what she wanted from inside. Amie hesitated then picked up her handbag, the smaller of the suitcases into which she had packed the fruit and water, and reluctantly stood in the roadway blinking at the bright lights that shut out all but her immediate surroundings.

Perhaps they're going to escort me to the Club and everyone else will be there she thought. Surely they won't hurt me, I have no quarrel with either side and they must know that. The thought gave her courage and she stood waiting to see what they were going to do. She clamped her teeth together to try and stop them from chattering, and held her arms stiffly by her side.

The Captain, if that was what he was, pointed to a group of people huddled by the side of the road and he gave her a push towards them.

Trying to maintain her dignity, Amie walked slowly towards the small crowd, searching frantically for a familiar face, but there was no one she knew. All the other people were black, so none were likely to be expatriates and maybe speak

English. She was dismayed not one of the Africans she had met at the school, or while filming for the Colonel was there either.

There was nothing else for it, but to sit on the ground and wait to see what would happen next. Without thinking, Amie got out one of her water bottles and took a sip. Immediately a murmur ran round the crowd and hands reached out to grab it from her. Before she even had a chance to quench her thirst, others were fighting over the bottle, pushing and shoving so half the water was spilt, before a few lucky ones managed to take a brief swig. Idiots, Amie thought briefly, why didn't they share it sensibly? There wasn't enough for everyone, but the water that was wasted, would have helped a couple more. It dawned on Amie it was the survival of the fittest, and she hugged both her handbag and the small case close to her chest. If she wanted food and drink, then she would wait until she was alone. I will survive, she thought in a sudden burst of fury.

Over the next few hours, a couple of other cars came round the corner and were stopped, and the occupants forced out. Each time Amie hoped it might be someone she knew, and each time she was disappointed. It felt as if they had been sitting there for hours and hours. The dew began to fall and everything began to get damp. Amie ached all over, partly from sitting on the wet ground, and partly from the places where she had bruises and grazes from the falling buildings earlier in the day. She wanted to doze off, she was exhausted, but she was too scared to, in case someone grabbed her bag and her case. To keep herself occupied, and stop herself from feeling so scared, and moving very, very slowly, she began to slide a few things out of her bag, her passport, money and a few of the boiled sweets Angelina loved so much. She would hide these in her bra and panties, so if they grabbed her things she would at least have something. Maybe her driving licence and her residence visa as well? Hang on a minute, she reasoned, there is just so much you can hide in your underwear! Despite her precarious situation, she smiled. If she ever survived this, there had to be a book in it surely?

Despite her intentions, Amie found her mind drifting off and she was almost asleep, worn out by the events of the day, when she felt her case being tugged gently. Immediately she sprang into full alert and tightened her arms around her possessions. She tried to twist round to glare at the perpetrator, but the people were all so tightly packed together, it was difficult to look behind her.

A short time later, one of the soldiers came over and shouted at them. All the others began to stand up and Amie struggled to her feet too. She squinted in the gloom at the gang of armed men. Were they government troops? They were all in fatigues, and none of them looked smart, but that didn't tell her anything, the regular army looked pretty scruffy at the best of times.

Slowly they were herded down the road. Sadly Amie noticed they were walking away from the Club, and wondered if her friends were barricaded inside. She allowed most of the others to push past her, hoping if she dropped to the back she might be able to slip away and make for the Club on foot. But the rebels, or whoever they were, had thought of that, and kept them herded together within a tight cordon of men on all sides. Amie trudged wearily on, jostled by the people all around her, assailed by the smell of unwashed bodies and fearful mutterings from the crowd. She understood for the first time that fear has a smell of its own.

When they reached the crossroads, they were told to wait and a few minutes later, several large trucks arrived. Using their weapons, the men poked and prodded the prisoners and urged them into the trucks. Amie scrambled up the makeshift steps and elbowed her way to the side of the truck, perching on a narrow ledge that ran the length of the vehicle. She was determined to watch carefully where they were going, so that if she got a chance to escape, she would at least know which way they had gone. But as soon as her truck was crammed full, they lowered a tarpaulin over the rear and set off at a brisk pace.

As much as she tried to work out where they were going, Amie soon lost all sense of direction, as they swung around one corner after another and the tuck bounced over the potholes and swerved to avoid unseen obstacles in the road.

While they'd been sitting on the roadside, the sounds from Apatu had momentarily ceased, but now there were renewed sounds of explosions and more rapid gunfire. Amie shivered, was this nightmare ever going to end? She lost all sense of time as well as direction, as the truck drew further and further away from the city. Her bottom first became numb and then sore, as they were bounced around like peas on a drum. It was only because they were packed in so tightly they didn't suffer greater injuries. On one side of Amie was a large woman nursing a young baby who had loud fits of crying, and on the other, a younger teenager, who deliberately leaned and pushed against her and breathed his foul breath in her face. One of the women began to cry and soon another one joined in, and the wailing got louder and louder until there was a wild cacophony in the back of the truck. If Amie could have moved her arms, she would have covered her ears to shut out the sound, but eventually a loud banging from the front of the truck and harsh voices, frightened them into silence.

At long last the trucks drew to a halt, and they were told to get out and the soldiers herded them towards what looked like a large hole in the ground. The bile rose in Amie's throat at what she perceived to be an enormous grave. There were several more soldiers still shoveling the soil away on the far side.

The captives were poked and prodded as they unwillingly

slid down the sides of the large crater and then told to sit. As Amie fell rather than walked down, she was suddenly filled with a deep despair. She would never see Jonathon again, she would never see her family either, get to hug her father or have a cuddle with her mother. She was totally alone and she didn't know what to do. Any moment, she expected one of the soldiers to raise his gun and start firing. She couldn't stop shaking. She still had hold of the one small case and her handbag, would these be buried with me, she thought irrationally? She was surprised the soldiers hadn't confiscated them.

There was a commotion among the soldiers as a car approached, its headlights illuminating the whole area. It stopped at the edge of the clearing and one of the soldiers raced over to open the rear door. A large black man, dressed in army uniform festooned with gold braid, got out and conferred with the soldiers for several moments, and then walked over to the pit. He barked out a command and someone rushed to hand him a torch. Slowly he shone it on the crowd huddled beneath him and panned slowly across. When it swept past Amie she looked up, but the light beam went past her, and then it swung back again, and shone right in her face. She tried to figure out something, anything, about the man behind the torch, but the light totally destroyed her night vision.

The new, important arrival barked out an order and one of the soldiers scrambled down into the pit and grabbed Amie by the arm pulling her after him. She did not even have time to wonder if this was good news or not before she was half pushed, half dragged in front of the man in charge.

"Who are you? What are you doing here?" he asked in passable English. A sense of relief washed over Amie.

"I was driving near town.... and..... and.... your m..men st..stopped me." she stuttered.

"You are from where?"

"From England and I.... I wasn't doing any harm, nothing wrong...." Amie trailed off.

"You are working here in Togodo?"

"Yes, no, yes, I mean my husband is. He is building the new desalination plant to bring fresh drinking water for everyone." Amie knew she was whining, but somehow she couldn't help herself.

The Commander, as Amie now thought of him, gave a sarcastic laugh. "For everyone, yes, yes, that is a joke." Then he turned to his men and from what Amie guessed was giving them a severe reprimand for taking a white woman, at least that is what Amie hoped.

"Can I go back to Apatu, please?" she asked, hating to beg yet desperate to escape. "I want to go home."

"To your England?"

"Yes."

"That would be most difficult, the airport has been closed."

Amie's hopes of a quick escape were dashed. The Commander turned to confer with several of his men and for a brief moment, Amie thought of trying to make a run for it, but she didn't know which way to go, and she was aware of the dangers out there. It wasn't like running off into the English countryside at night, the worst you could suffer there was the cold and damp.

The Commander gave an order, and several of the men lined up along the edge of the pit. Raising their guns they began to fire on the hapless prisoners below.

Amie cried out in terror and turned away, she just couldn't bear to look. Their shrieks of pain and terror filled the air, and there were sounds of scuffling as those closest to the edge of the pit tried to climb out and escape. One man fell to the ground right beside Amie, his body riddled with gunshot wounds, it jerked uncontrollably. Amie shrieked and jumped away, shaking from head to toe. Her teeth were chattering and she felt herself losing control of her own body. Slowly she sank down onto the damp ground and tried to curl up into a small ball.

Then there were shots from a little further away, and several of those who were standing around suddenly turned away and faced out into the darkness. At the edge of the clearing, further shadowy figures were approaching, guns aimed at the Commander's men who for several moments were too shocked and surprised to return fire. Then all hell broke loose.

13 CAPTURED

Amie kept as close to the ground as possible and slithered backwards over the damp earth. Bullets flew to either side of her and over her head, but she didn't think she'd been hit. Somewhere she'd read or heard that when you *were* shot, it didn't hurt for a while, as the body went into shock. I'm alive, I'm still breathing, she told herself over and over again. She wasn't aware she'd already been in a state of shock for several hours.

The firing went on and on and on, lighting up the darkness in sudden bursts of light before everything was plunged back into darkness. It was hell as Amie had imagined it, total chaos, screams, cries, shrieks, women wailing, men shouting and pleading, the stench of blood, faeces and urine. The rattle of the machine guns went on and on and on, and so did the shouts and the screams and the shrieks and the cries of agony.

Then, just as suddenly as it had started the shooting stopped, leaving a silence that was deafening, broken only by those poor souls in the pit who were still alive, and the sounds of some of them still trying to scramble out.

Amie looked up slowly, and could hardly believe her eyes. Colonel Mbanzi! He was here, surrounded by several of his soldiers, one of whom looked like the driver on their second trip into the bush. Well he can't expect me to film this for him, Amie thought wildly and irrationally. She couldn't make up her mind whether she should stay right where she was, or rush over and ask for protection. At least now she knew it was the rebels who'd brought her here and who were responsible for the massacre.

Slowly she looked around. Colonel's Mbanzi's soldiers were dragging the dead and injured rebels, and piling them up to one side. Several more of his men had climbed down into the pit, pulling out those who were still alive. A few more troops appeared with portable lights which lit up the bush, and illuminated the carnage. More soldiers were posted around the edge of the clearing, to keep watch for the wildlife that would surely be attracted by the strong smell of blood.

With the immediate danger over, Amie shuffled into a sitting position. She was still not sure whether to approach the Colonel, he had never shown any empathy towards her, but the decision was taken away when he turned his head and saw Amie. He walked over to her.

"What are you doing here?" he asked. That's the second time I've been asked that thought Amie.

"I was in town, and the.... er...." what should she call them, soldiers, rebels? "There were explosions and I drove home but there was no one and I can't find any of the other foreigners and then I was stopped in my car..."

"They have all gone, left before the airport was closed."

"My husband, Jonathon, did he get out, has he gone!" Amie felt frantic, was she the only foreigner left in Togodo?

"The evacuation was very efficient," stated the Colonel, "we know how to deal with these filthy rebels and we do not intend for them to hurt our foreign workers."

The relief that swept through Amie was enormous. She was safe, the Colonel would not let any harm come to her. He had enough sense and intelligence to realize it was not in the best interests of his country to murder foreign workers. It made sense he would get Amie repatriated as soon as possible, maybe by boat, if the airport was closed.

She took a deep breath and was just about to thank Colonel Mbanzi not only for saving her life, but for making sure she was safely out of the country, when he suddenly seemed to grow larger, fly off the ground and disappear.

I'm hallucinating was her first thought, but then she realized that from out in the darkness, someone had aimed a weapon and annihilated her rescuer. Amie watched, as if in some horror film, bits of what had once been Colonel Mbanzi flew in all directions. She slithered backwards, keening softly to herself. This couldn't be happening to her. She was going mad and so was the rest of the world.

More rebel troops poured into the clearing, shooting any government soldiers they could see and all Amie could do was to shuffle further and further away from yet another scene of carnage. For some reason she could never explain, her hands remained firmly gripped to both her suitcase and her bag, as she dug her elbows into the ground and pulled herself along. Rocks, small stones and tree roots dug into her, ripping at her clothes as she moved slowly backwards inch by inch. Her breathing was ragged and she couldn't stop herself from whimpering quietly. She had no other plan but to reach the safety of the darkness outside the clearing beyond the lights.

As soon as she was enveloped in the darkness she slowly got to her feet, though her first instinct was to bend over and run, it was all she could do to walk. Keep walking, keep walking, she told herself, keep walking, get away from all this. Someone, somewhere, must know I'm not with the rest of the evacuees. Where was Jonathon? Back in England by now? Why did he leave on a plane without her? She felt waves of self pity engulf her, she was all alone and no one was about to help her.

Back by the pit the rebels had regained the upper hand. The wretched people who only a few moments before, had been saved by the government soldiers, were now forced back into the hole in the ground and speedily dispatched, along with any remaining government forces who had failed to escape. The rebels swarmed all over Colonel Mbanzi's car, whooping with glee as they found several cell phones and several more rifles in the boot. They collected up all the weapons and ammunition they could find, and commandeered the extra vehicles. All in all it had been a successful night.

"Where is the white girl?" the rebel Commander asked, but no one had seen her. "We must find her, she will be useful as a hostage. If we threaten her life, then England will supply us with more weapons to help us defeat this corrupt Kawa government," as he said the word Kawa, he spat into the dust.

"Find her," he instructed his men. "Find the woman and bring her back to the city. She will be useful."

If Amie thought she was going to escape, she had underestimated the rebels. She had only traveled a mere hundred metres before she was surrounded by yet another group of soldiers. They grabbed her arms, none too gently this time, and forced her back towards the clearing.

When the soldiers arrived with their hostage they were told to shove her into the nearest vehicle. As her carry on case snagged against the door post, one of the soldiers wrenched it out of her hand and walked away with it.

"No, stop, that's mine," pleaded Amie, but it only came out as a whimper. Tears flowed down her cheeks as she huddled on the back seat of the car, she had lost all hope.

At some point Amie either fell asleep or blacked out, for when she opened her eyes it was daylight. She was aching all over and parts of her felt numb. No, it wasn't some terrible nightmare, this was real. She thought about trying to escape, but there were soldiers all around, rebels or soldiers, it was impossible to tell one from the other, and for now, she was past caring, they were all her enemy. Even while she was trying to plan a daring escape, she realized she had neither the will nor the ability to do so. Her body was frozen in shock and with the shock, came indecision and so Amie just sat there.

Three large trucks drew up and several of the rebels climbed up into the back. Two came and pulled Amie out of the car and pushed her into the front seat of the leading vehicle, crammed between the driver and another soldier who climbed in after her. They set off at a brisk pace heading towards the city.

As they reached the suburbs, it seeped into Amie's brain the destruction and looting had spread out from the centre of the town and into the residential areas. She could see groups of people entering the houses, and trucks, cars and even supermarket trolleys were being used to carry away a wide range of household goods. One looter had piled his trolley so high the television perched on top, tumbled off and fell into the road smashing into pieces, and the convoy had to swerve violently to avoid driving over it.

In the centre of town, the streets were strewn with rubble, some buildings swayed precariously, threatening to crash down at any moment. Rubbish and spent cartridges were strewn over the ground and here and there, bodies were spread-eagled in the gutter or curled up next to abandoned buildings, or just lay in the road and on the pavements.

Strangely, the area around the government buildings at the top of the main street remained unscathed. Amie could see the British Embassy as they drove past, untouched by the war, but the front gates were hanging open and she could see it was completely deserted. The complex that housed the offices previously occupied by Colonel Mbanzi and his government troops had also escaped damage. As they turned the corner near the palace, she saw they were making for the police headquarters and the prison.

A rough-looking group of soldier rebels were on guard outside the main entrance, but as soon as they saw the trucks approaching, they rushed to open the large gates into the courtyard and close them again behind the vehicles.

Amie was pulled out of the truck, but as her feet touched the ground, her legs gave way and she collapsed in a heap. The nearest soldier forced her to her feet, and pushed her from behind into a nearby doorway. She saw a long, stone corridor painted a dull yellow, with rooms opening off on both sides. Naked light bulbs hung precariously on frayed lengths of wire, casting long shadows on the walls and floor.

They were joined by two more rebel soldiers, one took hold of her other arm while the third held a large bunch of keys. They marched her along the corridor, turned right and then hustled her down a set of steps, at the bottom of which, was a large grilled door, which reminded Amie of the safety gate on the front door of her own house. It was only then she realized with horror, they were going to lock her up.

The second corridor was lined with solid metal doors on the right and the left, but they stopped by the first one, and taking his time to choose the right key, the soldier unlocked the door and the two men supporting Amie tried to shove her inside.

She saw a cell about two metres wide and two metres long, with a mattress on the dirty, stone floor, one thin blanket, and a bucket in the corner. She turned, and frantically tried to fight and push her way back upstairs, but they firmly propelled her inside, and slammed her against the wall. She was still clutching her handbag, but they wrenched it away from her and the next moment, she felt hands all over her, almost caressing her skin, as they removed all the things she had hidden in her clothing. Then they turned and walked out, slamming the door behind them. The sound reverberated in the stillness of the prison.

She burst into tears, things couldn't get any worse. She fell back on the thin, soiled mattress and cried and cried until there were no more tears to shed.

Upstairs in one of the largest offices, the rebel Commander waved to a chair and waited for his Captain's report. "She's safely locked up downstairs?" he asked.

"Yes Sir."

"She's given us enough trouble," the Commander snorted. "So, what do we know about her? You have removed everything she had with her?"

"Yes Sir. She was hiding her passport and some money and her residency papers in her underwear. This is her bag, but it does not have anything in it of any use, except maybe her cell phone." The Captain placed Amie's bag on the table along with her documents. "We understand she worked for Colonel Mbanzi, in his Communications Department," he added.

"Doing what?"

"It appears she headed up the film unit. She was seen in many different places with her camera and she was taken to film the village and the ambush."

"So she's not an amateur then?"

"No Sir, we don't think so." The Captain referred to his notebook. "She had a team with her, Ben Mtumba and Themba Rebasi."

"Themba is one of ours, so we don't need to worry about him, but this Ben is related to the President, ex-president now. You must find him, I want him as well."

"Yes sir," the Captain made as if to leave but the Commander indicated he hadn't finished.

"You must do a thorough search of the house, and I want those tapes. Or have you already found them?"

"No sir, not yet. She did have a case with her, but they weren't in there, but we will have another look in the house. She was carrying a small suitcase but it has disappeared, someone took it."

"Leave her to me," replied the Commander. "I'll have a little chat with her later. You may go."

The Captain hesitated. "If I may ask, what are you going to do with her Sir?"

The Commander was silent for several seconds then smiled. He leaned back in his chair. "She will make a useful hostage which will deter any of the interfering outside countries getting too involved in a dispute that has nothing to do with them. They already have their greedy eyes on the wealth we've found up north, and can't wait to get their hands on our natural resources. Offers to develop and mine and refine and produce are pouring in every day. If we'd not taken action, that scum Mtumba would have let them have it all, and for what, a pittance! No, they have no idea what they are dealing with now. Once they realize we're in power they'll dance to a very different tune, oh yes." He paused, "Go, go and find those tapes and anything else incriminating you can find. This is going to be the biggest show trial the county has seen in years, once we can prove Britain has been deliberately spying on us. Yes, this should work out very well indeed." The Commander waved the Captain away and picked up the phone.

As the British Airways 747 landed back in Britain, there was already a large crowd from the media waiting outside the fence. It had been entirely by chance a British plane was standing on the tarmac at Togodo airport when the rebels entered Aputu. The word to evacuate immediately was out, and it was a chaotic and frightened crowd of people who made for the plane as if their lives depended on it.

Jonathon was frantic. He'd been in his office when the attack started and he received the call to go straight to the airport, but at that moment, a bomb exploded nearby, and the building began to collapse around him. He was knocked unconscious by the falling masonry, and had it not been for Alfred, his Fixer, he would have suffocated. Alfred dragged him out from under the beams, threw him over his shoulder, raced outside, dropped him into the back of the company pickup truck, and drove like a fiend to the airport. Jonathon was not even aware he'd been carried onto the plane, and it wasn't until they were banking to the south over Ruanga he came to, to see a friendly steward bending over him.

"Where am I?" he asked. They explained what had happened, while he dragged himself to his feet and lurched down the length of the plane, supporting himself on the backs of the seats looking for Amie. He didn't see Diana, or Richard or Kate, and he didn't see Amie either. There were lots of people missing. He grabbed the steward's arm.

"There are people missing!" he gasped. "We must go back for them!"

"Sorry sir, that's impossible, they opened fire on us as we were taking off, it would be suicide to return," the steward replied. He took Jonathon firmly by the arm. "Let me help you to your seat, and we'll get that cut on your head seen to."

Charles rushed up to say his wife wasn't on the plane either, but the story was the same. They would not put the lives of over a hundred people at risk, for the few people who were missing.

Jonathon was forcibly returned to his seat and buried his head in his hands, trying to hide the tears which filled his eyes. He had no idea where Amie was, and he was desperately afraid of what might have happened to her. He didn't even know if she was alive. It was all his fault, he should never have accepted the job in the first place. He remembered how reluctant she was, and how scared when they first arrived in Apatu. He'd wanted to climb the corporate ladder, prove how capable he was, and now look where his ambition had got him, and her. What was he going to tell her parents and her sister? They would never forgive him for not taking care of her. He began to plan how he could get back to Togodo to go and look for her, and he knew just who was going to help him do that.

At Heathrow, the cameras began to roll before the door to the plane opened and the first of the evacuees walked slowly down the steps. No one was quite sure who had leaked the information to the press, but it was going to be a great story. Not for years had the entire expatriate population of a developing country, including all the embassy staff, been flown out due to civil unrest.

It was a subdued group which was taken for de-briefing. What had happened in Togodo? Who was in charge now? Did everyone get out? Did anyone have a complete list of all the British in Togodo?

Amie had no idea how long she was left in her cell, but time seemed to have little meaning. As the sun was going down, they opened a flap at the bottom of the door and pushed in a filthy, dirty tray. There was an enamel mug of the ubiquitous sugar with tea added, two large lumps of bread with a scraping of jam, and two bowls, one of thin gruel in which floated a mixture of vegetables and chunks of some kind of meat, and the other with maize meal porridge. Although Amie would have liked to refuse, she was so ravenous she fell on the food and wolfed it all. The tray had appeared so fast Amie hadn't even had a chance to call out and ask why she was locked up. How long did they intend to keep her here and what did they want from her?

She tried to cheer herself up with the thought at least they were not going to starve her to death. Death, she shuddered. Was Jonathon alive? Was he safe? If she ever saw him again, she would never, ever complain when he left his clothes on the floor, or was too tired to talk to her at night, or when he was in a grumpy mood. All those things were so insignificant now. Sitting here in this small, filthy cell was the reality.

It wasn't until the following morning they came to escort her upstairs. These guards were more deferential, they didn't grab her arm, but beckoned politely and walked beside her back up the steps and along the corridor until they reached the Commander's office, they knocked on the door and the Commander stood up to welcome Amie.

"Please sit down," he said politely. Amie sank into the soft chair on the opposite side of his desk, it felt like a cloud after the thin, bare mattress in her cell, she was still badly bruised from the truck ride. It was not a large office, housing only the desk, a few shelves filled with files, and a couple of easy chairs which looked somewhat out of place. The most impressive piece of furniture was the large, leather office chair occupied by the Commander.

"I must apologize for the scarcity of our accommodation," he smiled at what he thought was a good joke. "As you can see, we have a shortage of good rooms after all the bombing."

Amie didn't laugh or smile. It was not a situation she found funny in the least. Yesterday she had felt really frightened, but overnight her mood changed and now she was beginning to get really angry. These people had no right to treat her like this. She'd done nothing wrong and she had a right to be sent home. This was abuse on a major scale, her human rights had been violated for no reason at all.

"Oh, you must think me very rude, let me introduce myself. I'm Commander Nyatasaki of the Free Togodo Forces."

Amie did not respond.

"I'm sure you are curious as to what has happened in the last few days, so I am happy to tell you we have overthrown the previously corrupt government, and we will set up a new, democratic parliament, yes, just like you have in your Westminster, with elections and everything. But first of course, we must put all the systems in place and ensure this time we will give benefits to *all* our people, not just those corrupt and ignorant Kawas."

Does he really believe this? thought Amie in a flash of

clarity. If he has such contempt for the old ruling tribe, will he give them a vote, and then provide them with a good education? She didn't think so.

The Commander paused for a few moments as if he expected Amie to say something, but she remained silent.

"Now while you are a guest in my country I need a little information from you and then we will be happy to escort you to the airport and see you safely on your way back home." He paused. "Are you happy to answer a few questions?"

"I suppose so, if I can," Amie said at last.

"Good, good. Now the first thing we want to know, is how long you have been working for Colonel Mbanzi?"

"But I never…." Amie stopped. In truth she had done what the Colonel asked, even if it had been under duress.

"It wasn't proper work. I mean he only wanted some programmes made for the Trade Fair."

"And these were video programmes you recorded with your camera, yes?" Amie nodded.

"Yes, and what did these programmes show?" the Commander prompted.

"The upliftment schemes, the hospital, electricity supply, computers in schools, that sort of thing."

"And you were impressed with all these new innovative projects yes?"

"Well," careful Amie she thought, you can see the trap. "I guess it's early days and the projects have not been going all that long and it takes time…" she trailed off.

"Quite, quite, so let's say you didn't think much of the efforts made by the previous government."

"But I didn't say that at all!" protested Amie.

"Ah, so you *were* impressed then, very good. Of course being closely aligned with the former rulers, you would see things from their point of view."

"No, no you don't understand. I was quite neutral about all of it. Colonel Mbanzi asked me to record certain projects and then give him the programmes to show at the Trade Fair, and that's all I did!"

"Oh, no, no, no, no, no, I don't think so," Nyatasaki said softly. "I believe you also went out into the bush and recorded some let's say 'scenes' in the bush. Am I right?" The Captain leaned back in his chair and stared at Amie.

Amie did not know what to reply. She sat thinking for several minutes.

"I didn't want to film those, those scenes," she replied. "When they took me out to the village I had no idea what I was going to see."

"And?" the commander waited patiently.

"And, I was told to film and so I did. I was too scared not to."

"But of course you got well paid for this."

"No, no one ever mentioned money to me. They, er they said it would help my husband in his work, get permissions early and plans passed and so on." Amie could tell he didn't believe her.

"I find it most unusual Britain would send a woman to Togodo as a spy," said the Commander.

Amie gasped. "No!" she cried and half rose out of her chair. "I'm not a spy! I'm just an ordinary housewife, I'm nothing, I mean I couldn't... I wouldn't know how...."

"Enough for today I think," the Commander interrupted her. "Maybe when you have had time to think a little more, you will be persuaded to tell us the truth." He barked out an order and immediately the door opened and Amie was conducted back to her cell.

The days merged one into another. Sometimes Amie was left to her own devices, the only break in the monotony was the food pushed through the flap in the door morning, noon and night. Often they didn't even empty the bucket left in the corner of her cell for days. From the few sounds she could hear of the outside world, things seemed to have returned to normal, under what she assumed was the new 'rebel' government. If there were any counter insurgences she wasn't aware of them.

Every now and again they would take her upstairs, sometimes to be questioned by the Commander, sometimes by his underlings. On each occasion, the situation seemed to be getting worse. They had found the spare tapes which she had squirreled away in the house at Spring Glen to take back to England and make her own programmes showing, as she thought at the time, 'the real Africa, without the propaganda.' They had also discovered the bank statements which showed the large amounts of money in her account, and they so obviously didn't believe her, when she protested she had no idea who put the money there.

The Commander didn't hit her, but stared at her from behind the desk, and patently didn't believe a word she said. On other occasions, she was taken to a smaller room and questioned again and again and again. The questions were always the same.

"When did the British government ask her to spy for them? What did they want to know? Who put such vast sums of money in her bank account? Why was she withholding tapes in her own home which showed Togodo in a bad light? Why did she want to show the poor people and the bad housing and the broken roads? Where were the tapes she made from the two bush visits?"

And Amie always gave them the same answers, but they either didn't believe her, or they simply refused to believe her. Then their mood changed, they got angry, and they began to hit her, punching and kicking and twisting her arms. She was battered and bruised, but there was nothing she could tell them, except maybe why she had hidden those extra tapes. She was wise enough to know that admitting she was going to try and put them together to show the 'real' Africa, was not going to help her cause.

She had little idea of the passing of time. Had she been locked up for days, weeks, months? What was happening in the outside world? Was anyone trying to get her out? Had her home country just washed their hands of her? Surely Jonathon and her parents were knocking on doors, talking to the newspapers, campaigning to get something done? She briefly remembered that Britain had a policy of not giving in to blackmail, and since everyone had been evacuated, there was no longer any representation from the government. Just how important was one British housewife? She feared no one outside her immediate family and friends was too worried about her. She remembered cases of other British nationals locked up abroad for years and years. Sometimes they were released and sometimes they were never heard of again.

Day by day, Amie sunk deeper and deeper into a depression. The sheer monotony of prison life was mind destroying. She saw no other prisoners, although occasionally she heard bloodcurdling screams from somewhere inside the building. She was beginning to think it would be better to end it all than continue to live like this.

Until one day they came for her soon after the first rays of the sun began to pour over the far distant hills, spilling down the slopes onto the earth below. She heard them approach, their footsteps echoing loudly on the bare concrete floors. As the marching feet drew closer, she curled up as small as she could and tried to breathe slowly to stop her heart racing.

The large fat one was the first to appear on the other side of the door and he was accompanied by three other warders. They unlocked the old, rusty, cell door and the skinny one walked over and dragged her to her feet. He pushed her away from him, swung her round and bound her wrists together behind her back, with a long strip of dirty cotton material. She winced as he pulled roughly on the cloth and then propelled her towards the door. The others stood back as she was pushed into the corridor and up the steps to the ground floor.

She thought they were going to turn left towards the room where they made her sit for hours and hours on a small chair, but this time they didn't turn left, they turned right at the top of the steps and pulled her down a long corridor towards an opening at the far end. She could see the bright sunlight reflecting off the dirty white walls. For a brief moment she had a sudden feeling of euphoria, they were going to let her go! She could hear muffled sounds from outside in the street and shouts from the other side of the prison walls.

It was surreal there were people so close to the prison going about their everyday lives. On the other side of the wall, the early morning suppliers who brought produce in from the surrounding areas and the market stallholders were haggling over prices, shouting and arguing at the tops of their voices. But all these sounds could have been a million miles away, for they were way beyond her reach.

Hope flared briefly. Her captors had finally realized she was innocent. They'd never openly accused her of anything sensible, and she still didn't know why she'd been arrested. She kept telling herself she'd done nothing wrong, and she convinced herself the nightmare was over at last.

All the doors on either side of the corridor were closed, as they half carried, half dragged her towards the open door in the archway at the end. The closer they got, against all reason, her hopes just grew, and grew. They were going to set her free. She was going home.

As they shoved her through the open doorway, she screwed up her eyes against the bright light, and when she opened them, it was to see a bare courtyard, surrounded on three sides by high walls with no other door leading to the outside world.

Then she saw the stake in the ground on the far side, and brutally they pushed her towards it. She was too weak to resist, and it was difficult to walk, so she concentrated on putting one foot in front of the other, determined not to give the soldiers or police or whoever they were, any satisfaction. She would show as much dignity as she could.

The skinny one pushed her against the post and took another long piece of sheeting from his pocket and tied it around her chest fixing her firmly to the wood. She glanced down at the ground and was horrified to see large brown stains in the dust.

Not freedom, this was the end. She squeezed her eyes tight shut, determined not to let the tears run down her cheeks, but the sound of marching feet forced her to open them again. She saw four more men, all dressed in brown uniforms, with the all too familiar guns who lined up on the other side of the courtyard opposite her. They were a rough looking bunch, their uniforms were ill fitting and stained, and their boots were unpolished and covered in dust.

She was trembling all over. She didn't know whether to keep her eyes open to see what was going on, or close them and pretend this was all a dream. She was torn, part of her wanted it all to end now, but still a part of her wanted to scream, 'Let me live!! Please, please let me live!!'

The big fat man barked commands and she heard the sounds of guns being broken open as he walked to each of them handing out ammunition then, with the safety catches off, they prepared to fire.

To her horror, she felt a warm trickle of liquid running down the inside of her thighs, at this very last moment she had lost both her control and her dignity. They'd not even offered her a blindfold, so she closed her eyes again and tried to remember happier times, before the nightmare started. Briefly she glanced up at the few fluffy white clouds floating high in the sky as the order to fire was given.

The noise was much, much louder than she expected more of an explosion than gun shots. And then there were more loud bangs, all around her. Apatu had erupted yet again. She opened her eyes to see that the wall of the prison had gone, and the line of soldiers, who moments before had raised their rifles to kill her, were gone, lying lifeless under the masonry that had once been a wall of the prison building.

For several moments, Amie was too shocked to move. She looked over to the market, where people were running in all directions, screaming, shouting and wailing. Some stopped to attend to the wounded, while others just took flight, running away as fast as they could.

There was nothing to stop her running away either. She tugged at the strip of cloth holding her to the post, but instead of tearing the cloth, the post came free, and she stumbled forward and fell flat on the ground. She paused to catch her breath and then desperately tugged at the post, until she had managed to slide the cotton over one end. Slowly she stood up. While her brain was screaming at her to get away as fast as possible, her body would not respond. She took one tentative step forward and fell flat. She pulled herself up on her knees, stood upright and took another step, wobbled, and then another, slowly she tottered towards the outside world.

On the other side of the prison walls, she was tempted to sit and recover, but the fear that maybe they would come and drag her back inside the undamaged part of the building, gave her strength. All around her, bombs were falling, and shots rang through the air, and several aircraft flew overhead, strafing the people as they ran for safety.

But which way should she go? She paused for a few moments with her back to the prison wall, or what was left of it, and tried to decide which was the quickest way out of town. She would just have to trust to fate to take her in the right direction. If she made for the beach, if the worst came to the worst, maybe she could cross the border into Ruanga a wild idea she knew, but she simply didn't have a better one. The best course was to try and head for the shore south of Apatu, away from the northern areas the rebels might be patrolling. Then she would just keep going.

A few minutes ago the market had been a bustling hive of activity, women buying their fruit, vegetables and meat for the evening meal. Now it was a scene from hell. Shrieks and screams resounded through the air and people, those who still could, were running in circles. A few of the women were trying to save what produce they had left, others simply ran over the plastic sheeting treading on oranges, bananas and raw meat as they tried to get as far away as possible. Others were sneaking around on the periphery, stealing as much food they could stuff into their pockets.

Amie ducked down and ran too, she had no idea where her strength came from, nor her energy, but her instinct for survival kicked in. As she ran she kept as low as she could, and slipped into doorways whenever she saw someone coming. She couldn't see any soldiers, or were they rebels? Was this a counter attack by the remnants of the former Kawa government? A splinter group of the new government? Peace keeping forces from another country? It didn't matter, Amie was not going to put her trust in any of them.

As soon as she felt far enough away, she stopped for a moment to take stock. Uncurling her fingers she poked and prodded herself and flexed her arms and legs. It didn't feel as if she'd been shot, though there was plenty of blood on her jacket, it didn't seem to be her own blood. It was a miracle she'd been so close to so many guns and escaped unscathed.

It took her some time to reach the outskirts of town, and she hardly remembered how she got there. She had one bit of luck when she sheltered in an open shop doorway. The owner was lying dead on the pavement outside, and the place was empty. Behaving in a way she wouldn't have thought possible only a few weeks previously, Amie stepped over the body, ducked inside and grabbing some plastic bags she filled them with bottles of water, biscuits, energy bars, sweets and soap. She had no money to leave on the counter, but hoped she would be forgiven for stealing. It's in a good cause, she told herself, and the poor guy, wouldn't need any of it now.

She had a further windfall in the shop next door. Maybe only a few hours ago, it had sold the usual wide variety of general products serving the local population, a little bit of everything like an Aladdin's cave. It too was deserted and Amie was able to grab clean clothes including a warm jacket, a blanket, a torch, and several boxes of matches. They also had a range of rucksacks and Amie stuffed all her new found possessions into one of them and crept back out into the street.

It was almost as if she had this part of the city to herself. The streets were deserted and as she made her way towards the southern suburbs, she met no one. They probably all ran out into the bush, she thought, on the run, which is exactly what I am, a criminal on the run. If I was innocent before, I'm not now.

When Amie reached the last suburban street where it met the undeveloped open bush, she hesitated. This was a new danger, another enormous leap out of her comfort zone. It was unlikely she would meet many wild animals this close to town, but they were out there. She firmly pushed these thoughts to the back of her mind. Maybe the creatures would have been frightened off by the sounds of the gun fire, or maybe they would be attracted by the smell of blood? Either way she hoped she might just go unnoticed and unmolested.

She took her first tentative steps out into the unknown.

14 DANGEROUS TERRITORY

When they'd stayed up at the game lodge, the air had been filled with a variety of noises, grunts, growls, the occasional roars in the distance and the ever present cicadas. Now, the only sounds Amie could hear were her own footsteps and her heavy breathing. The rucksack which had seemed light in town now began to weigh a ton and her shoulders began to ache.

She decided to keep walking until the light failed and then she would hide up. It would be too dangerous to try and find her way in the dark. So far she had been beyond exhaustion, but as the landscape began to mist over and undulate, she realized her strength was finally giving out.

She found a depression in an old Baobab tree and taking a long stick poked around in the hole thoroughly. She could hear Dirk's voice inside her head. Never, ever sit or lie down without checking first if you have stumbled into another creature's home. Investigate first.

Satisfied the opening contained nothing more threatening than the couple of stray moths she'd dislodged, Amie wriggled back into the hole pulling her rucksack behind her. She took off her jacket and rolled it up as a pillow, draped the blanket over her knees and lay down. It was not a comfortable night, despite the protection of the Baobab tree, as she jumped at every little sound. She dozed on and off and in between she recited her times tables, tried to remember long lost pieces of poetry, and made mental lists of all the people she had known, anything to keep her mind off the possible dangers lurking close by. At first she twitched every time she heard movement among the leaves, but finally she was too tired to keep watch any longer and fell into a deep sleep.

When Amie woke, the dawn was just breaking. She didn't feel refreshed, but a drink of water and a couple of energy bars helped. She should start walking now, before the sun got too high, later it would be too hot to walk and she would have to rest up again. She was less likely to be seen at this time of the morning, although the Africans were early risers, but the biggest problem was she was not really certain which way to go. Geography, geography lessons, what did I learn in geography? she asked herself. The sun rose in the east, so she needed to veer left to find the coast but maybe it was best to keep a little inland and walk parallel to the sea.

Before she abandoned the shelter of the baobab tree, she would put her hand on the gnarled trunk, and whisper a heartfelt thank you. Dirk had told them the Bushmen always apologized to their prey just before they finally dispatched it, and it seemed to Amie that this great tree had protected her through her first night alone. She had never heard it mentioned that the original people who inhabited this area, had ever thanked the trees and plants, but she felt it couldn't hurt. She hoped she would remember all the other things Dirk had taught them on that weekend all those months ago.

Slowly she wriggled out of her refuge and dusted herself down. She changed into the clothes she had taken from the shop, and groaned to see she had grabbed a tight blue, sleeveless dress, it was not at all suitable for walking about in the bush, but it would have to do until she could wash her old clothes which now stank, she had been wearing them for so long. She hoisted the rucksack onto her shoulders and began to walk. The sun should move from my left to my right, she thought, and if I can keep in that general direction, I should be making for Ruanga, away from the rebels' homeland, away from Budan to the north which may also be at war with Togodo now, if they want to claim the new mineral wealth. She would make for Ruanga where hopefully President Zanda's people were still living in peace and harmony.

At first her legs were stiff and her whole body ached as she shivered in the cool of the early morning, but she picked up speed as the sun began to warm the land. She lined up a landmark in the distance, a tall outcrop of rock that stood out higher than anything else, and keeping her eyes firmly fixed on that, she made it her first goal.

The terrain was easy to cover, flat sandy soil, interspersed with low shrubs and trees. The land stretched as far as the eye could see ahead of her and on either side, on and on and on into the distance. Behind, she could just make out the shapes of the taller buildings in Apatu that were still standing. The only obstacles she had to walk round were the giant termite mounds, some almost as high as herself. For the most part, she could walk in an almost straight line, and by the time the sun made it too hot to go any further, Amie felt that she'd made progress.

She collapsed under the shade of a large bush and took several more sips of water, and ate four biscuits before reluctantly packing the rest away in her rucksack. She had no idea how long her meagre supplies would have to last, but she would use them sparingly. She was very tempted to use a little of the water to wash herself, but decided that was not sensible. She would save what little she had for drinking.

Amie walked for six days, sheltering at night under bushes or in depressions, covering herself with leaves before wrapping herself in the blanket to keep out the cold. Her dress clung to her back where she'd sweated during the day and she'd come across no water in which to wash or replenish her supplies. She was down to her last bottle.

She'd caught glimpses of the sea a few times on her left,

but she was too scared to walk along the wide beaches. She would be so exposed and vulnerable since she had no idea who controlled the beach area. She realized with surprise that she was behaving like most of the other African animals, resting up when it was dark and again during the heat of the day, and only walking at dawn and dusk. The only problem with that was she was active when they were, and so she kept on the alert. She had no idea what to do if she saw a lion or a hyena. Climb a tree? She just hoped they wouldn't be hunting too close to the coast. She tried not to let the rhythm of her footsteps and the repetition of simply going forward, to dull her senses. She needed to stay alert to any dangers.

She came across several animal tracks in the sand, but she couldn't tell one from another, which was probably a blessing she decided. But now water was going to be her biggest problem. She was still close to the coast, and Amie desperately tried to remember how far inland the salt water might permeate the soil. She would have to turn further inland away from the sea, and try to find a river bed, it was her only hope. She'd not seen any sign of dwellings in the last three days, and that suggested there was no fresh water supply in the area. No water, no people, no wild animals she reassured herself, but that doesn't solve my problem.

Reluctantly she veered off to the right and began to make for the low lying hills. Water courses must drain down to lower levels, she tried to reassure herself. All water makes for the sea, but the hills seemed so far away and she was worried she would go too far inland. Under the unrelenting African sun, she began to perspire and she knew that was the fastest way to lose more body fluids. She found a low lying shrub and crawled under its welcome shade.

As the sun began to lose its heat she dragged herself to her feet and began walking again. The hills seemed farther away than ever and she began to despair. All around her the flat sandy plains stretched in every direction, and she was beginning to feel disorientated. She stoically put one foot in front of the other and trudged on. The landscape began to undulate in front of her eyes and she was vaguely aware she was approaching a line of trees that curved round a slight depression in the ground.

Trees often grew by rivers, she thought just as she tripped over a tree root and found herself rolling down a gentle slope. She landed in a flat sandy area, cursing and swearing as she knelt up and rubbed her arms and legs. Was this a river bed? It wasn't very deep, but it was wide, the only way she was going to find out was to dig.

That was the next problem, she didn't have a spade or even a tea spoon and that only left her hands. Taking off her rucksack, Amie began to scoop out handfuls of sand. It wasn't as easy as she expected, for as soon as she dug down a little way, the sides of the hole caved in and she had to work further and further outwards to make the hole deep. It was beginning to get dark and she felt very vulnerable, but she was also so thirsty she kept digging.

She lost all sense of time as she threw scoop after scoop of sand to one side. Her breathing became ragged with the effort and her arms began to ache. The hole was maybe half a meter deep and as fast as she grabbed one load of sand the hole seemed to fill up again with two more.

She was concentrating so hard, that at first she wasn't aware the sand now felt damp. She stopped for a moment and watched as a small pool of water seeped into the lowest part of the hole. With this encouragement, she renewed her efforts until she could see a small puddle of water. It suddenly occurred to her it might be salty and she held her breathe as she dipped her fingers in and licked them, brackish maybe, but not salty, it was drinkable. She gave a whoop of joy and began to widen the bottom of the hole.

It took her far into the night to find enough water to refill four water bottles. She was angry with herself for throwing away two empty bottles at the beginning of her journey, it had never occurred to her to keep them, but four were better than one, she told herself. If she remembered correctly, you could go a week or more without food, but three days was the limit without water, even less probably in a hot climate.

That night, she climbed up into the lowest fork of a large tree that bordered the dry river bed. She was worried the scent of the water she had so thoughtfully excavated might attract the game. As a reward for all her hard work, she treated herself to a whole bottle of water. The brackish fluid tasted better than champagne. Her muscles ached, her stomach rumbled, but sheer exhaustion put her to sleep. Her last thoughts were that in the morning, she would have another good long drink before she set off again.

When Amie opened her eyes as the dawn broke the next day, she was amazed she hadn't fallen out of the tree. She congratulated herself on her survival skills, until she looked down and saw a lioness by her water hole. Her blood froze, there *was* wild life out here and she had become so relaxed and sure this area was safe! She found herself holding her breath, as if the very act of her breathing would attract attention. She was not very far off the ground and she thought the lioness would have no problem climbing up after her. She would only have to stand up on her back legs and stretch a little to reach Amie.

For now though, the lioness lay quite contentedly in the river bed, yawning a few times and giving her paws a good lick. She seemed neither aggressive nor hungry, and Amie could only hope she had hunted recently and would not be looking for another meal now.

Amie knew she dared not move until the animal had left and that meant she would lose at least half a day's travelling south, that's if I'm not the next meal, she thought sadly. Despite her terror, Amie could not help but admire the sheer beauty of the animal as it lay in the sunshine. The wind blew through the tree rustling the leaves, another danger, was Amie downwind? The light breeze was blowing gently into her face, so she reasoned she must be downwind. It would be a disaster if the lioness could smell her, so she had to hope and pray the wind wouldn't change direction.

It wasn't until the sun was well over the hills when the lioness finally stirred, stretched, and slowly began to move away. Her stomach looked very distended and Amie wondered if she was pregnant. Dirk had told them lionesses often left the pride before giving birth, to protect the cubs from the lions. They would rear them for the first few weeks on their own before taking them back to the family group.

Amie stayed for a while in the tree. She was loath to descend, but she knew she couldn't stay where she was indefinitely. Her legs were cramping up from sitting still for so long, and she could only hope the lioness was close to giving birth, maybe lions were like humans who often didn't feel like eating shortly before going into labour.

I'm rambling, she thought to herself as slowly and painfully she lowered herself to the ground. She had noticed the lioness had walked away upwind, so hopefully she wouldn't get Amie's scent. Every hair on her back tingled as she slowly worked her way up river, and again turned towards the mountains. The sweat began to pour out of her as she walked quickly and quietly away from her night's refuge. The rest of the pride might be close by, she could be walking straight towards them. How far did lionesses travel to give birth to their cubs in safety? And why had she seen virtually no other animals until now? Could the lioness be nomadic, not part of a pride at all, a solitary female? That's what I am going to believe Amie told herself firmly. I can't go back, so I go forward.

It was one of those rare days when the clouds wandered across the sky, giving some relief from the heat of the sun, and Amie kept walking. She had planned to refill her empty bottle from the river before she set out, but the thought of sharing the same water supply as a lion put her off. Who knows what diseases she might ingest? She still had a few biscuits and sweets and a couple of energy bars left, and these would have to last her as long as possible.

She felt she made good progress that day, the hills looked much closer and while she had been too busy watching the lioness, she had not taken much notice of the position of the sun. She just kept trying to remember her brief glance at the Internet maps she had looked at on her lap top back in England. She thought the range of mountains, or small hills, she had no idea how high they were, marked the border between Togodo and Ruanga.

Not long before the sun began to sink low in the sky, Amie stumbled onto a dirt road. This was not what she was expecting, but she hoped it ran south from Apatu. It was a wide, gravel road but didn't look as if it was busy. Amie hoped she could follow it south. It made walking a lot easier, easier to see snakes, she rationalized, but did it lead back to Togodo? Maybe it went to the border? For several moments Amie dithered as she tried to make up her mind whether to follow it or not. She wouldn't necessarily be safer on the road, but if a vehicle came along, she would hear it and see the dust long before she saw it and could always dive off the road. She decided to take the chance.

It had now been several days since she'd last seen another human, but while she was feeling almost desperate to see someone and have social contact with one of her own kind, she was also terrified of meeting anyone. She had no trust in any Togodian and she kept wondering if she was the only European left in the whole country. It was an uncomfortable thought.

She heard a vehicle approaching, coming fast towards her and immediately, Amie raced off the road and into the bush. She hid behind a small thorn tree and watched it go past. It looked to be some sort of army truck carrying a load of soldiers in the back, it was impossible to tell what side they might support and she briefly wondered how they could tell either.

She waited several more minutes before she had the courage to scramble back up onto the road. As each kilometre passed, the rucksack became heavier and heavier. She carried it in one hand and then the other to relieve her aching shoulders, but she was never tempted to leave it behind. She still had two and a half precious bottles of water left, and a few biscuits. She had treated herself the previous evening by drinking as much as she could, reasoning she could refill in the morning. The lioness had put paid to that plan. She had drunk half a bottle today, so she needed to find another source of water tomorrow for the next day.

She had no idea how far she had walked, or how many kilometres Apatu lay behind her, but as she put one foot in front of the other, she reckoned she was covering more ground than before. She was getting into her stride, and the cloudy skies allowed her to keep going throughout the day. It was approaching the wet season and she only hoped she would reach the border before the rains began.

It was late in the afternoon when she paused briefly, she had a weird sensation everything looked familiar. There was a clump of fever trees on one side, and almost opposite, a smaller dirt road leading off to the left. She paused, should she bear left and head back a little way towards the coast? Without the sun, she wasn't sure which direction she was now heading, as the gravel road had twisted and turned in several places. It might be easier walking under a cloudy sky, but it was also easier to get lost, or walk around in circles.

Another approaching truck made up her mind for her, and she darted down the side road and hid in the undergrowth. There were faint tyre tracks on the side road, so trusting to luck, Amie set off. Every now and again she thought she recognized a landmark, a particularly tall tree, or a flowering bush or another dry river bed, but then doubts set in. Still, she reasoned if she walked for long enough, she was bound to get somewhere, deliberately forgetting she had no food, and very little water left. Should she stop and try and refill her water supplies? There was a small ridge ahead of her, so she decided she would walk as far as the top and try to get some idea where she might be. She could always come back and start digging before it got dark.

She noticed several buck among the trees on either side of the road. They looked up in alarm as she approached and didn't take their eyes off her, but they only moved away a few paces, obviously she wasn't a threat she observed with a wry grin. Just wait until I get really hungry, she laughed nervously. Am I getting braver, or am I losing sense with reality? She asked herself.

As she reached the top of a small rise, she could see gateposts in the distance. Now she knew she was hallucinating, Nkhandla Game Lodge was right in front of her. That can't be right, surely the lodge was north of the capital, and she thought she'd been walking south. Maybe it didn't matter now, she had found sanctuary and she was safe at last.

As she walked between the gate posts, she felt the weight of the world falling from her shoulders, from now on everything would be all right. Dirk and Helen were such old hands they would know exactly what to do and how to help her. She couldn't wait to tell them of her adventures.

The first sign things were *not* right, was the absence of vehicles in the front driveway. Maybe they hid them out of sight, reasoned Amie as she mounted the outdoor steps to the bar area. The next thing she noticed was the bare shelves behind the bar, last time she was here there were rows and rows of bottles, now they were gone, and so were the people, there was no one around. She noticed that everywhere was covered in dust, leaves, small branches and animal droppings.

Some instinct kept Amie from calling out, as she slowly tip toed across the verandah and peered first into the lounge and then the dining area. Everywhere she looked had been stripped bare. There was no furniture, no tables laid, no food in the fridges, nothing. She began to despair, the place she had thought might be a refuge was deserted. Who had been here? Where was everyone?

She looked out of the back door, but there were no signs of life in the servants' quarters either. Climbing the stairs off the main reception she crept slowly towards the living area where she knew Dirk and Helen stayed. Here at least the large bed lay undisturbed although no bedding remained and the built in cupboards and drawers were empty. Amie felt like a thief or a peeping tom, but she was desperate to find some clue as to what had happened or an idea as to where her hosts had gone.

Back downstairs she went to the desk, and rifled through the drawers. The booking log was still there, showing that guests were expected in a few days time. They were going to be disappointed, but then it was unlikely they could even get here with the airport closed, and riots in the capital.

Amie swung around sharply as she heard a rustling noise behind her, but it was only a bird which had flown in from the balcony. It was just as nervous as Amie, as it took off immediately and flew back outside.

Amie left the main building and went to look in the nearest banda where not so long ago she and Jonathon had stayed, even thinking about him brought tears to her eyes. As in the other rooms, most of the furnishings had gone, only the bed, made of solid tree trunks and too heavy to move, was left in place. Amie sat down on the bare springs and wept.

Amie's stomach began to rumble and convulse and she

realized it had been a long time since she'd last eaten. She had almost lost track of time, so she went back to the kitchen hoping to find something to eat that might have been overlooked. In the bin she found some hard, stale biscuits, and in the larder there was a jar of mince meat left over from the last Christmas mince pies, a product she knew most locals didn't like. Wrenching off the top she scooped it out with her fingers while nibbling at the biscuits.

She left her rucksack in the kitchen and wandered out of the back door. She noticed several brown stains on the grass and guessed the worst, she'd seen enough blood in the last few days to recognize the smell, and as if to confirm her fears, as she walked towards the garden fence, she came face to face with a hyena. She froze. What had Dirk told her? Never stare directly into the eyes, keep them lowered to show you are not a threat. Amie found this incredibly difficult to do. She was almost mesmerized with fear as she and the animal weighed each other up.

The hyena moved a step closer and Amie took a step back. Should she try and make a run for it back to the kitchen and slam the door shut? Should she make for the nearest banda and shut herself in there? What if she tried to threaten it by shouting and waving her arms, would it run away? As she took another step backwards, she almost stumbled over a large brick lying in the grass. Slowly, she bent down, picked it up and threw it as hard as she could at the animal. Much to her amazement, it landed on the hyena's head and letting out a loud yelp, it ran off and disappeared out of sight.

Amie took a deep breath and went quickly back inside. It was obvious that Dirk and Helen were not here, she thought they had probably been murdered. Had she not been so dehydrated she would have shed tears for them, but her survival mode kicked in again and she decided to make a thorough search of the lodge and outbuildings before she continued her journey.

Her most important find, was a rain barrel of fresh water, so for the first time in ages, Amie had a good wash, rinsed out her clothes and drank until her stomach would hold no more. Before it got totally dark, she took everything upstairs, closed the bedroom door jamming it with a wedge of wood she'd found in the yard, and lay down for the best night's sleep she had had in a long time.

When she woke the next morning, Amie couldn't remember where she was, then it all came flooding back. During the night nothing had changed. As she got dressed Amie made a mental list of what she would like to find. Batteries for the torch she'd taken from the store in Apatu, and she needed some extra empty bottles she could fill with water, even though they were so heavy to carry. And food, yes, any food she could lay her hands on.

She spent the whole morning looking in every nook and cranny, every cupboard and drawer and every shelf. After she finished in the main building, she investigated all the bandas but whoever had ransacked the Lodge had done a thorough job. Her total haul at the end of her search was a pile of old and rather dirty rags, a large sheet of polythene, extra water bottles and a two more jars of mince meat.

It was just as she was gathering everything together ready to leave, she noticed the map on the wall. She rushed over to look at it. It clearly showed the position of the Lodge and she was incredibly relieved to see it *was* south of the capital. Maybe it was because the workers here had been from the northern tribes, Amie assumed they'd travelled north from Apatu that weekend. And the distance to the border with Ruanga? It looked a long way, but it was impossible to measure it because the corner of the frame had been damaged and Amie couldn't make out the scale markings. It did show the border was marked by a river, but it didn't indicate how wide it was, or if it had water in all year round.

The range of hills appeared to be inside Ruanga, so if they were the ones Amie could see in the distance, then maybe she didn't have too far to go. She'd been through so much, had so many traumas, she was becoming fatalistic about her life and how long she might expect to live. She would do her best to get back home, but if she didn't make it, then she would just be another statistic on the Dark Continent.

Reluctantly, Amie walked down the steps into the front parking area and set off again. It didn't make sense to stay, even though it gave her a semblance of safety. No one was going to look for her here, or come and rescue her either. She needed to get herself to safety, and she was the only one she could rely on now. She continued to walk south.

Thousands of miles away, back in England there was a debate raging in the media. News of the ransom demand for Amie had been leaked to the press. There were two sides to the story. On the one hand some journalists were of the opinion that if you travelled to live and work in a foreign country, often for large sums of cash and all living expenses found, you were aware of the risks you took. To expect others to put their lives in jeopardy to rescue you if the foreign country erupted into civil war was unreasonable. You were responsible for your own bad judgment. Under no circumstances should the Prime Minister sanction payments for hostages. If they paid up even once, then every British person who left these shores would be a sitting target.

On the opposite side of the coin, the headlines screamed it was a disgrace! Her Majesty's Government had a duty as the protector of all its citizens wherever they might be. The SAS should be sent in immediately to rescue the poor innocent people who had been caught up in the fighting and subsequently imprisoned. They dragged up the Don Pacifico affair, when in 1850, Lord Palmerston, the British Foreign Secretary had dispatched a squadron of the British Navy to blockade the Greek port of Piraeus for two months, in retaliation for harming David Pacifico a British subject in Athens. Born in Gibraltar, only his property had been destroyed, but Great Britain ensured he was well compensated. In those days, the papers screamed, it counted to be a British subject, it meant something. Those were the days when Britain was indeed Great!

Have you read what it says in your passport recently? Another newspaper screamed.

> HER BRITANNIC MAJESTY'S SECRETARY OF STATE REQUESTS AND REQUIRES IN THE NAME OF HER MAJESTY ALL THOSE WHOM IT MAY CONCERN TO ALLOW THE BEARER TO PASS FREELY WITHOUT LET OR HINDRANCE, AND TO OFFER THE BEARER SUCH ASSISTANCE AND PROTECTION AS MAY BE NECESSARY.

Did that have any meaning in the world today? No! Today, the government cared nothing for the safety and welfare of the very people who paid its salaries and taxes.

In Castle Bridge, Amie's parents worried constantly about her. Most of the time, they were under siege from the crowd of reporters and TV crews who pushed and jostled outside, asking repeatedly for quotes, information and their feelings about their daughter. The press tracked down old school friends, teachers, ex work colleagues and anyone who had ever been in the briefest contact with Amie, to fill their newspapers and TV talk programmes. They had phone-ins on radio, and a few rather thoughtless people even laid wreaths on the grass outside the Reynolds' house, sending Amie's mother into floods of tears.

No one from the family, or the press, was privy to the talks that were held at high levels behind closed doors. General consensus was that Britain's policy was not to succumb to blackmail by a foreign country over the safety of its citizens. If there were other demands beside the ransom demanded by the new rebel government, these were not made public. Britain had not recognized the new regime in Togodo, maybe it would never recognize it. Even if President Mtumba and all his ministers had been totally corrupt, to the outside world, they were the legally elected choice of the people.

It was a stalemate.

As she trudged further south, Amie often thought of her husband, her family and friends, but she would have been astonished to learn about the furor her arrest had caused back home. She pushed all thoughts of loved ones to the back of her mind, it only made her cry and feel sorry for herself, and her priority now, was to survive.

The terrain changed. Now there were fewer trees and more shrubs, and it made her journey a little easier. On the other hand, there was less shade, and she began to worry her water would not last until she reached the river. She had eaten the last of the food she had stolen in the capital, along with all three jars of mincemeat.

She was surprised that this part of Togodo seemed to be uninhabited, she saw no one. She hadn't decided what to do if she did meet people. Would it be better to hide or safer to ask for help? As she walked she tried to calculate her speed and work out how far she covered each day. She knew she would have to find food somehow and soon. In her head she heard Dirk telling her that any part of the Baobab was safe to eat, and on the second day she veered further inland when she spotted one of Africa's majestic trees. She stood looking up at the tall, wrinkled trunk of the tree that looked as if it had been planted upside down. She would never be able to reach the leaves or fruit, even if it had been the right time of year. She sank down and looked around. There was a variety of plants growing nearby, but which ones were safe to eat?

She chose a thick fleshy plant, and tore off a leaf. The sap was clear and not creamy, so that was a good sign. She rubbed the leaf on the inside of her lower lip and sat back in the shade to wait. She had to judge the time as her watch had also been taken from her when she was thrown into prison. Feeling no ill effects, she next placed a small piece on her tongue to see if it tasted putrid, or it burnt or stung. The minutes ticked by, so far so good. She then nibbled a small piece of the leaf and waited as patiently as she could. It took a lot of self control, as by now she was so hungry, it was tempting not to chew as many of the larger leaves as she could, as quickly as she could.

She dozed off in the heat of the midday sun and when she awoke, she decided she had proved this one plant was harmless. It might even do her some good. She ripped several more leaves off the plant and munched, pretending it was roast beef, or a large slice of quiche. She giggled, though whether from fear, or genuine happiness that she'd found a source of food, she wasn't sure. Before she set off the following morning, she ripped up several of the plants and packed them into her rucksack. She reasoned they would shrivel up very quickly, and hoped they had propagated as far as the border.

The next day, she saw a puff adder lying in the sunshine. These were the snakes that did not get out of your way, ignoring the sound waves made by approaching feet. In her hurry to avoid it, Amie ran back several steps and gashed the back of her leg on a sharp thorn bush. She looked in horror as a thin trickle of blood ran down towards her ankle. Now she had two problems. The scent of blood travelled far across the veld, and might attract predators, and there was also the danger of infection.

She walked away from the slumbering snake putting a safe distance between them, and sat down to clean out the wound and bandage it. Using as much of her precious water as she dared, she dabbed at the wounded area as best she could, and then tried to tear off the bottom of her dress to use as a bandage. It looked so easy in the movies, she thought as she tugged and tugged, but the material would not give way. She tried to bite the seams, but only succeeded in hurting her teeth, so in the end she was forced to abandon her efforts and hope the gash would heal quickly.

She began to worry about getting heatstroke. Her legs were cramping more and more frequently, she often felt dizzy and her head ached badly. Her earlier strength had drained away, as she doggedly put one foot in front of the other, but too often, the landscape began to undulate in front of her. She was fearful of losing direction, what if she was not walking towards the border?

She stumbled over to one of the smaller thorn trees and attempted to scramble up into the first fork off the ground, but she simply didn't have the strength. She munched the remaining leaves and took several sips of water. Her supply was running very low and she knew she would have to find more very soon, but the shimmering ground looked completely flat in all directions, and there wasn't a dry river bed in sight. She rested up until the sun began to sink in the sky and then forced herself to her knees and using one of the empty water bottles, she dug a shallow hole in the ground. No sign of water at all, but maybe she could catch a little dew.

Using a sharp stone, she cut one of the water bottles in half and placed it upright in the bottom of the hole. Over the top, she placed the large piece of plastic she had found at the Lodge, and weighted it down with large stones. Placing one stone carefully in the middle of the plastic directly over the bottle, she could only hope. Thank you Dirk, thank you Dirk for passing on the knowledge, she said to herself over and over and over again.

Exhausted by her labours, she foraged around, and was relieved to see more of the 'safe, succulent, plants' as she thought of them. The ones left in her rucksack had shriveled up and didn't look edible by now. In the cool of the evening, she found the energy to climb a little way up into the tree, dragging the rucksack with her. She was tempted to leave it on the ground, but was afraid an animal might find it and destroy it.

She slept fitfully that night, waking every few minutes with cramped arms and legs, or feeling sore where the tree trunk or the bag was digging into her. I'm getting weaker, she thought. Several weeks of prison food had not exactly equipped her for long treks, and she knew her spirits were sinking lower and lower. She wasn't sure how much longer she could go on. She had no idea how long she'd been walking, or where she was, or how much farther she had to go. She had not thought beyond getting to Ruanga, and she had no idea what sort of reception she might receive there, or how she would get to the capital and contact an embassy or… Let me get there first, she thought, just let me get there.

As soon as it was partly light, Amie slid down from the tree and went to examine her homemade still. Lifting the corner of the plastic very carefully, she could see a few drops of water run down the underside towards the waiting bottle. She gave a whoop of joy, but when she'd removed all the plastic, she was dismayed to see there was maybe two tablespoons of water in the bottle. It didn't look particularly clean and it certainly wouldn't be enough to sustain her. Nice idea Amie, she said to herself, but you will just have to walk for longer and faster each day, rest up for less.

It was a stupid decision.

Even though she knew how hot the sun could get, and what effect it would have on her hydration levels, Amie had underestimated the extent to which it would affect her sense of direction and her will to continue walking.

That day she covered a lot less ground, and with a sense of dread, she sipped the last few drops from the water supply she'd brought with her from the Lodge. She found she was wandering, weaving from side to side, and losing focus on the range of hills which sometimes appeared to be ahead of her, and sometimes to her right or her left.

Her mouth felt dry and her tongue several sizes too large. She ached all over and it was becoming harder and harder to walk. The gash on the back of her leg was throbbing, and she thought it was probably infected. Several times she stumbled, she'd lost the energy to step over obstacles, and had trouble focusing, as she tried to weave around the shrubs that suddenly sprang up in front of her.

Her headache got worse and worse and she wanted to vomit, although there was very little in her stomach. She picked some more leaves and squeezed the liquid out of them, as she caught the meagre amount of sap in her mouth, but she was not as careful as she had been before, and because her vision was fuzzy, she chose the wrong plants.

15   THE LITTLE PEOPLE

There was a loud roaring in her head and a tickly feeling on her cheek. She stirred and heard scuffling nearby in the dark. She gasped and tried to curl up as tightly as she could, only to find her back was wedged against something solid. She kept trying to roll out of danger but there was nowhere to go, and she didn't have the strength. She lay still for several moments, trying to gather her wits about her. She was just too scared to open her eyes, but they seemed to be covered and she didn't have the energy to move.

She began to understand how life was cheap in Africa, the cards were stacked too high. If it wasn't tribal opposition, or becoming a victim of crime, there was also the rawness of nature, the scorching sun, the lack of water, or the savage, wild animals. At that point, Amie discovered a whole new admiration for those peoples who had survived for generations in these conditions. She was ready to accept her fate, and reasoned that in the state she felt, it would be a blessing her misery was about to end.

The tickling began again, and was she imaging it, or was that giggling? After a few brief moments the fog closed in again, and the darkness returned.

The next time she woke she could see shafts of daylight through the gloom at the edges of the covering over her eyes. She tried to pull herself up, but it was just too much of an effort. She tried to focus on the light. The African sun was always bright and shared its heat, but here she was cool and comfortable. She realized her head was no longer aching, her legs weren't cramped and for a change, the world stayed quite still. She closed her eyes again and the tickling on her cheek was repeated. There were more noises, a scuffling and a few sharp squawks and the sound of a slap. A couple of wails which quickly faded, and then there was silence.

As Amie drifted off once more it was beginning to dawn on her she had been found and taken somewhere, and she was no longer in danger. She fell into a deep, peaceful sleep.

She came to, to find herself flanked by a row of smiling black faces. She stared at them in amazement. They were not like the Africans she'd known in the city, these people were not Kawa, or Luebos or Tsaan. These people had lighter skin, and looked to be quite small. Their hands and feet were delicate and they appeared relaxed and friendly.

Looking round, Amie saw she was in some sort of grass shelter, lying on a bed made of leaves and rough matting. She struggled to sit up.

The lady closest to her held out a gourd and indicated she should drink from it. The liquid was white and a little creamy, just the sort of drink she should avoid, according to Dirk, but there was no reason not to trust these smiling people. As she sat up and grabbed the gourd in both hands, they all clapped, and the ladies ululated softly. The drink was very bitter, and Amie gasped and tried to give it back. The lady closest to Amie shook her head and looked stern, she refused to take it, making her gestures quite clear, Amie was to drink all of it.

As she slowly swallowed each mouthful, Amie's mind was spinning with the questions she wanted to ask, but it was unlikely any of these smiling people would have one word of English between them. The three people closest to her were women, they sat patiently on the ground, never taking their eyes off her, Amie seemed to be a source of fascination to them all. The one who looked most senior, had on a clean, but torn, white school shirt, and a skirt that had once been bright and colourful. Two of the others were bare breasted and wore skirts of faded material wound round the waist. They all sported jewellery made from seed pods and other natural materials.

The elder woman hesitantly indicated Amie should lie back down, but she was anxious to get up and explore where she was. She shook her head and waved her arms to show she wanted to go outside.

The elder woman shook her head quite firmly, then hesitantly, she put out her hand and pushed Amie quite firmly back down. Before she could object, Amie saw the world go round, fade and then, once again, she remembered nothing.

Amie had no idea how long she lay in the hut. She was aware that each time she opened her eyes, there was always someone on duty, who handed her the gourd and insisted she drink from it, and each time Amie blacked out again, even though she fought to stay awake. She had to find out where, how ..... but she didn't have the energy or the will to resist them, it was pleasant to float away, with no worries, no pain and no responsibilities.

Eventually, the little people, as she thought of them, decided her recovery was complete, and when she woke, they allowed her to stagger to her feet and they led her outside the hut to sit for a short time in the late afternoon sunshine.

Amie noticed that wherever she was now, there were more trees than out on the savannah, and here and there, small patches of woodland had been cleared and planted with maize. The haphazard collection of huts was hardly a village, and Amie counted five huts from where she sat, and there were maybe thirty people altogether, and yes, they were *all* quite short. At first, she thought some of the women were large children, but from the wrinkles on their skin and the grey hair on others, she saw they were fully mature. There were four young children who were very cute but shy. They ran about in the clearing, hiding behind trees and peeping out at her. They giggled every time she looked in their direction, and when she put her hands in front of her eyes and then suddenly removed them saying "boo," they dissolved into peals of laughter.

Whoever these people were, thought Amie, they were happy and content, and probably lived off the land, in harmony with nature, and I thought there were no more peoples like this left anywhere in the world, except for maybe the Amazon basin.

That evening, they brought her what tasted like maize meal porridge mixed with small pieces of meat on a large leaf that served as a plate. It was a bit tasteless, but Amie smiled and nodded and chewed and chewed the tough meat chunks hoping it wasn't anything too disgusting. What I don't know, won't worry me, she reasoned.

The days fell into a comfortable, lazy pattern. Everyone rose with the sun, and after a meagre breakfast, most of the men picked up their bows and arrows and melted away among the trees. Amie was amazed by their ability to appear, or disappear without seeming to move, one minute they were there, the next, they were gone.

The women spent part of their day tending the few crops they grew, and pounding the ripe maize in the traditional African way. Holding long, smooth sticks, they stood in pairs, taking it in turns to crush the dried maize in the large gourd at their feet. But most of their day was spent foraging among the trees for roots, berries, nuts, tubers and mushrooms.

The first few weeks, Amie was left very much alone, except as an item of interest for the children. Most of the women were away for a long time each day, and whether from a sense or boredom, or a willingness to join them, Amie indicted she wanted to help.

The chief woman appeared to be rather reluctant to include her in their daily foraging, but when Amie persistently followed them into the wooded areas, watching what they picked and then copying them, she smiled and made no more objections. They gave her a basket made of stripped tree bark roughly woven together, to show she had been accepted as one of the gatherers. Not that Amie was much use at all. During one hot and exhausting morning, she had only gathered a handful of plants and roots, and when she showed them to the chief woman, she smiled and shook her head. She took all but two leaves out of Amie's basket and threw them away.

To Amie's horror, they also collected caterpillars, Mopani worms and termites. Her stomach heaved at the thought of eating such fare, while trying to rationalize she had probably been eating them for days.

Collecting water also took up much of their time. It was quite a walk deep into the woods, to a large depression in the ground. Here it was cool and moist, but every day, the women had to dig deep into the leafy forest floor to reach the water table. Using small wooden ladles, they carefully spooned the water into the large gourds, until they were full to the brim. While the outward bound journey was fun, the return one was hard work. Amie had complained to herself about the weight of less than a dozen plastic bottles of water, but the full gourds were much, much heavier, and they were also slippery to carry. For part of the journey back to the village, the women carried the gourds on their heads, but where the trees grew closer together and closer to the ground, they had to carry them in their arms.

On her second trip to 'help,' Amie slipped on a tree root and dropped the gourd and watched in horror as the water spilled out all over the ground. She looked up fearfully, not sure how angry the women would be. There was a brief, tense silence and then first one, and then the rest of the women all burst out into peals of laughter, and putting down their own containers, rushed over to help her up, poking and prodding her to make sure she was not hurt. I don't think I would have been so forgiving, thought Amie, after all that hard work, but the women still smiled and with much clucking and clicking assured her it was all right.

Preparing the food for the evening meal also took a lot of time, as the women scraped and peeled and boiled whatever they had managed to find. The women used natural tools made from bone, stones and pieces of wood, but Amie noticed there were a couple of blunt, rusty knives among the kitchen implements. So, there *is* some contact with the outside world she thought, but somehow, for the moment, she was in no hurry to rejoin it. Life here was so peaceful, so relaxing and Europe, the city, and even the suburbs seemed fraught with problems and danger.

Over the following days, Amie learned many words from the tribe. To herself she described them as pygmies, simply because they were so short. She had never felt so clumsy before, but none of them, not even the men, came up to her shoulders. They had a simple grace, like forest dwelling ballet dancers, as they negotiated the narrow woodland paths, skirting fallen tree trunks, leaping over large boulders and weaving gracefully, to avoid the low hanging, overhead branches.

It was easy to learn the words for concrete objects like maize, hut, individual plants and names. The chief woman was called E'lft and her man was X'ome, as best as Amie could pronounce it. In time she learned all thirty names and was amused to see, that even here, in a primitive society, there were many similarities with people anywhere else in the world. There was a hierarchy, although it was fairly fluid and everyone seemed to be involved in making decisions, at least this was what Amie guessed. It was very difficult to make out what was going on when they all got talking together.

Her closest friend was A'ncah, a girl about the same age as Amie. She would sit patiently and teach Amie how to prepare the pumpkins, how to make the potent homemade beer, and how to adorn herself with the seeds they fashioned into jewellery from the plants that grew nearby. A'ncah had an almost uncanny way of reading Amie's mind, and often brought her a drink when she was thirsty or food when she was hungry, even outside meal times. She would accompany Amie to the water hole when she wanted to wash herself, and keep watch for any marauding animals in the undergrowth. The two women grew very close.

But it was a lot more difficult for Amie to discover the words they used for work, or go, or other verbs. If she pointed and waved her arms to indicate 'to go' she was never quite sure if they were telling her the name for a tree in the same direction, or if they really understood her at all. She shadowed one of the smaller children and tried to work out what the adults said to him, but even when she heard the sounds, they were almost impossible for her to pronounce. On the other hand, they also had problems trying to say 'Amie' and their attempts made her laugh. Generally though it was quite frustrating, and Amie missed being able to talk and exchange ideas.

Amie also felt guilty about taking up space in one of the huts, sharing it with seven other people. She was not sure she would ever get used to such intimate community living, there seemed to be no concept of privacy at all, and so she tried to get across the idea that maybe she should build her own hut. However, either they did not understand her, or they simply did not want another hut in the village. Amie gave up and waited until she was alone before performing what in her culture, were nature's more private tasks.

Every now and again, the men did not go hunting, but sat around in the village while they prepared their arrows. Amie could see the arrow heads were made of metal, and wondered where they'd got the metal from. There was no evidence of any type of mining, yet the arrows were well formed and very sharp. On one occasion, she bent down to pick one up, but X'enu shouted loudly at her and she snatched her hand back. Had she broken a tribal taboo? Were women forbidden from handling the weapons?

X'enu clucked at her. He pointed to the arrow head and then drew his finger across his throat. Amie understood, of course, the arrows must be tipped with poison. She shuddered to think what might have happened if the men had not been there to guard their arrowheads.

All the members of the tribe seemed to be very healthy. There was the odd cough or cold, and occasionally someone gashed an arm or a leg, but there was always a leaf, a tree root or the sap from a plant that was used to help healing. Even when little K'ungu got bitten by a snake, the nearest woman picked him up by his arm and swinging him onto her back, disappeared among the trees. When they returned a short time later, she had plastered a thick paste over the bite and bandaged it with leaves. By the end of the day, K'ungu was running around with the other children with no apparent ill effects, although the women shouted at him when his antics threatened to dislodge the leaf bandage tied on with lianas.

The children belonged to everyone in the tribe, going from one to the other for cuddles and attention. If they misbehaved, they were smacked quite hard, and their wails ignored until they did as they were told. Amie noticed too, even the smallest child was expected to help. There were small brooms made of grass for them to sweep inside the huts and around the village. They were sent to gather stones for the fires and when everyone went into the forest to collect wood, they were expected to pick up small pieces to be used as kindling.

Amie was surprised at how few children there were, and wondered how many died in childbirth. Some of the women didn't look as if they had had children, and she watched M'agha with interest, she was at least six months into her pregnancy when Amie first arrived. Yet when her time came, as happens all over the world, the elder women took her into her hut and shortly after, appeared with the newborn wrapped in bark cloth. Amie had been at the hospital when Sam had had both Dane and Jade, and there had been a lot more commotion than this! How stoic these forest dwellers were she thought in admiration.

The women were adept at making fire too. Ruefully, Amie remembered her Girl Guide test when she couldn't even light a fire using matches. Here, a few minutes with a couple of flint stones, and the kindling burst into flame. Amie grew to have great respect for their way of life. If only we could all live in such harmony, she thought, but there are far too many of us on the planet for that now.

The men would return in the late afternoon with a variety of the game they had hunted, never too much, for the food would waste very quickly in the heat, so it had to be hunted most days. The dead deer, especially the small duikers did not bother Amie too much, but the day they brought back two monkeys appalled her. Eating deer was one thing, but monkeys, that was as close to cannibalism as you could get! That evening, she shoveled the overcooked meat around on her plate, wondering how many times in the past she had happily eaten one of our closest cousins, but she dared not throw it away. It would never do to attract unwelcome visitors by leaving leftover food around.

Even here, in this idyllic setting, there were still dangers, from the stinging ants, the mosquitoes and the snakes. The first time a snake slithered into the village, Amie was amazed at how calm the women were. Most of the men were away hunting, and it was Awai who calmly picked up a stick, and purposely guided the creature back into the fringes of the forest. Amie was impressed with their lack of aggression, these people only killed to eat. She tried to remember all the tales she had read about the Bushmen or San people, but surely they lived out in the desert areas? She didn't think this tribe was closely related, but they had a similar culture of living in harmony with nature.

There was great excitement the day the men brought the honey home. They crept out of the surrounding trees carrying large bundles of leaves, inside which were golden yellow honeycombs. The children rushed to poke their fingers into the sticky goo, and were only half heartedly chastised. That night they all sat and munched and slurped the sweet honey, and dipped a variety of nuts, forest fruits and small red bananas into the sweet stuff. Amie thought she had never tasted anything quite so good before.

Amie lost all sense of time as one day followed the next. There was seldom any change to the daily rhythm of life. One week blended into the next until one morning there was a buzz of excitement, although she could not guess what was causing it. The men had not gone hunting, the women were fussing around sweeping, clearing, tidying and checking the levels of beer in the gourds.

Not long after midday, first one, then another and then three more men slipped into the clearing. These were men Amie had not seen before and much to her amazement, they were wearing European clothes, cut off jeans, faded shirts and two of them wore flip flops. So they *are* in contact with the outside world, she thought.

The men had returned with precious hoards of sugar, tea, pieces of metal suitable for honing into arrowheads, bundles of cloth, a stack of cigarettes and parcels of different powders and crushed stuff Amie could not identify. The prizes that caused the most excitement were the two bright red plastic buckets and a plastic bowl. Amie wondered if the women would come to blows as they pounced on these treasures, but after each one had a turn to examine each article in minute detail, they were placed back in the middle of the circle. It was obvious they would be happy to share the spoils.

Amie eyed the folded bundles of cloth with acquisitive eyes. She didn't have the courage to suggest she take one, but she couldn't take her eyes off them. When she had escaped the rioting and then been taken into custody, she'd been wearing a summer skirt and top and a light jacket. In prison they had taken everything away from her except her clothes. After her escape, she had taken or rather stolen, new underwear and the blue dress from the abandoned store in town, but she had been wearing these same things for so long she'd lost count of the time. She had learned to ignore the dirt, and the tears and holes in the fabric, but each time she washed them they disintegrated a little more.

A'ncah's sharp eyes missed nothing, and leaning over, she whispered in E'lft's ear. The elderly woman nodded and spoke softly to Marabi who seemed to be the one in charge of the working group. His face lit up and he reached forward and handed Amie one of the bundles of cloth. Amie didn't know what to say, she had not learned a word that meant thank you. She looked round the circle and smiled and nodded and mouthed 'thank you, thank you,' over and over again. The rest of the tribe thought this was very funny, and they burst into ribald laughter, thumping each other and rolling from side to side. Their generosity, and their good humour were too much for Amie, and she burst into tears. There was a sudden silence, as everyone stopped laughing and A'ncah put her hand gently on Amie's arm.

"No, no, I am not crying because I'm sad," she sobbed, "but because you're all so nice." No one of course understood a word.

Looking worried, E'lft glanced at X'ome and on his nod, handed a second bundle of cloth to Amie, maybe she wanted another one?

"No" exclaimed Amie, "I am very happy, look," and she gave them all a big smile. After a few moments hesitation, they seemed to understand from her body language that she was pleased. Everyone relaxed, and then the men clapped and the women ululated.

After the evening meal there was much laughing and talking, as the men told of their time away from the village. Copious amounts of the homemade beer were consumed and then most of the elder people settled down to smoke. For a moment, Amie thought sadly of Diana and her addiction, but then realized the men weren't smoking ordinary cigarettes, they were smoking marijuana! She was very reluctant to try one, but they pestered her again and again and persisted, until she agreed to try one puff. It didn't seem to hurt, so she took several more puffs. It gave her a relaxed feeling, and leaning back against the side of her hut, she drifted off to sleep.

As far as Amie could understand, these five men had travelled quite some distance and found work of some sort, and all the gifts they brought back were rewards for their labours. So, they could not be too far away from civilization she thought.

Lying in her hut that night, Amie thought about the outside world. Until today, it had seemed a life away, a place on another planet, but now, almost insidiously it had crept back into her world. Seeing the plastic buckets and the bowl had jolted her back into the present. She knew several months ago she had been desperately trying to get back home, but since she'd woken in the village, time seemed to have stood still. She had been aware of the seasons, but had not measured them. It was enough that each day slid peacefully into the next.

Her mind, body and soul had been ravaged by the riots, the horrors she'd witnessed, her imprisonment, her struggles across dangerous terrain, and the loss of everyone near and dear, but here she'd found peace. Did she even want to leave? This was not her world, this way of life belonged to these simple forest people. Not so simple, she reminded herself, they have skills I'll never possess if I live to be a hundred.

There had been times when she had been deliberately excluded from their simple ceremonies, such as when T'gutu died. They kindly but firmly pushed her away when she went to join the procession carrying the old man's body into the forest. Amie shared the women's tasks, she did not want to be a burden on them, but deep in her heart she knew she would have to leave one day, but maybe not just yet, give me a little more time to heal, she whispered into the darkness.

Amie was not aware that the time left to her here was drawing swiftly to a close, and she would have no part in the decision.

16 BACK TO REALITY

The working men had been back in the village less than one full moon, when the attack came in the middle of the night. The village was surrounded by a band of angry youths carrying sticks, spears and pangas. They were hell bent on trouble. Everyone tumbled out of the huts, or buried their way underneath the leaves and melted into the forest. One moment they were there, and the next moment they were gone.

Amie huddled on her leaf mattress in the hut and shook with fear. She looked around wildly for somewhere, anywhere to hide, but before she could even decide what to do, she was face to face with a young African boy. He looked at her in shock, then yelled out to the others, and two or three more crowded in through the doorway and gaped at Amie. She could tell finding a white woman in a situation like this was a shock to all of them.

The oldest of the group nodded towards the doorway, and when Amie didn't move, he leaned over, grabbed her arm and pulled her out into the clearing. There followed a heated discussion, and she could only guess they were trying to decide what to do with her. A few of the boys rooted through the other huts, and finding the new plastic buckets and bowl retrieved them, along with the remaining bundles of cloth. Amie prayed they wouldn't confiscate the new dress she'd fashioned from her share of the spoils. It looked as if maybe the workers had perhaps taken more than their due when they returned to the forest, for once the newcomers had taken what they wanted, they set off back the way they'd come, taking Amie with them.

At first Amie tried to pull back, or run off to try and hide among the trees, but two of the youths took a firm hold, one on each arm and once they had moved some distance away from the clearing, Amie knew she would never be able to find her way back.

They travelled for most of that night. Walking three abreast, Amie slowed them down considerably as they followed a path through the trees, and it was long after the sun had risen, when they finally left the cool of the woodland area, and set off across the savannah. Amie had no idea where they were taking her, but she was fairly sure it would be somewhere much closer to civilization.

As the sun rose high, they stopped by a small stream to drink and eat some of the marula berries off a nearby tree. One of the boys took a dirty plastic bottle out of his pocket, and offered Amie some water. She accepted gratefully. She was familiar by now with the marula trees, and helped herself. A couple of the boys were also catching Mopani worms and eating them, but Amie still preferred hers toasted to raw and she declined to join them.

As soon as the sun began to lose its heat, they set off again. Amie's feet were a lot tougher than they had been, her shoes had disintegrated months ago, but the swift pace of the party was beginning to wear on her. They no longer held her, guessing she would not know which way to run, but she struggled to keep up, fearful of where they were leading her, yet even more fearful if they left her behind. There was safety in numbers, and at no time could you forget this was still the domain of African predators. They met no one on the journey, and just as the first stars began to twinkle in the sky, they arrived back at their own village.

Amie immediately recognized the mixture of first and third

world. Here many of the huts were built of earth blocks and had thatched roofs, but one was covered in corrugated tin. The space in the middle of the houses was littered with pieces of old magazines, empty plastic bottles, and broken plastic jugs, buckets and bowls. The people she saw were all in western dress, with the woman wearing colourful turbans. Small, semi naked children were running around, chasing the chickens, but everyone stopped in amazement, as they watched their boys return with Amie.

In different circumstances, it could have been described as Amie's fifteen minutes of fame. There was much excitement and chatter, as they all crowded round and stared at her. Unlike her pygmy family, they did not reach out to touch her blond hair which by now hung way below her shoulders, nor did they poke and prod her. They were obviously used to seeing white people, but not from the forest.

There was a disturbance from the largest hut, and an elderly man appeared and walked over. There was a sharp exchange with Amie's captors, and then he came over to Amie. She guessed he might be the Chief.

"You English?" he asked.

For a moment Amie stood there nonplussed. It seemed such a long, long time since she'd spoken in her native language that for a moment, she was lost for words.

"Yes," she said at last.

"You are from the trees?" and the man pointed back the way they had come. Amie nodded. She didn't know what to tell them. Instead of relief at finding someone who spoke her language, she realized she needed to be careful what she said. If she admitted to being from Apatu, they might take her back, and she had no idea who was now in charge. There was no one there to help her, she had no passport, and no means of identifying herself.

"Where are we?" she asked.

"You don't know?" the Chief was puzzled.

"I walked a long way," Amie hoped he wouldn't pry, but of course he did.

"Where you walk from?"

"It's not important, what I need to know now, is where this place is." Amie spoke slowly and carefully, it took a while for her to remember all the words which were once so familiar, and spoken without a thought.

"This place, Bubezi," the Chief replied. He beckoned her to follow him, and pointed to a chair outside his house. He sat down facing her, and one of the women brought over two enamel mugs. At the first sip, Amie recognized the ubiquitous tea with at least three, if not four spoons of sugar.

The Chief stared at her for several minutes, he sipped his tea slowly, before he asked, "You run from rioting, yes?"

"Yes," admitted Amie, it seemed pointless to deny it, why else would a white girl on her own, be wandering around in the African veld?

"What has happened there? Who is in charge of the government now?"

The Chief shrugged. He was obviously not interested.

"President Zanda, he is boss," said a voice behind her.

It took a moment for this to register and then Amie exclaimed. "Then we are in Ruanga!" Several of the onlookers nodded vigorously. "How far to city?" Amie waved her arms around trying to indicate distance.

"Two, three days," said the Chief. "Your name?"

"Amie, and yours?"

He didn't give his name but replied, "Themboniso will take you to city tomorrow."

"But, but how?" Amie was trying to sort out her feelings about going back to a city, and at the same time, she couldn't see any means of transport in this small village.

"We go," and the Chief stood up abruptly and walked into his hut.

Themboniso it seemed was one of the young men who

had brought Amie out of the forest. He suddenly appeared by her side and repeated the word. "Tomorrow."

Amie stayed where she was, everyone else was disappearing through doorways, or chasing the children off to bed. Just as Amie was trying to decide where to try and curl up for the night, one of the younger girls approached and with a smile, took her to a hut at the far end of the village.

Once she had ushered Amie inside, she nodded and disappeared from view. Amie looked around, this one hut was three times the size of the one she slept in in the forest, and it looked as if she had it all to herself. That was a strange feeling, not to be cuddling up to other bodies to keep warm, although her recent family was not known for its high standards of personal hygiene. Funny what you can get used to she thought, as she shook out the foam mattress and the blanket before lying down.

For some reason an old television programme flashed into her head. They had sent a famous personality to stay in an African township with a family for a week. He had lasted one night, and after that, with tears in his eyes, relocated with his host family to a hotel in town. People can be so resilient if they have to cope, was Amie's last thought before she fell asleep.

The following morning, the village, like all those in Africa, was up with the dawn. As she stretched and put on her cloth dress, Amie wondered if she would ever sleep late again, being active with the sun, and sleeping after dark had become second nature to her.

She opened the door of her hut and peered outside. Already the children, refreshed after a long sleep, were racing around, and the women were lighting the fires to boil water for the morning tea. Amie noticed with wry amusement that all but one were using matches, and the exception, had a gas lighter just like the one she'd bought for Pretty to light the stove in the kitchen.

After using a water barrel to rinse her face, hands and feet, she wavered uncertainly in the hut doorway, until the woman who had served her tea the night before, waved her over for breakfast. It was another cup of over-sweet tea in a none too clean mug, and a huge jam sandwich the size of a door step. Amie found she was hungry and ate the lot.

Although Themboniso had said he would take Amie to the city 'tomorrow,' she was aware he might not mean that quite literally. Tomorrow could be the next day or even a few days later, but immediately after breakfast he indicated she was to follow him, and he set off in such a hurry, Amie barely had time to thank her hostess for the food and drink. She had to run to keep up with him as he strode out across the veld. While he appeared to be making no effort to walk fast, somehow he covered the ground at an alarming rate.

Finally, exhausted, with sweat pouring down her face and under her arms, much to Amie's relief they reached a gravel road. Themboniso didn't stop however, but turned left and continued at the same reckless pace along the ungraded road. Amie struggled not to lose him, the bare stones hurting her feet, which were used to the gentle, cool, forest floor.

It wasn't too long before the sound of an engine came roaring up behind them, and Amie was amused to see that Themboniso imperiously waved it down, like a policeman on point duty. The battered pickup truck skidded to a halt and protracted negotiations went on, which gave Amie time to catch up. She arrived by the truck, panting with exhaustion, just in time for Themboniso to indicate she was to climb up among the sacks of pumpkins, maize and other bulky packages, which provided no comfort on the bumpy ride. Themboniso sat in the front cab with the driver, reminding Amie of her second class citizenship on this continent.

A few kilometres further on, they turned abruptly onto a tarred road, narrowly missing a speeding Mercedes by millimetres. The Mercedes owner blasted his horn loudly, but it didn't faze their driver, who gaily waved two fingers in the air, as the car swerved violently to avoid them.

Themboniso might have meant the trip into the city was two or three days on foot, but in the truck, it was going to take less than a day. As she saw the towering buildings in the distance come closer and closer, Amie became aware of her appearance. Her hair was completely tangled, she'd not been able to comb it properly, and even her new dress looked exactly what it was, a piece of faded cloth wrapped around her like an old and tired sari. Her feet were bare, she had no possessions, and she was not at all sure what she was going to do once she arrived in the town, was it the capital city even? Finding the British Embassy seemed a good idea, but if this was just a small town, then how much farther was it to the capital, and how would she get there?

The closer they got to town, the more people they passed walking along the side of the road, herding goats, dragging old supermarket trolleys piled high with goods, groups of children on their way to or from school. They passed the inevitable shack lands as they approached the centre of town, rows of dwellings made of old packing cases, topped with corrugated iron and weighed down by old tyres. Welcome to the city thought Amie and realized she was neither excited, nor relieved, but scared. The hustle and bustle sounded so loud, the crowds were so dense, she felt alienated. Will I ever get used to urban living again? she wondered.

The truck came to an abrupt stop and Themboniso jumped out, and beckoned to Amie to follow him. Feeling battered and bruised, she fell rather than climbed off the back of the vehicle. They were in one of the outer suburbs and Themboniso set off purposely along the well kept streets, flanked by houses very similar to the ones in Spring Glen. They turned several corners until they reached one of the larger houses, surrounded by a high wall. He rang the bell beside the large gate and spoke to the intercom. The gate clicked open and Amie followed him up the front path and round the side of the house, past the sparkling blue swimming pool and up to the back door.

A housemaid, not unlike Pretty, was standing outside. She peered at Amie as if she was an alien and there was a sharp exchange of words. At first she seemed uncooperative, but then she suddenly disappeared and returned several moments later, and waved them both inside.

Even though Amie had lived most of her life in similar surroundings, she felt awkward and out of place. She was ashamed and embarrassed about the way she looked, and paused at the entrance to the lounge.

"Where is she then?" demanded an imperious voice.

The maid came over and grabbed Amie's arm, pulling her into the room. Amie saw an elderly woman in a wheelchair, who picked up her glasses and peered at her visitor.

"Gracious," she exclaimed, "you *are* a wild, white woman! I didn't believe what I was hearing!"

"I'm sorry to arrive like this you must think it frightfully rude but…" Amie trailed off.

"Come and sit down child, and tell me all about it," the lady indicated a chair opposite.

"Oh no, I am such a mess and so dusty and – what must you think of me?"

"You are a sight for sore eyes, but first I want to hear who you are and where you come from. Wait!" She turned to the maid and asked if Themboniso was still waiting outside the back door. The maid nodded. "Then tell him to wait until the Master gets home. They can negotiate the business side." She turned to Amie with a smile. "You do realize, Themboniso wants payment for bringing you into town? But he's suggesting an enormous amount. He used to work for us as a garden boy, but he was so unreliable we had to let him go. He must have seen you as an easy way to make a bit extra," she laughed.

"Of course, I will repay you as soon as I get home, but now I've nothing at all, only the clothes I stand up in!"

"I can see that! Now, while Emily makes us coffee, you must tell me all about it. What have you been up to?"

Amie told her story as briefly as possible. For some strange reason, she felt very protective towards her forest family, and she was deliberately vague as to where they lived. While she recognized her new acquaintance wanted to know where she came from, Amie was also now desperate to know what had happened in Togodo, and she also wanted to know where she was.

"Goodness, I don't even know your name," her hostess said, "I'm Alice Robbins, my husband works on the mines here. This isn't the capital, I'm afraid, that's Atari, and it's about two hundred kilometres farther south. Umeru is just a small mining town, we don't have all that many amenities here, everything is centred around the mines."

"I'll need to get there somehow," said Amie, "I've no passport, and I must get home and I must contact my family, let them know I'm safe."

"Well that I can arrange immediately, of course we must let them know," said Alice with a smile. "But would you like a hot shower and some clean clothes first? Make you feel a little more human?"

"A shower, what a wonderful idea! That sounds like heaven!"

"Let me come with you, and see what I can find for you to wear. It won't be as smart as your present dress of course, but....." they both laughed.

Amie liked Alice Robbins. She took everything in her stride and Amie was reminded of the resilience of those expats she had grown to love.

"I think I have an African comb around somewhere, it's going to be a job getting those tangles out of your hair."

"I need a good hairdresser and a few hours with a

manicure set," said Amie looking at her nails.

"That can all be arranged," said Alice as she wheeled herself swiftly into the bedroom. Her maid hovered uncertainly in the doorway.

"Emily, fetch some clean towels, but first, hand me down the blue dress from the wardrobe and some clean underwear."

Amie wanted to stay under the shower for hours, it was sheer bliss to feel warm water running over her skin as she scrubbed off the dirt. Some patches remained stubbornly grubby, and she guessed it would take several more showers until she would feel totally clean all over. Looking in the bathroom mirror, she was surprised to see how brown she was, and noticed with alarm how rough and calloused her hands and feet were.

"You can tell you've been away from civilization for a while," Alice smiled. "While you finish off, I'll go and get the computer up and running. I'm sure you can't wait to see your family."

Amie hesitated for a second, she thought she would prefer to speak to them without video, would her appearance scare them off? It seemed ungracious though not to accept the offer, an Internet call was free and she thought it rude to refuse.

When she went back into the lounge Alice was waiting for her. While it was so nice to be clean, Amie found it strange to be wearing European clothes again. She felt constricted, and she kept wanting to take off the sandals Alice had left out for her to wear.

"Give me their names and we'll see if we can connect," Alice said, but either her family were not online, or they didn't notice Alice's request to network.

"Never mind," Amie's hostess said. "We'll try them on the landline." This too was a failure, for there was number unobtainable at the Reynold household, Sam and her family didn't answer either, and the phone in Jonathon's parents' house just rang and rang. Amie wanted to burst into tears. She had hyped herself up to make contact, and now she couldn't. She was tempted to ask if she could call a friend, but it didn't seem right to give the news to anyone else before she spoke to her family. She would just have to be patient. Hopefully, everyone would be home when it was supper time in England.

While they sat and waited, with more coffee and cakes, Alice filled her in on the news from Togodo. From what she'd heard, the revolution had continued for months, with first one side in control, and then the other. The news that large deposits of valuable minerals had been discovered in the north, along with years of neglect by the ruling Kawas, had prompted the minority tribes into attacking the government. As far as anyone knew, there were no foreigners left in Apatu, and many had fled into neighbouring Ruanga. Quite what the situation was no one was sure. Alice didn't think there were any foreign embassies operating there, but several major mining companies were more than eager to negotiate with whoever was in charge of the country, but as that kept changing all the time, nothing had been agreed so far.

"When my husband gets home from work, I'll ask him to try and find out who might still be here, though I'm sure any expatriates who escaped over the southern border would have reached the capital and be back home by now," Alice observed. "We get very little news from Togodo, as it has not been on good terms with Ruanga for years. Opposing tribes of course, but I do know the race is on here to prospect for minerals as well, the capital is knee deep in exploration companies disappearing out into the bush with equipment."

For some reason she couldn't explain, even to herself, Amie couldn't stop fidgeting. Suddenly she looked up.

"What date is it? I've sort of lost track of time." Alice told her, and Amie, still finding it very difficult to think straight, sat and calculated for a few moments. "But I've been, it's, it's over a year!" she exclaimed. "Surely I can't have been living rough all that time, could I? No, not a whole year! It can't be that long, it can't be!"

"The troubles started almost eighteen months ago," Alice commented. "For a while we were worried about our safety, but I can't imagine what you've been through. It's an amazing story, yet you've survived, I think you are very brave."

Tim Robbins arrived home from work later that evening to find Themboniso, sitting patiently on the back doorstep, still waiting for him.

"After all my years in Africa, I will never understand the African's unending patience," he exclaimed as he walked into the lounge. Amie stood up to greet him, although Tim was just as friendly as Alice, she still felt shy, awkward and out of place.

"How are you?" he greeted her. "I hear you've had quite an adventure, and you can add to that, you've just cost me the price of a dinner for four in the Savoy!"

"Oh, oh, I'm so sorry," wailed Amie. "I will make sure you get it back, I didn't mean to be a …"

Tim interrupted her. "My dear girl, you're not to give it another thought! I'm only too pleased to help, it's the least I can do. We'll be dining out on this for years to come won't we Alice?" bending down he kissed his wife.

Alice smiled. "We will, and Amie feel free to stay with us as long as you like."

"Thank you, but I should get back home as soon as possible," even as Amie said this, she was aware of a strange reluctance to return to Castle Bridge. That wasn't normal surely? Didn't she want to see her family and friends? Get back to a more normal life? She was amazed to realize that she wasn't sure.

Just then the lights flickered and the power went out. Tim checked the phone and shook his head.

"It doesn't look as if you'll be talking to anyone back home in England tonight," he said ruefully. "When the services break down, we often don't get them back for days. We don't have cell phone reception out here either, so your re-entry into the world will probably have to wait a bit longer. What I will do, is get you transport to the capital, to our head office, I'm sure Matheson and his family will put you up, and help you sort out emergency travel papers. You don't have a passport now I take it?"

"No," said Amie. "They took everything away when I got put in prison."

From then on events moved at great speed. Alice helped her pack a small suitcase with a change of clothes and a few toiletries, and smiled and sadly waved goodbye as a company car arrived to collect Amie and take her to the capital. She met up with the Mathesons and stayed with them for a couple of days, while the officious staff at the British Embassy sorted out her travel documents. She sat in a small room for hours, answering a battery of questions. Where had she been? What company had her husband worked for? What had she been doing for all these months? Why had she not got in touch earlier? Could she prove she was British?

There were further problems as the phone number and address she gave them for her parents were no longer valid, and it was only when they managed to contact Gerry and Sam, that they finally believed her story.

If the noise and chaos of Atari frightened Amie, the chaos and frenetic activity at Heathrow Airport was deafening. She had not expected crowds of reporters and TV cameras and flash bulbs going off in her face. She was jostled and bumped, as they fired questions at her as she walked out into the arrivals hall, looking wildly around for her family. It was obvious someone in Atari had tipped off the media and now

Amie was the centre of very unwelcome attention.

At last she managed to push her way through, brushing aside the microphones waved in front of her face, and in tears, she fell into her mother's arms.

"Take me home," she sobbed. "Get me out of here."

Amie's parents were just as bewildered as she was, and they protected her as best they could, as the media hoard followed them all the way into the car park, and then knocked on the windows asking for comments, or for Amie to make a statement, or tell them where she had been, and what had happened. It was all terrifying and she buried her face in her hands and bent over in the car seat willing them all to go away.

No one said anything much on the journey back home. Amie wondered where Jonathon was, but she was too afraid to ask. She sank into a silent word and hoped and prayed her parents would understand.

Instead of pulling up at their old house, she was surprised to see that while she'd been away, they'd moved to a much smaller house on the other side of town, but here too, there was another crowd of media hawks, screaming and shouting with a barrage of questions. She refused to look at them, and shrank beside her father as he elbowed them out of the way, and shielded her as they went in though the front door.

The photographers thought nothing of trampling on the flower beds, trying to peer in through the windows to get more shots of Amie, and her mother rushed over and drew the curtains. Then, even before they had a chance to sit down or put the kettle on, the phone started ringing incessantly. One newspaper, magazine, television and radio station after another, asked to speak to Amie. They wanted her to appear on the Breakfast Show, the Tonight Show and make herself available for interviews. Finally, Amie's father took the phone off the hook.

"And I thought we were ex-directory now," her mother

observed as she put coffee and cake on the table. "Jonathon's parents just took the receiver off the hook and left it off." She stopped suddenly, berating herself for mentioning Amie's husband.

"I wouldn't put anything past what they can find out," responded Amie's father. "How do you feel?" he asked kindly.

Amie didn't know what to feel. She was not in familiar surroundings, her parents seemed awkward, not sure how to react to her, and she also felt totally out of place. She shook her head and tears ran down her cheeks. She was home, why was she feeing this way? What was wrong with her?

17   THE RETURN

There was a loud banging on the front door, and someone put their finger on the bell and kept it there.

"Now who the hell is that!" exclaimed Raymond Reynolds as he marched to open the door. Sam, Gerry and the children were standing on the doorstep waiting to be let in.

"Hurry up! At last!" exclaimed Sam as she raced into the kitchen. "Those reporters were about to eat us for breakfast," she laughed. "Amie, it's really you!" She swept Amie up into her arms and gave her a big bear hug. "It's so good to have you back, now you can get back to a normal life. Not, that it will ever be normal for you from now on. All those TV interviews, and having your face in all the newspapers and now you're famous, they'll probably have you on all the celebrity shows as well. Hey, we have someone famous in the family at last, maybe we can get to meet other famous people if you take us along to the studios. Hey that would be great!"

"Calm down Sam," said Mary Reynolds, "it's all a bit of a shock for Amie right now."

"Yes, but in a couple of days when she's settled back into things, then the fun will start," Sam brushed her mother's warning aside.

In contrast to Sam, Amie's niece and nephew were standing quite still, staring at her as if they didn't know her at all.

"Come kids," said Gerry, after kissing Amie on the cheek and giving her a little squeeze, "let's go find Grandma's box of toys in the other room."

As they left the kitchen there was an awkward silence. Amie looked at them all.

"No one has mentioned Jonathon. Where is he?" she asked. "Why hasn't anyone mentioned him? I asked about him in Atari and they wouldn't or couldn't tell me anything! Is he dead?" Amie had been so afraid to ask, she didn't want to hear Jonathon was dead, she couldn't bear it. Somehow, while she'd been in the bush, she'd accepted her fate and the fate of all her other friends, and in her own way she had mourned losing him. She'd not thought far ahead, about ever leaving, it was if she had been in one long dream. Now she was back home, and the world was crowding in on her again, and she needed to know the worst.

There was a sudden pause, the world stood still and Amie's family looked at each other in dismay. She looked at each one in turn, and searched their faces.

"He's dead isn't he?" she asked. "You can tell me, I have to know sooner or later."

Mary Reynolds cleared her throat and said, "Amie, we don't know. We don't know where he is. He left Apatu on the last plane out of the airport, and by the time he realized you weren't on the plane they were already in the air."

"They carried him onto the plane when he was unconscious, I think he'd been knocked out by a collapsed wall or something," Samantha butted in quickly.

Amie's father glared at her, and then her mother continued. "He was home for a short time, and, well we thought he'd gone a little crazy. He was determined to go back and look for you, and find out what had happened. He said you knew someone high up in the government, and maybe they would try and protect you."

Visions of Colonel Mbanzi being blown into little bits, floated in front of Amie's eyes, as the voices of her family rose and fell.

"Then he had the most awful row with his parents," Sam

interrupted again. "It was such a big fight he moved out and came and stayed with us for a few days. Then he caught a plane and went back to look for you."

"How, how long ago was that?" asked Amie faintly.

"Must be about four or five months now. He spent weeks and weeks petitioning the government, and the Foreign Office, and the police, and anyone else he could think of to go and find you, but they all said there was nothing they could do."

"Did you know the Togodian government told the British Government they would release you for fifty million pounds?" Amie's mother asked.

"No!" Amie was shocked. Then a thought struck her. "You didn't…?"

"No, not the reason why we downsized, it just seemed sensible with Sam having her own place and you…." she trailed off.

"Me missing, presumed dead."

"When Togodo asked for an amount that size, there was no hope of raising it."

"But some charity did open a bank account and start a collection, but it never reached anything like that," added Sam helpfully.

"I'm not sure the government would have been able to hand me over," said Amie. "It's a long time since I was in Apatu." The rest of the family waited silently to hear more, but Amie was exhausted. She guessed they would call it post traumatic stress syndrome, but for now, all she wanted to do was sleep.

The next few weeks were a blur. Amie got up and dressed and ate the food her mother put in front of her. She played a little with the children when Sam popped in, but she refused to go out, except for one brief visit to Jonathon's parents which was so uncomfortable she couldn't wait to leave. Her parents dragged her out to see a psychologist, but she didn't want to face the world and she didn't even want to watch television. Certainly in the first few days after she got back, she was the flavour of the month, with all kinds of experts talking about where she might have been, and how she might be feeling and how long it would take her to get back to normal.

What's normal? Amie thought. Living in the bush seemed more normal than this world, with its suffocation with material possessions, and too much food to eat, and racing around to work harder to climb the corporate ladder and earn more, and then buy even more stuff to show the world how well you were doing. It all seemed so pointless, so pathetic, like rats in the proverbial trap.

Amie no longer had an email address. Her box had jammed full months ago, so when she received a large, bright pink envelope in the post, she was intrigued. Inside was a large comic 'Welcome Home' card and a letter.

Dear Amie,
I guess you're thoroughly fed up with all the media hype and may not want to hear from me, but I thought for old time's sake I would write and ask you if we could meet up. I have a proposition you might be interested in. Name the time and place.
Best wishes
Dave – ex cameraman from Video Inc.

Amie read the letter twice before putting it back in the envelope. She remembered Dave as one of the best cameramen she had ever met, and she was intrigued as to why he was no longer with Video Inc. They would have been mad to get rid of him, so what had happened? She felt the first spark of curiosity she'd had in ages. She'd refused to meet up with her other old friends, preferring to hide out in the house, but now this letter from Dave sparked her interest. There was a mobile phone number under his name, and without giving herself time to think, she went straight to the phone, replaced the receiver quickly before any of the media had time to get through, and dialed his number.

Dave answered on the third ring and he sounded just the way he'd always done when he was Amie's hero when she worked behind the reception desk at Video Inc. They agreed to meet at a small café just round the corner from her parents' place the following afternoon.

Amie saw the pleasure in her mother's eyes when she announced she was going to have coffee with a friend around the corner. She saw it as a sign that finally, Amie was on the road to recovery. The sessions with the psychotherapist had seemed a waste of time, but maybe there was nothing wrong with her. They had taken her for a complete check up at the London School for Tropical Diseases, and everyone was amazed at how healthy she was, even if she had lost a lot of weight.

If Dave was shocked by how thin Amie was when she walked into the cafe, he didn't show it as he stood up to shake her hand. "How are you?" he asked gently.

"I'm not sure I know," Amie replied. "I seem to be somewhere between this world and the next, though I know that sounds silly."

"No, it doesn't," replied Dave. "Experiences, especially traumatic ones have that effect. I've seen it before."

The waitress came to take their order and there was a short silence before Amie said, "I was surprised that you aren't with Video Inc anymore."

"No. I had an offer to go back to Africa and make a series for a large international company, and so I went freelance and things just rolled on from there."

"Oh, I see," said Amie.

"I left shortly after you went to Togodo and I've been on

the move ever since, I've seen quite a bit of the world in the last few years." There was a short silence then Amie held up the letter.

"And this? What did you....?"

"First I want to ask you what you want to do now. Have you thought of anything?"

"No. Part of me wants to go and look for Jonathon, but that's not possible."

"What's stopping you?"

"My folks for one thing, I'm staying with them and I've not got much money, no job and no prospects, unless I sell my story to one of the media people."

"And you don't want to do that?"

"I'm not going to go on some talk show and be treated like some freak," Amie's voice rose in indignation, causing many of the other patrons to turn round and stare at her. Several of them began whispering and pointing.

Dave stood up suddenly, threw a note on the table and grabbed her arm. "Let's get out of here," he said. "We'll take a walk in the park."

They walked out of the café without waiting for their order. It was one of those rare English afternoons when the sun shone and the temperatures were in the low twenties as they entered the park and found a nearby bench.

"OK, let me tell you what I have in mind. I don't want you to say anything until I've finished, and then I still don't want you to say anything until you've had time to think it over. Understood?" Amie nodded.

"One way or another you are not going to shake the media off totally. Even a couple of years down the road, your name will come up in some production planning meeting, and they will approach you again. A young girl missing in the wilds of Africa for over a year, is just too good a story to pass up. You do realize that don't you?" Amie sighed and nodded again.

"So, my proposition is we go back together, for two reasons. To find out what happened to Jonathon and to tell your story on camera. This way, once it's told, everyone will leave you alone, and at the same time, you might be able to find Jonathon, or at the very least, have closure."

"But, but I can't" exclaimed Amie.

"Would going back be too traumatic for you?"

"No, no it's not that. I do want to go back," exclaimed Amie, suddenly realizing this was the truth. "But I've no passport, no money no resources, I don't have a choice."

"I'm offering you a chance, a way to go back," said Dave quietly, "but I do want you to think about it. I want you to be sure, because it won't be easy."

"I don't even know about, about the logistics. Is the airport open in Apatu, would they arrest me the moment I stepped off the plane? I wouldn't know where to begin!"

"That's where I come in, and a small team on the ground here, and I wasn't thinking of arriving, waving cameras aloft at a major airport, but something a little more subtle."

While Amie had longed to go back and look for Jonathon, until now, it had not been a real possibility. Also, she wanted to know what had happened to all the other people she had grown close to. Dave's words had reawakened her mind, and all of a sudden she couldn't wait to get started.

"I don't need time to think," she said. "I do want to go back. Most people would think me crazy after everything that's happened, but there's something about Africa that pulls you, and it won't let you go."

"I've only been there maybe half a dozen trips for a few weeks at a time, but I do know what you mean. You long to return."

"Yes, I want to know what happened to Jonathon and to Angelina and Pretty and William, they can't all be dead."

"There is something else I should mention, and you might not like this. You do know there was a price on your head from the Togodo government?"

"Yes, fifty million pounds," Amie smiled ruefully. "No one person is worth all that."

"The British Government wouldn't pay a fraction of that for any hostage, you know their rules. But it occurred to me you should not go back as you."

Amie gasped. "You mean a disguise, pretend I'm someone else?"

"Exactly. How does that sound?"

"Sensible. I could cut my hair short and die it black and wear dark glasses," and Amie laughed for the first time since she'd returned home. Dave's proposal was a big adventure, and she began to feel alive for the first time in months. Not only would she be helping to make a world class television series, but she would be back in the place she loved, and maybe even re-united with the man she loved as well.

"I'll do it," she said firmly. "Just tell me what you want from me."

"Whoa," said Dave. "I want you to think this through properly. What I'm suggesting isn't totally legal, although we wouldn't explain how you got back in to Togodo, but...."

Amie took Dave's hand. "Dave, when you've been through all the things I have in the last months, this doesn't frighten me. Yes, I do have a story to tell, and maybe it will make some of those stuffed shirts watching African wildlife programmes, in their comfortable armchairs, sit up and think!"

Dave stared at her in amazement, and then he smiled and gave her a big hug. "I think we're going to make the best television series in history," he said. "How soon can we start pre-production?"

"How about now?" replied Amie with a smile.

The next few weeks were tricky for Amie. She hated to deceive her family, and the few friends that had dropped round, but she was telling no one of her plans. Her days were spent at the small office Dave had rented, where she was introduced to Sandy his production secretary, Bill who was normally in charge of sound, Neil whose speciality was lighting and Petra who was a general gofer.

Bill was over six foot tall, with sandy hair which flopped over his face. He was quiet and shy and very different to Neil, whose roots were in the West Indies, his black face was seldom without a smile and he was full of fun. Sandy's parents had emigrated to England from Nigeria when she was very young, and though her origins were also from Africa, she never remembered living there, so she was both curious and eager to see the land of her ancestors. Neil thought it unlikely he would ever know from where in Africa his family had been taken as slaves, but like Sandy he was keen to see what he still thought of as his original homeland.

The two biggest decisions they faced was how many of them should go, and how. It was decided that Petra should stay, so they would have someone to keep in touch with back home. No one else was told about the project, Dave reckoned the fewer people who knew the better.

The next decision to make was should they masquerade as investors, and fly in openly and take it from there? Or, should they slip in from Ruanga and keep a low profile when they reached Apatu?

Amie was in favour of the second choice. She was fearful they would get stopped before they even had a chance to start, and if they were going to tell most of the story, then they would be able to take visuals of Ruanga, and they would be in the right place to film the Mathesons and Tim and Alice Robbins as well. She thought both families would be happy to cooperate. But there was one thing she was adamant about.

"I think I can find the forest people again," she said, "but I want everyone to promise their location is kept a secret. Obviously the tribe nearer town knows where they are, as some of the young men go to work for them now and again, but I would never forgive myself if they were later besieged with foreign camera crews and their lives were destroyed." Everyone understood and agreed.

"I can guarantee that," said Dave. "All the people here you can trust, you have my word."

Days were spent making lists and buying supplies. When Amie's new passport arrived, she simply didn't ask where it had come from. She had borrowed a black wig for the photograph, as she only planned to dye her hair the night before they flew out. Her parents were going be upset enough, when she told them she was going to shoot on location out in the wilds of Alaska, where she would be out of contact for a couple of weeks. She hated lying to them, but thought it much better for their peace of mind.

She knew the more carefully they planned, the better the production, but it was quite thrilling for Amie to play a major part. After her time spent in both rural and urban Africa, she had lots of advice to give about what they would need and what was superfluous.

The next few weeks flew past, and when the tickets from London to Atari arrived, she realized it was all happening, and felt both fearful and full of excitement at the same time. It was either going to be a big adventure, or a total disaster, and no one could tell which way it was going to go.

The night before they flew out, they checked into a hotel near Heathrow Airport, and Amie turned herself into a brunette. When she looked in the mirror, she hardly recognized herself, and on the way down to dinner, Sandy walked past her without even noticing who she was.

Dave, Bill and Neil had checked the camera equipment again and again. They were taking two small cameras with HD quality and the lighting and sound equipment were the smallest versions on the market. There were also back up cameras which were even smaller, which could be used for filming in secret.

"We need to pretend what we have here, is only tourist stuff," Dave reiterated. "We know no journalists have managed to get into Togodo up till now, so we should be the first to get footage out." Looking at Amie he added. "You could almost pass for a local, with your tan, but I've packed a burka for you to wear, and a long black wig. I've also got some instant tan for Bill and myself, so we are not too conspicuous!"

"This is getting to be like a spy movie," said Neil. "The professional film makers would have a fit."

When Amie had said goodbye to her parents in Castle Bridge, they were both worried she wasn't ready to go back to full time work. They sensed an underlying manic quality in her behaviour, but she was an adult and they could hardly force her to stay at home.

The moment they opened the doors on the plane after it landed in Atari, Amie took a deep breath of warm air. She felt she had come home, although that was nonsense, she'd only lived in Africa for a few years, compared to all the time she'd lived in England.

There was the usual chaos at the airport, but at customs, they barely glanced at the passports before stamping them and waving them through. Everything had arrived in one piece, and even while they were waiting for their luggage, Dave was busy filming, using one of the hidden cameras he was carrying in his shoulder bag.

The drive into the city was a bit hair raising, but Amie was reminded of her own early feelings as she saw Sandy and Bill's reactions when they saw the shack lands and the appalling poverty.

"Oh, those poor, poor people!" Sandy exclaimed. "How can they live like that?"

"You do get used to seeing the poverty and the poor,"

Amie remarked. "I know that sounds callous, but this is life for millions on the planet, in fact for the vast majority. In Europe, we really live in a rarified bubble."

"Surely not," said Neil, "how can you see all that and not want to help them?"

"Amie's right," Dave interjected. "There are too many to help, and if you just give hand outs those are not appreciated and a lot of them will not attempt to haul themselves out of poverty through their own efforts."

Amie looked at Dave in surprise. He understood the problems in Africa, he had a lot of insight for someone who had never actually lived there.

Once they were settled in their hotel they gathered together for the evening meal. Amie was going to contact the Mathesons and explain what they wanted and ask that they re-enact the time she spent with them.

"I had fair hair then," she told them. "I'll look totally different!"

"That may be a good thing," Bill replied. "You won't be mobbed when you get back home."

But where was home? Amie wondered. The moment she had set foot back in Africa, she had immediately felt at home.

The Mathesons were only too happy to co-operate, and they spent the following few days re-enacting Amie's arrival in the capital, and shots of her talking to the family and then walking into the building where the British Embassy had its offices. Amie didn't dare walk right into the Embassy, but luckily it was on the fifth floor of a high rise building, so all she had to do was walk in the downstairs entrance. Dave then took a close up of the embassy sign on the wall. They drove back to the airport and showed her walking into the departures terminal with her one small case.

The following day they set off north to Umeru, the mining town where Alice and Tim lived. It was a weird experience for Amie, she was going back in time and re-running earlier months of her own life. This time she was the star of the movie, where before she had only ever operated behind the camera.

In Umeru, they all received a warm welcome. Alice was thrilled to see her house guest again. They spent several days there filming a faithful account of Amie's stay, with Sandy doubling up as a makeup artist as she turned Amie back into the waif and stray she was when she first emerged from the bush. She made such a good job of wrecking the new wig, Amie suggested she had really looked better when she first walked out of the bush.

They had to improvise by using the current garden boy instead of Themboniso, and Edgar was very puzzled by what they wanted him to do, but like most Africans he was willing to co-operate and very easy to direct. He was especially pleased not only to have a break from gardening, but also with his payment for an interesting few days work.

"Nothing as exciting as this has ever happened before!" Alice exclaimed.

The evening before they left, Tim Robbins took Dave aside and handed him a long package wrapped in cloth.

"Take this," he said "it's a Remington sports rifle and there is ammunition in the gun bag pocket. You don't know what you're going to meet on the other side of the border. Hopefully you won't have to use it, but at least it might give you some protection."

"But I can't..." Dave began, but Tim cut him off.

"I know you couldn't fly in with any firearms, but this is just in case. Anyway, when you come back safe and sound, you can return it. Let's go outside and you and the other guys can fire off a couple of shots to familiarize yourselves with it."

Even though Amie knew they were only firing off test shots, every time there was a bang, she winced.

"Now for the difficult bit," Dave said the next day as they

prepared to retrace Amie's journey into the bush. "Do you think you can remember where Themboniso's village was? I was counting on Edgar to tell me, but he doesn't know Themboniso at all."

"I think so," Amie replied. "I know we drove for almost a day on the gravel road and then turned off inland and walked for maybe three hours? You lose all sense of exact time living in the bush. I do remember there was a very large Baobab tree where we hit the road, so I should be able to identify that."

Loading the two hired Land Rovers with all their gear, including tents, plenty of water and food, they set off north. Without mentioning it to the others, Amie was worried about finding the village, but much to her surprise it was easier than she thought. Life was simpler with modern transport, as the vehicles ate up the miles. When she thought about it later, Amie was not absolutely certain at first they had found the right village, but she would recognize the Chief again if she saw him. Most of the villages were very similar, and as she had only spent one night there, she didn't recognize any of the people. Themboniso was nowhere to be seen, but the villagers they did meet, were very friendly. They were kept waiting for a long time in the sun to see the chief, who was the only one who could give them permission to film, or even stay in the village, but while they waited, they were offered several cups of sugared tea.

"How can they drink this stuff?" gasped Bill.

"Shush," said Amie, "we don't want to offend them. It's something you get used to, trust me."

As they sat in the shade under a tree, Dave carefully moved his shoulder bag in different directions. He was secretly taking footage of the huts, the chickens, the children running around and daily scenes around the village. Often his view was blocked by the row of people who came to stand in a line and stare at them.

Finally, the Chief said he was ready to talk to them and he walked outside his hut and sat down. The crew was escorted across the middle of the village and squatted down on the ground.

Between them, Amie and Dave explained they wanted to take pictures so Amie would remember the time she had spent with them, in return for a variety of things they had bought in Atari. The Chief debated this for some time, but as he eyed the spoils and the money they offered, he said they were happy to co-operate.

Once again, Amie pretended she was being brought into the village and once again the local actors played their parts well. If we make this too realistic, she thought, it will all look like a fairy tale. They had one piece of luck when Amie saw one of the little bush dwellers working in a nearby field. Marabi and Amie embraced each other like family members, and Amie waved her arms about to show that she and her friends wanted to go back with him to the forest.

He smiled and nodded his head and seemed to indicate by making the signs she knew stood for the sun and the moon, they could leave in a couple of days. This gave the crew enough time to return to Atari and replenish supplies before returning again to Themboniso's village.

While they waited patiently, Dave took lots of extra footage of daily village life with one of the larger cameras, much to the delight of the children who couldn't get enough of looking at themselves on the playback monitor, and Amie sat and drank in the familiar sights and smells of the land she had grown to love.

Riding in a truck was a first for Marabi, and his pure pleasure at the experience reminded everyone of the huge gulf between their two cultures. Amie was not sure if he did not direct them in a very wide detour, as they bounced across the savannah, avoiding thorn bushes and termite mounds. There were no roads to be seen, but the terrain was relatively flat. However, once they reached the edge of the forested area, it was not possible to drive the vehicles any further. They unpacked their supplies and shared them out, while Bill disabled the Land Rovers by removing the rotor arms. Marabi led the way through the trees, knowing by instinct exactly which way to go.

When they reached the collection of leaf houses, and Amie saw her old friends, she burst into tears. They were all still there, except for little D'epto who had died a few weeks earlier. E'lft and X'ome welcomed them solemnly and shyly. They seemed much in awe of these tall strangers.

A'ncah shrieked with joy and threw her arms around Amie, ululating loudly. Her actions melted the ice and the rest of the tribe in turn welcomed her with tears of joy, and presumed she had come back to stay.

Amie introduced the other members of the team, though few of the little people were able to pronounce such difficult names as Dave, Bill, Neil and Sandy. They laid out a cloth on the ground and indicated their visitors should sit, and several of the women brought out home brewed beer, fruits, berries, and small pieces of dried meat.

After much smiling and pointing and arm waving, Amie began the protracted negotiations about the filming. This was a lot more difficult than she had imagined it would be. The tribe members were very suspicious of the camera and when Dave demonstrated how it recorded their movements, there was a near riot.

"Isn't it known some people believe that taking a picture also takes away the soul?" Neil asked quietly.

"Yes, in many parts of the world," replied Dave, "but if they've never seen a video camera before, how do you explain it to them?"

No progress was made on that first day, but the tribe was happy to offer them a hut for the night and happily shared their food. Amie explained it would be better to use the hut, rather than try and put up one of the tents. The villagers would be insulted if the crew appeared to prefer their own accommodation, and practically, there was not much space between the trees to anchor a tent anyway.

Amie was surprised to see Sandy was coping quite well, but the person who was finding it all very foreign was Bill. He was totally out of his comfort zone, and kept a sharp eye on the ground looking for snakes and insects, and an even sharper eye on the trees.

Amie tried to reassure him. "In the months and months I lived here, I only suffered a few bites and scratches," she told him. "It's unlikely any large or dangerous animals would come close to the villagers here, they will keep their distance."

Bill however did not look convinced. Amie began to feel quite sorry for him as he nervously followed her to the water hole where it was customary to wash.

It was obvious the tribe would not co-operate with filming. Each time they saw the camera, they rushed past, eying it suspiciously, so Dave resorted to filming their activities secretly. Not realizing he had a camera running in his shoulder bag, the women proudly showed off how they made beer, prepared the food and washed their clothes. They set about building another leaf house and took their guests foraging among the trees, pointing out what was safe to eat. The men were happy for Dave and Neil to go hunting with them, but thought it strange Dave insisted on taking his bag with him. Amie couldn't help feeling guilty. She knew they were being deceitful, but if this was the price she had to pay to get back to Apatu and look for Jonathon, she would go along with it.

After a week in the forest, Dave pronounced himself happy he had enough footage, except for the shots of Amie he needed. While the tribe still refused to co-operate in any role play, Dave was forced to film her mostly on her own, and she was sad to think that anyone watching it, would think her new family were unfriendly and left her alone.

While Dave, Neil and Amie stayed in the forest, Sandy and Bill had driven the second Land Rover to and from Umeru several times, replenishing supplies and charging batteries. The Robbins were only too happy to offer them all the help they could. They arranged for the recorded tapes to be sent back to England in the mail bags used by the mining company. If they were making for a possible war zone, Dave did not want to lose the footage they'd already shot. He also contacted Petra back in England to give her up to date reports. She was the only one they could tell, since no one else knew what they were doing or where they were going.

Amie was not surprised when Bill had volunteered to drive back to Umeru for supplies. She could see he was uncomfortable so far away from civilization and took every opportunity to go and stay with the Robbins, sleeping in a comfortable bed and eating familiar food. As for Amie herself, a large part of her wanted to stay with the tribe. The peace she had discovered living with the forest people, returned the moment she walked back into the main clearing. She welcomed the simple, friendly, unconditional love they all showed her. She admired their way of life, living in harmony with nature. She loved the way they quite literally, left only their footprints behind them, and she was quite in awe of their extensive knowledge of plants and their many healing qualities.

Sadly Amie said a fond farewell to her friends, feeling both pleased and guilty at the same time, as they handed out the buckets, bowls, mirrors, cloth and other goods they had brought from Umeru. Is it best to leave them totally in the past? Amie wondered as they walked back through the cool forest. They do have some contact with part of the modern world when they hire themselves out as labourers, but there are so few peoples these days that live so simply and happily. It was only the thought of finding out what had happened to

Jonathon that allowed her to tear herself away from the tribe, as the Land Rovers headed north towards Togodo.

"If you found yourself almost by accident in Ruanga, I guess that means there isn't a border fence all the way along," Dave remarked as he set up the GPS.

"I don't remember any fence. I don't remember a whole lot about the journey," Amie replied, "only that it was a nightmare. I must have crossed at some point, but where, I have no idea."

"Well we can follow the road for a while and then maybe cut inland when we approach the border. I only hope this mapping is accurate," Dave studied the route on the small screen. "Sandy, can you find the paper maps as well? I don't want to rely only on one source of information."

They made good progress on the road going north for two days, with only one or two other vehicles travelling either way, until Neil who was navigating, directed them off into the bush.

"We'll pull over well out of sight of the road and set up camp," he suggested.

"Good idea," agreed Dave, "and then tomorrow we can film Amie doing her walking across the savannah bit."

"Dave, I'm not an actress," Amie moaned. "You don't need too much footage do you?"

"I can cut it down if I used the camera from your point of view, but I want to show how you found food and collected water."

"Yes, I can see those are important parts of the whole story," Amie admitted. Now she was back on the open plains, away from the peace and comfort of the forest people, much of the horror of her long walk became more vivid, and she shuddered at the memory.

But this time, she had company and with five of them together, Amie felt safe and to her surprise, she began to enjoy her acting role. Sandy made her up to look as if she'd been living rough for days and now her feet had grown soft again, she did not have to pretend the agony she felt walking barefoot.

Dave shot a little footage each day, and in between, they broke camp and moved a little further north. At last he pronounced himself satisfied, and Amie was impressed when she saw what he'd captured on tape, it looked very real.

"Not so much acting as re-enacting," she remarked, watching the monitor. "I could never have behaved like that if I hadn't lived through it."

"I think this is going to make a great series," said Dave happily. "It's going to make a lot of money for all of us." Amie realized she hadn't even considered the financial side of the adventure. She knew Dave had good contacts, and yes it *was* a good story, maybe they could even sell it in America. But for her, the most important part of the trip was to find Jonathon. If she was honest, it seemed most unlikely, but inside, she had this really strong feeling he wasn't dead. In the past, she'd always scoffed when people said they just knew their missing family member was still alive, when it was patently obvious they weren't. But she couldn't shake off the feeling he was still in Apatu.

At some point they must have crossed the border into Togodo, as they began to see burnt out villages, abandoned vehicles riddled with bullets, and neglected crops in the fields. Dave insisted on stopping and recording many of the scenes, while Bill remained in the truck, ready to take off at a moment's notice. If he'd been nervous before, now he was really scared. Amie noticed Dave have a quiet word with him, since his fear began to permeate throughout the group, and everyone found themselves looking over their shoulders every few minutes.

A few days later they approached Apatu and they could see the remaining high rise buildings in the distance, they were not far out of the city, and they were not sure what they would find there.

18 APATU AND BEYOND

"Strange they should build such tall buildings when there is so much space and empty land everywhere," remarked Neil.

"It's a sign of prestige, I think," said Dave. "In first world cities, they were built to save space…"

"… so they copied the idea to look modern I guess," added Sandy.

The last night at camp, they sat to discuss their strategy. Amie drew a basic map of the city as she remembered it, reminding them there were many parts she was not familiar with, and even the bits she remembered well, might not be accurate. She drew in the main street, the area where the Club had been, the orphanage, Spring Glen School, her house and the desalination plant, all areas that Dave needed to record.

"We can mock up the prison stuff in the studio if necessary. We'll keep that bit simple and not labour it. The main focus of the series is to show your survival, and we don't want to get embroiled in politics. From now on, we use the miniature cameras and the small radio mikes for natural sound."

"How dangerous is it going to be?" asked Bill nervously.

"We can't tell, but I think Sandy and I should go in and do a recce first," replied Neil. "We will blend in better and be less obvious."

"Fine with me," said Sandy. "This is the biggest adventure

of my life!"

It was hard the next day as Amie watched the two African members of the crew set off to investigate the city suburbs. She could not sit still, jumping up every few moments looking for something to do. To keep her occupied, Dave had her pretending to dig for water and re-enacting her testing the plants to see if they were edible. Bill was horrified when Amie picked up a Mopani worm, crushed it and ate it, declaring that no matter how hungry he was he would never, ever, put one of those in his mouth. Even Amie chuckled at his reaction, releasing the tension she felt being so close to Apatu, and yet so far away.

When Sandy and Neil returned late that evening, it was to report everything in the capital seemed quiet. There was no fighting, although there were troops here and there carrying AK47's, but generally everyone seemed to be going about their everyday life. It was impossible to tell who was in power, the previous government, or tribe members from the north who'd been labeled as rebels.

No one had stopped them or asked questions, and the traffic in the main streets was busy and chaotic. They both felt it was not safe for everyone to go into town, they had seen no white faces at all so it would be wiser for Amie, Bill and Dave to keep a low profile.

Bill immediately volunteered to stay with one of the trucks and guard their supplies, which didn't surprise anyone, but there was a lot of discussion whether Dave should enter the city.

"You'll stick out like a sore thumb mate," Neil pronounced firmly. "Even with that tanning stuff we brought it just wouldn't work. But when we go back in tomorrow, Amie could wear that burka so she will be mostly covered up anyway."

Reluctantly Dave agreed it made good sense. Although there had been no information about Togodo in the international press, he'd thought a few foreign businessmen would have flown in, in the hope of getting lucrative contracts with whoever was now running the country.

Amie was both nervous and excited the following morning, as swathed in a suffocating black burka which only showed her eyes, she climbed into the Land Rover with Neil and Sandy. Looking in the rear view mirror, she could see the look of relief on Bill's face as he was left behind with Dave. Today, Amie would be using the small spy camera and as they drove into town, she rubbed more dirt and sand onto the back of her hands, hoping it looked more natural than the dark brown tanning lotion they had rubbed into her skin.

Some of the city was as she remembered it. The main street was much the same, except some of the rubble had still not been cleared away. There were several empty spaces once occupied by shops and offices, and the Grand Hotel did not look quite so grand any more. There were two broken windows on the ground floor, and several gouges in the walls which had taken direct hits from the mortars, and the paint was also peeling off the walls. The army and government offices appeared intact, and the usual bored looking guards on duty, were lazing against the gate pillars smoking and chatting to each other as before.

They drove up and then down the main street, to allow Amie to record the destruction. They then drove past the large open air market, and the vendors were still there, sitting under the blazing African sun with their wares spread out on plastic sheeting in front of them. Apart from the piles of rubble and burnt out vehicles here and there, life in the market was going on as before, everyone had to eat. They recorded the prison ruins. It looked as if no one had even tried to repair the building.

Next they headed out to the Club, which had been very badly damaged. It looked deserted and there was no one around. They all decided it would not be wise to get out of the car, and a few shots of the exterior of the least damaged part of the building would be sufficient for the programme. Amie could see that the once sparkling pool was now a sludge brown, and the tennis courts were unusable. The nets had gone, and the once smooth surface was full of large potholes and in one corner were the remains of fires which had been lit, probably for cooking.

When they cruised slowly past Spring Glen Primary School, Amie could see it was still being used as a school, but it now resembled the orphanage. There were children everywhere, none of them in uniform, and the fencing had been removed. The once pristine playground, sports fields and gardens, were now strewn with rubbish, and there was graffiti daubed on most of the walls and many of the windows had been broken. Amie sighed, how could such a well run place deteriorate so quickly? Did no one have any pride in their surroundings?

Nothing had happened at the orphanage at Tamara, it had been left as a piece of waste ground, more litter, more building remains and Amie had to shake herself out of her despondency before she began to roll the camera. Everywhere they went, Amie kept a sharp look out for Angelina, but the chance of finding one small child in a city this size, even if she had survived, was remote. So too were her chances of finding Jonathon, but her mind closed off and she would not let herself think about it.

When they reached Spring Glen Mall, they decided to take a chance and get out and wander around inside. There were very few people shopping, but the Mall itself seemed to have escaped any damage. Only half of the shops were still open and Amie looked sadly at the vacant corner cafe where once she had enjoyed so many morning coffees.

There was one destination left, and Amie had been saving that for last. She had this ridiculous, wild hope she would walk back into the house in Spring Glen and find Jonathon, William and Pretty carrying on their lives as normal.

They cruised slowly down the street, it looked as if there had been very little fighting in this suburb, and suddenly, there was Amie's old house. It was not exactly as she remembered it, the paint was peeling off the walls, the gates were wide open, and one of them was left hanging by a single hinge. The garden had grown wild, but it looked as if someone was living there.

"Drive round the block," she told Neil. "I can jump out and get to the back wall."

"I don't like that idea at all," he complained. "We're relatively safe in the truck, I can always make a quick getaway. Can't you film from here?"

"I've already run the camera from this angle, and I'll only be a moment," Amie replied. "I just need to see who's living there."

"You're mad," grumbled Neil, but he obligingly drove round the block and stopped outside the back of the neighbouring house. Amie jumped out, falling headlong as she grabbed at the unwieldy burka which wrapped itself round her ankles. She untangled herself and crouching low, crept along until she was level with her old back garden. She peered through the holes in the ornamental bricks in the wall. There were two small children playing in the back yard, and then a couple who were obviously Togodian, appeared in the doorway and called them inside. For a heart-stopping moment, Amie thought they had seen her, as the man glanced up at the back wall and frowned. Then he turned away and walked back inside the house. Amie was frozen to the spot, but a stage whisper from the truck snapped her into the present, and she climbed back into her seat and they set off back to camp.

Amie was bitterly, bitterly disappointed. Her common sense told her this was all a wild goose chase and she felt unreasonably angry with Dave for conning her into this trip. He, along with everyone else knew it was impossible to find one lone white man in the middle of an African war torn city. Amie had dreamed up so many scenarios, each more fantastic than the last. They had met up with Alfred the Fixer and he would know where Jonathon was. Work had even started on the desalination plant again. President Mtumba was back in power and everyone was happy, and so on and so on.

But Togodo was not the same, and she should have realized this. There must have been months and months of killing, looting and raping. The economy would have been put back decades, and all the new, uplifting projects put on long term hold. She had just been blinded with an unreasonable hope, and now she needed to face the truth.

Sandy and Neil had got shots of the now abandoned desalination plant on their first recce into town, so there was no need to drive out that way again. Work had ceased and the little that had been built was now in ruins. As they bumped and swerved around the potholes on their way back to camp Amie held back her tears, pleased for once the voluminous burka covered most of her face. She was so angry with herself. Why, why, she wondered did hope still fester long after all reasonable hope should have been snuffed out?

She was morose that evening as they prepared the evening meal on the last night they were going to spend near Apatu, tomorrow they would be turning back south.

They had chosen a well concealed dip in the land to camp. They had lit no fires, nor used lights after the sun went down, and so far their presence had not been noticed. Amie couldn't help thinking that before the revolution, there were always people wandering around in the outlying areas, but now, most of the citizens she had seen today, seemed to be subdued, and scurried along looking fearful. It made sense in the aftermath of a tribal war, who knew who their enemy was? Everyone belonged to a tribe, an accident of birth, but it could make all those from other tribes your enemy.

Early the next morning, they pulled out just after the sun came up. Amie travelled with Neil and Dave in the front vehicle, while Sandy kept Bill company in the one behind. They would stay off the road for as long as possible to avoid any possible confrontation. As they bumped along, driving around the low scrub and termite mounds, the dust blazed a trail behind them. They saw no animals, not even the odd buck, and the African savannah stretched ahead as far as the eye could see.

As the sun began to sink low in the sky, they turned off the veldt and continued on along the road, making better time while still taking care to avoid the enormous potholes which had not been attended to in months. They had been travelling for about an hour, when Bill suddenly said, "I can see vehicles behind us. We should get off the road!" He indicated to Dave, who didn't argue, but immediately turned left and they bounced over the uneven ground as quickly as they could, but when they doused the lights it slowed them down even more until they rolled to a stop.

"Keep going, keep going," urged Bill, dying to put his foot hard on the accelerator.

"It doesn't make sense, we can hardly see where we're going in the dark, and if we hit a tree or a boulder, we're in big trouble. We'll just sit tight until they've gone past, they may not even be soldiers, maybe just ordinary people travelling south," Dave sounded a lot calmer than he felt. Everything had gone smoothly until now, was it all going to fall apart as they were leaving?

Looking back to the road in the distance, they saw two large trucks come to a stop close to where they'd driven off the road. Several figures with torches jumped down and walked along the edge of the road looking for tracks amid the now settling dust. Their shouts echoed faintly across on the wind.

Amie found herself holding her breath as she watched the

lights sweep over the ground, blurred by the dust kicked up by the Land Rovers when they left the road. No one spoke, no one moved, as they watched the lights come closer and closer towards them. Is there still a price on my head? Wondered Amie in a panic, while Dave was trying to decide if it was wiser for them to get out of the trucks and try to hide further away. Time seemed to stand still as the voices grew louder. Neil tried to ease his legs as they began to cramp up and Sandy was clenching her hands to stop them from shaking so much. Quietly Dave reached under the seat and brought out the gun. He had no idea if he would have the courage to actually fire at anyone, but the feel of the cold metal in his hands was reassuring.

Suddenly there was a loud roar, and the dark figures froze. Cries of "Simba! Simba!" went up, and a couple of shots were fired into the air. There followed another roar and then a short silence, before their pursuers made a run for the trucks still parked on the road, jumped inside, and raced off into the distance.

"What was all that about?" asked Neil.

"There's a lion somewhere close by," said Amie. "I guess they weren't going to hang around if they couldn't see where it was, and there may be more than one, possibly a whole pride of them."

"And you walked this on foot!" exclaimed Neil. "You were so brave!"

"Not really," murmured Amie, "just desperate."

They discussed whether they should sit tight and wait until it was light, or press on. Bill, Amie and Sandy thought the soldiers, if they were soldiers, might return in the morning and look again for tracks in the daylight and were in favour of moving on. Dave thought it unwise to drive too far without lights, while Neil argued that if they drove slowly using only side lights it was the best of both worlds. A suggestion to walk in front of the trucks with a flashlight to make sure the terrain was safe, was vetoed immediately, as everyone remembered what was out there.

"I didn't think lions hunted at night," said Neil as they inched their way forward.

"They hunt from late evening, through the night and into the early morning," replied Amie. "They'll stop if they make a kill large enough to feed the pride. They may also have disturbed hyenas or jackals with their kill, and invited themselves along to share in the spoils," she added. "We could be in their territory for quite a long time, as they cover a vast area. To be safe, we should light a fire and then they'd keep their distance …"

"…but that's not an option right now," Dave cut in. "We're safe as long as we stay in the trucks."

They crawled along at a snail's pace for the rest of that night. Twice they were forced to get out and use one vehicle to winch the other out of a deep rut, or a soft sandy dry river bed. Although they kept a sharp look out, there was no further sight nor sound of the lions, and by the time the sun rose again, Dave reckoned they were about fifty kilometres from the city.

"Not very far," observed Bill gloomily.

"No, but we can make faster progress on the road, and maybe after we've had a bit of breakfast, we get back on the road and hope to get almost as far as the border before nightfall." Dave's suggestion was approved by everyone, it was nerve wracking driving over the rough terrain, exhausting hauling the vehicles out of trouble, and even though the wide gravel road hadn't been graded in years, at least they were not going to get lost.

Even Amie's spirits lifted a little as they made good progress south, bumping over the ridged and rutted surface. They had a tense few minutes as a vehicle approached, but it was only an ancient pickup truck overloaded with water melons and pumpkins. As it went past without slowing down, everyone breathed a sigh of relief.

It was late afternoon before they saw a sign for the border post ahead.

"Time to turn off," said Dave. "Does any of this look familiar to you Amie?"

"No, I must have been a long way east from the main road, I was trying to keep closer to the sea. I thought that would make sure I wouldn't get lost."

"When we came north a couple of weeks ago," said Dave, "I didn't think to notice how far from the city we were." He tapped the GPS, but the screen stayed blank. "Damn thing has given up on us as well." As he was speaking, he turned down a side road and looked for a gap between the bushes wide enough for the vehicles to go off road and still stay parallel to it so they wouldn't get lost. They travelled on for a couple of hours until they found a small grove of trees which provided some camouflage.

While Sandy and Neil opened cans of meatballs and baked beans for supper, Dave and Bill studied the map to see if they could work out where they were.

"Sorry it's going to be cold fare, again," said Sandy as she dished up the plates, but better safe without a fire."

"It's ridiculous," said Amie as she took her plate. "I feel more of a criminal now, than when I was on the run from prison."

"Well they wouldn't be too thrilled if they found all the camera gear," said Bill. "We could get into real trouble for having that, and what about the gun, surely that's illegal as well?"

"I think they'd be more upset by the cameras than the gun," remarked Amie.

"And driving into Togodo without going through the border post?" asked Sandy.

"We could just as easily pretend we were lost and thought we were still in Ruanga," replied Neil.

"And if our captors don't speak English, and if they just blow us away without talking to us?" whined Bill.

"Cheer up Bill, we'll face that if and when it happens," said Dave. Bill was getting on everyone's nerves, and his fear was contagious. Dave made a mental note never to include him on a shoot again, I'll suggest he hone his editing skills, he decided, then he can sit in a safe, air conditioned studio at home.

After all the tension and the bumping around and keeping a lookout for danger all day, everyone was very tired and as the last of the twilight disappeared, they all settled down for the night. They had only put up the tents once or twice the whole time they'd been in Africa. By unspoken agreement everyone felt safer sleeping in the trucks, not only because it took a long time to erect the tents, but they could speed away from danger if they were ready to leave at a moment's notice.

Amie couldn't settle, even though it was her turn to have the back seat to herself. She turned one way and then the other, but although she was exhausted, she just couldn't sleep. First one leg then the other cramped up, so, slowly and as quietly as she could, she opened the back door and slipped out. She was bending and stretching to gain some relief, when she thought she heard voices whispering close by. She froze. The whispering stopped, leaving a deafening silence. Then she heard a soft crack behind her and she felt something brush against her arm. Amie swung round and took a deep breath to shout a warning, but not before a strong arm closed tightly round her chest and one hand covered her mouth to cut off her screams.

There was chaos in both vehicles as the rest of the crew struggled to wake and leap into action, but they were too late, they were already surrounded. The pale moonlight glinted on the barrels of several guns, and they all put their hands up and stood waiting. There was a long silence as their attackers took in the situation. There were at least five of them, and two more dark shapes were just visible in the shadows. For several moments, no one moved. The crew held their collective breath until a voice said

"Good God, what are *you* doing here?" The crew were too stunned to say anything. Neil's mouth fell open, Dave gasped, Bill whimpered and Sandy looked shell shocked. Amie couldn't say anything at all, her mouth was still covered.

"Amie? Is it Amie?" a voice came from behind Dave. "I don't, don't believe it! Is it really you?" Jonathon stepped out of the shadows just as Amie fell into a dead faint.

By the time she came round again, everyone else had the full story and Amie had a lot of catching up to do. When the revolution was at its height, Dirk and Helen had left Nkhandla Lodge to the looters and taken refuge in one of their furthest bush huts. Since Dirk's family had been in Togodo for so many generations, he had nowhere else to go, and Amie remembered Helen telling her that once she had come to love Africa, she didn't want to live anywhere else.

All of the hired help at Nkhandla were from the north and they remained loyal and helped protect their employers, ferrying in supplies as needed from a nearby village. The rebels had taken over the government, whether they would do any better than Mtumba and his bunch was doubtful, but things did seem to be getting back to normal.

As Amie already knew, Jonathon had returned to look for her and Charles had come with him, something she didn't know. They too had flown into Ruanga, hired a vehicle and driven through the unmanned border on a dark night. They had bumped into Jefri and Kahlib on the road and been brought back to the camp. They had made three trips into Apatu to try and find out what had happened to their wives and the other missing people, but with no success. When they received word there were strangers in vehicles close to the bush hut they came to investigate.

"It's like a fairy tale," exclaimed Amie as she hugged Jonathon. "I'm never going to let you out of my sight again," she said happily. Then she remembered, "I'll have to tell Charles, I was with Kate when she died. I don't think she suffered much, but the shop we were in was bombed and the walls collapsed on top of her. It was so awful, poor Kate. She had just tried on this gorgeous evening dress and I was telling her how good she looked, and the next moment, she was gone."

Jonathon rocked her to and fro as she wept. "I think Charles had a feeling she didn't make it. Most people were on the last plane out, but not everyone has been accounted for. But all the time I had a feeling you were still alive. I just couldn't give up hope."

"So, what do we do now?" asked Amie. Somehow the thought of returning to England wasn't very appealing. She thought of the crowds, the media, the unwanted attention, the pushing and shoving, the concrete jungle and the constantly grey skies.

"I think we should stay here for a while. Who knows, the new government might decide very soon to continue with the desalination plant, or there may be opportunities in other parts of the world."

"But how, how can I stay in Togodo!" exclaimed Amie. "They accused me of being a spy!" Jonathon laughed and hugged her close to him.

"A spy! Then they caught the wrong Fish didn't they?" he laughed. "We're reasonably safe here in the bush. Living off the land with Helen and Dirk has been the best time of my life. I miss nothing from home at all, except the folks of course. You don't want to go back do you?"

"I don't think so, but I don't want to make any decisions right now. Can't we spend a little time together first and see how things go?"

"It's a deal," agreed Jonathon. "Come on," he added

drying her eyes and pulling her to her feet, "let me show you the buck we killed this afternoon."

Dave and the rest of the crew left the following day. Jefri went with them to show them a border crossing that was always unmanned. They would call in at the Robbins and get in touch with the families to let everyone know they were safe and well. They left one of the Land Rovers behind along with the rest of their stores and supplies. Helen was ecstatic with the bar of soap and bottle of shampoo Sandy gave her.

"You have no idea what you miss, until you can't get it." she said cheerfully. "And it will be nice to have another woman to talk to. We can have our own coffee mornings under the Baobab tree."

"Yes," agreed Amie happily. "I can't wait to tell you about my tribe in the forest, they were just the greatest people, except they don't speak English and you do, and that makes it all just perfect."

It was several days later that Amie realized what Jonathon had said, and his words took on a new and sinister meaning. They caught the wrong Fish? She remembered the extra year he'd spent away after getting his degree, and his failure to come home during the vacations. She remembered this desalination plant moved more quickly and more efficiently than any of the other new projects in and around Apatu. She remembered the long evenings when he did not come home until very late. Maybe she didn't know Jonathon as well as she thought she did, maybe she didn't know fully what he actually did either. She didn't know whether to feel proud of him, or scared of what might happen to them in the future. For now, she would simply take one day at a time.

ABOUT THE AUTHOR

Lucinda E Clarke has been a professional writer for the last 30 years, scripting for both radio and television. She's had numerous articles published in several magazines and currently writes a monthly column in a local publication. She once had her own newspaper column, until the newspaper closed down, but says this was not her fault!

She has won over 20 awards for scripting, directing, concept and producing, and had two educational text books published. Sadly these did not make her the fortune she dreamed of, to allow her to live in the manner to which she would like to be accustomed.

Lucinda has also worked on radio - on one occasion with a bayonet at her throat - appeared on television and met and interviewed some of the world's top leaders.

She set up and ran her own video production company, producing a variety of programmes, from advertisements to corporate to drama documentaries on a vast range of subjects.

Altogether she has lived in eight different countries, run the 'worst riding school in the world,' and cleaned toilets to bring the money in.

When she handled her own divorce, Lucinda made legal history in South Africa.

She gives occasional talks and lectures to special interest groups and finds retirement the most exhausting time of her life so far; but says there is still so much to see and do, that she is worried she won't have time to fit it all in.

Amie is her second book, 'Walking over Eggshells' her autobiography was published in 2013 and is available on Amazon in Kindle and paperback.

© Lucinda E Clarke 2014

To my readers

If you have enjoyed this book, or even if you didn't like it, please take a few minutes to write a review. Reviews are very important to authors and I would certainly value your feedback. Thank you.

Connect with Lucinda E Clarke on Facebook
Or by email lucindaeclarke@gmail.com
Twitter @LucindaEClarke

Readers reviews for LUCINDA E CLARKE'S
"Walking over Eggshells"

Although at times heart-breaking, this is not a book full of doom and gloom. There is adventure and humour and the author provides a wonderful insight into the expatriate lifestyle in Africa.

This book shows the strength of the human spirit when it goes into Survival Mode. A great read.

"Walking over Eggshells" is such a good read that I want to recommend it before I am through with it. Each time a chapter closes, I can't wait to find out what will happen in the next one.

I had no idea what to expect when I purchased this story. Having started reading it, I simply couldn't stop. This is a compelling story of a mother's cruel and systematic mental abuse of her only child. The fact the author survived this ordeal to tell the story speaks volumes about the ability some people have to overcome adversity.

That Lucinda E Clarke can write and write well is not in question. This memoir left me breathless at times. She writes of her adventures, mis-adventures and family relationships in an honest but entertaining manner. As each chapter opened I could not wait for the continuing saga and adventures to recommence. I think the success of this memoir is the authors sense of humour and determination to press forward despite suffering a childhood (and indeed adulthood) at the hands of a mentally abusive mother. I was never depressed by her story but sometimes saddened and almost angry on her behalf. I wholeheartedly recommend this book, buy it, delve in and lose a few days, well worth it.

I felt a touch of envy as I realized Lucinda lived the adventurous life that most of us only dream about. It became a fascinating journey as she allows the reader to join her on her writing career. Through the hills and valleys, the ups and downs, Lucinda captures the best and worst of the emotions and qualities which make us human. It was an amazing read and a literary journey worth traveling. Thank you, Lucinda E Clarke, for one of those rare once in a lifetime reads

Made in the USA
Charleston, SC
25 August 2014